THE INTERCEPT

THE INTERCEPT

Dick Wolf

Doubleday Large Print
Home Library Edition

WILLIAM MORROW
An Imprint of HarperCollins*Publishers*

THE INTERCEPT. Copyright © 2013 by Dick Wolf. All rights reserved. Printed in the United States of America. No part of this book may be used or reproduced in any manner whatsoever without written permission except in the case of brief quotations embodied in critical articles and reviews. For information address HarperCollins Publishers, 10 East 53rd Street, New York, NY 10022.

ISBN 978-1-62090-857-0

**This Large Print Book carries the
Seal of Approval of N.A.V.H.**

Dedicated to all those who keep us safe 24/7/365

ACKNOWLEDGMENTS

Thanks to David Highfill and Richard Abate, for their professionalism, enthusiasm, and guidance. To Cliff Gilbert and Bob Philpott, for their decades of advice and having my back. To Chuck Hogan, for his critical insights and creative generosity. To Peter Jankowski, who keeps the train running on time in my television life. But most of all to my children, Olivia, Serena, Elliot, Zoe, and Rex, and my wife, Noelle, who make my life truly blessed.

THE INTERCEPT

PART 1

BACKGROUND NOISE

September 2009

New York City

Bassam Shah had driven through a day and two nights from Denver, stopping only for gas, eating fried pies, drinking Red Bull, and urinating into a plastic milk jug between gas station fill-ups.

At dawn, in the chaos of merging lanes on the New Jersey side of the George Washington Bridge, orange traffic cones squeezed the cars to the right. Port Authority Police cars blocked the available lanes, routing all visitors to the city to a checkpoint just beyond the tollbooths. Commuter congestion into New York City was building at that early hour, though still not at its heaviest.

Two men in blue Windbreakers and baseball hats waved flashlights up ahead, peering into a car's rolled-down windows. They wore wires in their ears.

Shah saw no dogs. For that, he was relieved. He was ten cars back from the search point.

He watched the driver, a man traveling alone like him, get out to open his trunk. The searchers—now he saw the words PORT AUTHORITY POLICE on the backs of their jackets—shined their lights inside. They lifted the mat off the spare tire, conferred . . .

. . . then let the man drive away.

Shah had to risk it. The decision was not a difficult one. If he fled, they would stop him and search him intimately and rejoice at their success. Instead, he made himself small, exactly as he had been trained to do, settling into the persona of a grateful immigrant.

His story—he was driving into New York to check on his family's coffee cart—had the benefit of being the truth. It was verifiable. Truth by admission was imperative in a situation such as this one.

He eased the Ford Taurus forward, warm vent air breathing on him, soothing him. It was a muggy early autumn morning. He counted down as each driver was quizzed, each car scrutinized.

When his time came, he lowered his window and faced his interrogators.

"Where are you going?" asked the younger of the two black cops, shining his light in Shah's face.

"To Queens," Shah answered. He felt his confidence ebb as the words left him. Something felt wrong here. But to be this close and fail was impossible. He had felt certain the police were watching him in Colorado. But his cross-country drive had been uneventful. He had to push past his self-consciousness.

"You are coming from where?" the cop asked.

"Denver," answered Shah. "My home. Near there—Aurora."

All true. No lies.

The cop nodded. Truth or lies, it did not seem to matter much to him. "Step out of the car, please."

Of course they would make him get out. Shah was an Afghan, twenty-four years old, with caramel skin. His neck beard, hair, and eyebrows were all reddish brown. Physically, Shah fit every little box on their desperately simplistic checklist of profiling characteristics. The embodiment of what many Americans considered a dangerous man.

He clicked open his seat belt obediently, attempted a smile, and emerged before the great bridge in the warm air over the Hudson River.

The other policeman leaned inside the open car door, scouring the front seats with his flashlight as though it were a laser ir-radiating the floorboards and upholstery in search of clues.

"Mind unzipping that?" the cop said, stabbing his light beam at the Nike gym bag on the backseat.

Shah could have refused. He knew his constitutional rights under U.S. law; indeed, most every Afghan in the States knew these laws by heart. These men had no warrants, but they could "ask" him to accompany them somewhere else for more searching. All they needed was a pretense. Such was the thin thread upon which Shah's free-dom now hung.

He pulled out the bag, feeling the heat of the high-candlepower flashlight beam upon his tan hands. He opened it, removing a long head wrap, bunching it in his hands. He pulled out two robes thick with a few days' body odor. He pulled out a half-burned candle and sticks of incense.

In other words, he had exactly what these men expected an Afghan to have.

They peered further inside, touching nothing with their blue-gloved hands. Shah's laptop case was on the seat next to the bag; he showed it to them, and they were satisfied. They asked him to open the trunk and he complied. They discovered nothing there except the spare tire, a basic tool kit, and some grime.

And then it was over. They nodded to the driver's seat as a gesture that they were done and looked to the next vehicle. Shah deferred to them without making eye contact, got into the rental car, buckled up, and drove away.

All along the bridge, spangles of light glistened off the morning dew that coated the thick steel cables. Below, the running lights of barges on the Hudson River dimmed as though in awe of the dawning sun.

He felt great exhilaration at having passed the checkpoint, which was meant to discourage interlopers, but in fact seemed to him now like a threshold.

He was inside now. And it had been easy.

At the same time, Shah's anger began to rise anew. He cursed the deference the bridge trolls forced him to adopt. He was a man who valued his dignity. So he took in the beauty and magnificence of the view with a sneer.

As the city passed across his windshield, Shah's confidence returned, knowing that the detonators were securely fish-lined into the passenger-side air-conditioning vent.

In lower Manhattan, on the twenty-third floor of FBI headquarters at 26 Federal Plaza, not far from City Hall, the Joint Terrorism Task Force meeting was already under way. Jeremy Fisk, a detective assigned to the NYPD's Intelligence Division, arrived late, hobbled by a sprained ankle.

He had missed a layup in his over-thirty league the previous night—he played twice each week at ten P.M., a ridiculous time for an amateur to pursue any sport, but the only time he could reliably make with his schedule—and came down on someone else's foot and rolled his. He had sat on the court floor gripping his shin just above his hyperextended ankle, waiting for the swelling to begin and cursing himself.

That's it, he'd thought, for the thousandth time in his life. Enough with the basketball. They said that biology is destiny, and so it was that a formerly tall-for-his-age fourteen-year-old now spent two evenings a week with like-minded desperadoes throwing himself around a basketball court. He loved the game, but never the sheer exhaustion of running up and down the court—an exhaustion that came more easily these days. Fisk had topped out at five-eleven, never playing college after the JV team at Villanova, riding the bench because everybody else was better and, eventually, taller than he was.

Fisk limped over to the wall. The briefing room was overcrowded with representatives of the various agencies that comprised the JTTF. There were similar task forces in over one hundred cities nationwide, but New York's was, appropriately, the biggest. Besides the host agency, the FBI, full-time federal participants included the U.S. Marshals Service, the Secret Service, the Bureau of Alcohol, Tobacco, and Firearms, the Diplomatic Security Service, Immigration and Customs Enforcement, the Internal Revenue Service, the army, the Naval Criminal Investigative Service, and more than a dozen others, in addition to state and local law enforcement departments.

Such task forces are often derogatorily referred to as "alphabet soup," due to the large number of acronyms. To Fisk's eyes, the JTTF was worse. It was alphabet, minestrone, potato leek, French onion, clam chowder, gumbo, and Scotch broth . . . many great tastes that did not belong on the same menu.

Fisk's department, the Intelligence Division, was not part of the JTTF. It functioned as a separate intelligence-gathering agency within the New York Police Department. He was here as little more than a courtesy.

Fisk shifted his weight off his hurt ankle, leaning against the wall behind a liaison from the Postal Inspection Service. At the head of the room, Cal Dunphy, the current top FBI special agent assigned to the JTTF, was bald by choice, his broad jaw forming his head into a perfect oval. His eyes briefly flashed on Fisk when he entered, but nothing was said. Dunphy pulled notes from a file and consulted them through the lenses of his rimless eyeglasses.

"We're in his car and on his phone. We're in his laptop. Mr. Shah is moving with full confidence, and yet has no idea that we've got a flashing beacon on his back, bright and strong."

The FBI and Intel had had many operational differences of opinion in the past. The chief source of friction was their shared jurisdiction: a good old-fashioned turf battle. Two well-financed ops groups with similar but not identical agendas, going toe-to-toe in the greatest and most targeted city in the world. And neither side had either margin or tolerance for error.

They did not work well together. Recently, and too often, they had stepped on each other's toes, compromising the other's investigation. Various attempts had been made at improving communication and coordination, but nothing altered the fact that they were two dogs fighting over the same piece of meat.

So each agency kept the other at arm's length. The FBI had Shah all to itself in Denver. Now Shah was in the Big Apple, on Intel's terrain. They had learned enough from the mistakes of the past to establish a baseline of coordination, resulting in Fisk's presence at this briefing. But that didn't mean they were suddenly on the same page.

As Dunphy went on, it was clear to Fisk that the FBI was merely going through the motions. They were sharing the results of their surveillance info but not the sources. They wanted point on Shah. They certainly didn't want Intel tracking him independently.

A couple of different liaisons asked questions that were intended to make them appear smart and involved, but without any true interest in moving the issue forward. Groupthink. Fisk saw Dunphy glance his way. Dunphy, to his credit, knew Fisk wasn't going to let this ride.

Fisk stuck out his hand, as though hailing this train that was going around in circles. "This whole thing makes me itchy," he said. "I don't like it. He's here now. Right in the city. We know what he's got. We know what he's here for. I think letting him dangle like this is too goddamn risky. You say you're confident of his timeline—"

"We've got three days, Fisk."

"Having a GPS tag on a fox who's already in the henhouse doesn't reassure me much."

Dunphy all but sighed. "Nothing would reassure you, Fisk."

"Grabbing him now would."

"And give up three critical days of intelligence gathering? Who knows what we can get from this guy? This is crux time. Invaluable. This is the fruit at the bottom, Fisk. The sweet stuff. I understand your skittishness, but we're holding a strong hand here—"

"It's not skittishness; it's common sense. You're telling me this guy is on a controlled burn. I've seen those things get out of hand many times. All it takes is a sudden shift in the wind."

Dunphy smiled. Fisk knew what that smile meant. He saw parents use it on their kids in the park. "We've got the best meteorologists in the business."

"Predicting the weather is not the same as making it rain," said Fisk.

The FBI had conducted various undercover terror stings since the dawn of domestic terrorism. For every terror plot that arose organically, which is to say without domestic law enforcement interference—the underwear bomber in a jetliner over Detroit, or the planned attack on Fort Dix, New Jersey—two others originated with the prodding of undercover federal agents. Not unlike actual terror cell leaders, they radicalized vulnerable Muslim suspects by fomenting anti-American dissent and supplying the conspirators with dummy materials, such as fake C-4 explosive or harmless blasting caps. These paper conspiracies were then passed off as major law enforcement victories, vanquished threats to homeland security. But it was no exaggeration to say that the FBI had instigated more terror plots in the United States since 9/11 than Al-Qaeda.

Fisk continued, "My concern is that everyone is on board with your plan—except the terrorist himself."

"Noted," said Dunphy, pissed off now, and finished with Fisk. "Anybody else?"

Fisk had heard enough. One of the pleasures of not being beholden to the JTTF was the ability to walk out of a meeting—or hobble, which was just what Fisk did.

Just under an hour later, Jeremy Fisk limped into the Intelligence Division office in Brooklyn. The building was almost all the way out to Coney Island, a long D train commute from Park Slope. Surrounded by automobile junkyards, the unmarked one-story brick building gave no indication of the important work going on inside.

Not only were the windows made of bulletproof glass, but the entire building was sheathed in ballistic Sheetrock. Cars moved in and out of the lot all day, the electric gate in the fence sliding open and closed, yet strangely no one else on the block questioned it.

Fisk made it to his cube, the ankle tender but not bad, wrapped tight in an Ace bandage. He settled into his chair, switching on his computer—then sat back a moment and closed his eyes. Awaiting the boot-up of his computer was the most restful interlude of his day. He heard the day shift ambling in, listened to coffee cups being set down on desks, chairs being rolled back, jackets being shrugged off. Then for a few moments the symphony of the office faded away and Fisk drifted beneath it, clearing his mind for the day's challenges.

The NYPD's Intelligence Division had grown out of the New York City terror attack of September 11, 2001. After being rehired as police commissioner four months later, Ray Kelly determined that federal law enforcement communities had failed New York. He could not understand how every law enforcement and security agency missed a plot involving dozens of people taking flying lessons, crossing borders, shipping money all over the place. Nobody was going to take care of New

York, he realized, except New York's Finest themselves.

A great many police forces across the country had traded on the emotion and fear of 9/11 to bolster their budgets and departments—from large cities to small towns, law enforcement expenditures rose precipitously throughout the first decade of the twenty-first century—but only one municipal agency created its own mini-CIA.

The Counter-Terrorism Bureau of the NYPD and its partnership with the JTTF was the public side of the NYPD's efforts. The true face of counterterrorism, the Intelligence Division, was rarely seen. As such, the often controversial details of Intel's inner workings were closely guarded secrets.

Just weeks after the last fires were extinguished at the newly christened Ground Zero, Commissioner Kelly hired David Cohen, a thirty-five-year veteran of the Central Intelligence Agency, to become the NYPD's first civilian intelligence chief. His job was simple and yet chilling: defend the preeminent city in the world from attack.

At that time, the Intelligence Division was primarily used for escorting various visiting dignitaries around the city. Cohen, with the commissioner's full support, transformed Intel from a cushy preretirement assignment into a specialized unit that analyzed intelligence, ran drills and undercover operations throughout the five boroughs, and cultivated a broad network of informers to feed the division its insider data. While undercover work is a staple of big-city police departments, no other urban law enforcement organization in the nation worked as aggressively to infiltrate potential terror cells.

To do so, Cohen brought over various former espionage colleagues, first to screen and hire officers, and then to educate those officers in the tradecraft of information gathering, interdiction, and threat assessment. The goal was to locate and neutralize pockets of militancy before they became fully radicalized terror cells.

Fisk had been a detective bureau investigator for two years before being promoted for a spot in Intel. Being fluent in Arabic certainly helped. Fisk's mother was Lebanese, hailing from a wealthy family who had openly despaired when she married his father, a Texas-born diplomat. While Fisk's salary remained the same at Intel—he was Detective Two, no matter where he worked inside the NYPD—he wasn't hampered by budgetary concerns as he had been on regular duty. No hassles about buying or repairing equipment: funding was available and easily procured. What he had not been prepared for were the opportunities for travel, with assignments taking him to London; Lyon, France; Tel Aviv; Toronto; Egypt; even Iraq.

He was, for all intents and purposes, an intelligence officer inside the NYPD.

Covert intervention was equal parts art and science. The adrenaline flowed differently when you were investigating crimes before they happened, rather than reacting to immediate and developing crises. The Tantric anticlimax of serving search and arrest warrants—of taking the puzzle apart before it was quite put together—was the only drawback to Intel.

Success meant that nothing happened. No bomb detonated, no bridge collapsed, nobody screamed in the night. It meant that the city kept moving. Keeping men and women going to work, children playing in parks, elderly people complaining about the weather: this was his job.

Fisk opened his eyes, returning to full consciousness. The office buzzed around him. The city sentinel rested but never slept.

His computer had booted up. The wallpaper on his monitor was a spectacular view of Manhattan looking north from Governors Island.

He dug in right away, scanning reports from his rakers. They had been busy yesterday; they would be even busier today.

Rakers were real cops, undercover, many of them new to Intel. The term came from a controversial remark an NYPD spokesman once made about sending ethnically matched agents into neighborhoods to "rake the coals looking for hot spots." Most Intel cops got their start as rakers, including Fisk. Those vans that pull up outside a New York deli or convenience store at ten thirty at night, their drivers dollying in racks of soda and candy—for eight months that had been Fisk, delivering goods throughout the five boroughs . . . but mostly listening and watching.

So-called mosque crawlers were civilians on the payroll who hung around, watched, and—when they thought they had something—reported. Some were motivated by ancient hatreds. Some had had relatives killed by the Taliban or Al-Qaeda. Some needed the money. And some—many—had chosen informing as a lesser evil over arrest.

ACLU-style activists railed against perceived abuses of privacy by the Intel Division's secretive surveillance methods. It was profiling, pure and simple, they charged—something cops had been doing for centuries. Show me a better way, Fisk always thought. But as the saying went, there were no liberals in a foxhole.

Fisk sifted through the reports, keeping track of what amounted to gossip from Muslim neighborhoods. Whose brother was in town from overseas? Whose friend wasn't around suddenly? Why were these two men and a woman having coffee at that bookstore in Astoria where nobody ever went?

Before Intel, most cops working terrorist cases didn't even know that Muslims prayed in congregation on Fridays. Intel's special Analytic Unit, comprising experts from both academia and intelligence, figured out things like why a man whose family had been wiped out by a drone in Afghanistan a week ago might be somebody to look at closely. One of the many lessons of 9/11 was that there needed to be a central brain trust to process all incoming data, to interpret what the rakers were seeing and hearing. The AU tracked the big picture, the nuances and connections that were beyond the ken of each individual shoe-leather Intel cop.

Much of Fisk's daily work involved slogging through reports from his informants and reading memos that the FBI decided to share. Days like this one were few and far between. This thing with Bassam Shah was hot.

Fisk walked to the heart of the Intel building, known officially as the Global Intelligence Room, though nobody ever called it anything other than The Room. It was a sunken pit roughly the size of an Olympic swimming pool, open on one side where a wide three-step staircase led up to cubicles and offices.

A dozen flat-screen televisions hung from ceiling mounts on the side walls, broadcasting Al-Jazeera and every other foreign news service from big satellite dishes set next to the backup generators outside. Headlines from the world's news sources ticked in red across LED displays under the TVs. On the front wall, an electronic world map tracked threats with coded lights for New York, Tel Aviv, London, Riyadh, Islamabad, Baghdad, Manila, Jakarta, Tokyo, and Moscow.

On the floor beneath the map were banks of consoles with computer screens rivaling NASA's Mission Control. Linguists in headphones, fluent in Arabic, Pashto, Urdu, Fujianese, Spanish, French, and other languages, tracked and logged pertinent items coming across the newswires and broadcasts. They fed useful information to the officials in perimeter offices who maintained the threat board. Those officials briefed response teams and field agents who followed up on the ground in New York City.

Fisk sat in on an Analytic Unit meeting updating Shah's progress. Intel Division was shoe-leather detective work and big-picture tea-leaf reading.

"How'd the briefing go?" asked Louise, a language tech who was an expert on Arabic dialects.

"Wonderful. A lovefest."

"Did they kick you in the shins again?"

"Basketball injury," said Fisk, smiling. "But, yes."

"You ask for it."

"Listen, I want somebody the JTTF doesn't know. A fresh face."

"Uh-oh. What are you going to do?"

Fisk feigned offense. "My job. Any recommendations?"

"Depends. Are they going to get in trouble for you?"

"That depends."

"On what?"

"On Bassam Shah."

Bassam Shah left his Ford Taurus in a mall parking garage, taking only his laptop bag from the backseat. Before leaving the car, he fished the detonators out of the air-conditioning vents, leaving them on the floor in front of the passenger seat. He left the car keys in the cupholder and the driver's door unlocked before walking away.

The detonators were removed almost immediately, just minutes before an FBI surveillance car secured a spot within eyesight of the Taurus. The runner, who was unaware of the larger plan, quickly slipped into another vehicle two flights down and drove away.

Shah hurried through the shopping center, hopping a taxi that took him to a prearranged address. He entered the front door of the high-rise apartment building and immediately went to the basement below, utilizing an old tunnel known to drug dealers and illegal immigrants. It delivered him to a second building, where he exited at the rear and crossed backyards to a bus stop.

Gone were his laptop and one of his phones.

Shah entered the subway, riding for an hour. He sat in a corner seat, placidly but carefully watching riders get on and off.

He switched trains twice, watching for familiar faces, seeing none. Still, he could not relax. He tried to tell himself that this was normal. He boarded a 7 train, wearing ear buds whose plug end was tucked into his empty pocket. His jaw was trembling and there seemed to be nothing he could do to stop it. Anticipation and adrenaline had set his muscles to shaking. He wished he had a player into which he could plug the ear buds, only to counter the alarms going off inside his head.

He was finally able to soothe himself by focusing his thoughts on the task at hand. He imagined the subway car filling suddenly with a blast of orange flame. The shock wave tore the steel hull apart as it blasted through the underground tube, obliterating every human in its wake. His mind went further, well beyond the blast radius, into the fear that would ripple throughout the city and the country at large.

Paralysis would ensue. Then necrosis. Then death.

No one and no place is safe. Not in New York City, not anywhere.

That was the message.

Physical exhaustion caught up with him, coupled with the rocking of the subway car, lulling him to sleep. He awoke fighting, wild-eyed, when a Transit Authority driver shook him from his slumber. As the uniformed woman bustled off to call the authorities, Shah rushed out of the car and up an out-of-service escalator and quickly onto the street, chastened by his own inattention. Too much was at stake.

He walked the rest of the way to Times

Square. The sunshine warmed him and he met no one's eyes. The city planners had recently restricted traffic from the major intersection, setting up tables and chairs, in an effort to make the Crossroads of the World more of a plaza. Shah was looking for his family's cart.

Until the 1970s, Greeks owned and operated most food cart franchises in New York City. The business had fractured throughout the 1980s into the 1990s. Most vendors still rented their carts from descendants of the old Greek owners, but now different nationalities specialized in certain products.

Fruit stands and downtown hot dog carts were manned by Bangladeshis. Dominicans ran the uptown hot dogs. Vietnamese ran smoothie carts citywide. Brazilians and Colombians operated the fragrant nut carts. And Afghans ran almost every coffee and pastry cart in town.

Shah's father, a cabdriver, had purchased his cart in 1997, just before it became prohibitively expensive to do so. In May 2001, he left the family to attend a funeral in the Andarab district of Baghlan Province and never returned. The family's search for him was initially confounded by the travel and information restrictions imposed after the 9/11 attacks, but he was never heard from again. His disappearance remained unsolved and festered like a wound in Bassam Shah's mind.

Shah had, over the course of that decade, come to associate his father's vanishing with the terror attacks. All this ruminating had led him to the certainty that his father had been somehow involved in the Holy War. He believed that his father was still alive and had been pulled into the resistance movements in the mountains, most likely crossing over into Pakistan.

At the training camp Shah had attended in Waziristan, his instructors hinted as much. Their discouragement of his desire to continue the search for his father served to confirm his thoughts. Cells must be kept separate for security reasons, and Shah pledged himself to the larger cause.

The coffee cart cleared thirty thousand dollars a year. Shah himself had operated the cart alone for much of the middle of the decade, his dependably friendly morning face for the arriving armies of financial district bankers and clerks masking the tumult inside. In those days, which seemed so long ago now, he had kept a stack of Korans in a box beneath the cart, and handed a copy to anybody who would take it. But when questions about his father's fate took over his thinking, consuming his daily life, he realized he needed to leave the cart and seek his own path.

He moved to Denver for a year for religious observance in a mosque outside the city. Shah subleased the cart to a fellow Afghan, a cousin who was eager to work and who appeared content with his subsistence living, even happy—and essentially blind to the plight of his countrymen.

Shah returned to New York every few months to check on his cousin. His visits were always the same. Sell a few cups of coffee, greet the occasional old customer, and help his cousin tow the cart back to Greenpoint in Brooklyn for storage at the end of the day. But recently he had treated these visits as less than a courtesy call and more of a reconnaissance mission. Also, returning to the city recharged his resolve, erasing any doubts he had as to his duty.

He found Ahmed working beneath the

cart's faded umbrella just off Seventh Avenue, a strategic position equidistant from the many Starbucks around Times Square. Midafternoon was a slow period, when customers tended to be caffeine-craving tourists off their usual time clock or nearby office workers in need of a stimulant between meals. Shah plucked out his ear buds and greeted his cousin, who was excited to see him. He inquired about the business and made small talk, but not much more. He treated Ahmed coldly, which was not his intent, but Shah knew he was not himself. He saw that Ahmed noticed his lack of spirit, but Ahmed said nothing.

Under the pretense of examining the cart for possible repairs, Shah examined the area beneath the cart where he used to store his Korans. Ahmed's Puma backpack was the only item there.

Ahmed brought up a problem he was having with the coffee distributor, and Shah nodded as though any of this mattered. An approaching man called his name—"Bassam!"—nearly sending Shah into a panic. But Shah saw that the old man was a former customer, recognizing his nicotine-gray face and the sneakers he wore with his suit like the female commuters.

The customer was effusive, wanting to know how he was, and Shah responded as though from the bottom of a murky pond. He was so many leagues away from any sort of common social interaction. And this man was a Jew, and Shah felt a sting of foolishness for allowing himself to befriend him so many years ago.

"Is anything wrong, are you all right?" asked the man. "You seem different."

Shah shook his head or nodded, he did not even know which. No matter how he responded to the man, his mind was saying *Go away*.

And finally the man did, and Shah could tell Ahmed was looking at him warily. Shah told him they were packing up a little early that day. Together they pushed the cart two blocks through the square, then three blocks west to the parking lot on Forty-third Street. There they loaded the cart onto a rusty trailer hooked to a 1999 Toyota Camry and towed it back to the storage building in Greenpoint and locked up. Shah handed Ahmed his backpack and a wad of bills.

"Tomorrow is yours, cousin. Enjoy a day away. I would like a day's work with the cart. Here is your day's proceeds in advance."

Ahmed leafed through the bills, less than one hundred dollars. He was more confused than grateful. To his credit, a day off meant nothing to him. He worked without complaint. But he was pleased to receive his pay. "Would you like me to help you in the morning, fill the dispensers—"

"No, I will do so myself."

Ahmed wanted to insist. Routine was everything to him, and he seemed almost offended by Shah's generosity. But eventually he took his backpack and, with a warm but uncertain nod, started for home.

Fisk was at his desk later in the day when an attractive young woman tapped the top of his monitor. She had short, dyed black hair that looked like she had trimmed it herself: a note of harshness in contrast to the soft features of her face. Still, he bought the screw-you, punk look. It must have served her well, passing as a hard-case radical in neighborhoods where it looked good to be Caucasian and pissed off at the United States. She had spent the past seven months talking revolution and seeding dissent in order to draw out others eager to make such talk a reality.

"Krina Gersten," she said, introducing herself. "I was told you asked to see me?"

Fisk nodded, thrown off by what looked to him like a hickey on the side of her neck, just above the collar of her military-style jacket. He felt his eyes flash to it, and then, rather than pull back guiltily like a kid caught staring at cleavage, he squinted, getting a closer look.

"Snakebite?" he said.

She smiled, touching it gently, like a burn. She had a fine neck, which was why the mark stood out so vividly. And her smile showed a tiny space between her two front teeth, giving her face a little extra character and attitude. "You're the first person rude enough to comment on it."

"I make an incredible first impression," said Fisk. "You see, the trick is to suck out the venom without swallowing it and becoming poisoned yourself."

"You've had experience with this?" she said.

"With snake venom?" he said. "Just ask my ex."

Gersten smiled at that—not amused, necessarily, or even impressed, but rather appreciative of the banter. Intrigued. Fisk could see that, to her, flirtation was less an invitation than a challenge. "'Ex' as in ex-wife?"

"Ex-fiancée," said Fisk. "She was a snake charmer."

"Right," said Gersten. "Sounds like a fun gal."

Fisk held out his hand. "Jeremy Fisk."

Gersten made a point of giving him a good, firm, professional squeeze.

"Easy there," he said, pulling back his sore hand. "Death grip. Dad in the military?"

"Not the military," she said.

"Uh-oh," said Fisk, knowing what was coming next.

"That's right," she told him. "A cop."

"Christ. Second or third generation?"

"Me? I'm the fourth."

"Gah. Okay. Thanks very much for the warning."

"You have no idea," she said. "What about you, Detective Fisk? What's your story?"

"Me? Just your run-of-the-mill first-generation public servant."

"Yeah? So where'd you draw the cop gene from?"

"Mutation," he said. "A defect."

"Okay," she said, sizing him up, deciding. "You're interesting."

Fisk liked her immediately. Later he would learn that her father had been a sergeant in charge of one of the department's scuba squads when he suffered a heart attack underwater. Gersten had been thirteen at the time. She still lived with her mother across the Narrows over on Staten Island, which was like a ghetto for New York cops and firefighters. She had also done a tour in Iraq with a national police transition team, following college at CUNY. So for her the cop life had been the one and only course on her life menu.

The big dance was bad business with another cop, but immediately they had that undercurrent of attraction that kept things fun and interesting. Gersten came recommended to him from street raking for her skills, her work ethic, and the fact that she took shit assignments without complaint and wound up excelling at them.

"Did I see you limping?" she asked.

"You might have. Basketball."

"Hurts getting old, huh?" she said.

He smiled at her insolence. "Maybe you can make heads or tails of this. I had this dream last night. I was at a cocktail party at the police academy, which also resembled my high school. Anyway, I watched as the bartender planted a bomb beneath the bar. I saw all this from across the crowded room . . . but I couldn't get to him, all because of this limp."

"Was he Middle Eastern?" she interjected.

"Of course he was," said Fisk. "You make pizzas all day, you dream of pizzas. You work mosques and shawarma shops all day, you dream of Middle Easterners."

"Tell me about it."

"So finally I get near the bar—I'm the only one who can hear this thing ticking—and I go around the end and dive underneath . . . and there's nothing there. Just the tanks for the soda taps. I look up—and now the room is in flames all around me. Drapes on fire, walls melting—but people still socializing and chatting."

"Good booze," she surmised. "Open bar, I take it?"

"I was hoping for a little more insight than that, Doctor."

Gersten said, "In my dreams now, I am always aware that I'm dreaming. Never used to be that way before I switched over to Intel. Now I'm always conscious that it's not really real. That I have to be in control, even in my sleep. Takes all the fun out of it, don't you think?"

"Ever vigilant," said Fisk. "The nature of the job."

"The nature of the beast. Not fair, though. I can't even get away from this stuff in my downtime?"

"No such thing as downtime," said Fisk. "Remember, you're not paranoid, you're *alert*. I go to movies now, I can't stop thinking about all the people in the dark around me—who are they, what are they doing."

She nodded. "They're enjoying the movie."

"The way it's supposed to be. That's our job. Allowing them to do so." He sighed. "I used to like movies."

"And I used to like sleep," said Gersten.

They caught themselves bitching. Fisk said, "Okay, now that we've had our cry . . ."

He brought her up to date on the Shah situation. Just the highlights, for the time being.

"You know the imam who runs the funeral home in Flushing?"

Gersten nodded. "Samara Abad Sa-lame."

"The FBI's had him in their pocket for a while. Got into a bit of trouble last year with his taxes. Not enough to get him hauled in, but just enough to soften him up for a visit."

Gersten got it. "They went salivating," she guessed.

"Exactly. Now, Salame has given them the goods so far. And they've made him available to us, and he's been on target, so much as we know. But his loyalty is ultimately neither to the FBI nor to us. So I don't think it's too much of a leap to con-sider the fact that he might not be telling the FBI everything. Now, Analytic got me lineage charts on a guy currently in Gitmo who is apparently Salame's brother, though maybe by a different mother."

Gersten said, "Family concerns trump all."

"Exactly. And Shah is also a cousin of his."

Gersten said, "Let me ask you this. Do you think Shah was baited in Denver?"

"You mean, was he encouraged or other-wise coerced to act? Probably." Fisk waved

it away. "I can't care. That's the FBI's problem. This is our job here. Actual lives are
at stake. No matter what brought him to
this point, there is absolutely no question
he is planning and preparing a terrorist
act. He's a dictionary-definition terrorist."

"Sounds to me like I'm getting off the
street," said Gersten.

"For now," said Fisk. "See, they—the
FBI—they wanted to let this guy run some
more, see who he meets here in New York,
gather up more intelligence crumbs."

"You think it's not worth it."

"Nope. Not since Shah shook free of
surveillance three hours ago."

Gersten's mouth hung open. "Holy shit."

"We've got people who knew his family.
I've got a bead, not on where he is, but
where he might go. The FBI might have
this information too."

"Good," she said. Then, reading his
face, she reconsidered. "No?"

"This is Intel's turf now. I need someone
like yourself. Someone who doesn't look
cop. Somebody who can dupe not only a
terrorist, but perhaps the FBI as well. What
I need to know right now is, will that be a
problem for you?"

Of all the answers he could have received, Fisk did not expect her to smile.
She said, "Now things are getting interesting."

"Peavy?" said Fisk. "Where are you?"

"The studio." Peavy was a military
sharpshooter, a veteran of four tours of
duty over the past decade with eighty-five
confirmed kills to his credit. He taught at a
Krav Maga studio on the Lower East Side.
"I'm in."

Fisk said, "You don't even know what it
is yet."

"It's either a job or tickets to the Yankees."

"The Yankees are out of town," said Fisk.

"This official or not?"

"Depends."

"On what?"

"On how it comes out."

Peavy said, "Let's not do this over the
phone."

At eight o'clock the next morning, Shah entered the unlocked door of a house in Flushing, a residential neighborhood of single-family homes. Majid Kazir arrived less than ten minutes later, looking dazed and dark-eyed from having stayed up all night. He pulled a can of Diet Coke from the refrigerator and sat down at the table, plucked open the soda can tab with a long thumbnail, and drank as though to wash away a bad taste in his mouth. He badly needed the caffeine.

Kazir smelled of bleach. "Mother is finished," he said.

This was Kazir's mother's house, but Kazir was not referring to her. The beauty salon attached to the structure belonged to his mother, was staffed by his two sisters, and was managed by Kazir. Kazir's hair was kinky but flat. He had no use for beauty products himself, but the shop did a steady business and his mother and sisters were always pleased.

The shop had been closed for four days. Their trip to visit relatives in Pennsylvania had been arranged by Kazir to take place this week. He needed the house to himself.

As the manager, one of his responsibilities was to procure supplies used in the treatments. He had been patiently amassing a modest stockpile of hydrogen peroxide, acetone, and acid from various beauty supply stores over the past eight months. The three ingredients in acetone peroxide, or triacetone triperoxide, could form a primary high explosive. The compound's notorious sensitivity to impact, heat, and friction earned it a nickname among the Islamist underground organizations.

Mother of Satan.

Shah said, "Mother is packed and ready?"

Kazir nodded, suppressing a carbonation belch. He looked at his still-trembling hand. Kazir had been heating and mixing the ingredients all night. "Mother was a bitch tonight, my friend."

Kazir finished his soda and tossed the empty can into the sink. Shah had been put in contact with him through the network. Kazir did not come to him espousing jihad and anti-American sentiments—which was good, since those are all hallmarks of a law enforcement plant. Kazir was serious, and he was quiet. His only hot point of anger was the place of women in American society. He detested their independence, which he claimed was the reason he had so much trouble finding a wife. Indeed, his own mother and sisters venerated him as the man of the household, so much so that he was required to contribute very little to the family business. Even this, he resented.

He believed that he was meant for bigger and better things. This was his first stride toward greatness, following in the footsteps of his Moroccan countrymen, who had orchestrated the Madrid commuter train bombings. Outwardly, he appeared to pay Shah's bid for martyrdom much respect, but Shah suspected that Kazir would never exhibit the same level of commitment as Shah—that is to say, the ultimate commitment. In this endeavor, Kazir had taken great care that his participation not be discovered.

Kazir had been trained as a chemist in the same camp Shah had attended, in the high mountains of Waziristan on the Pakistan and Afghanistan border. Shah had confidence that the explosive would not fail him—nor he it.

Shah pulled the cell phone from his pocket. "Here." He placed it on the table before Kazir, who regarded it as one might regard a cockroach.

"What is this?"

"A telephone," said Shah. "It contains my statement. My video. You will upload it precisely at eleven A.M."

Kazir looked at the flip phone. "You videoed it yourself?"

"Of course." It was an older device with the chipset of a pay-as-you-go convenience store phone. He had used its low-res camera to record his final words while locked in the bathroom stall of a Middle

Eastern restaurant on Twenty-eighth Street. His other phone, his public phone, he had "lost" along with his laptop. Those devices could not be trusted.

"Dispose of this when you are done," said Shah.

"I do not like handling electronic devices," said Kazir.

High-impact explosives, yes. But smartphones, no. Shah shook his head. This man refined hydrogen peroxide and acetone into explosive crystals as powerful as C-4. But he was paranoid about handling a microprocessor. Shah was not unhappy to leave this world.

"I have been very careful, I assure you," said Shah. "Where is it?"

Kazir nodded to the back entrance. Shah rose and found a gym bag there, a small duffel. He lifted it, tentatively at first. It was heavy, but not prohibitively so.

He thought to say something more to Kazir, who remained slumped in a chair in the kitchen. But there were no words.

In the end, he tucked the pack beneath his arm and simply headed out the door. His farewell would be one not of words but of deed.

Fisk looked through the high-powered monocular spotting scope mounted on a tripod resting on the rubber-coated roof of the Marriott Marquis hotel in Times Square. The scope's end was topped with a nylon visor to eliminate any telltale glints of sunlight.

He was set up between the blowing strands of hair of a model's image atop a giant Victoria's Secret billboard advertising their newest padded bra.

Next to the scope was a tented monitor showing a shaky, human's-eye view of the Crossroads of the World below. Fisk was connected to the monitor by headphones.

He bowed toward the spotting scope, panning the square at late morning. Tourists in pairs and in groups, hundreds of cameras going—both 35 millimeter SLR and phone-based—and signboard walkers working to push passersby into comedy clubs, tour buses, and restaurants.

Fisk looked back up. He did not want to loosen the hinge that would allow him to use the monocular to scan the other rooftops, only to have to reset on his target on the square. But he guessed that the FBI had their own people at vantage points around Forty-fifth Street. As usual, he wondered what they were waiting for. Were they still relying on Shah's supposed three-day timeline?

For that matter—what was Shah waiting for?

Fisk returned to the scope, trying not to get antsy. He eyed the Naked Cowboy posing for pictures with tourists near the bleacher seats at the TKTS discount tickets booth. He watched a walking blue-green Statue of Liberty working the ticket sale lines. He scanned the knot of potential shoppers surrounding a pair of giant

M&M's in white gloves and shoes, one red, the other yellow. He looked at the tables of knockoff handbags and cheaply made souvenirs along the fringes, operated by nervous-looking black marketeers.

Then he went back to his target, the coffee cart owned and—today, at least—operated by Bassam Shah.

"Okay," said Fisk, speaking into a small microphone jutting out of his earphones. "This is ridiculously dangerous. Enough waiting. Time to initiate contact."

Krina Gersten wandered the square with a map in one hand and a guidebook in the other. Somebody tapped her on the shoulder, an Asian tourist wanting to get a photograph with the mime dressed up as Lady Liberty. Everybody wanted their picture taken with the green-painted lady holding a foam torch. Gersten obliged and took the picture, watching the coffee cart out of the corner of her eye.

Tourists everywhere. Gersten played her part, accepting every flyer offered her for discount pizza and free stand-up and strip club admission and bus tours.

She wore a Bluetooth headset on her

ear. The call was open. She could hear Fisk, and he could eavesdrop on her in real time.

In the Y in the insignia on the front of her stiff new New York Yankees ball cap was a tiny pinhole camera, relaying her perspective to Fisk.

"Time to initiate contact," Fisk said.

"On my way now," she muttered.

She walked to the coffee cart, waiting behind a hassled office worker on a break who was arguing into his cell phone. Shah worked the carafe, squirting in flavored creamer and two Splendas. The customer slipped him three one-dollar bills and walked away yammering.

Gersten stepped up. She could see the sweat on the Afghan's brow. He looked at her strangely, distractedly. He looked ill.

"Hi!" she said brightly. "Do you have any hazelnut decaf?"

He appeared puzzled. Then he checked the labels on his own carafes.

"No decaf."

"Okay, I'll take the caffeine, I guess. I'm on vacation, right? Probably need it anyway."

He did not respond or acknowledge.

She didn't believe he even heard her. He lifted a thick paper cup from the tower on the cart spike and filled it.

"Black, please, with two Splendas," said Gersten, once he finished the pour. She watched him tear open the yellow packets of artificial sweetener. "Sorry to intrude, but . . . are you okay? You don't look so hot right now."

Shah looked at her briefly, hard. Part of it was an ethnic predisposition against independent women, perhaps. But part of it was certainly suspicion.

He did not answer, swishing a thin wooden stirrer through her coffee.

"I didn't mean anything," she said. "Just concerned. Hey, can I take . . . ?"

She went around the side of the cart, trying to get a full view of it. She was reaching for a coffee lid, but Shah quickly stepped in her way, blocking her with his body.

"I get!" he said. "I get!"

"Okay, jeez. Sorry."

He handed her the coffee. Gersten juggled her maps and travel guide, taking out a few dollars, which she straightened out and handed to him.

"Thanks," she said. "Have a great one."

She walked back toward the TKTS ticket booth, her map tucked beneath her arm. The coffee cup was not warm in her hand. She sipped it immediately and found it tepid—and horrid. The worst cup of coffee she had ever had.

"I think it's happening," she said.

Peavy, the sniper, lay atop the third-story theater marquee and watched the coffee vendor through his scope. They had set up overnight, erecting a low, tented roof for cover, draped in the same obscuring fabric as the advertising material that covers transit bus windows. Peavy and his spotter could see out, but no one could see in.

Times Square was a great spot for a high hide. If people looked up, they looked way up. Probably no more distracting location in the world.

Wally, his spotter, had trained in from D.C. the day before, no questions asked. Wally's talent had been forged in urban situations overseas. The FBI's Hostage Rescue Team—Fisk said they were possibly perched nearby—was very good at range shooting, famous for their vaunted "aspirin" test, the ability to hit a baby aspirin at one thousand meters. Not so much in urban landscapes.

HRT used .308 sniper rifles. Peavy's weapon was a Barrett M82A .50 caliber semiautomatic. Fifty-seven inches long, weighing thirty pounds when empty.

It was not empty now. Peavy was loaded and locked over Times Square.

No question Fisk was a dedicated mofo, borderline insane, Peavy thought. But not as insane as posting up for a kill shot in the middle of Manhattan, going up against the Federal Bureau of Investigation. Which made it fun.

He had a nice 240-degree angle. The coffee vendor was far right. Wally kept him updated on wind changes. Buildings made it tough. The BORS ballistic computer on top of his Leupold scope eased the level of difficulty. This computer, the size of a pack of cigarettes, factored distance, trajectory, and barometric pressure automatically, rendering an accurate firing solution in seconds. He had already zeroed for elevation.

Right now the target was out at six hundred yards. Peavy relaxed his shoulders, waiting for Wally to relay Fisk's order.

Shah unhooked the canvas covering from its grommet on the roof of the cart, draping it over the service side. He eyed Lady Liberty walking past, then the Naked Cowboy on the corner, posing. A person dressed like a 1950s Puerto Rican gang member in skinny jeans and a T-shirt with a pack of cigarettes rolled under one sleeve was trying to interest tourists in a revival of *West Side Story.*

They all looked suspicious to him. And every customer that morning seemed like a plant. Anxiety was sapping his determination.

No more. There was no perfect time. He had to do it now.

He dropped the canvas covering on the other side and unlocked his wheels. He pulled out the wooden wedges and started rolling the cart, pushing it south through busy Times Square toward the subway entrance.

Fisk saw two male "tourists" fold their maps and start moving in the same direction as

Shah moved with his cart. The FBI was stirring, but still not pouncing.

Fisk said to his Intel cops, "Stay close." He said, "Peavy, you tracking?"

"Don't worry about me," came the sniper's voice.

Fisk had watched the entire exchange with Shah from Gersten's point of view. He saw the nervous anticipation in Shah's face. Most of all he wondered what Shah had in the bottom of his cart. What Shah didn't want Gersten to see.

"Stay close, everyone," said Fisk, pulling down his headphones. He pivoted too quickly, forgetting his sore ankle, and started off at a limp. "I'm coming down."

Gersten trailed Shah from a distance, still pretending to be following her map. He was pushing the cart along with his head out to the side to avoid oncoming tourists. He crossed Forty-fourth and kept going south.

She was screened by a cluster of tourists, and just as she got around them, she saw Shah looking back, spotting her looking his way.

Shit. She had no other choice but to

own it. Thinking fast, she waved her map and jogged toward him, catching up.

"Hey, hi, this coffee—it's so terrible. Can I just get a refund?"

He stood very still. His eyes held the most vacant expression she'd ever seen. The brown pupils were glassy, looking dead from the inside out, and she recognized the stare of a true fanatic, someone in a self-induced psychotic trance. She knew then that she was looking into the eyes of a terrorist.

His skin had gone ash gray with blotches of red on his neck, like hives. He struggled to speak.

"Go away," he whispered.

Gersten hesitated. She waited for Fisk's order. Shah pushed his cart ahead a few more yards—then abruptly set it down.

He reached into the shelf beneath his cart, removing a gym bag, and started running.

Fisk finally got out of the hotel, dodging tourists and hawkers, and he hobbled across the crowded square. He hustled along on his bad ankle until he spied Gersten and her Yankees cap way down past

Forty-fourth standing with Shah. Fisk raised his hand and waved, pointing his men to intervene—but they were already a few steps behind the FBI, closing in from four different directions.

Peavy pivoted. Wally gave him a new range, which he punched into the optical ranging system computer. The mark had been moving right to left, pushing his cart, moving at a slow rate. When he took off running with the bag in hand, Peavy exhaled and kept him in his sights.

"Tell me," he said to Wally, who was hooked up to Fisk.

"Nothing yet."

The mark was darting in and out of people, and Peavy had him all the way. The sniper's motto was "Don't Bother Running—You're Already Dead."

Wally tracked him with the glasses. "What's he got in the bag?"

"Nothing much," said Peavy. "Just a few pounds of boom." He watched the rabbit run, needing to rerange. "Dammit, Fisk."

Shah turned and took off, and Gersten broke into a run after him.

He hoisted the gym bag strangely, running with it held behind his head.

Gersten had just dodged a surprised and unaware cop when, all at once, two men in suits tackled her.

FBI agents, yelling that she was under arrest.

"NYPD!" she said, trying to kick the assholes off her.

Fisk arrived, grabbing the agents by their collars, waving his shield and yelling. Then he continued on, forgetting his pain now.

He looked beyond the intersection, searching for Shah's target. When he cut to the right, staying on Seventh Avenue, Fisk knew.

"The Forty-second Street subway entrance!" he said into the small mic in his sleeve.

Wally heard something. His head swiveled slightly, his right middle finger fine focusing the binoculars.

"Six eighty at the subway entrance . . ."

Peavy adjusted the scope one click without taking his eye off the target, who was running with the gym bag behind his head. A 400-grain solid brass 50 caliber round leaves a Barrett at 3,200 feet per second. Shock and blood loss make a hit anywhere on the body a kill shot, but only a head shot guaranteed immediate neurological and muscular shutdown. And Peavy was a perfectionist with 127 confirmed kills. Through the scope, he held Shah in the crosshairs as he sprinted toward the stairs. Wally gave the command.

"Send it."

"I want the head." Peavy's trigger finger tightened with ball-bearing smoothness.

Fisk saw Shah knock over a child, running full-out for the subway entrance. His momentum caused him to stumble, reaching out with the hand that held the gym bag for balance.

Fisk heard nothing: no report, no echo.

At the top step, Shah's head disappeared in a pink mist. The terrorist's body twisted midstride and pitched forward headlessly, coming to a stop.

The gym bag landed near him—not softly, but softly enough.

Fisk stopped, stunned. He was estimating the blast radius of the explosive.

Gersten caught up to him, FBI agents passing them, rushing to the dead terrorist. She looked at Fisk. "How did you do that?"

Fisk turned and looked back toward Times Square. He did not know where Peavy was set up—only that he was probably gone from the firing spot already.

He said, "Friends in high places."

PART 2

October 2009

Abbottabad, Pakistan

Arshad Khan, a heavyset, fiftyish man in a blue nylon tracksuit and Puma high-top basketball sneakers, looked very much out of place among the gamers and tourists at the All-Joy Internet Café.

He sipped his hot tea and prowled the Web for newspaper stories, YouTube videos, and blog postings about the Bassam Shah incident in New York City. There was little information of value, but it satisfied his curiosity.

Photographs of sunflowers culled from a Google image search filled another open window on the monitor bike-locked to the café counter. He spotted eight new ones that he did not recognize from previous downloads, and saved them to a two-gigabyte Lexar flash drive, its activity light flickering as it stored the images.

Finally, after shifting his posture to cover the screen from casual observers, he opened a third window—a small one—and quickly browsed familiar pornography sites, ones not blocked by the café. He captured free JPEG images and video clips almost at random—lactating women, lesbian sex, gay men masturbating—until the thumb drive was full.

He unplugged the drive, paid the teenager at the door for his hour at the machine, and wished him peace. Khan spoke Urdu with a Pashtun accent, but given his casual appearance he could have been from anywhere in the Arab world. He crossed the street, savoring the cooler air beneath the canopies of the ancient oriental plane trees as he strolled. Many of the trees were five hundred years old, a fact he found reassuring. Modern life was full of so many tentative realities, but time and history belonged to no man. The future, however, was always in play.

He entered the parking lot of a squash complex, home to the game that Pakistanis had seized from their English colonial masters and dominated for fifty years. Khan unlocked the driver's door of his brick-red Suzuki minivan, heaved himself inside, and sat there with the engine on and the air-conditioning blowing.

For ten minutes, he methodically scrutinized everyone entering and leaving the café. Khan would not return to this particular Internet café for at least another month, rotating his weekly visits among the six scattered around Abbottabad. He also monitored all passing cars, bicycles, tuktuks, and their drivers. He scanned the rooftops of the low buildings in this part of town. Abbottabad was one of the communities hardest hit by the catastrophic earthquake four years earlier, and no one wanted to risk the construction of more than two stories of concrete block.

When he was satisfied that he was not being followed or observed, he pulled out of the parking lot, driving three miles northeast on Kakul Road to the suburb of Bilal Town, near Pakistan's national military academy. The high, burning sun gave rise to mirage vapors in the distance, but he was content that he was unfollowed and alone. He had made this commute many times before.

His property was roughly triangular, and he entered the grounds through a gate in the twelve-foot-high concrete wall at the western point. He pulled into a narrow alley about twenty yards long, then got out to close the first gate and open the second. This admitted him into a parking apron. Khan drove the Suzuki into one of the four bays of a garage and closed the door.

Khan saw three bicycles with wicker tool panniers in the adjoining bays. He frowned. Always easier when bin Laden was alone. Outsiders did not come often. They usually disguised themselves as workmen and stayed through most of a day, leaving after Asr when the streets of the neighborhood filled with similarly homebound laborers and servants.

Still, the presence of strangers in the house made him wary. He wished he could delay his visit, but that would only raise unwarranted suspicion. He pulled from the passenger-side floor two large yellow plastic bags containing twelve-pack cans of Coke, fresh mangoes and apricots, and a jug of bleach.

With the flash drive in his trouser pocket, Khan walked through another mantrap gate into the main courtyard. He had had the house constructed soon after the earthquake. To his neighbors curious about its high walls, razor wire, and security cameras, Khan explained that the house was also home to his uncle, a gold dealer who needed the extra protection.

The main building comprised three stories over a square footprint about fifty feet long on each side. As with the outside walls, the house was constructed with steel-reinforced cinder block, which had been further strengthened with troweled concrete to a thickness of one foot. There was no telephone or Internet connection.

Khan went in through the ground-floor entrance reserved for men, so there was no risk of encountering an unveiled woman. The interior was barnlike, with very few wall coverings and no unnecessary furniture. Ahead, a narrow staircase rose through a small opening in the ceiling to the second floor.

To his right, he heard voices coming from the parlor, a traditional room for business and reception, always near the doorway in any Arab dwelling of substance. Ever since Khan had agreed to shield and shelter bin Laden, he had disciplined himself to have stone ears.

But these voices were too loud to ignore. Emotional speech in this dwelling was rare. The visiting workmen were usually so softly spoken, they had to lean close to one another to be heard.

"Why have we not made more progress with the water tunnels?" Khan heard one of them snap.

When the man he was addressing remained silent, the sharp-tongued speaker went on.

"You have said we have loyalists on the maintenance crews. How difficult can it be to seed the anthrax?"

"The workers are never alone." This was another voice, with a distinctly Yemeni accent. "We have already lost a man, rest him peacefully. Handling the anthrax is as dangerous to the warrior as it is to the targets."

The first voice. "Can we reliably expect

a result within six months? That is the greatest question. Money, as we all know, is an issue. Our purse is light."

"I think not. We began this endeavor in the hope that success with the water tunnel would make the Trade Center victory seem like a stolen bicycle by comparison. But fortune has not favored us."

A third voice, this one slightly off, the speaker an Arab though not using his first language. "We have the poison payload. We now also have a Shadow 600 drone purchased from the Romanians, rated and waiting in Toronto. It has an engine and fuel tank that will get it to New York, Boston, or Philadelphia from the Canadian border, flying below air traffic radar coverage. Maybe even, with the grace of Allah, enough to reach Washington, D.C. The drone is big enough for a payload of dust, salted on leaflets or confetti. Times Square at their New Year celebration. That would be most impactful."

Khan had failed utterly in his resolve to hear nothing. In fact, so mesmerized was he by the confrontational back-and-forth, he did not detect bin Laden's bare footsteps descending the stairs.

Bin Laden always waited until everyone had assembled before joining a meeting. He encountered Khan in the hallway and glared at him at first before his long face softened. He had entrusted Khan with his life, and this was not without great consideration. Before Khan stood the most wanted man in the world, the living object of the wrath of the world's most powerfully evil nation.

What did it matter that Khan overheard the strategists of his inner circle discussing their plans? Khan had sworn to take his own life rather than be captured and tortured. And he would do it too. By the grace of Allah.

Bin Laden reached out to his friend's shoulder. He extended his other hand palm up.

Khan smiled in relief, at first mistaking this gesture for one of friendship. Then, realizing his mistake, he reached deep into his long pocket and handed bin Laden the Lexar flash drive.

"As always, we are safe," said Khan.

Bin Laden nodded, slipping the drive into the folds of his robe. "You would be more comfortable in the kitchen," said bin Laden.

Khan nodded, said thank you, and turned and walked to the kitchen. He was most relieved to have escaped the tension in the entry parlor, and looked forward to a repast before midday prayers.

He heard bin Laden's voice rise in fury as he encountered his advisers—"You foul my house!"—before Khan quietly closed the kitchen door, moving to the teakettle on the stove.

Bin Laden stood before the men seated in the antechamber parlor. They looked at him like surprised students caught brawling by an imam.

Bin Laden moved to his cushion and folded his legs, sitting down among them.

"You foul our one purpose under Allah by compounding your failures. The same plans I hear over and over. Ambition without results. Bomb this. Bomb that. Nothing original, nothing intelligent. From the moment of approach, you are all wrong."

He looked at each face in turn, wanting to strike a chord deeply in them. For this was not simply a disciplining. He was disgusted. He was angry.

"Failure has somehow become noble.

How is this? A wrong we need to right." He kept his voice low and patronizing, addressing them as though explaining rules to disobedient children. "We have achieved our preliminary goal, inciting the United States into invading Muslim countries. We have drawn the enemy into engaging long wars of attrition. But we are far from achieving our ultimate aim—that of collapsing the world economy that is controlled by the Americans, and installing in its place a Wahhabi caliphate to rule according to God's law.

"Our strike at the heart of capitalism eight years ago was a triumph, not because it killed three thousand people, but because it instilled fear in the hearts of the American people. For what are three thousand deaths to a nation of two hundred seventy-five million? A trickle from the bucket. Our victory was in striking down a symbol of their wealth, their strength, their prestige. Their perfidy. We weakened them, not in number but in spirit. We humbled them.

"And since that time, what? A few bodies in the London attacks? That could have been just as easily carried out by common gangsters. And now this most recent embarrassment in New York. We could not even manage to get one single soldier of God into the city subway. Instead of a blow to remind them that they will never, ever know peace, we allowed them another burst of confidence. Another victory to show their people."

The Yemeni spoke. "Plans are increasingly difficult now," he said.

"You are only seeing what they want you to see. The Americans are devouring their treasure in order to prevent us from doing what we have already done. Their airport surveillance makes it exceedingly difficult to succeed with an airliner, yes. But, I ask you—why should we wish to repeat ourselves? We have failed to innovate. If we have learned nothing else from the past decade, it is that we must be more bold, rather than less. We declared jihad against the United States government because it was unjust, criminal, and tyrannical. Not because it was easy. Thirteen years later, it is no less so."

"With respect, my friend," said one of the others, "the enemy has learned well."

"That, I reject. It is not they who have

learned well, it is we who have learned poorly. I have been praying on this recently. We have given up our greatest advantage, and that is the element of surprise. Always in battle, the moment arrives when courage and a calculated risk turn the tide. Years ago in Afghanistan, we learned when we chose to sacrifice thousands in order to close Khyber Pass to the Russian supply convoys. It worked. By the light of Allah, we wore them down. We bled them slowly, the work of a thousand leeches, until they retreated. We have now drawn the Americans into the same trap. They are stuck, bleeding like a pig, and yet still refuse to change their way of life that so offends God." Bin Laden removed an empty hand from the folds of his robe, pointing at each man in turn. "We are at the moment of Khyber Pass now. We will part today with a vision of beautiful success, and a divine plan to achieve it."

The room was silent for a long minute. The man who spoke halting Arabic lifted his hand, asking permission to speak. Bin Laden nodded.

"We must direct our energy toward a target of such powerful symbolic importance to the Americans that its destruction will resonate for generations."

Bin Laden nodded. At the very least, he was confident that his words had gotten through to them.

Another said, "They are waiting for a direct attack from us."

"Precisely. And we should never give them what they anticipate."

"But our resources have dwindled."

"All the more reason to act smarter, to move more swiftly. With an economy of effort. We must think in a new way. What is our goal? Anwar."

Anwar, the younger man directly to bin Laden's right, said, "Not the destruction of lives, but the destruction of a way of life."

"A people." Bin Laden returned his hands to the folds of his robe. "We must lead them like the dogs they are, manipulate them through their weakness. Their existence is an affront to all that is good in the universe. We need a single target of supreme consequence. A strike that will break the soul of the Western demon. Our enemy has raised its heavy shield in anticipation, inviting us to strike it directly, like fools." Bin Laden sat up, seeing clearly as though visited by a bolt of divine inspiration. "Instead, we will feint to expose their vulnerability—and then strike deeply and cleanly. Remember, a strike to the ankle is just as fatal as one to the throat. For the giant still falls."

PART 3

May 2011

Ramstein Air Base, Germany

PART II

May 2011

Ramstein Air Base, Germany

Airman third class Donnie Boyle had been in Mortuary Affairs ever since he finished basic training the year before. He had bargained with the recruiter in Boston and gotten an assignment to Germany, but at the time he had no idea this kind of job even existed.

At first, handling the dead gave him the same evil dream night after night. In it, the mangled parts he unloaded off aircraft from Iraq and Afghanistan reassembled themselves into men and women, sat up, and asked him if they could bum a cigarette. He always told them he didn't smoke, which he didn't, whereupon the bodies came apart again and sank down into a pool of greenish liquid.

Boyle got over the dreams in about a month, but he still hated the job. It ate away at him like an ulcer. Two or three times a week, a giant C-17 Globemaster touched down bearing a load of brushed aluminum coffins. Each was draped with an American or English or Australian flag. Long before Boyle got to Ramstein, they had discontinued the arrival ceremonies with Class A uniforms, bands, and salutes. It had gotten to be too much to bear for everyone involved. Now they unloaded the planes with a forklift. A forklift. But respectfully.

From the runway apron, the dead were transported by flatbed truck into a refrigerated hangar. That was where the forensic specialists took over. After the deliveries, Boyle and the other guys who worked on the ramp helped open the coffins. You never knew what you were going to get. Inside could be anything from what looked like a man or woman taking a nap, to something resembling a large, burned pot roast, to anything in between. Sometimes, there was so little left—no dog tags or labeled uniform—they could not positively identify the dead soldier in Kabul or Baghdad.

The main task in Ramstein was figuring out who had died for his or her country. Because everybody assigned to Mortuary Affairs already had top secret security clearance, it was easy to pull out Boyle with two other guys when the contents from bin Laden's house arrived. The assignment orders were UFN—Until Further Notice. Word was it would be three days, tops.

Three days away from the coffins. It was a stone gift.

The first load from Pakistan came in on a white Gulfstream jet with no markings at all, not even a tail number. The crew did not disembark. The jet sat dark on the airfield, way across at one of the grass-covered humps where they used to store nukes.

Within the hour, a camo Marine Corps C-130 touched down and taxied over to the Gulfstream. Boyle and the others rode a cart out to facilitate the offload into the bunker.

From the outside, the bunker looked like a World War II ruin. They entered through a fifteen-by-fifteen-foot storage locker with piles of broken machinery and aluminum sheeting all over the floor. At the far end of the clutter, a steel door opened into a ten-by-ten-foot air lock. On the side walls of the chamber, white Gen-Nex painters' coveralls, tie-on face masks, and booties hung on hooks. Boyle suited up, pulling blue latex gloves from a box on the door rack. Tedious work, but so was popping open coffins.

No forklifts here. Boyle and the other two men worked like movers, slogging through a long day toting sealed crates, taped cardboard boxes, steel picnic coolers, and an endless number of bags of rocks and dirt. Every time they went inside, they had to suit up; every time they went out, they had to shed the coveralls, masks, gloves, and booties.

The room beyond the air lock was not what he had expected from looking at the grass bunker outside. It was a clean, brightly lit compartment, about fifty feet by fifty feet, with computer stations in the center and deep wall racks set against white-enameled tin walls. To Boyle's mind it resembled a morgue for possessions.

Perpendicular to the storage racks were metal tables, each with its own laptop computer and tray of instruments. Scalpels, scissors, tongs, piles of plastic bags, magnifying glasses, tins and vials of liquid, a dissection microscope. The interior was air-conditioned to sixty-four degrees Fahrenheit. The artificially cold air scratched his throat, and the steady hum of the blowers gave him the sensation of being airborne or underwater.

Two guards in field armor and battle hats stood watch, each wielding an M16, making radio checks into their boom mics once every fifteen minutes. The offload took eight hours. Afterward, the airplanes refueled and taxied away, made a running turn into their takeoffs, and disappeared into the rainy night over Germany.

An officer showed up while Boyle and the others were finishing the last of the Gatorade. His orders to them were to forget what they had just done. In the morning, they would be needed to run errands to and from the bunker. The officer didn't say for whom.

"Without question, what you people are about to examine here represents the greatest intelligence haul in history," said Dennis Geeseman.

He stood at the squadron commander's briefing podium, a thick file tucked beneath his arm, facing four men and two women sitting apart from each other on black leather recliners in the pilots' ready room. It was just after midnight. Geeseman hadn't slept in thirty hours, but the task invigorated him and he was cruising on adrenaline—just like the old days. He looked crisp in his blue suit, white shirt, and lavender tie. He was the ranking FBI agent on the evidence strike team of the Joint Terrorism Task Force. He was in charge.

"Okay, quick intros." Geeseman opened his file on the podium, lifting out the top sheet, reading from it. "Ellen Bonner from Bureau forensics."

Geeseman paused to find a hand raised, a woman in her mid-thirties wearing loose traveling clothes in the front row.

"Special Agent Bonner will handle DNA extraction and preliminary categorization of organic and nonorganic samples. Phil Elliott from the Defense Intelligence Agency?"

Elliott half stood and waved his hand. He had small, smart eyes.

"Elliott will take the hard copy from the household effects, evaluate, read, and extract whatever might connect the dots. Jeanne Cadogan from Central Intelligence Science and Technology will pick apart the household items."

The only other woman present, Cadogan neither stood nor raised her hand.

"Clothing, cookware, and anything else that might establish ties to other locations and persons," continued Geeseman. "Jerry Fisk from . . ."

"Jeremy," Fisk said, interrupting him.

"Jeremy Fisk," Geeseman corrected himself, giving his head a slight who-gives-a-shit tilt to the left. "NYPD Intel Division. He'll be available to Phil and Jeanne for translation. He will also scan everything for names already linked to ongoing investigations in New York and London. He's worked in both cities, the two hottest targets, as everybody here already knows. And last but not least, Barry Rosofsky and Devon Pearl."

Geeseman gestured to two men who looked like they had been sent by a movie studio casting department to play computer hackers. Rosofsky was the plump one, Pearl the emaciated pale one, each wearing jeans, T-shirts, and shy smiles. No eye contact.

"They are here from the NSA to analyze and catalog computer drives, CDs, anything digital that had been within bin Laden's reach." Geeseman looked up. "As you know, I am Dennis Geeseman with the FBI. I'm going to supervise and float where you need me. I've got passable Arabic,

Fisk, so if you get behind I can help. Here's how this is going to work. We've got no clerical in the bunker, no support staff at all. You'll each be logging your own findings on the laptops. Anderson and Storch over there"—Geeseman indicated a pair of uniformed air force enlisted men standing against the back wall—"will assist your commo and tech. We will flash to Fort Meade and Langley if we get anything urgent, through the signal intelligence station on the other side of the base. We have transportation outside for hand-carrying outgoing messages. There are no lines in or out of the bunker for this job. We're sealed in tight, for obvious reasons.

"You're looking for anything hot, anything unexpected, any hard intel such as names, locations, dates, or lists," said Geeseman—repeating their dispatch briefings for effect. There was no such thing as too much communication, a fact he had learned the hard way. "Basically anything that might lead us to any outstanding, still-active plots. We don't know what we're getting vis-à-vis code work. We're not expecting to find a laundry list of terrorist agents in place or senior Al-Qaeda leadership, of course . . . but then again, stranger things have happened. Lots of eyes and ears will be on this stuff for weeks and weeks, but we are the first ones to unwrap this present. This is hour one. Let's make absolutely sure we don't let something timely and obvious slip through our fingers. If so, we'll all feel shitty a few weeks from now. Remember, a quick revenge strike is not out of the question. These guys are epic grudge holders, and we just pissed them off royally.

"We're going to be here for two days minimum, maybe twice that. They have rooms for everyone over at the bachelor officers' quarters if you want to sleep. There will be vehicles outside the bunker when you need them. We're bringing in food, but if you want something different, it doesn't hurt to ask. These guys love any excuse to run out to Kaiserslautern, and if it's exotic but feasible, we will have airmen outside in the morning to fetch whatever you need. It's only seven in the evening where we came from, so I assume everybody wants to get going right away. Questions?"

"How do we sort the stuff?" Cadogan

asked, dropping the formality of a briefing into a conversational tone. "And who gets what first?"

"This is not a race, please keep that in mind. The containers were marked and numbered by the follow-up team after the SEALs got his body out of there. So we have rough categories with best-guess labels. You will see numbers that correspond to the lading inventory that each of you will be issued inside the bunker. The SEALs grabbed obvious discs, drives, and computers. Those are clearly identified in their containers, so Rosofsky and Pearl, you're all set to start there. We got a lot of random debris from a trash-burning pit in the compound, so Bonner, maybe you want to grab that. We may get lucky with some genetic material. Maybe a little hard copy. For the rest, just take what looks like it might fall into your areas of examination. If, once you get it open, you change your mind, feel free to pass it on—just please make sure it goes to the right person. Don't concern yourselves with chain of custody— that's for those who will come after us."

The residual adrenaline rush of dashing for the Lufthansa flight to Frankfurt and the chopper to Ramstein, and the wild exhilaration following bin Laden's death, kept everyone going inside the bunker. They were a dream team of detective skill and talent, the best in the country at what they did, but at first they couldn't help sounding like a bunch of kids playing Clue. Every few minutes, another exclamation of discovery or surprise broke the steady drone of the air-conditioning fans.

"Oh, baby, will you look at this," said Elliott, holding up a black diary bound by a simple elastic band. "He had a fucking Day-Timer. A Day-Timer. My mom had one of these." He plucked off the band, turning the pages. "The marks in it aren't a language, but the cryppies at Meade should have a field day with this."

Off to the copy machine it went.

A few minutes later: "One of his wives shopped in Thailand within the past few months—or got this from somebody who did," chirped Cadogan, holding up an ivory-colored silk undershirt. "The label is brand new, no dye stains from washing. Now how the hell did they get her there and back?"

Bonner, working silently, took smears, chips, and samples from glassware, food cans, serving utensils, hair combs, lumpy remnants of bar soap, and the contents of two small plastic bathroom garbage pails. Joining the excitement, she at one point blurted, "I've got blood, I've got semen, I've got hair. There is so much here that, once we sort it out and get exemplars, we'll have positive biological IDs on everybody who ever set foot in the place."

Rosofsky and Pearl worked at back-to-back computers. As they moused and clicked and typed, they vented the intensity of their concentration by talking mindless, dependable smack about seventh-generation video game consoles, the Nintendo Wii versus PlayStation 3. The first few flash drives they cloned gave them the general picture. Pre-takedown surveillance had found that bin Laden's house had no electronic link to the outside world, incoming or outgoing. He depended on a courier to bring in news, field reports, and amusement.

But he had to have some way to issue his commands to Al-Qaeda cells, as well as receiving outside intelligence. After ten years of looking for bin Laden, one thing his trackers had long ago confirmed was that he paid close attention to the details of plans all over the world. This included the London subway attack, USS *Cole,* and the first World Trade Center bombing. So the team was primed to look for portable, disposable media that could port into and out of any computer or modern electronic display.

Rosofsky and Pearl scanned the CDs and flash drives for the obvious. Timetables, maps, names. Anything that could help them later when they proceeded into more complex digital terrain.

They skimmed downloaded news broadcasts, many of them featuring OBL himself delivering his pronouncements after attacks. They found a folder containing practice tirades, what was essentially a terrorist blooper reel. There were a few random documents in the mix, some of them text files, some PDF scans of handwritten pages, but nothing obviously juicy. Fisk and Geeseman were passed the Arabic documents and read what they could. They were data compilations on dozens of cities, much of it copied verbatim from sources such as the CIA *World Factbook* and Wikipedia, like terroristic book reports.

None of it alluded to a specific attack or target—nor did they expect it to. Any intel acquired so easily would be immediately suspect.

They skimmed through entire two- and three-year-old issues of *Time, The Economist,* the *New York Times,* the London *Times, The New Yorker, Wired,* and *USA Today.* They were looking specifically for any breaks in formatting, any edits within the text—any hidden transmissions.

After working for a few hours without anything to show for it, they set all that aside. Pearl opened a new folder on his screen. "It's got to be in the pictures," he muttered.

"Agreed," said Rosofsky, bobbing his head across from him, as though listening required motion to penetrate his brain.

"Then you'll also agree that Mario kicks Sonic's ass every hour of every day from now into eternity and infinity."

"I will concede that the Wii is indeed a fantastic console. For six-year-olds who scare easily."

"I'm starting with the porn," said Pearl, so completely immersed that he was unaware of the non sequitur. The first images opened on his screen.

Fisk bailed out for a break once words started swimming before his eyes. He went to the base, grabbed a Twix bar from a vending machine, and sat down at the phones, staring off into space, munching chocolate and caramel and cookie. Once his focus returned, he allowed himself one call. He checked the time difference in New York, then pulled on a headset and dialed anyway.

The phone was answered on the second ring. "Ze condor flies at midnight," said Fisk in a hammy German accent.

"Caller ID comes up as 'Germany,'" said Krina Gersten. "I half expected to hear the chancellor's voice."

"Everything sounds a little dirtier when spoken with a German accent, don't you think?"

"You've been working hard, I can tell."

One Friday evening more than six months earlier, after a long noncourtship of flirtation and denial, the inevitable had happened. They returned late from a day of interviewing baggage handlers at JFK about a missing shipment of magnetic relays, the type that were ideally suited for delayed bomb fuses. They came back together on the Long Island Rail Road from Jamaica in order to avoid the rush hour traffic in a cab. Not much happened on the commute back: each was tired, recharging on the long ride when they switched to a crowded subway car. They got out at Grand Central, since each of them lived on the East Side of Manhattan. It was only as they clicked along the black-and-white tiles on their way through the vast train station that Fisk slowed and raised his eyebrows to her, suggesting a detour with just a look.

They closed the Oyster Bar after two bottles of Australian Riesling, dozens of oysters, a pair of thick crab cakes, and previously untold life stories. Then they found a waiting taxi outside as though it had been part of the plan all along. They held hands in the back of the cab, Gersten resting her head against Fisk's shoulder, riding in buzzed silence to Fisk's two-bedroom co-op in Sutton Place.

Inside the apartment door, once it finally closed and it seemed that conversation was again permitted, Gersten said, looking around, "Family money?"

"Yes," Fisk said. "And the money I make from being an international gigolo."

She nodded, smiling. "Who's making the bigger mistake here?" she asked, kicking her shoes to the side and leaning against the wall. "It's me, right? Always the woman."

"Don't say that. I don't want you to do anything you're going to regret."

She looked at him with one eye almost closed, as though viewing him through a surveyor's instrument. "Exactly what you should say at this moment."

"Don't profile a profiler," said Fisk, shedding his jacket and spilling change on the kitchen counter. "I do have ulterior motives, however."

"When did you know?" she asked.

"Know what?"

She pointed her finger back and forth between them. "This."

"When?" He opened his refrigerator, bending down to look. He pulled out two bottles of Amstel Light and went to the cupboard for crackers, something solid, anything. "Hard to say. But I know this. I lock into that first moment we met like it was yesterday. Your hair was still choppy."

"You liked that."

She was right behind him now. He straightened and turned. The co-op apartment kitchen was typically cramped. Gersten seemed shorter than he was used to, and then he remembered that she had kicked off her shoes. That started to get him hard. "I think there was something in that moment. But then we both knew it was a bad idea, and so went about wasting months and months pretending to be professionals."

"Pretending," she said, licking a bit of lingering oyster sand off her lip.

Fisk showed her the Amstels but she shook her head.

"Bathroom," she said.

He pointed.

She went.

He put down the bottles and waited.

She returned. He feared that the spell was broken, that she was going to beg off now, having had that conversation in the mirror. She would make plans for tomorrow, then back out via text, avoid him at work Monday morning, always avert her gaze whenever she saw him, and pretend that this night had never happened.

She stood at the kitchen entrance, unfazed by the fact that he hadn't moved an inch while she was gone.

"Mouthwash," she said.

He thought about that one. "I'm probably out," said Fisk.

"Oh, well," she said.

She didn't move. Neither did he. Good sign.

"You know, I'm pretty good at keeping secrets," Fisk told her. "Kind of what I do for a living."

"Really?" she said, with an exaggerated searching glance at his ceiling. She was terribly attractive when she was unsteady. Probably because so much of their job demanded absolute steadiness. It was nice and dangerous and sexy to see her off-kilter. "That's funny." She pushed a hair away from her eye. "Me too."

"Covert operations," he said.

She winked, then pressed her forefinger to the side of her nose. "Exactly."

He gave the enterprise some thought.

"Operation Friday Night Friction," he said.

She shook her head. "Too crass. Who do you think I am?"

He thought some more. "Operation Class Not Crass."

"Better. Getting warmer." She shifted her weight from one stocking foot to the other. "This is such a sweet mix of wrong-right."

He nodded. "Sour and sweet."

"It's good right here. The threshold. I want to hold on to this moment."

"Not me," he said.

"I want to know things about you," she said. "This is just part of it for me."

"Absolutely," he said. "Me too." And then, because he didn't feel like he had convinced her, he added, "The fact is that I would say just about anything right now to keep this night going—full confession. But just reminding you, underlining it, so you know—this didn't start tonight, for me. And because of that, it won't end tonight. No matter what happens."

She nodded, taking his words to heart. "We intersect, but don't disappear—deal?"

He puzzled over her words as she leaned her shoulder against the doorway. "Fucking profound," he said. "Where'd you get that from? That's good."

She said, "Are we going to stay here, or do you maybe have a bedroom?"

"I have a bedroom," he said.

In they went. Everything else disappeared. It was quiet and they were serious. They were locked in on each other.

No artificial light in the room, just the city night through the open window blinds. Whispers and slow, careful movements, each one watching the other.

Intensity built. Caresses became squeezing, rhythm became thrust.

"Goddamn, Gersten," said Fisk—as at once she went from supine to straddling him.

The fucking became frantic, even rough. Her gym-hard body on him, her hair brushing against his face. His hands gripping her hips. Almost like a fight, except that there had to be two winners.

He watched Gersten's face in the shadow of the city night. He felt her fingertips chewing into the tops of his shoulders. He watched her lose herself, lose all inhibition, moaning. It ended with the headboard banging into the wall . . . and then silence.

A siren four floors down on East Fifty-fifth woke him, not the sunlight. He squinted and found her sitting on the floor against the wall near the door, wearing a pair of his gym shorts and a V-neck undershirt, checking her phone. Her hair hung over her eyes and her legs were crossed. A glass of water stood on the floor next to her.

They were both hungover and elated simultaneously: the sour and the sweet.

Junk TV became their focus that day, as neither one wanted to be the first to delve into a critical conversation.

"You have anything today?" Fisk asked her.

She studied the television, curled up sitting on his sofa now, a throw pillow beneath her bent left leg, chin on her bare knee. "Yeah," she said, though her eyes didn't sell it. "Actually there are some things I could do . . ."

"I wasn't asking so you'd go," he told her. "In fact, I was hoping maybe you could stay."

She took her chin off her knee and looked at him. Profiling him for sincerity.

"Know this," she said to him, "I swore to myself I'd never get involved with another cop. And I never have. Never."

Fisk shrugged. "What makes you think we're involved?"

Her eyes narrowed, taking the joke as intended. Fisk noticed the small gold detective's shield replica, about the size of a nickel, dangling from a plain dog-tag chain around Gersten's neck.

"Your father's?" he asked.

She nodded, touching it with her forefinger. "His badge number. Four six three two. My mother gave it to me when I graduated from the academy. I take off everything else but this."

Fisk tugged the pillow slowly out from beneath her bent leg. "Prove it," he said.

"Miss me?" he asked now, many months later, speaking on the secure line from Ramstein Air Base.

"Intolerably," she sang, a mix of exaggeration and honesty. "Everything good?"

"You know the drill. FBI is running it. They still hate me but they need me. And Geeseman's still two parts asshole, one part haircut."

"He's probably monitoring all comm, FYI," she told him. Gersten still lived with her mother, but stayed most nights at Sutton Place, even when Fisk was gone. "Wish I was in on it. That is some hot shit, you lucky dog. OBL. I'm walking around picking up trash dropped by snotty NYU Muslim kids again tomorrow."

Fisk smiled. "Muslim beards are the new hipster goatee. You fix the faucet?"

"Nope. Couldn't get it. Dropped a note to the super."

"Lazy," he said, stifling a yawn.

"It's not my sink," she said, and he could tell she was smiling. "All right, I can hear the exhaustion in your voice, and that you want to get back to it. Find something big, will you, hero?"

"I'm trying."

"When you get home, I'll properly debrief you."

"Ah," he said, smiling. "Do me one little favor. Say that again in a German accent."

Fisk pulled on sanitary garb again and moved through the air lock, returning to the bunker and the forensic search. Pearl and Rosofsky had never left, a quad montage of pornographic movies on the screens in front of them. A dizzying exhibition of the twenty-first-century incarnation of the human reproductive imperative, flickering past them at four frames per second.

"Learning anything, boys?" Fisk asked, watching over Pearl's shoulder.

Pearl said, "I got numb to this stuff years ago."

"Do you think you're about ready to try it with a real human woman?"

"Someday maybe," joked Pearl, sitting back, arms crossed, his eyes never leaving the skin game before him.

"Patterns, anything?"

"Definitely some random movies in here. A pattern, I don't know. It would take a psychologist to say with authority what the big Laden got off on, and what was sent his way with messages encrypted. But I'm happy to report that sniffing OBL's underwear ain't part of my job description."

"Just sniffing hard drives."

"Exactly." Pearl pointed off to the right. "Hard copies are on Geeseman's table. The big beard was definitely using steg for moving info."

"Thought so," said Fisk.

Steganography means "hidden writing." An old example from tradecraft would be a message written in lemon juice in between the lines of an innocuous letter; the lemon juice would turn brown when the paper was heated. In the digital age, a computer deconstructs the binary code for an image, translating symbols into complex images. A message may be embedded in such a file by adjusting the color of, say, every one thousandth pixel to correspond to a particular letter in the alphabet, and then transmit it. The alteration of the image is so minuscule as to be invisible to the human eye. If the viewer did not know the message was there, finding it among countless images on a person's computer was virtually impossible.

Four years after 9/11, a twenty-five-year-old named Devon Pearl, newly hired by the National Security Agency after being caught hacking into their system, read a terrorist training manual recovered from a Taliban safe house in Afghanistan. It contained a section entitled "Covert Communications and Hiding Secrets Inside Images."

Pearl found that no one at NSA was an expert on digital steganography, and so he became one himself. By late 2006, he developed the first practical search engine for ferreting out digital images that contained code anomalies indicating the presence of embedded steganographic messages. Pearl's sniffer program—he was now on version seven—could finger-walk through roughly one thousand still images per minute. For video, depending on the level of complexity, it could process five minutes in one. The program spit out a list of corrupt files with even a single pixel out of place. He then ran another program to weed out normally corrupted files—bad transfers—from the systematically manipulated ones.

It was possible now to encode plain text or mini-programs within images or movies that could crash a hard drive. A potential case of domestic terrorism the year before had turned out to be a rogue church of fundamentalist Christians using steg in gay porn to spike the computers of those the church deemed "sinful." Members of an Al-Qaeda cell captured earlier that year in Milan were found with the usual array of pornographic downloads on their phones and computers, but also dozens of screen grabs from eBay sites selling diaper bags, used cars, furniture, and Hummel figurines. All part of a complex file-sharing communication network of terrorists who were piggybacking on legitimate Internet sites.

Pearl's voice followed Fisk over to Geeseman's lab table. "There's not much yet, but after we defog the image, some of it is in plain text. No hard intel yet. But it's clear that they've been busy."

Fisk picked up the thin packet of printouts. He flipped through images of New York—no surprise, more than 50 percent of the traffic analysis at NSA headquarters at Fort Meade was Big Apple. The city had become an international terrorist obsession. By comparison, every other potential target in the United States was small potatoes.

These images were postcard views, though. Commercial photographs. Not handheld surveillance.

Geeseman walked over, perhaps concerned that Fisk was going to move something out of place on his lab table. "Refreshed after your break?" asked Geeseman.

Fisk suppressed an eye roll. Geeseman was a closet cigarette smoker who could not last more than two hours at a time inside the bunker. He and Geeseman had a purely professional relationship. Fisk's rule-breaking reputation in New York had surely preceded him. "I had a quick hot tub and a rubdown, and now I feel like a million bucks."

"I see you found the first scans."

"Looks like the wonder twins are making progress. What about the others?"

"Slow and steady. Bonner, Elliott, and Cadogan are up to their ears with fantastic samples, but not much right-away intel. They're going to spend the rest of the day cataloging for stateside forensics. We've got a C-17 picking it all up tomorrow about this time. Going to Dover for distribution to the task force agencies. Most of it'll end up with Meade and Langley."

Fisk shook the New York scans. "And Intel Division."

"Of course," said Geeseman.

Geeseman moved on, but Fisk remained with the scans, flipping through the last pages. The images were printed six to a page, not unlike mug shots, and Fisk's eyes went to the flowers. Three different images of sunflowers. He recognized one image of a vase bouquet from a book on his coffee table back home. The other two were similarly post-impressionist and, if not Van Goghs also, dutiful knockoffs.

But the color copies were somehow duller than the crisp New York cityscapes. As though they were second- or third-generation scans of printed material.

Fisk called back to Geeseman. "Hey, did OBL keep a garden?"

"A what?"

"These pictures of sunflowers here."

Geeseman walked back to him to take a look. "He or his wives kept a vegetable patch near the animal pen. Thing was immaculate."

"Just vegetables?"

Geeseman reached for a laptop, quickly shuffling through images of the compound. "See for yourself."

Fisk zoomed in. "Immaculate" was the right word. But no decorative flowers in sight.

Geeseman was already at Pearl's side. "Flower pictures?"

"Flower power," said Pearl, his fingertips clicking over the keyboard, producing on-screen type faster than Fisk could read.

Image windows opened, one after the other.

"Lookie here," said Pearl.

Rosofsky rose from his chair, peering over the top of the back-to-back monitors. Pulling out his earphones released the tinny noise of human humping.

"Dammit," said Pearl, his keystrokes

now coming in staccato bursts as the printer whirred to life across the bunker. "Distracted by tits and ass, was I. They always hide their steg in the porn. Fucking sunflowers."

Fisk's eyes danced to each window popping up on the screen. "What are we seeing here?"

"Okay," Pearl began, like a lecturer on the first day of Intro to Steganography. "The trick to this thing is that both the sender and the receiver of any kind of code, cipher, or embedded message in an image have to know where to look. They need the combination. Now, OBL and his minions were definitely sending a lot of comm in the porn files, and we may find some seriously good intel there eventually. Or . . ."

Fisk said, "Or maybe they were clogging up the porn with junk messages, static. Hiding the real message within a mosaic of nonsense ones."

Pearl pointed upward as though Fisk had just won an auction. "When you've got something special going, you designate a particular category of image, say tug jobs in the case of porn. Or you just start with something innocuous and new. In this case—pictures of sunflowers."

Pearl clicked through a stream of images of sunflower fields, potted sunflowers, sunflowers on bonnets, sunflowers in paintings by Van Gogh and Monet. He was also reading his output underneath.

"Okay, these messages are embedded but also enciphered. Now, I'm not a cryppie, but I'm going to make an educated guess that this is a virtually unbreakable one-time-pad system. We'll know more when they crunch the stuff at Meade, but this is sophisticated, random stuff. No doubt there will be several hundred people working on this tomorrow."

"No doubt," said Geeseman, seeing the intel equivalent of dollar signs. "Let's flash what you have directly to NSA. Right now."

"Easy enough," said Fisk. "They're regular digital files. Can fly right through the wires and airwaves just like anything else, once I offload them onto a clean drive."

"Gimme," said Geeseman. "I'll dispatch on the secure link from the comm station."

Fisk said, "Hold on, let him finish this. Let's make sure we give Meade the entire package at once."

Pearl was nodding, like a jazz musician riding a particularly sweet groove.

Geeseman exclaimed, "We've got Al-Qaeda by the fucking beard."

Fisk focused on the screen. "Anything, any kind of pattern at all. Location, people, methods . . ."

Pearl said, "I really can't read the code. But I can see this."

He keyed in a command, and the corner of one of the sunflower images blossomed on the screen to ten times its original size. Its provenance was clear. Fisk had been right. "Metropolitan Museum," it read.

Pearl said, "The Metropolitan Museum of Art in New York. Don't think that's an accident."

Now it was Fisk's turn to nod. "Bring it, fuckers. We're on to you."

"Wait."

Fisk looked at the side of Pearl's head. "What do you mean, wait?"

Pearl continued to work his keyboard. "Oh, lookie here."

"Look at what?"

Pearl said, "If this really is a one-time pad, somebody over at the NSA owes me a fruit basket."

Geeseman said, "Pearl, talk English."

"Those cryptanalysts better put me on their Christmas card list forever." He stopped typing and turned. "Somebody screwed up and embedded one image in the clear."

Fisk's eyes widened. "And with that, they can—"

"Maybe crack the other messages. It's a way in, at least. Don't know if this was from or to bin Laden, but . . ."

He clicked his mouse and a message appeared in a window on the screen:

They must be made to believe
that we repeat ourselves out of a
desperation to act.

By teardown time, Fisk was properly exhausted. No other finds topped the sunflower code discovery, currently being pored over stateside. The air lock was struck, the movers going in and out with hand trucks, transporting the detritus of the late Osama bin Laden's possessions to the waiting Globemaster.

The helicopter to Frankfurt was set to lift off in forty-five minutes. Maybe enough time to get a shower, but more likely not. Geeseman was walking around all rooster-chested, thrilled to have such sensitive and potentially lucrative intel going out under his name. He was giving the movers a hard time, following them around like a grandmother making certain her crystal would not be broken.

"Heavy stuff on the bottom," he said, and Fisk caught one of the airmen rolling his eyes.

Fisk rubbed his. He was stuck between feelings of satisfaction for the discoveries they had made, and frustration for the discoveries they had not. His tired mind was tailing off into a useless spiral, so he forced himself to go get cleaned up at the officers' quarters. He changed clothes and was ready just in time for the ride out to the chopper pad, taking a seat in the front next to the driver.

It was the same airman whom Fisk had seen rolling his eyes at Geeseman's officiousness. "It's Boyle, right?" said Fisk.

"Right, sir." He twisted his shoulder toward Fisk so that Fisk could confirm this by reading the name tape across his left breast pocket.

"Did you put the heavy stuff on the bottom, Boyle?"

"Yes, sir," he snapped. Then his gaze flickered to Fisk. He saw Fisk smiling, and then Boyle relaxed. He checked the mirror to make sure Geeseman was not in the vehicle with them. "Just like I learned in grocery-bagging school, sir."

Fisk nodded, pleased to find a guy with a decent sense of humor. "So what do you do when you're not hauling around a bunch of nosy civilians?" he asked.

"Mortuary Affairs, sir."

"What's that? Undertaker?"

"Kind of, sir," said Boyle. "All the bodies from both wars come through here on their way home. Not the best assignment, though in a sense it is an honor to be doing it . . ."

"Grim work," said Fisk.

"That's the word for it, sir. Just seeing the dead for real . . . it's something I thought I'd never understand."

"Does that mean you understand it now?" asked Fisk, the chopper coming into view ahead.

"Not exactly, sir. I understand that the big picture doesn't mean a damn thing to any of those men and women anymore."

Fisk nodded. "You're dealing with the pixels, just like we are. Everyone else gets to stand back and take the wide view."

"Sir?"

"Nothing, Boyle. I'm practically talking in my sleep here. My mind's still back in that bunker."

"Intense work, sir."

"Eh. Sounds like you've put in your share of hard days, Boyle."

"I have, sir. But it's okay. I'm good with it. Nothing compared to what you all were doing in there. Not that I know for sure, but I think I have an idea. Of course, we're at opposite ends of it. But you've got a hell of a lot better chance of impacting this fucking thing than I do." Boyle winced at his curse word. "Sir."

Fisk thought back to bin Laden's words, which might turn out to be his final statement, his ghoulish message from the grave. *They must be made to believe that we repeat ourselves out of a desperation to act.*

Fisk could not quite decipher it right now. He only knew that it meant one thing.

Something was coming.

PART 4

CHATTER

A Few Years Later

Thursday, July 1

"Boston Center, Scandinavian 903 heavy is with you. We're out of Atlantic Uniform, flight level three six zero, direct Newark."

"Scandinavian 903 heavy, Boston Center. Good morning. Maintain three six zero. Expect descent clearance at 1655 UTC."

"Roger, Boston Center. Maintain three six zero, clearance at 1655. Scandinavian 903 heavy."

Captain Elof Granberg raised his arms over his head in a groaning stretch, his fingertips pointing to the cabin ceiling. The pressure in his bladder had just reached a level of discomfort, which he knew would intensify once he stood. He reached for the direct passenger cabin intercom on the center console.

"Almost done, Maggie," he said to the flight attendant who picked up on the other end. "Initial descent in about twenty. Anders and I will pay our visits, then you can let the pax move around a bit before sitting them down for landing. Please let me know when we're secure."

Granberg then leaned across the console and tapped his copilot on the shoulder. "You take the first head call, Anders. I have the airplane."

"You have the airplane," copilot Anders Bendiksen said. Bendiksen unbuckled his shoulder harness, pushed the straps off his shoulders, and slid his seat back, standing to wait for the flight attendant to confirm that there were no passengers in front of the cockpit door.

The intercom handset buzzed. Bendiksen picked it up.

"All clear for you."

"Thank you, Maggie," said Bendiksen. "Coming out now."

* * *

The mandatory protocol for cockpit door opening in American airspace had been in place since the attacks on New York and Washington. One flight attendant blocked the aisle leading from the front of the passenger cabin, standing before the drawn privacy curtain. A second flight attendant was a backup, standing on the other side. The armored door to the flight deck could be opened only from the inside, or outside from a keypad. The code was changed for every flight, and was known only to the pilots.

On U.S. domestic flights, a wire screen was unfurled and secured, sealing off the vestibule from the first-class cabin while the pilots moved about, one at a time, outside the cockpit. On an international flight aboard a twin-aisle jet like the Airbus 330, the guard post was a ten-foot-long vestibule in front of the flight deck door. On one side was a bathroom, on the other, a bar and coffee galley.

A half-bulkhead separated the vestibule from the business-class cabin. The aisles began on each side of it, running aft through business, economy extra, and economy-class sections to the rear of the airplane.

As the purser on the SAS nonstop from Stockholm to Newark, Maggie Sullivan took her position as the forward blocker. Maggie was a solid five-four with dark hair in a French plait and a long, angular face bred from centuries of black Irish seafaring stock. She possessed that perfect combination of politeness and firmness common to the best flight attendants and nurses—but as a sentry, she was hardly imposing.

Her colleague that flight, a slight Nordic blonde named Trude Carlson, stood behind her. Seven years before, they had together attended a daylong instructional seminar from a martial arts trainer who taught them incapacitating kicks, chops, and pressure-point gouges. The aim, the trainer told them, was to delay an assailant at least long enough to secure the door to the flight deck, and therefore the controls of the airliner. Self-sacrifice, should it be necessary, was implicitly part of the job.

They had performed the door-opening procedure so many times that it had become a ritual rather than a tactic of true vigilance. So when the cockpit door opened, Maggie and Trude were chatting through the curtain about their plans for the unusually lengthy seventy-two-hour layover. They planned to visit the TKTS discount ticket booth in Times Square and were discussing the current must-see Broadway shows. And Trude had an old flame who lived on the Upper East Side who might have a friend for Maggie.

The cockpit door was thrust open and Anders Bendiksen appeared. "Hej-hej," he said, with the singsong lilt of the customary Scandinavian greeting.

Trude chirped "Hej-hej" back to him, glancing over her shoulder.

"Good group this flight?"

"Not bad," said Maggie, still steamed about the man in 11D who had spilled tomato juice on her shoe. Her stocking squished with every step, and she would never get the odor out.

Anders opened the lavatory door and ducked inside, sliding the OCCUPIED lock behind him.

The passenger was on Maggie before she even turned her head back toward the seats.

No outcry. No noise from the business-class cabin. No warning.

A blur, his first contact with her. An arm across her chest, crushing her breasts. Lifting her off her feet, startling her painfully. Jerking her inside the privacy curtain.

His other hand was at her throat. She felt something else there: the icy sting of a sharp blade.

Trude froze. She got her hands in the air, but they were empty. She felt powerless and stunned. This was not happening.

"ON YOUR KNEES!" he shrieked, his English heavily accented, and further warped by rage. He pulled Maggie deeper into the vestibule, out of sight of the majority of the passengers. "BOTH OF YOU! NOW!"

Trude looked around for help, for a weapon, for anything. A pitcher of coffee sat in the galley, but it was nowhere near scalding, and anyway out of her reach. She looked at Maggie's face and saw a long-stare look in her eyes that frightened her as much as the intruder.

"Now!" the man ordered. "She dies now! Obey me!"

Trude fell forward to her knees. The

man lowered Maggie, pushing her down to the floor. He thrust out his other hand, showing them a contraption molded out of toy plastic, with wires extending from it into the cuff of his black cotton shirt.

"I have a bomb!" he declared, showing them the detonator trigger. He spoke loudly enough to be heard in the lavatory, and perhaps even inside the flight deck. He pounded once on the lavatory door with his knife hand.

His eyes were wide, his face intense, like a man staring into a blazing fire. He was young, in his very early twenties. Obviously of Arabic descent, though dressed as a Westerner, his skin tan, his face beardless.

Maggie remembered him in a microsecond flash of her brain cells. He had boarded, took the front row aisle seat on the right side in business class, held an open magazine during takeoff, wrapped himself in a blanket, and slept all the way from Stockholm. His seatmate, a woman, was geared up with the expensive kit of a well-off executive road warrior. Loose-fitting designer gym suit, plush eyeshades, Bose headphones, and a neck pillow leaned against the cabin window. She had slept most of the way too, dropping off soon after take-off. Neither of them took any service at all until water at wake-up before preparing for landing.

"The code!" the man screamed at the door of the lavatory, striking it again with his fist. "I want the cabin code! If you come out, I detonate! Five seconds—or the first woman dies!"

Maggie looked at the man's shoes, his knees, his crotch. Seeking a weak point.

But she would have to get past his knife first.

The man kicked the lavatory door so hard Maggie thought he might have damaged it. "Answer me!"

Anders said from behind the door, "I hear you." His voice was loud enough to be heard, but modulated for calmness. "I do not have the code. Only the captain has the code."

"Liar! You do have it! She dies now!"

He reached down to Maggie, the knife blade pressing against her trachea, the detonator held high. She felt a burn, then warmth running down her neck.

She had been cut. She didn't know how badly.

Trude screamed. The man kicked at her, striking her shoulder, knocking her onto her side.

Anders was saying from behind the door, "Let me come out! I can talk to the captain!"

"Give me the code now!" yelled the intruder.

"I am coming out!" said Anders.

He was trying to open the door, but it was jammed.

"Give me the code!"

At once the vestibule entrance erupted. The hijacker, who had turned his head toward the lavatory, did not see the onrushing passenger explode through the privacy curtain.

Charging, screaming.

Maggie, more out of self-preservation than foresight, grabbed at the man's knife hand. Had she not, the momentum of the passenger hitting him would have run the knife blade right across her throat.

The first passenger in, a fit-looking blond male, grabbed the man's other hand, the one gripping the detonator. He tore it from the bomber's hand ferociously—and then two more men entered from behind, hitting them, driving the blond and the bomber against a stowed serving cart in the wall compartment, then down to the floor.

Another man dug for the knife. A woman pulled Maggie back to the wall.

Two men pinned the bomber to the floor. He was writhing and growling madly.

The blond rolled over onto his back. He held the detonator, but his other hand held his own crooked wrist, his mouth twisted in pain.

Wires dangled from the detonator. The men on the floor yanked up the bomber's shirt, tearing the cotton fabric, searching for an explosive device.

There was nothing but hair and belly.

It happened so quickly, it took time to realize that it was already over. The bomber lay with his face mashed into the floor, a knee upon the back of his neck. Everyone was panting, sweating, exuding adrenaline.

Trude began sobbing into her open hand, staring at Maggie. The female passenger who had joined the men in charging the hijacker instinctively pressed her bare hand against Maggie's bloody throat. Trude pulled down linen tray cloths to stanch the blood flow.

Maggie sat blinking and gasping, allowing them to minister to her. She broke out of her daze when she saw that the hijacker was in reach, extending her leg and heel-kicking the prone bomber.

"You cocksucker!" she screamed. "Evil! Fucking! Cocksucker!"

She looked down and saw her white service blouse soaked red with blood, and she burst into tears. The woman rescuer probed her neck to find the source of the bleeding. The cut was small. The bomber's knife had nicked a vein, but the flow of blood wasn't pulsing. The woman stripped off her own zippered warm-up jacket, mashed it into a compress, and pressed it to Maggie's neck with the towels.

"You're okay," she told Maggie. "It looks like he missed the artery. You're okay."

Banging on the lavatory door. One of the rescuers, an older man, banged back, yelling, "We are safe out here!" he barked. "Stand back as far as you can!"

The man put his shoulder into the broken door, throwing himself at it, but couldn't bust through. Trude was on her feet and went around with him and both of them rushed the small door.

It gave inward this time, the lock cracking out of the frame. The door struck Anders, but he was ready for it, having braced himself with his arm and leg.

He stepped out of the tiny bathroom and looked down at the foiled terrorist, who lay immobilized on the floor wearing tan pants and a ripped white shirt.

"Merde," Anders said.

The enormity of what had just occurred was only now becoming apparent to everyone inside the crowded vestibule. Anders reached past Trude to the intercom on the wall next to the bar and coffee station.

"Captain? This is Anders here. We've had an attempted hijacking."

"I heard it, Anders."

"Everything is under control at the moment. Maggie is hurt."

"How badly?"

Anders looked at Maggie. The woman passenger lifted her jacket from the wound. Anders nodded, smiling at Maggie.

"It looks like she is going to be fine," he said.

"Are you secure?"

Anders looked back at the two men lying

on top of the bomber. He saw the blond holding the supposed detonator, and his own crooked wrist.

"He said he had a bomb, but it . . . looks like it was just a hoax. Just a trigger with wires. And a knife."

For ten seconds, the line was silent.

"Here are my orders," said Captain Granberg when he came back on. "Move all passengers from business class to the rear of the plane except those controlling the hijacker. Tie him up with lap belt extensions and the plastic slip ties from the emergency electrical repair bin. You know the one."

Anders said, "Overhead, just forward of the galley."

"When you have him tied, carry him back to the last row in that cabin, recline the inner middle seat, lash him tightly in it. You supervise at all times. I want him handled humanely, but securely. Be sure he cannot move. Remove his shoes and his pants also. Post at least two guards over him. Do not let him get his hands anywhere near his own mouth or throat. Do you copy?"

"I copy," Anders Bendiksen said.

"For security reasons, I will not be opening the flight deck door again. You will remain posted at the door in view of the attacker. I have already squawked the hijack code on the transponder. I will now get clearance for an emergency descent and landing."

The captain's voice came over the Airbus's cabin loudspeakers.

"Ladies and gentlemen, this is Captain Granberg. We have successfully averted a cockpit intrusion in the forward cabin."

The gasp that went up throughout the length of the aircraft was unlike any human noise the crew had ever heard.

"There is no danger currently. Please remain in your seats unless instructed directly by First Officer Bendiksen, myself, or members of the cabin crew. I repeat—please do remain in your seats. The airplane is still in perfect condition, and we will be diverting for landing with law enforcement members standing by. Please do not be alarmed by the flashing lights after we land, nor the medical support equipment. We have had one minor injury, and I am assured it is not serious or life-threatening.

As soon as possible, we will resume our journey to Newark. I would like to apologize for this inconvenience on behalf of the airline, and for your missed connections with ongoing flights. Thanks to all of you for your patience and understanding, and flight attendants, please prepare the cabin for landing."

Bangor International Airport, some 230 miles northeast of Boston, is the largest, easternmost airport for incoming European flights. A former air force base, the remote airport offers relatively uncluttered skies and, at more than eleven thousand feet in length and two hundred feet in width, one of the longest, widest runways on the East Coast.

Once the stopover point of choice for refueling international charter flights, with the advent of longer-range jetliners Bangor International became, in the air-rage era of the 1990s, a convenient drop-off point for drunk or unruly passengers or medical emergencies.

After 9/11, it became the go-to destination for transatlantic flights diverted due to terrorist concerns. Most often this applied to passengers discovered to be on the Homeland Security Department's no-fly list once a plane was already in the air. A few other times the airport had received aircraft beset by inebriated or psychotic passengers.

The apparatus was therefore already in place, and the response team drilled and ready—but when word came that it was not merely an undesirable passenger but in fact a thwarted terrorist hijacking, the extraction proceeded with additional electricity.

Captain Granberg set down the big Airbus just after 1:00 P.M. Eastern and followed Bangor ground control orders to taxi, park, and shut down his main engines on a hardstand approximately one mile away from the passenger terminal.

Granberg watched from the cabin while a swarm of emergency vehicles—in chartreuse green, as opposed to cherry red—took positions around his plane with fluid choreography. For a silent minute, none of the fire trucks and ambulances and foamer tanks moved. Then ground control advised Granberg to open the galley access door on the starboard side of the vestibule. Granberg relayed these instructions to Bendiksen, who opened the door into the gray Maine light.

The tactical team boarded the plane from an elevated food service truck nuzzled up to the galley door. Four members of the Bangor Police Department hostage extraction team in black body armor, accompanied by two special agents from the Bangor FBI field office and two emergency medical technicians, entered the plane. Automatic weapons drawn, the team rushed past the flight crew and the remaining passengers who had captured the hijacker, through the business-class cabin curtain into economy extra, greeted by the passengers' gasps.

Once they were aboard, Captain Granberg opened the cockpit door and emerged from the flight deck, surveying the damage in the vestibule. He followed the extraction team, showing his captain's bars.

"We'll take him off first, Captain," said the team leader. "The injured attendant and those involved in the fight next." He nodded toward them. "You will then taxi to the terminal to unload the rest of the passengers."

Granberg acknowledged the orders and, after a quick appraisal of the would-be hijacker—anger starting to set in now—he returned to the cockpit.

With an efficiency that comes only from drills and endless rehearsals, the extraction team released the hijacker from the improvised bonds, replaced them systematically with Velcro straps around his ankles, thighs, waist, and shoulders, and pinned his arms to his sides. In a move the hijacker tried to evade with a violent shake, they covered his head with a black, breathable cloth bag and cinched it closed at his neckline. Three of them hoisted the prisoner to shoulder level like a rolled-up carpet. In step, they moved swiftly up the aisle and out onto the food service truck, into the cargo compartment.

The compartment was lowered into the driving position, and the hijacker was secured to a bare steel gurney with two thick

leather belts. The truck pulled away, escorted by two police cars, roof racks alive
with flashing blue and chrome-white lights.

The fourth team member led the five
passengers and Maggie, the injured flight
attendant, to the elevated platform of a
second truck, which was similarly lowered
and driven away under escort. Trude Carlson and Anders Bendiksen remained
aboard the aircraft, as did the paramedics
and the two FBI agents. The Airbus door
was shut and secured, and Captain Granberg started up the engines again, turning
the aircraft around and taxiing to the passenger terminal.

The airport detention facility was on the
south end of the main terminal. The driver
of the food service truck, a policeman in a
black Windbreaker, backed down a sloping ramp into a subterranean garage. A
corrugated steel door slammed down behind it, and the clanging reverse caution
alarm of the truck stopped.

On the opposite end of the garage, wide
double doors opened to a room with a steel
picnic table bolted to the floor surrounded
by four cells, two of them fronted by bars,

two with pale green steel doors. Beyond the cells were two interrogation rooms, ten-by-ten concrete chambers with drains in the floors, all of these post-9/11 renovations paid for by Homeland Security. The extraction team rolled the would-be hijacker of Flight 903 into the first interrogation room, turned off the light, and closed the door.

The pinioned man was held fast. No room even to squirm. The straps felt like they were crushing his bones—his ribs especially. The pressure on his lungs was immense. He breathed shallowly, fighting for oxygen in the stifling blackness of the hood. Sobbing hurt too much.

After ten minutes of immobility and silence, he became convinced he had been left alone to suffocate and die. He imagined himself already buried. Even as his mind wanted to fly into panic, he fought to be strong.

The FBI's terrorist reaction team was airborne even before SAS Flight 903 landed. Four agents, three men and a woman, specialists in urgent interrogation techniques, flew at two hundred knots in a UH-60 Black Hawk from Boston. Covering the distance to Bangor took them a little over an hour.

The tactical assumption was that a terrorist incident is rarely a solitary event. The loose strictures of the U.S. Patriot Act allowed the team expanded interrogation tools. They could go into his head like an extraction team, removing information by force if necessary. Time was at a premium. Minutes wasted on back-and-forth exchanges with a knowledgeable suspect could mean the difference between saving or losing countless lives if a massive plot was under way.

The team entered the interrogation room and worked quickly. The subject's head jerked to the side at the sound of the door opening; isolation had softened him up. The team carried in their own chair—steel, with plates at the feet of all four legs for bolting the chair into the floor. That was not necessary here. They manhandled him into the seat, leaving the hood covering his head.

They bound his wrists to the chair arms, his calves to its front legs, then removed the other restraints. He was fingerprinted digitally, each fingertip and full palm.

The woman rolled up his left sleeve. He tensed at the preternaturally smooth touch of a latex-gloved hand.

The hypodermic needle went in. The chamber filled with a sample of his blood. The vial was capped and taped, the puncture wound left without a bandage. A thin stream of blood rolled down to the crook of his elbow.

After the silent ministrations of physical identification, the first word came at him with the force of a slap.

"Name?"

A man's voice, speaking in a common Saudi dialect.

The hijacker clenched his teeth within his hood.

"Name," again. Then: "We already know who you are. We have your passport. Name?"

He gritted his teeth. His heart was leaping out of his chest.

He felt the chair go back at an angle, and was startled he was going to fall. He prayed, giving himself to God as he had every day of his life.

"We have water," said the voice. "Would you like the water?"

They did not mean a drink. They meant torture. Waterboarding.

The hijacker held his breath, expecting a torrent at any moment.

Instead, another tugging at his left arm. He felt the prick of another needle.

Only this time—no blood was taken.

Within moments, he felt groggy and elated. He sank into a warm bath . . . or, rather, the warm bath sank into him.

His name came soon after, without much effort. Awaan Abdulraheem. The words walked out of his mouth like freed prisoners. Awaan felt a tug at his hair and the hood came off, giving way to a beam of light.

He felt a devil inside of him, a chatty demon, delighted to talk.

"I am from beautiful Yemen," he said, his voice like a song. "*Arabia Felix,* as the Roman conquerors called our fertile home on the Red Sea. My people have grown mangoes on the outskirts of Sanaa for five generations. I am twenty years old. I am mujahideen. I serve one true God."

Awaan began to weep, crippled by his failure. What had they done to him—turning him into someone else? Demons. Their questions elicited responses as though through dark magic.

"I am not a pilot. I learned how to turn the dial on an autopilot to get the plane to New York. My strike into the heart of that city of devils would have been my gift unto God!"

They want to know about the others. Hold on to yourself, he thought. He focused on his mother back home. How proud she would be. He was not the misfit they all thought he was, after all. He was capable of great things.

"I am an obedient soldier," he said, his tears hot and stinging. He bore down, re-membering his pain, nattering on through a forced smile. Hold fast, he told himself. Answer literally.

Who else planned attack?

"The plan grew from only my heart. No others."

They pressed, wanting more from him. Wanting everything. He choked back his own words, convulsing, struggling for air. He gagged, finally, and a bilious stream of vomit splashed warm into his lap.

Once SAS 903 had declared the attempted hijacking and was diverted for landing at Bangor, the FAA shut down the airport to all traffic with the exception of law enforcement aircraft. Inside the main terminal, no more than one hundred passengers due to meet or depart on midday flights were inconvenienced.

Airline workers joined with the small food service shops to make the 230 unexpected visitors as comfortable as possible. By the time the Airbus taxied to the jetway, they had coffee, sandwiches, and soft drinks set

up on a buffet in the main arrivals hall inside the security screening gates.

The mood was distinctly cheerful, even
exuberant, as the passengers deplaned:
all of them grateful that the worst had not
happened, that they were on the ground,
that they were alive. Airport representatives were coordinating with the airline and
Homeland Security to reroute passengers
and their luggage. The airport lockdown
kept media at bay, and the passengers
were encouraged to call their loved ones
but not to contact any media outlets for
the time being.

Maggie and the five heroic passengers
who had come to her aid were escorted to
a lounge converted into a mini-emergency
room, in accordance with airport disaster
planning. With the FBI agents and police
standing guard, each person was greeted
by a physician and a nurse. Maggie's bleeding had stopped, but she was dizzy from
both blood loss and stress, and experi-
encing shocklike symptoms.

Trude, the other flight attendant, had
become hysterical once the passengers
and crew had exited the airplane. She was

dosed with antianxiety medication, but when that did not settle her down, she was taken to a local hospital for evaluation. The pilots were both questioned, but because neither was in fact an eyewitness to the attack, their value to the investigation was limited.

The blond man who had snatched the bomb trigger from the hijacker's hand was thought to have broken his wrist and received immediate medical attention.

A female FBI agent took the floor, speaking loudly. "Could I have everyone's attention, please? Very quickly, we want to get the injured treated right away, and everyone else looked over. I need to ask that your cell phones be turned over to us at this time, so that we may contact your families and associates for you. You of course will be able to contact them yourselves at a later time.

"I need to insist that no one talk to anyone else until we have had a chance to debrief you. This is very important. You have all been instrumental in disrupting a terror attack, saving the lives of your fellow passengers. It is imperative that we begin our investigation into this incident with uncorrupted witness accounts, so we'll ask you to bear with us for the next few hours.

"Other than that, once you have been evaluated and medically cleared, feel free to help yourselves to sandwiches, coffee, tea, and sodas. Restrooms are through those doors, and you do not need an escort but we do ask that you go one at a time. Any other questions or issues, please seek out one of the officers. Thank you."

Jeremy Fisk and Krina Gersten rushed over to Teterboro Airport just in time to hitch a ride on a Treasury Department jet carrying three quick-reaction investigators from the Joint Terrorism Task Force from New Jersey to Bangor, Maine.

Intel Division was being included because the flight had been bound for Newark Airport, and the plot apparently involved a target within the New York metropolitan area. The mood on the jet was cordial, but mistrust continued between the JTTF and Intel. In the wake of the averted Times Square subway bombing, the heads of both departments had publicly pledged their support for each other, but the reality hadn't trickled down to the street agents.

Fisk had been on his way to lunch when he got the alert. He was told to take one other Intel cop with him, and the decision was an easy one. Krina had been relegated to various shit assignments recently. As a female cop investigating a largely Muslim population, there were some obvious limitations on her assignments, but over time Fisk had come to defend her allegation that there was more to it than that. She never complained, except privately to him. Cop work was still largely a boys' club, and as she told him, she had been dealing with this sort of thing her entire career.

They touched down smoothly, taxiing right up to the main terminal. An airport representative escorted them to a common room outside the detention center, where the terrorist reaction team had nearly finished their postmortem. The fellow FBI agents acknowledged one another, then everyone took a seat around a conference table while the lead agent spoke from his notes.

"Looks like this guy Abdulraheem was the whole thing," said the agent. "We've got everything he had. His story is so common among these young wannabe terrorists that it can't be a legend. He loved the attention he got in Sanaa, Yemen, when he was recruited into one of those puppy cells at his mosque. They sent him to Peshawar for indoc, gave him a cutout contact, and told him to wait until he received orders. For a year he waited. And waited. And maybe went a little crazy. That's how they do it, they test your fidelity, your patience. Abdulraheem failed the test. The wait was too much. He took a page from the nine-eleven playbook, bought an undetectable obsidian knife, jumped on the friendly old Internet, and watched some British flight school's taped lectures on controlling an airliner's course and altitude with the autopilot. That was it. He made his move alone on SAS 903, that is confirmed. His target was undefined in midtown Manhattan. He was planning on figuring that part out once he got inside the flight deck. This actor's gonna be with us for a long, long time at Club Gitmo. Very small potatoes, seems to me, but who knows? He might know a few more names. He's proven he doesn't have the stuffing to wait the long wait. If he's got anything else, it will come out, sooner rather than later. But the critical threat here is over."

Gersten and Fisk sat through the rest, Fisk noting his thoughts on paper. The briefing broke up, and he and Gersten went into the interrogation room alone, spending a half hour's face time with Awaan Abdulraheem.

With his language skills, Fisk took the lead, speaking to the subject in Arabic while Gersten played the intractable female presence. Fisk laid down a few baseline questions, in order to establish a rudimentary rapport, but the narcosynthesis of the mild hallucinogen the subject had been administered had not fully worn off yet. For Fisk, it was like interviewing a sleepy drunk.

Abdulraheem was loquacious, neither fierce nor defiant, and often pathetic, like a neglected child who had been bad and looked forward to the attention punishment would afford him. The drug contributed to Abdulraheem's mood, clouding his true character, but to Fisk it was evident that the would-be hijacker was not very bright. He was hardly the embodiment of the fear, suspicion, and anxiety one might expect, as he would no doubt be portrayed by the media.

As they huddled outside afterward, Fisk translated a few of his answers for her. He could not mask his annoyance. He understood the need for immediate intervention, but mood-altering drugs should be a method of last resort. Especially when the administrator was unsure of the proper dose, as had been the case here.

"Bottom line?" said Fisk. "Not a major player."

"A lone wolf?" said Gersten. "The odds are against it."

"I'm not making any final pronouncements," said Fisk. "Maybe he's dogging me—maybe he's Keyser Söze. But I don't think so. More likely he's double-digit IQ, led more by religion than reason."

"He got himself on the plane," said Gersten. "He got a knife on there."

Fisk nodded, rechecking his briefing notes, finding the passenger list. "And he—or someone else—paid for a business-class seat."

Before Fisk and Gersten finished, the task force released the other passengers and crew, and SAS Flight 903 departed for Newark, its original destination. Each passenger answered direct questions about departure points and destinations, and each was completely rescreened by TSA. In all, their total inconvenience time was seven hours.

By the time Fisk and Gersten got to the five remaining passengers and one crew member, the balm of free food, relief, and camaraderie had worn thin. Someone made the mistake of telling them about the plane continuing on without them. Now the flight attendant and five passengers just wanted to be someplace else—anywhere but Bangor, Maine.

Fisk was immediately impressed that a group of people this disparate could come together in the heat of the moment and swiftly overwhelm the hijacker. He supposed that this was part of the legacy of 9/11: when faced with an onboard threat, very few airline passengers would risk waiting to let things play out. These five happened to be the first into action.

He knew he risked a backlash if he inconvenienced them much further, but he needed to get some additional perspective on Abdulraheem. Like radioactive matter, eyewitness accounts degraded over time, so he put on his most friendly face and went around the room to each in turn.

The Six, as the preliminary report in his hands had christened them, all gave approximately the same response when asked about their heroic moments in the vestibule outside the cockpit of SAS 903.

Alain Nouvian, a fifty-one-year-old cellist returning to New York from a brief concert tour in Scandinavia, was a small-eyed man with an unruly comb-over of dyed black hair. He approached the questioning with great care, like a man interviewing at a job fair. "I . . . I didn't think. I didn't think I had it in me to do what I did. It looked like I was dead no matter what . . . and I wasn't going to just sit there. To be frank, I'm still coming to grips with my actions. This is the most alive I've felt in thirty years. There was a test earlier today, life or death . . . and I acted. As they say, I rose to the occasion. That maniac was going to blow up the plane, for Christ's sake—or at least crash it into something. Instead, I crashed into him."

Douglas Aldrich, a sixty-five-year-old retired auto parts dealer from Albany, had been returning from a four-day visit to his daughter and grandson in Göteborg. "Instinct. I don't even have to think about it. I was more worried about getting some feeling back into my legs at the end of the flight—you know, that thrombosis stuff. I was standing in the aisle trying to stretch out these old muscles when I heard the commotion. I'm a Vietnam vet, which was a long time ago, but today it felt like yesterday. I don't think of myself as a brave man. There was no orchestra music, you know what I mean? No moment of heroic decision. I—and I think the others—just did what I had to do. The people I'm thinking about right now? Those others on the plane. Who just sat there. All the people in business who didn't stand up when this terrorist attacked. That's what's spinning my mind at this moment. Them getting into their beds tonight. Lying there in the dark with their thoughts. Tell you what—I'm going to sleep like a goddamn baby."

Colin Frank, forty-five and paunchy, was a journalist working on an assignment for *The New Yorker* on a piece about the rise in popularity of Swedish crime literature. His reading glasses were perched high on his forehead, one of the lenses showing a threadlike crack. He had not yet come to grips with what happened. "I haven't the slightest idea why I did it. I'm being honest—I remember nothing. My body was moving without thought. It's like a switch was flipped. One minute I was in my seat reading Henning Mankell—and the next I was on top of a terrorist at the front of a plane. I went from reading a crime thriller to starring in one—kind of seamlessly. It didn't seem extraordinary, the situation . . . and at the same time it didn't seem real either. Like I was still in the book." He smiled, lifting off his glasses and admiring the imperfection in the lens, as though needing evidence of his actions. "Sort of like reading a baseball book and then finding yourself rounding home plate. Right place, right time, I guess. I just feel so goddamn lucky to be alive."

"When do we get to Newark?" asked Joanne Sparks, thirty-eight, the general manager of an IKEA store in Elizabeth, New Jersey. A fit frequent-flyer business-class traveler, she was returning from the company's home office in Stockholm and had been seated next to Abdulraheem for the entire flight.

"Soon," answered Fisk.

"How soon?"

Unlike the others, Ms. Sparks addressed Fisk and Gersten not as an interviewee, but as an equal, with the candor and polish of a combatant on a television talk show.

"I'm not aware of the exact details, but I—"

"So we're not going right home. Are we."

Fisk smiled, changing tactics. "Probably not. Again, it's not my call. But my guess is you six will be bundled onto a government aircraft and flown to LaGuardia for further questioning. This is a big deal, you should realize."

"How long?"

"How long in New York? At least a day."

"Bullshit. What am I, under arrest?"

Gersten jumped in. "No, ma'am. You are not under arrest. You are material witnesses to a terror attack—"

"He's a fucking malcontent with delusions of grandeur. There was no boom at the end of those wires. There was nothing. False alarm."

Fisk said, "It's not that simple. But I suggest you take up your complaints with the FBI."

"The FBI?" said Sparks, doing a double take. "Wait a minute. Then who are you?"

He explained himself again. "I'm just trying to get some context on the hijacker. You were seated next to him for the entire flight. Is there anything you can give me?"

Sparks threw up her hands. "You know how often I travel? I board, the eyeshades go on, the shoes come off, I'm gone." She softened a little, Fisk's earnestness working on her. She was angry about the inconvenience, but proud of her courage. "Look, it was pure reaction. Pure fucking gut reaction. Adrenaline, whatever. Fight or flight. Or rather—fight on a flight, right? This guy . . . he had been asleep the entire way. And I mean sound asleep, to the point that I presumed he'd taken something for the flight. In fact, when he first got up and went right at the flight attendant, my thought was, you know, Ambien. I've seen that before on a plane. Jesus. You fly enough, you see crazy things. But there it is. I can't give you much more than that. Didn't pay him the slightest attention, nor he me. It was like he was dead next to me for hours, then all of a sudden he was up like a zombie and trying to take over the plane. Crazy motherfucker."

Magnus Jenssen, twenty-six, was a Swedish schoolteacher on a sabbatical, planning to tour the East Coast of the United States by bicycle before running the New York City Marathon in early November. He was sitting up on a gurney in the makeshift examination room, his left wrist in a gel cast, his arm snug in a white muslin sling. He was fair-haired with antifreeze-blue eyes, handsome, fit. "I don't know why I jumped," he said, his accent strong but his pronunciation clear. "He had a bomb. Or certainly seemed to at the time. He was hurting the attendant. I saw that trigger device in his hand and it just looked terrifying. That someone could press a button and have that kind of power over me to end my life and everyone around us. It was too much to bear . . . and again, all this in an instant. I really zeroed in on that switch. I locked in on that device and I pounced. Too hard, I guess." He turned his arm at the elbow, wincing. "This will make it difficult to bicycle. I may have to adjust my travel plans, no?"

Fisk said, "I cracked mine playing basketball a year ago. Six weeks to heal, another four to six for physical therapy, and you'll be good as new."

Jenssen nodded warmly, appreciating the encouragement. He had a smile for Gersten as well, but a little different, flirtatious. Fisk couldn't blame the guy; in fact, he admired his panache. This guy had foiled a terror attack and had a broken wrist to show for it. The media was going to anoint him a hero. He was in for a good weekend in New York that could stretch on for weeks and weeks.

The thirty-two-year-old flight attendant Maggie Sullivan hailed from the shipbuilding village of Georgetown, Prince Edward Island, Canada. A white bandage covered the wound on her neck, and she proudly wore a Bangor Police Department sweatshirt. "The Fourth of July weekend," she said. "Is that what he was thinking?"

"I can't confirm that," said Fisk. "But it looks likely."

"Stupid, stupid, stupid. Do either of you smoke?"

Fisk shook his head. So did Gersten.

"Me neither," said Maggie. "My dad used

to smoke cigars. I kind of want one now. Don't ask. This is me, post-frazzled."

Gersten said, "Are you ready for a hero's welcome?"

"Why not?" said Maggie, smiling, pushing back her short chestnut brown hair. "Damn! I wish Oprah still had her show!" Maggie laughed, a throaty growl with the sudden intake of breath particular to that part of Atlantic Canada. Gersten laughed harder than Maggie did. The flight attendant was easy to like.

"I just wish I had gotten in one really good shot at him," said Maggie, making a fist and grinding it into the air in front of her. "Right in the nuts."

PART 5

EAVESDROP

Friday, July 2

On the flight back to New York, Fisk and Gersten sat shoulder to shoulder. Fisk listened to the unexpurgated initial interrogation of Awaan Abdulraheem, which had been downloaded onto his iPod, while Gersten read the translated transcript on her laptop.

By the time they pulled out their ear buds, both had arrived at the same conclusion.

"This guy is way wrong for this," Fisk said. "It's not adding up."

Gersten nodded. "But what's it mean?"

Fisk looked out at the lights of New York

unrolling below them. "A diversion?" he suggested.

Gersten said, "From what? Some other event?"

"No. I'm thinking more on the plane."

"On the plane?" She mulled this over. "Like what?"

"I don't know. I'm trying to find a reason. A reason why someone would train, sponsor, brainwash, coerce—but, bottom line, get this stooge on a plane to try to take it over."

Gersten said, "You'll have to tell me, since you speak the language, but the translation made it sound to me like he was a true believer."

Fisk nodded. "He thought he was going to get in the cockpit with the bomb bluff and take them down. He believed he was going to succeed. No question. But air security was set up precisely to stop crackpots like this."

"You're convinced he's not a lone wolf."

"I'm not convinced of anything just yet. But I'm sure as hell ready to be."

Gersten took a sip of bottled water. "The other passengers were all vetted and cleared."

"I know. Luggage and cargo too. Let's get the list from Newark customs and break it down, take another long look at everybody else on that plane."

Gersten sighed. "I was looking forward to getting home, taking a hot bath . . ."

"A hot bath? It's ninety degrees out."

"I wasn't planning on taking it alone."

Fisk smiled. "I'll owe you one. How about that?"

She leaned across Fisk to take in the view of Flushing Bay and the approach strobes guiding them into LaGuardia. Doing so allowed him to sneak in a quick nuzzle behind her ear, then a kiss.

Gersten said, "Deal."

Crossing Queens and Brooklyn from La-Guardia Airport in an unmarked car took them forty-five minutes. Little traffic on the streets at three thirty in the morning except taxis and cop cars. People without air-conditioning sat out on their stoops at that late hour, too hot to sleep. It was going to be a classic Fourth of July weekend in New York City, with asphalt-baking temperatures in the upper nineties and hothouse humidity. Even before dawn, the temperature had barely dipped below eighty degrees Fahrenheit.

The duty driver delivered them through

the automated gate at Intel. They carded in, quick-timing it toward Fisk's office.

The terrorist thwarting had gone real-world. This was the end of the first news cycle, the early newspaper editions already in the trucks and on their way, their online editions posted and commented on, the morning network news shows readying their broadcast rundowns. Success meant nothing to them. The predictable issues would be the question of how 125 Intel detectives, a dozen brainy analysts, hundreds of informants, as well as the FBI, CIA, NSA, and all the rest, did not catch even the faintest whiff of this hijacker's plan.

The former Border Patrol had, after 9/11, become a muscular police force with a new name—Immigration and Customs Enforcement—a more complicated bureaucracy, with lots of planes, helicopters, and cars. ICE was part of the Department of Homeland Security, the premier agency of the terrorist age in America, with the second-largest budget in the government after defense spending.

Fisk and Gersten received fingerprints, retina scans, passport scans, and travel histories for every passenger on SAS Flight 903. Gersten took the top half of the alphabetized list, Fisk the bottom. He rinsed out two mugs and filled them with coffee and sugar. They only had a few hours before the bosses came in and meetings would pull them away.

He gave Gersten his desk and dragged his chrome-legged Naugahyde couch over to the credenza, spreading out pages and opening his secure laptop.

There was no art to their process. It was profiling, pure and simple. They filtered for Arabs, for Muslims. They filtered for anybody whose travels had taken them anywhere near Yemen, Pakistan, or Afghanistan in their lifetime. This was the only game plan available.

A little after five, they compared results.

"Pretty clean plane, all in all," Gersten said. "Mostly summer tourists."

"Same here. You first."

She said, "I've got a Pashtun author, last name Chamkanni. Says she's going to a writers' colony in New Hampshire, which checks out. Got a Pakistani family, thirtysomething parents, two kids under five. Last name Jahangiri. Declared themselves as traveling to a family reunion in Seattle. They look fine, already made their connecting flight. The Seattle branch of the family runs a squash club, and the grandparents filled a blog with pictures of the grandkids—looks tight. Worth following through, though.

"I got only one maybe. Saudi passport, Baada Bin-Hezam, thirty-two years of age. He's an art dealer coming to New York to consult on the repatriation of a collection of early Arabian artifacts looted by the Brits when they occupied Iran. This guy gets around. London and Berlin earlier this month. Stockholm just to change planes. Fits his occupation, of course. ICE has him coming out of Sanaa to Frankfurt three months ago, soon after bin Laden went down."

"And he's not no-fly?" said Fisk.

"No. Nothing about him looks especially hinky, except now that we're looking for something."

"The genius of profiling," he snarked. "Turning square pegs into round ones."

Gersten stretched her neck and felt it crack. "What did you get on your list?"

Fisk rubbed his tired eyes. "Not much.

Two families, very low probability. Really only one guy I want to look at a little bit. Engineering student at Linnaeus University in southern Sweden. From Tunisia originally. Lukewarm. He's got a cohesive CV. He's published legitimate papers on wind turbines."

Gersten said, "I think the Saudi is worth a thorough look-see."

"I guess I do too. Any idea where he is now?"

She pulled his sheet. "Cleared customs in Newark at twelve thirty this morning. No track after that."

"He use a credit card for his flight?"

She checked. "He did."

"Let's Patriot Act that account, shall we?"

The Intel chief, Barry Dubin, arrived early, as he did most days. He was bald, an egghead with a trim, mostly gray goatee. A former spook, he was steady and competent but humorless. He draped his jacket over the back of his office chair as always. Fisk noticed that his flag pin was upside down.

"I was at the Mets game last night. Left

after five innings to get some shut-eye, but they showed the news report about the foiled hijacking between innings and Citi-field nearly collapsed from the cheering."

Fisk said, "The thing is, they're not used to hearing fan applause there."

Dubin smiled and nodded, though it was clear to Fisk that he did not understand the joke. "It was goddamn hot too. What's on your minds?"

Gersten stood next to Fisk. Fisk could not get a read on whether Dubin knew about them or not. They had taken great pains to hide their relationship, mainly for reasons of convenience—but this was an intelligence agency, after all.

Fisk said, "Well, the FBI is doing back-flips. Their end zone dance. But I—we—have a bad feeling about this."

"I assume it is more than just a hunch."

"It is now."

Dubin listened without comment while Fisk took him through the interrogation, his impressions about the Yemeni hijacker's limited intelligence, and the speed with which he broke under questioning.

"It was too easy," Fisk said. "This guy is so malleable. To me, that's the scariest thing about it. We're thinking there could—stress 'could'—be more to it."

"More suspects?" Dubin puzzled this out. "Maybe he had terror cell buddies on the plane? They scrubbed the op when it went bad in front of the cockpit? Decided to wait for a better day?"

"We thought of that, but this Abdulraheem isn't the clam-up type. Now—maybe he's an evil genius and a great actor. But I don't think so. I heard somebody who was scared and proud at the same time. He thinks he's a success story, and he's going to spend the next phase of his life at Guantanamo."

"Okay. So who are you looking at?"

"We've got one potential associate, a Saudi who—"

"What flavor?" interrupted Dubin.

Gersten said, "Don't know yet. The name on his passport is Baada Bin-Hezam."

Dubin said, "Assuming that's his real name, he sounds ethnic Yemeni Kindite."

Fisk nodded. "Same as bin Laden."

Dubin said, "It's a bit of a leap, but I'm still with you. Walk me through it."

Fisk nodded, putting the pieces together as he talked. "We know that before he was taken out, bin Laden was definitely down on what he thought of as thug bombers, like this Abdulraheem. We got great stuff from NSA after they worked over the loot from his house. OBL didn't care about high body counts. He wanted high-viz targets with symbolic value. That, he declared, was the holy route toward his ultimate goal— uniting the world under the extremist Muslim version of God's law and the Koran."

Dubin shrugged. "Al-Qaeda is in a shambles now, post-OBL. Who's to say this guy isn't a lone gunman, a rogue jihadist?"

"It seems definite he is a for-real camp-trained mujahideen. So sure, maybe he's just a comet shooting through the jihad universe. A rogue vector. Or is he a true pawn? Part of an operation—one he maybe has no knowledge of—that is still in play?"

Dubin said, "You're saying the tip of the spear who doesn't know he's part of a spear?"

Gersten said, "Where did a mango farmer from Yemen get business-class airfare?"

Dubin shrugged. "You tell me. What did he say?"

"He said something along the lines of 'God provides.'"

"But what's it get him? A failed or aborted hijacking?"

Fisk said, "He made a lot of noise. Pulled a lot of attention to himself. Maybe someone put him up to it as a diversion to get the real actor safely in country."

"An unwitting diversion. A little far-fetched, but fair enough. Fisk, I hope you didn't have any beach plans this Fourth of July weekend. You head up the search for this Saudi. I don't like unanswered questions, this weekend of all weekends."

Fisk and Gersten each nodded, knowing exactly what he meant. The Freedom Tower.

"We've got the new One Trade Center building dedication, and before that, the fireworks show, which is always a logistical game of Twister. I don't want any drama. I don't want any unnecessary distractions. I want you to get on him fast. If he's easy to find, then it's nothing and you'll have saved yourself some weekend. If he's hard to find . . ."

"We're on it," said Fisk, as they turned to leave.

"Actually, Gersten, I want you to stay behind a minute."

Gersten stopped, surprised. "Sure," she said, with nary a glance at Fisk, who, after a moment's pause, walked out and closed the door behind him.

Gersten was in his office doorway three minutes later. She looked deflated, as though a disappointment had allowed all the exhaustion to catch up with her.

"Oh, shit," said Fisk. "What is it?"

"Adventures in babysitting. That's me. The passengers and the flight attendant."

"You've got to stay with them? Dubin's order?"

She moved in from the doorway so as not to be overheard. "Girls are good at babysitting, right?"

Fisk shared her disappointment. Still, he tried to make it right. "It is necessary," he said. "I mean, they are the only witnesses to this thing. And the media take on this is, from the standpoint of public cooperation, almost as important as the actual investigation."

"Then have Public Affairs do it." She swatted at the air, as though sexism were a fly. "I'm telling you . . ." She put her hands on her hips. "Am I a cop, or aren't I?"

"You're a good cop. What's the assignment? Specifically?"

"Three watches, twenty-four seven. Patton and DeRosier are with me. They're at the Hyatt next to Grand Central, and we are going to be holding their hands starting at ten A.M. today. Their first press conference. The mayor and the commissioner."

"Okay, look—" he started to say.

She shook her head, stopping him. "Don't tell me that just because two other men drew the assignment I'm overreacting."

Fisk set his hands on his hips. "What I was going to say is that two other men drew the assignment and maybe you're overreacting."

She shook her head, staring off to the side, tapping her foot.

Fisk said, "You want to be on the Saudi with me. Believe me, I want you to be on the Saudi with me."

He moved forward to console her and she put her arms up, stepping back. "I'm not oversensitive, Jeremy. I'm fucking pissed, and that's all there is to it. I don't want to be consoled right now."

Fisk nodded once. "Okay."

"I'm sick of being treated like an intern around here." She turned toward the door, walked to it, then pivoted back. "But an assignment is an order, and you know what? Fuck Dubin. I'm going to get me a long, hot bath at some point this weekend and live out of the Hyatt's minibar, and smile and walk these heroes around like a preschool teacher on a fucking TV station field trip."

She turned and walked out. Fisk knew it was best to just let her go. She didn't like a lot of the assignments she drew, but obeying them and excelling at them was never an issue.

"Ladies and gentlemen, the mayor of New York, the Honorable Michael Bloomberg."

City Hall's public relations chief, a young woman in a crimson business suit, backed away from the podium clapping her hands, but not before tilting down the microphone.

Mayor Bloomberg took her place and smiled and waited for the applause to fade. "I think it's safe to say, this is a day New Yorkers will never forget," he began. "It reminds me that while New York is a city that has seen the darkest moment in our nation's history, it has also produced some of the greatest moments. Moments of tri-

umph and uplift. Moments of pure heroism. And we will add to the ranks of those
heroes the men and women who will be
joining me here today."

Gersten, having quickly changed outfits
and thrown together a weekend bag, stood
in the wings on the opposite end from where
The Six would be making their entrance.
She looked out at the press corps and the
onlookers—including hotel employees and
construction workers present for the building's ongoing renovation—and she could
feel the energy in the ballroom. The moment was electric. She had underestimated
the public impact of The Six's actions.

Mayor Bloomberg continued. "As all of
you know by now, shortly after noon yesterday, a hijacker armed with a knife who
said he had a bomb attempted to storm
the cockpit of Scandinavian Airlines Flight
903, which was thirty minutes away from
landing in Newark. This criminal, a Yemeni
national, failed in his attempt because six
people of varying backgrounds, men and
women of three nationalities, who might
never have come together but for this dangerous incident, refused to yield to terror.
The FBI, along with officers from the New

York City Police Department's Intelligence Division, have confirmed that the hijacker intended to murder both pilots and take control of the aircraft using its autopilot. This man had no knowledge of how to land the aircraft and, indeed, had no intention of doing so. Had he succeeded in the attempt, we might be holding a very different news conference today. We would be adding up the number of casualties and property damage estimates. Instead, we are celebrating life and the indomitable spirit of freedom."

He shuffled his papers, then set them aside.

"And so, without further ado, the heroes of Flight 903."

Before he could even finish the sentence, the Hyatt Grand Central's ballroom erupted. Gersten was unprepared for the force of released emotion in the reception. Hoots and hollers from the construction workers in back. Journalists rising to their feet. She had underestimated the visceral reaction—so much so that she felt exposed by not clapping, and eventually joined in, a smile coming to her face.

The six heroes of SAS 903 filed toward

the front, also clearly stunned by the response. They passed NYPD commissioner Ray Kelly, who was clapping hard enough to crush coal into diamonds. Mayor Bloomberg stepped back from the podium as the full-throated cheers from the audience of journalists and citizens washed over them.

Finally, the mayor retook the podium. "It is now my distinct pleasure to introduce these heroes to you all. We have prepared brief biographies of each of them, which most of you picked up on the way in this morning. Please hold your applause until I finish the introductions.

"First, to Commissioner Kelly's immediate left, SAS flight attendant and purser, Margaret Sullivan."

Maggie stepped forward at the urging of the others. Gersten saw that she had done her best with her makeup, but a night with little or no sleep showed through. She had changed into a clean Scandinavian Airlines uniform, and her face looked nearly as pale as the collar of bandages on her neck—though her smile, its sincerity, was wide and bright.

"Next, Mr. Alain Nouvian, a musician

with the New York Philharmonic and a native Long Islander."

Nouvian executed a head bow, as at the end of a well-received performance. It brought a smattering of applause despite Bloomberg's admonition.

"Next to Mr. Nouvian is Joanne Sparks, who, as the manager of an IKEA store across the river in New Jersey, has probably furnished half the apartments in this city."

That got a generous laugh. Sparks had changed out of her travel clothes into a sharp cream suit. She even received a few catcalls from the hotel employees in back.

"Mr. Douglas Aldrich is from Albany, where he owned a NAPA auto parts store for thirty years before retiring to dote on his grandchildren, one of whom lives in Sweden."

Aldrich acknowledged the introduction with a half salute to Bloomberg and a chuckling wave at the audience.

"Next to him, the man who was the first to confront the terrorist, ripping what was believed to be the trigger to a live bomb from the hijacker's hand, and fracturing his own wrist in the process. Mr. Magnus Jenssen of Stockholm."

The room broke into forceful applause. Jenssen barely acknowledged it, not rudely but rather modestly, averting his gaze from the camera lights and cradling his gel-cast-covered right arm. His face, given a rugged edge by stubble, was blank, a passive, nonplussed expression. Gersten had once read somewhere that among Swedes, facial expressions such as smiles, frowns, and glares are parceled out much more sparingly than anywhere else in the world. Jenssen was dressed in the same casual clothes he had on when they took him off the plane in Bangor, a black turtleneck with one sleeve cut off to accommodate the cast, tan slacks, gray running shoes.

"And finally," continued the mayor after tapping the mic to silence the room, "Mr. Colin Frank is one of you. A native New Yorker, he works as a reporter."

Frank, still in his black suit and white shirt with the collar button undone, appeared to be the only one in touch with the surrealism of the moment. He pulled off his specs and waved awkwardly to the audience with a smile that acknowledged this absurdity.

Mayor Bloomberg said, "Ladies and gentlemen, these are your six heroes."

Gersten watched them absorb the applause. A monitor stood on a tripod near her, and she took in the camera view of the six of them. She could see how they would be presented to the world over the next forty-eight hours or so, almost like reality television contestants. Maggie the gutsy gal. Nouvian the artist. Sparks the professional woman. Jenssen the handsome foreigner. Frank the brain. And Aldrich the humble grandpa.

"Let the TV movie casting begin," she mumbled, wishing Fisk were there to hear it.

Police Commissioner Kelly then made a few brief remarks. He bridged the gap nicely from the courage of The Six to advocating the practice of vigilance as part of a New Yorker's daily life.

"Fear is a sickness that can cripple our lives," he said. "Vigilance is the antidote."

"Okay," said Bloomberg, returning to the podium. "Questions? Andy, you first."

Bloomberg had selected a man-in-the-street reporter for NY1, the popular local television station.

"Mr. Jenssen. It says here in your bio that you were coming to the States to go bicycle touring and then run the New York Marathon. Will this change your plans?"

"It does seem so," Jenssen said, as a hotel employee slid over to him with a microphone. "Not much chance for long-distance biking with this." He patted his cast. The audience reacted to his slight Swedish accent with a kind of childish awe. Accents impress Americans, and a true Swedish accent was rarely heard in the mass media.

"What will you do then?" the NY1 reporter followed up.

Jenssen did not appear to want to play the game. "I certainly would like to start with some sleep. Then walking, I guess."

"Are you married?" yelled a female voice from the back.

Jenssen squinted out into the accompanying laughter, but did not answer.

"One more," said the reporter, raising his voice slightly to get it in before the mayor moved on. "Why did you—all of you—risk your life and the lives of everybody on that plane by jumping from your seat and tackling a man who said he had a bomb?"

Jenssen tilted his head slightly, gazing down at the reporter with an expression of true confusion. "There is no why. It was too fast. I'll ask you, why did you wear that shirt today?" He watched the reporter look down at his shirt. "Exactly. There was no decision to make. No thought required. Just need and do."

The NY1 reporter waved his arm for more, but Bloomberg shook his head. Jenssen had already retreated from the microphone anyway.

"Over there. In the yellow dress. Yes, you. Go ahead."

"This is for Ms. Sullivan. Did you think you were going to die when the hijacker had the knife to your throat?"

Sullivan gasped and brought her hand to her throat amid a surge of camera clicking. "This is going to be a long couple of days, I guess," said Maggie, with a laugh and a nervous smile. "I . . . gosh, sure, I guess I did think I was going to die. How strange is that? I thought it was happening right then. I thought, Okay, this is how I am going to die. He cut me right away and

I . . . I felt it, but I didn't know how bad. No life passing before my eyes or anything like that. In fact, the only thing that passed in front of my eyes was Mr. Jenssen, racing in to tackle the . . . the jerk."

The corps laughed at her self-censorship, avoiding a curse word.

"He saved your life," said the reporter in the yellow dress.

Maggie's lips came together tightly in an attempt to pinch back sudden tears. She just nodded. Jenssen looked a little embarrassed.

The reporter then followed up with a comment instead of a question. "Well, we're all so glad you're still here," she said.

Gersten winced at the saccharine emotion, but a wave of applause rippled through the room. This was the sort of thing spoken at press conferences where the interviewees are celebrities—which is what The Six were now.

Another reporter. "Maggie, are you looking forward to going home?"

"As soon as they let us," she said, behind a laugh. "Somebody said something about talk shows, but I need to get some serious mirror time beforehand if that's the case."

More generous laughter.

There were more questions, and more stammered answers from bewildered citizens literally thrust into the spotlight. It was all congratulatory and lighthearted, yet there was a palpable sense of relief—mostly that no one had said anything outrageously dumb or offensive, thereby killing the public relations buzz—when Mayor Bloomberg called for the last question. He pointed to a television reporter flanked by her camera crew and producer.

"Hi, Colin," she said.

"Jenny," said Frank, recognizing the reporter with a knowing smile.

"The reporter becomes the story. How strange is it to be on that side of things, and I'm wondering if you think there might be a book somewhere in all this?"

Supportive laughter from the rest of the press corps.

Frank thought of a dozen pithy things to say and declined them all. "Here's something I never thought I'd hear myself say, Jenny: no comment."

The room erupted with laughter, even the mayor.

Fisk himself arrived at the Grand Hyatt just as some of the reporters were filing out of the lobby, while others were doing video pickups just inside the revolving doors. He stepped to the side, flapping the wings of his jacket in an attempt to cool himself down. His shirt was damp down both sides. He billowed it, getting some cool air moving. He could not remove his jacket because he was carrying. He figured he would start to dry out just about in time to head back outside.

He rode the short escalator to reception and eyed the bank of elevators. Half of the

expansive lobby was curtained off for renovations. He detoured into the gift shop for
an apple or a banana, and true to form
came out unwrapping a bar of chocolate
instead.

He pulled out his phone to text Gersten,
but then saw DeRosier and Patton at the
same time they saw him. "Everything all
right?" asked DeRosier.

"We'll see. Right now just cleaning up a
couple of questions. What floor?"

"Twenty-six. It's one of the ones still being renovated. How you liking the heat?"

Fisk rolled his eyes. "How you liking the
air-conditioning?"

DeRosier pressed the elevator call button. "Liking it just fine."

They stepped into one of the elevators.
Fisk pressed 26 and nothing happened.
Patton swiped his key card and the eleva-
tor started to rise.

Mike DeRosier was shaved bald and
broadly built, a former Boston University
hockey star who had played three years in
the AHL and Europe before letting go of
that dream in order to pursue his backup
plan in law enforcement.

Alan Patton was shorter than DeRosier,

and further differentiated by a thick head of black hair marked by a thin stripe of silver flaring up from his widow's peak, a "skunk stripe" he was unusually proud of.

Patton said, "Gersten's in a great mood, by the way."

Fisk smiled to himself. He played his part. "It's not such a bad assignment."

"Not for me," said Patton. "Anyway, from Gersten I'm willing to put up with the attitude." Patton turned to DeRosier. "She's wearing the tan pants with no back pockets."

Fisk watched them in the reflective gold doors. DeRosier nodded as the floor numbers rose. "Know them well."

"I think I would pay twenty dollars to see her in yoga pants," said Patton. "God, I love yoga pants."

"Yeah?" said Fisk. "How many pairs you own?"

DeRosier laughed.

Patton said, "You know how Jeter gives his one-night stands autographed baseballs? If I were him, I'd endorse a line of yoga pants. Just set up a rack inside the door of my penthouse, hand them to the hotties as they walked in."

DeRosier said, "You downward dog, you."

The doors opened on 26. The hallway to the right was curtained off, collapsed scaffolding and paint cans stacked against the wall—the renovation discontinued for the time being.

They turned left. Two uniformed cops posted to the hallway quickly tucked away their personal phones.

Two adjoining rooms had been opened up and converted into a hospitality suite for the floor. A small buffet table was set to the left with coffee, croissants, soda, and mini designer cupcakes from the shop downstairs. A wall television was on, pundits talking over footage of The Six's press conference.

"My god, I look like absolute *shit*!"

Fisk recognized flight attendant Maggie's voice from the adjoining room. Then laughter from her fellow heroes. Fisk looked in and saw that they were watching a second television, either sitting or standing, drinking Diet Cokes, stirring tea, snacking on coffee cake.

Fisk got Gersten's attention and she cut

in front of the television, joining him in the first room. DeRosier and Patton lurked within earshot. She was indeed wearing the tan pants, her badge clipped to the belt loop.

"How we doing?" he asked.

She looked back through the door. "Unwinding," she said. "Awaiting our next move." She looked back to Fisk. "How you want to do this?"

He looked around. "This setup is fine as is. I'll just speak to each one at a time. Keep it casual, relaxed. In and out."

Patton said, "Ah, the old in-and-out."

Gersten said, "You're lucky you're here now. I think once the fame bomb hits them, it's full-on diva time. This thing is exploding. That press conference?"

Fisk said, "Caught some of it."

"If it played half as big as it did in the room, we're in for a busy weekend."

Fisk pulled over two chairs. "I want to work on them in terms of no specifics, keeping everything general."

"And," she added, "I would be careful not to raise too many questions in their minds either, if you can help it. I know the mayor's office is setting up some things, TV things, and they're not pros. Last thing anybody wants is one of us stepping into the middle of an interview to cut them off."

Fisk agreed. "One question each," he said.

Patton's phone rang. He stepped away, and DeRosier seized the opportunity to go off in search of Danish pastry.

Alone for the moment, Fisk said quietly, "You okay?"

"I'm fine," she answered, rolling her eyes. "Momentary breakdown. I'm good. Whatever." She nodded through the door. "Their excitement is a little contagious, I have to say."

"Good. Oh—and Starsky and Hutch really like your choice of pants today."

She rolled her eyes again. "Ass monkeys."

Fisk shrugged. "They're not wrong."

She turned then and walked away into the adjoining suite, leaving him watching. He forced the smile from his face and switched off the television in the room so there would be no distractions.

Gersten brought him Maggie first. Fisk reintroduced himself and offered her the empty chair, himself remaining standing before the drawn window shade.

"One quick follow-up question," he said. "We're tying up loose ends and I'm wondering if you remember a Saudi Arabian businessman on the flight. He was seated in eight-H, window seat?" He watched her thinking. "Coffee-brown suit. Large, flat mole on the left edge of his jawbone."

Maggie closed her eyes, visualizing the airplane's interior. "I do . . . vaguely." Her eyes opened. "Why, what do you want to know?"

Fisk shook his head. "Anything you got."

"I didn't serve him. For meal service, I worked economy." She thought hard, struggling to give him something. "He was quiet . . ."

Fisk nodded. The last thing he wanted was for her to overreach, to invent something just so that she felt she was contributing. Just the facts, ma'am. "That's fine. Great. Thank you."

"Really?" Surprised, she stood. "That was easy."

Fisk said, "I think, given what you went through yesterday, everything is going to seem easy for quite some time to come."

Maggie liked the sound of that, and with a wink at Fisk, she returned to the adjoining room.

IKEA manager Sparks, retired auto parts dealer Aldrich, and cellist Nouvian all failed to remember the slim Arab in 8H. Reporter Frank believed he had stood behind him in line at the gate entrance, but could not give Fisk anything more than that the man carried his own neck pillow.

Fisk pushed it with the journalist. "I'm wondering if you saw him with or near the hijacker at any time prior to boarding."

Frank looked at the ceiling. Fisk had the feeling Frank wanted badly to be part of the investigation, out of professional curiosity. "No," he said, disappointed with himself. "Sorry."

"In fact I think I did." Jenssen, the wounded Swede, answered that same question, while looking pensively at a long-armed floor lamp.

Fisk said, "At the gate?"

"In the business-class lounge at Arlanda Airport. To be honest, I don't remember seeing him at all on the plane . . . but definitely in the lounge." Jenssen swirled the tea in his nearly empty porcelain cup. "I remember I was waiting for hot water. Now that I think about it, I believe they spoke briefly at the courtesy counter."

"They who?"

"The man in question and the hijacker."

Fisk studied Jenssen. He liked the schoolteacher's matter-of-factness. He could see that this man would not tolerate a hijacker taking control of his airplane any more than he would allow somebody to muscle in front of him in a line.

But this was important. Fisk wanted to give him a chance to varnish the story, just in case. He had to be sure. "Mr. Jenssen, are you positive?"

"I am, yes. I presume you are asking for a reason?"

Fisk nodded, allowing that, but did not elaborate. "Can you remember any other details? Try."

Jenssen focused his eyes on the unlit lamp as though constructing an image and examining it. It was another thirty seconds before he spoke.

"Something about the way they stood together made me think they were related in some way. Or acquaintances at the very least. A lack of acknowledgment, I think.

Like they were familiar. They had a short-hand." He closed his eyes. "I believe the man in the brown suit showed the hijacker something in a magazine he was reading. Our flight was called right after that." He opened his eyes and looked at Fisk with an expression that said, Anything else?

Fisk said, "How certain are you of what you just told me? Would you say fifty per-cent? Seventy-five percent? A hundred percent?"

"How certain I am of seeing those two men together in the departure lounge?" Jenssen said. "One hundred percent."

Fisk nodded. "One last question. How's the wrist?"

Jenssen smiled, looking down at his cast. "I'll know in three to four weeks."

Baada Bin-Hezam had been to New York often enough to know that the quickest way into the city from Newark Airport was the New Jersey Transit train into Penn Station.

He had threaded his way through hundreds of people waiting outside customs for the passengers of SAS Flight 903. Some of them had carried cameras and microphones, which they had thrust at any of the exhausted people who gave the slightest indication that they would tolerate the intrusion. Bin-Hezam had not ducked their glare, but instead had strode through it like a busy professional whose plane had landed long overdue. No one was interested in a man of Arab descent.

One of the greeters had had a clutch of red Mylar balloons, each in the shape of a heart. He had been a conservatively dressed man, trying to hand them to the rescued passengers. Other celebrants had held signs, many under the mistaken belief that the flight attendant and five passengers who had overpowered the hijacker were still on Flight 903. They were there to give them a hero's welcome.

NEVER FORGET!! 9/11/01
WE LOVE YOU!!!
THANK YOU, HEROES
USA USA USA

Bin-Hezam had avoided direct eye contact, making his way to the end of the crowd, while his peripheral vision had been carefully tuned to the telltale signals of police surveillance. A glance lingering too long . . . an ear bud . . . a sudden move as he had made his way to the escalator . . .

He had ridden the steep flight of mechanical stairs, up out of the melee to the arrivals hall. He had stepped off and proceeded to the tram that would shuttle him to the train station.

No one had been with him.

There had been a twenty-minute wait until the next scheduled train. He had found the lodging kiosk, a tilted bank of lighted square advertisements listing dozens of hotel selections. He had determined it best not to make lodging arrangements in advance. He wanted to shrink his electronic footprint down as small as possible. His only requirement had been that he sleep that night far from any established Muslim neighborhood.

He had selected the Hotel Indigo on West Twenty-eighth Street in Manhattan, a small boutique hotel tucked away in the middle of a block known as the center of the flower district.

Again, he had been unobtrusively vigilant during the train ride. He had disembarked at Penn Station, pausing for some minutes in a bookstore in order to allow his fellow passengers to filter through, then had headed for the street.

The summer heat had been instantly discomforting. He was unused to the humidity.

To him, water and moisture symbolized relief, but on the island of Manhattan it was oppressive and a bit disorienting.

The hotel was just a three-block walk from Penn Station, but Bin-Hezam had traveled a roundabout way just in case. His luggage was not heavy, but anything that restricted mobility in the heat was a burden. When he was confident he had not been shadowed, he had headed for the hotel.

On Twenty-eighth Street, he had passed many open shop gates and idling flower trucks, the sweaty vendors working busily on the last day of the work week.

As well they should, Bin-Hezam had thought. Many memorial flowers would be needed before the end of this weekend.

Past a young Hispanic bellman inside the hotel's chrome-and-glass doors, the clerk at the reception desk had been a young woman with dark ringlets and a false brightness that Bin-Hezam had found grating. A Jewess, of course. The neighborhood abutted the garment district, an old Zionist stronghold now flowing into Asian.

Bin-Hezam had masked his distaste, wiping his brow with a handkerchief and presenting himself for check-in. "I would like a suite for two nights, please," he had said, in his refined British art dealer voice.

"Do you have a reservation?"

"I do not."

"Because we are nearly full this weekend for the Fourth of July festivities." She had smiled with nonsensical enthusiasm and clicked her computer keyboard in search of accommodations. "We have a junior penthouse suite available on the top floor," she had said.

"That will be fine."

"Wonderful," she had enthused, as though by accepting her recommendation he had accomplished some great feat. "May I have a credit card and a driver's license or other form of picture identification?"

"I will pay cash," Bin-Hezam had said.

The girl had hesitated, having been thrown off her routine.

"Unless that is a problem?" Bin-Hezam had asked.

"No, of course not." She had recaptured her smile, resuming her singsong voice. "The rate for the junior penthouse suite is eight hundred dollars. If you do not wish to leave a credit card, we do require a two-hundred-dollar cash deposit, which will be refunded—minus incidentals—to you upon your departure."

Bin-Hezam had reached into the breast pocket of his rumpled but expensive brown suit jacket, retrieving a slim black leather billfold. He had selected sixteen crisp one-hundred-dollar bills and slid them inside his pale green Saudi Arabian passport, handing both to her.

She had smiled and counted the bills in front of him. In Manhattan, a foreign traveler bearing high denominations of U.S. currency was not at all unusual. "And the deposit?" she had asked, her voice inflecting the question mark.

"There will be no incidentals," Bin-Hezam had said, offering her a tight smile that communicated his insistence.

She had hesitated again, looking into his tea-colored eyes—a greedy Jew, of course—then had set aside the alleged hotel policy without further complaint. "All right, Mr. Bin-Hezam. That will be fine." She had counted out the sixteen hundred dollars again before depositing them into her under-counter tray. "Would you like to join our rewards program?"

"I decline."

She had smiled and nodded. "No problem." Another flourish of keystrokes and she had printed a receipt, returning Bin-Hezam's passport to him. "Would you like one room key or two?" she asked.

"Just one."

She had made the key and had slid it into a small folder, writing the room number on the outside. "Please enjoy your stay."

Bin-Hezam had slept, something he had not counted on doing. He had budgeted his time for a lengthier detention in Bangor or at Newark. More questions. More computer checks. He was immune to any form of scrutiny.

He had been hours ahead of schedule. The sleep would sharpen him for the next day's work. *Insha'Allah* it would all go this smoothly.

His room was so garish as to be painful to his soul, haute decor of a sort that reeked of competition among designers to prove who could combine the most outrageous colors in the most off-putting patterns. In this case, shades of purple with red counterpoints and aqua-blue details.

He had looked out his window before drawing the shade, the lights of the city peaceful, unsuspecting.

Bin-Hezam had set his wheeled carry-on upon the luggage stand. He had drawn back the zipper but had not unpacked. He had gone into the bathroom, another assault of form versus function, and quickly had shed his clothes. He had hung the suit on a towel rod while he had showered, hoping to steam out the wrinkles and some of the perspiration.

Afterward, he had put on a light cotton dishdasha from his luggage and knelt to pray, seeking God's blessing that he remain calm within this den of chaos. That he perform his duty with grace and cunning. And that he be brave at the end.

He had climbed into the bed. There, beneath the covers, Bin-Hezam had given himself over to a remembrance of the night he had been called to be. This had been his nightly routine while waiting for sleep to take him.

Like many before him, Bin-Hezam had once been visited by Mohammed in a dream. The prophet had shown him that hell was as real as Earth, and that the boy would be sent there when he died if he ever dared disobey his father.

He had shown Bin-Hezam fire that was a hundred times hotter than the noontime sun. It had burned off his skin, which grew back darkened only to be roasted off again and again. The burning had been agony. He had held his own innards in his hands while slung from a ceiling by chains of razor, the calluses of his feet just barely off the surface of the floor, near enough to it to be bitten by laughing scorpions.

His dry mouth had begged for sweet water, but the only drink he had been given was his own blood that never stopped flowing.

The following morning, young Bin-Hezam had reasoned that, because hell was real, not only must he believe that there is no god but one god and Mohammed is his prophet . . . but he could not tolerate anyone else who believed otherwise. To do so would be a sin. He had determined that he must do everything within his power to banish nonbelievers from the world, for the good of all mankind and the love of Mohammed.

Some years later, he had had the dream

again, prompted, he had been convinced, by the hideous photographic evidence of the abuses at Abu Ghraib. Young men like himself in that terrible prison, raped and defiled, tortured by the American Crusaders, including American women.

It had been a sign. Their pain became his pain, their chains his chains.

The Americans had tried to bring hell into this Earth. The jihadists at his mosque in Harad had taught him that the Crusaders and their Jewish masters would not rest until they had killed every last Muslim and unleashed the fire of hell.

Finally, his thoughts had turned to his dear parents, recalling his mother's delight every time she found perfect dates in the market, his father's firm instruction of Baada and his five siblings. His mother a goddess of kindness, baker of the best *fatir* he had ever eaten—and his father, a cobbler, a devout man but one never called to be a soldier of jihad.

Bin-Hezam had prayed for them. Secure in his purpose, saved from hell, he had drifted into a dreamless sleep mumbling his parents' names.

"Okay, Fisk," said Dubin, coming to the door, motioning him into the office. "I think you know the commissioner?"

Fisk shook the hand of the compact, buzz-cut ex-marine who ran the entire New York City Police Department. Commissioner Kelly made a point of meeting every one of his thirty-six thousand sworn officers, and Fisk had shaken his hand three or four times previously. But this was the first time he had ever seen the commissioner at the Brooklyn headquarters of the Intelligence Division.

The commissioner said, "Good to see

you again, Fisk," and abruptly sat back down in his chair, legs crossed, ready for business.

Fisk took a seat. Dubin remained on the edge of his desk.

"I wanted you to brief the commissioner personally as to this Flight 903 thing," said Dubin. "With everything going on this weekend, we can't take any chances."

Fisk nodded, unable to determine whether Dubin was kicking this upstairs or simply passing the buck. Was he covering his own ass, or did he truly believe there was enough evidence to warrant getting behind Fisk?

"Tell him what you told me," said Dubin. "Your theory. The long form."

Fisk turned to the commissioner. "It's not reached the level of theory yet. But I'll lay out the dots for you and I think you'll agree that they might connect."

The commissioner said, "Be precise. Tell me why you think what happened on that airplane might be the beginning of something instead of the end of it."

Fisk collected his thoughts before speaking. He knew he had but one chance to sell the commissioner on his fears.

"One," Fisk began, with a measured pace to be sure everything he said was fully digested. "Wide view first. If he was acting alone, then the hijacker Awaan Abdulraheem was on a mission that, at the very least, put him at a disadvantage to succeed. There is no way in this day and age that one man, acting alone, could take control of an American-bound aircraft with a phony bomb and a small knife. I'll leave out the chance that this guy might not be playing with a full deck, and could be more 'gee-whiz' than 'jihad.'"

He paused. The commissioner gave him nothing, no indication.

"Two. He is, by every indication, a jihadist, trained in Pakistan, versed in terror-speak—and yet with no financial resources of his own. If someone trained and sponsored him, then why wasn't he better prepared?

"Three. He has confessed. He broke down in ten minutes. I'm not saying he's a plant, but they screen these guys, they train them to stand up to us. They give them a script. It's our job to shake it. Normal and natural that they isolate these guys, so they can't give up the entire network. But they

prep their holy warriors, and this Abdulraheem was a songbird. A scared songbird.
I'd love to test this guy's IQ. I think he's a
puppet, a dupe. That he absolutely believed
that he was going to get away with heroic
martyrdom—but he was the only one."

Still no word or nod from the commissioner. Fisk looked to Dubin, who was no
help.

"Four. He shares tribal kinship with bin
Laden. Enough said.

"Five. He shares tribal kinship with another passenger on the same plane, a
man named Baada Bin-Hezam. Bin-
Hezam is a Saudi who is, or claims to be,
an art dealer."

The commissioner's eyebrows went up
on that one. "Where did you get the tribal
connection?" he asked.

"Our own Analytical Unit. Earlier today."

"Go on, Fisk," said the commissioner.

"Six. I worked on the Ramstein inventory from bin Laden's house. I had product
clearance for all the intelligence work that's
been ongoing at NSA, CIA, and the rest of
the task force. I was one of the ones shaking the pocket litter out of his pockets. Before we shipped it out of Germany, we

found some misencoded plain text in images of sunflowers. NSA got a lot more. Indications that point away from operations such as a lone airplane hijacker. Bin Laden was seriously lathered about the Bassam Shah attempt and isolated bombings in general. A lack of discipline, that's the take. OBL wanted a target worthy of high symbolic value. He openly questioned why they hadn't learned from past mistakes and anticipated our methods. Am I reading too much into that? I don't know. But a lightweight Yemeni with a fake bomb on an airplane cannot possibly be all there is to this thing. Goes against everything bin Laden was talking about. I think it's more than fifty-fifty we're being played."

"That's a serious contention, Fisk," said the commissioner. "Do we have a clear link to Al-Qaeda? And before you answer, let me tell you this." Kelly sat forward. "If you don't have a hard and direct link, and we act on this, we will be conducting one of the most difficult manhunts in this city's history—and in total secrecy. Because we will not use the media, because we cannot ever afford to be wrong. We cannot use non-Intel law enforcement because it will leak immediately. We cannot panic ten million people. And—this is just a fact—we cannot and will not squander all the optimism and confidence the foiled hijacking has brought to this city and this nation. No way I'm going to pop that balloon unless I'm damn well sure it's going to pop on its own. People are happier and healthier and more confident when they think they can't be beat. Just so you know where you stand, Fisk."

"Understood, Commissioner."

"Now. Do you have a link?"

"What you're really asking for is proof, and I don't have that. You know how we do things here. Al-Qaeda is not an organization with what we think of as military units. It's more like a method shared by many, rather than an orderly group of soldiers working together. There's top-down, but no schematic. Awfully hard to put two bad actors together at any time. So how do we track them? By figuring out who's related to who and which training camps they've attended—if they've attended any at all. Now, Abdulraheem could not have known the things he told us about training in Pakistan, unless he had been there.

The site itself was one of Al-Qaeda's most closely guarded secrets. Unless I'm misinformed, we didn't even know about it until we took down bin Laden."

The commissioner nodded. "If we had knowledge that this other passenger, this Saudi, had gone to the same camp—then it would be boom time."

"No way to know that," said Fisk. "Or highly unlikely, I should say. But here's the thing. The Saudi—Baada Bin-Hezam—has vanished. He stepped off the plane in Newark and disappeared into the wind."

The commissioner made a face, looking more sour than usual. "What do we have on this Saudi, besides the passport dope?"

"In terms of imaging, we have jetway camera captures from the boarding gate in Stockholm. I should have Newark Airport customs hall crowd pictures and passport control security video by tonight."

Dubin uncrossed his arms. "Can we get anything sent over here right away?" Then he answered his own question by picking up his phone and calling the photo tech section. He ordered the Stockholm images e-mailed to his computer immediately.

The commissioner stood, his hands on his hips. "Okay, I don't think we have any choice but to go after him. If we do pull back the curtain on this guy and find there's nothing, I'll still feel it was a job worth doing. These are the kinds of inferences we should be making."

The commissioner looked at Dubin, who took a deep breath and nodded. Fisk could almost feel the machine roaring to life.

"I don't like how cold we're going into this," said Dubin.

"But that is why we're going," said the commissioner. "Because it's so cold. Because this guy is invisible to us now." He turned back to Fisk. "This is your call, Fisk, so you're going to run it. But—quietly. He's an invisible man, so you run an invisible op. Figure out a way to make it look like a routine seek-and-find with your informants and other assets and resources. For the time being, only the three of us know how deep the water is here. Let's keep it that way. Assign analysts to different pieces of the puzzle. Only Intel cops get photographs of the Saudi for their own information. No mug-flashing in the neighborhoods—or limited. Definitely no spraying his name around. I'd like to think we've learned something from the Shah episode. Clear?"

"One other person knows," said Fisk, looking to Dubin. "Gersten."

The commissioner said, "Krina Gersten?" Fisk looked to him, hiding his surprise. "Her father was a good friend of mine, and a great cop. And her mother is a hell of a woman. Where is she on this?"

Fisk said, "She was with me in Bangor. She's leading the Intel detail covering the flight attendant and five passengers. We're protecting them, and we're also watching what they say to the media or anybody else."

"Good, leave her there," said the commissioner. "We need someone sharp inside the tent. Let her know what to look out for, and tell her to keep it under her hat. She has to know enough of what we know in case one of the so-called Six— and God, how I hate that name already— figures out what we're doing and starts blabbing."

Not since Chesley Sullenberger's "Miracle on the Hudson" had America anointed heroes so quickly. The Six, as they were becoming known, were for the most part in the throes of newfound celebrity. The twenty-four-hour news channels starved for breaking news had taken to the Internet, searching for any minutiae about the lives of the six formerly private citizens they could use to fill their airtime, biographical or otherwise.

TMZ went with a revealing bikini photograph from Maggie's Facebook page, taken about ten years before. Upon seeing it, she turned red and covered her face when the others reacted—Frank, Nouvian, and two of the cops hooted good-naturedly—but she couldn't stop laughing.

"Aruba," she said. "I was teaching aerobics back then." She discreetly set aside the cream cheese–smeared bagel she had been nibbling on.

Mayor Bloomberg had hired four temps from his own public relations firm, setting them up in one of the rooms on the floor to field media requests. The lead publicist, a tall, cheery woman with a practiced manner, took the floor.

"First of all, let me say what an honor it is just to be here with you. What you did was absolutely amazing, and the whole country is fascinated and basically in love with all of you."

She brimmed with genuine excitement, reflected back to her by most of them. Jenssen and Nouvian stood out as being not entirely enamored of the situation.

"We have been inundated with interview and appearance requests—just swamped. Exciting and appropriate. But so much so that we couldn't honor them all in a month if we wanted to. The mayor has asked me to coordinate things for you this weekend, to guide you through these extraordinary circumstances you find yourselves in."

"Oprah," whispered Maggie to the others, followed by an amazed giggle.

"Haven't heard from Oprah yet"—the publicist smiled—"though I'll be shocked if we don't. Now as I said, there are a lot of opportunities and things are starting to come together, but I wanted to meet with you first and talk about your desires and expectations."

"Such as?" asked Frank, the journalist.

"Well, often in a group situation such as this, people will nominate one to do the bulk of the speaking for them. It just makes it easier to have one voice, rather than six. So let me start like this. Does anyone want to volunteer?"

They looked at one another for a moment. Then Jenssen's good hand went up.

The publicist looked surprised. "You'd like to be the spokesman?"

"No," he said. "I'd prefer not to participate at all."

"Not at all?" she said.

"That's correct," he answered.

Nouvian's hand went halfway up. "I . . . I don't mind doing my part. But I've got a concert coming up in six days at Lincoln Center. That means a minimum of six hours of practice per day. Minimum."

"Okay." The publicist was confused now. She looked to Gersten for guidance.

Gersten stepped forward. "I'm sure it's hard for all of you to comprehend, cooped up here in hotel rooms in midtown Manhattan. But you are famous and probably on your way to becoming household names. Whether you believe it or not, you have become symbols of the best that Americans can be, of courage, of resilience. To put it another way, you are no longer private citizens, not anymore."

She saw them trying to comprehend this, each in his or her own way.

"Now, you can turn your back on that, you can close your shades when you get home, you can unplug the phone and close your Facebook pages. Or you can, I don't know, go around to the openings of restaurants and nightclubs for the next twenty years. The world is your oyster right now. The public wants to see you and hear from you and be inspired by you. So why not give them that? At least for this weekend."

"Look," said Colin Frank, not to Gersten but turning toward his fellow heroes. "I haven't said much about this yet, except for a conversation I had with Joanne." He nodded to the IKEA store manager. "But not only are we famous, we are going to be rich. Very, very rich, each of us, if we play our cards right. Now—I'm not saying we have to play anything up. On the contrary, the truth will out. But people will want to hear our stories. They'll want to read our books. They may want to . . ." He pointed at Maggie. "Wear the bikinis we wear." They laughed. "Eat the cereal we eat. Shop at the stores we shop at. Sounds crazy, but . . . do you see what I'm saying?"

"How much money?" asked Aldrich, the retiree.

"I don't know. Nobody knows. We should talk further about how we want to go about this, both together and separately. I'm not saying we're going to become Kardashians. Though I'm not saying we're not. Maybe you have a charity you want to get behind and support, driving its fundraising. I don't know. Am I going to write a book about this? You bet your ass I am. We are going to have people coming at us, vultures and opportunists, and we need counsel, we need advice. We need lawyers and managers—and I know this sounds crazy. But I've been thinking about this, now that things have settled down. We have something so few others have. We are not only witnesses to but participants in history."

The publicist interrupted him. "And that is a conversation I certainly encourage you all to have. And if I can be of any service to you going ahead, we can talk about that too, at the appropriate time. But Mr. . . ."

"Jenssen," he answered, sitting in the back of the room, sideways on a chair, his legs crossed, his cast in his lap.

"What do you think now? You expressed reluctance."

Jenssen scowled. "I don't share this excitement. Money is honey, as some say. A trap. Now, I like money. Everybody likes money. But money . . . if it becomes too much, you can give it away. Now, fame— you can't control it. Once you step onto that fame elevator, and those doors close—it takes you up or it takes you down, but it never goes sideways."

"Good," said Sparks. "I could use a little excitement." She threw another of her smiles at Jenssen. "I feel like getting on and pressing all the buttons at once."

Jenssen said, "People also apparently enjoy heroin. At first."

Gersten spoke up. "I think you need to think about this and talk together and try to figure it out. But for tonight . . ."

She looked to the publicist, who took her cue like a pro.

"For tonight, we would very much like to schedule one major interview with the six of you. Every broadcast network has expressed major interest, but only one has a highly rated news show on in late night, and that is *Nightline*. We would like for you to make your network television debut to-night."

Nouvian raised his hand like a child who had to go to the bathroom. "What if I just want to go home?"

The others turned toward him, sur-prised. Except for Jenssen, who crossed his arms and awaited the answer.

The publicist looked at Gersten.

Gersten said, "Going home at this point would be impossible."

"Impossible?" asked Nouvian. "Why? I am a free man."

"You are material witnesses to an at-tempted terrorist act, one that is still under active investigation."

"First of all," said Maggie, "we're not wit-nesses, we are participants. We have a say in this. Second—how is it still active? The hijacking is over."

Gersten said, "I have no say in this mat-ter. I am following orders."

"And so are we," said Jenssen. "Or so we are expected to."

Aldrich squinted like he smelled some-thing funny. "What's going on here? Are you telling me that if we stood up, the six of us, and walked to the door and out of here, we would be arrested, or detained?"

Gersten smiled. She did not want to say yes.

"Really," said Maggie, shocked.

"Under whose authority?" said Aldrich. "Is this Obama's doing? Is that dismantler of the Constitution pulling another fast one?"

"Under the law," said Gersten, "the Patriot Act gives us broad powers of investigation."

"You mean 'detention,'" said Frank. He turned to Aldrich. "It's not Obama. You can blame Bush for this one."

Aldrich didn't like that. He turned an angry red, but could only say, "This is utter bullshit."

Jenssen said, "So we are detained, we are prisoners here. Except where you want to trot us out on television to smile for the cameras?"

Maggie turned to them. "Come on," she said, "don't blame her." She was defending Gersten. "It's obviously not her fault. She didn't volunteer to give up her Friday night to take our abuse."

Gersten smiled, saying nothing.

Frank rubbed his unshaven face and said, "Look. Let's all play the game for tonight. It costs us nothing. The fact remains that we did do something remarkable, and we are, quote-unquote, heroes. So let's not overthink it. I feel a certain sense of obligation, but even if you don't—then look at it as a once-in-a-lifetime experience. Television is fascinating from the inside out. We'll go tell our story tonight, then get some much-needed rest and figure all the rest of it out tomorrow."

The publicist clasped her hands. "I think that's an excellent solution."

Sparks turned around to Jenssen, still sitting with his arms crossed. She squeezed his knee in a teasing manner. "What do you say, hero?"

Gersten smiled at how ironic it was that the most naturally photogenic person among them was also the most reluctant to go on television.

Jenssen slowly smiled, some of it for Sparks, the rest releasing considerable wattage into the room. "I guess I have nothing better to do this evening."

The mood lifted considerably. The publicist said, "We can tape at eight P.M. in their Times Square studio. To do so, we need to be in cars and moving at seven thirty, and until then you will have private time or a chance to connect with your families. Room service has been alerted to our schedule and will serve full dinners on dining tables in your suites at six thirty. Everybody clear on that?"

Nods and smiles all around.

Jenssen said, "Is there a gymnasium in this hotel?"

Gersten said, "There is, but we can't give you access today."

The publicist said, "We can try to build some time into the schedule tomorrow."

Nouvian said, "Wait a minute. We already have a schedule for tomorrow?"

The publicist realized she had said too much. "Maybe," she answered, as one of her assistants approached her with a piece of paper.

Maggie said, "If I'm going on national television tonight, I need some beauty work. And I mean, pronto."

"Seconded," said Sparks. "How about clothes that haven't been stuffed in a suitcase for two days?"

The publicist finished reading the page

she had been handed and looked up, smiling. "Then you will love this. Barneys New York has offered free shopping sprees for all of you. We'll get the website up, you can plug in your sizes, place your orders online, and two of my assistants will have it here for you by six P.M. As to makeup, there will be professionals at the television studio tonight. Does that get you ladies where you need to go?"

Maggie and Sparks looked at each other in silent celebration. Even Nouvian grinned.

Aldrich said, "What the hell's 'Barneys'?"

The others all laughed.

The publicist said, "I'll get that website up for you right away."

"Coyote" was the tactical field operation code name randomly spit out by the computer. Still, it struck Fisk as somehow appropriate. Every e-mail and piece of paperwork would be slugged with it. He started with a sketch of his action plan for Dubin's data files. How he planned to organize his people, his search and ID parameters, information security. Best to get the bureaucratic stuff out of the way early.

He held off putting his head down on his desk until the photographs came in. Dubin had ordered him to take a few hours in a duty bunk, but this wasn't Fisk's first long weekend, and he had an athlete's knowledge of his own capacity for fatigue.

His computer pinged the summons he had programmed for urgent e-mails. The photographs from the overhead Stockholm jetway camera materialized on his screen.

A collage of six black-and-white images showed a slim man in a dark suit, pointedly looking down as he passed under the camera. At one point, the morning light through the jetway window had startled him into looking up. That was the best shot.

He was a classically handsome Arab. Dark eyebrows across the top of an angular square face, broad shoulders. The body of a man who would get heavy later in life, but who now radiated strength and confidence.

The image improved upon Bin-Hezam's four-year-old passport photo, in which he sported a beard. But Fisk hoped Newark ICE would do better, and decided to wait for those before releasing these to the Intel machine.

The Newark customs hall photos came in on another computer chime. There were a dozen, most of them showing the Saudi at the baggage carousel. While the other passengers were visibly excited or relieved that their interrupted journey had come to a peaceful end, Bin-Hezam appeared like any arriving passenger disembarking from any airplane in any airport in the world. No expression, no pacing, no stretching. Head down, ignoring the exhilaration around him.

The shot from the eye-level camera at the immigration booth was the best of the bunch. He looked no different from any of the hundreds of young Arab men Fisk had known, though—unless he was reading too much into it—the man's desert-black eyes looked darker than most, borderline supernatural.

Fisk magnified the image 150 percent. The Saudi had a nickel-size mole at the left end of his jawline, looking like a dark welt. The mole gave them a little bit of an edge, as an identifying mark—but the haystack was still absurdly big.

Fisk ordered fifty prints each of the enlarged full-face photograph and the full-color, full-body shot from the baggage carousel. His action plan was uncomplicated and, he was afraid, potentially hopeless. He had to pull every raker and mosque crawler off whatever they were doing to canvass the Muslim neighborhoods in Queens and Brooklyn, betting everything on the Saudi's likelihood of surfacing there.

Bin-Hezam had to know somebody in New York. He had to stay someplace. With friends or family? The Analytic Unit had come up with no domestic relatives, but in many of these cases a fourth cousin twice removed demonstrated the fidelity of a parent or sibling. Still, a hotel was not out of the question, and Dubin had forwarded Baada Bin-Hezam's credit card information to the FBI.

Fisk's best friends now were shoe leather and blind luck. He pulled up the informant tracking sheets and dispatched e-mails to the detectives running each of the thirty or so men and women out on the streets of New York, with strict caution against further dissemination. Then, like a patient taking his medicine, Fisk forced himself to go head-down for a while, sleep taking him almost instantly.

Fifty minutes later he popped back up, briefly disoriented, waking out of a dream in which a coyote was loose inside the Intel Division's offices. He stood, needing to get his blood circulating, and inside of a minute felt alert and refreshed. He got a candy bar out of the break room vending machine and guzzled a caffeinated diet soda.

The day shift had handed their consoles off to the middies who would work until midnight. Dubin had turned the overtime spigot wide open and put everybody willing to work on the streets. That meant there were three times as many cops looking for Baada Bin-Hezam as there would have been on an ordinary shift.

It was a Friday night just after 6:00 P.M. The Jumu'ah weekly prayer was over. Many observant families stayed close to home in the evening, except for the Westernized young who were in the streets like the rest of New York on this hot summer night. Crowded avenues made it easier for his people to browse among the throng. They also made it potentially easier for Bin-Hezam to hide. But the heat generally brought people outside, so the odds were in his favor.

The agents at their computers flicked through screens of alternating text messages and GPS tracks, showing the locations of their people, passing on updates and summaries to Fisk. In the neighbor-hoods, years of sidewalk surveillance had given the rakers a sixth sense about who belonged there and who did not.

So far, no one reported any activity out of the ordinary.

Nearly one million of New York's eight million residents were Muslim. One in eight. There were 130 mosques in the five boroughs. Fourteen Islamic schools. Spe-cial parking rules in some neighborhoods for religious holidays. Shops and restau-rants mimicked those in Baghdad, Jakarta, Riyadh, Kabul, Karachi, and thousands of other settlements around the world in which there is no god but God.

The search on the street was a standard neighborhood canvass. Smartphones had rewritten the rules of surveillance. Gone were the days of clandestine meetings be-tween spies, informants, and handlers. The reports flickered across Fisk's screen from Muslim communities in Brooklyn, Queens, and lower Manhattan.

All the same. Negative for contact.

The demographic landscape of New York is forever shifting. The neighborhoods change as constantly and steadily as the

ancient glaciers that shaped the terrain under the city, their ethnic blends transformed
by migration, fear, whim, and greed. Bay
Ridge, Boerum Hill, Cobble Hill, Flatbush,
Sunset Park, and Greenwood Heights in
Brooklyn were home to vibrant cloisters of
Arabs and Turks, further refined by tribal
and family connections. Afghans and Pakistanis had settled in outer Queens, most
around the two mosques in Flushing. Bos-
nians and Indonesians claimed Astoria.

Fisk toggled his computer keyboard,
bringing up the surveillance camera feeds.
Five hundred digital video cameras fed
images into a control center in the old
Brooklyn Navy Yard. The two photographs
of Bin-Hezam had gone to the control center slugged with a national emergency priority, but no additional information. Only
the most senior of the camera techs had
ever seen a national emergency priority request. The order meant they had to drop
everything except violent-crime-in-progress
alerts to turn the cameras' attention to look
for a single suspect.

None of them had been told why. None
of them would ask. Everything they did
was need-to-know.

For any pair of human eyes working a camera sweep like this one, the level of concentration was similar to that of air traffic controllers during rush hour. One of the center's software programmers extracted the eight facial characteristics from the Newark Airport close-up that the computer needed to screen raw images from the cameras. The resulting filter algorithm was then applied to all incoming video. This action cut down the number of possible images of a known suspect by a factor of ten thousand to one.

The possible photos were pumped to duty agents at Intel by the dozens. Those screeners forwarded along any likelies to Fisk, who expected to see three or four faces an hour.

None of the first batch belonged to Bin-Hezam. No surprise. Success was never that easy.

Fisk felt himself slipping into the patient, confident rhythms of intense surveillance, digesting input from multiple sources all over New York. It was pleasurable, the familiar exhilaration of the hunt. These were impulses he associated with Krina Gersten, and he realized that he owed her a call. He speed-dialed her cell.

"Hey," he said.

"Hey-hey," she said, a bit of relief in her voice.

"Everything good?"

"Fine here." He heard her walking, and pictured her looking for a quiet, confidential spot to stand and talk. "They're in with friends, family, their thoughts, or the TV. We're packing them up soon to head over to Times Square to do *Nightline*. There was a mini-revolt, or the seeds of one, but they're all going along with the game plan for now. I don't suppose you're calling to get me off this day care detail."

"On the contrary," he said. "The commissioner likes you there. He knew you by name. I didn't know you were wired in with the deity."

"Lotta good it's doing me," she said. He heard her move the phone away from her mouth and tell someone, "Just a minute." Then she was back. "Yeah, him and my dad ran around a little bit. Staten Island back in the day."

"Maybe you can leverage that. Get a

message to him, get off that hotel detail. Or I could try . . ."

"First of all, my mom gets a Christmas card every year, but, I mean, that's the extent of it. Second, going over Dubin's head serves neither of our interests. I have to satisfy myself by living vicariously through you for now, and hope things change later. Where are you at? Pushing ahead with Bin-Hezam, I hope."

"Full speed ahead. The lid is off the box. Looking through city camera feeds and listening in on conversations. Nothing yet. Even given full access, we need to get so lucky to make this thing work."

"You're doing all the usual stuff, I'm sure," she said, thinking out loud. "Let's think targets. Obviously, there's this weekend. The fireworks."

"Three million people will be watching, spread out all along the West Side looking at the Hudson River. And then the dedication of One World Trade Center the next day."

"America's brand-new tallest building."

"The president is in town for that. The ceremony is just thirty-six hours away."

"Fireworks display is spread out from

Twentieth to Fifty-fifth Street. It goes for like twenty minutes."

"Twenty-five."

"That is a nightmare waiting to happen. By contrast, the ceremony's going to have a thick credential zone. It's going to be, what, a half mile around the site?"

"Something like that. Two juicy targets. Or, think about this—wait for the ceremony and its dignitaries to draw all security on the island, leaving the rest of Manhattan unusually vulnerable."

"Jesus," she said. "I'm sorry I asked." She was thinking. "Has to be high value, high visibility. Yankee Stadium?"

"Thank Christ, they're out of town this weekend. L.A. Angels. But don't forget— it's going to be big impact, but not neces- sarily high body count. Bin Laden wanted to dazzle and do damage."

"The Statue of Liberty. It's visible from lower Manhattan, from the Ground Zero area. Would be a huge fucking symbolic strike."

Fisk said, "That's heavy. But then again, as a target, it's as good as any. Let's face it, we could probably spend all night run- ning down New York City's greatest hits.

A tourist could. Right now it doesn't get us any closer to where and why. All we've got is who. Maybe who. We've got to go in that way. We've got to find some way to anticipate his movements and try to intersect with one of them."

"Anthrax," said Gersten. "Or some other bio agent."

"Always a concern. But nothing from the airport sniffers. Now, if he's got contacts here, and I assume he does—then it's possible."

"He must have help, right? Is he bringing something to somebody . . . or is he here to take delivery? His luggage was searched, so that's out. Is he here to facilitate something?"

Fisk said, "You know I hate to play into the bubble paranoia." He and Gersten had talked often about the skewed worldview that comes with hunting phantom terrorists seven days a week. "But maybe he's here to awaken sleeper agents. That makes sense to me. I keep going back to the big beard's words before his death. He wanted to implement a plan so clever we'd never see it coming. If bin Laden started turning the wheels on a major plan before he died, he would have wanted to use the best of everything. The deepest contacts, the brightest operatives. He would have burned his prime Al-Qaeda sleepers to make it work." Fisk heard himself pontificating. "Or, and I haven't taken this off the table yet, this Saudi is just some jet-setting art dealer, whose life is about to be temporarily ruined by one Intel agent's paranoia."

"Don't doubt yourself, Jeremy. Something's brewing here, something is happening. Get inside this guy's head. Do that by remembering that, if this is anything at all, it's something big. Something hard. Everything on the line, nothing ordinary. Nothing small. That's what bin Laden was planning, right? Something extraordinary. Taking this fight to the next level, the one beyond nine-eleven."

Fisk was nodding on his end.

"Dammit," continued Gersten. "I hate being on the sidelines."

"You're not," said Fisk. "This has been a big help. You've focused me. You sharpened my pencil."

"Yeah, yeah," she said dismissively.

"Keep thinking for me," he said, and hung up.

He reflected a moment on their conversation, briefly smiling. The National Security Agency's New York field office was monitoring cell phone communications per Intel's request, routing everything off the Flatbush, Cobble Hill, Astoria, and lower Manhattan cell towers down to Fort Meade's big machines. They could not process every call, legally or practically, so they were digitally scanning for Arabic words and certain terrorist keywords. He was smiling at the thought of his own conversation with Gersten being flagged. The snake eating its tail.

The bubble. The paranoia.

Thirty-six hours.

If there was to be a terror attack in New York City this weekend, Fisk had two nights and a day to find one man in a city of millions.

Gersten could have checked out and gone off duty at the end of her shift, but her talk with Fisk had reawakened the dutiful cop in her. She decided to accompany De-Rosier, the more tolerable of her two detail partners, to the television broadcast.

The hotel location of The Six had leaked out via media and the Internet, so the first thing they encountered upon leaving the Hyatt—besides a blast of early evening heat—was the bombardment of cheers and applause from a street-clogging crowd gathered to watch them cross the side-walk into the hospitality vans. The uproar was such that Gersten went on full alert, feeling more like a Secret Service security detail in that moment than a cop.

But the mood of the mob was ebullient. This truly was a hero's welcome. The only threat was that their enthusiasm could lead to a trampling.

Once aboard the air-conditioned van, The Six looked out the windows, shocked and amazed by their fans.

Aldrich eased into his seat and pronounced the crowd, in his words, "Crazy people."

"Love it!" said Maggie, waving as though she could be seen through the one-way windows. "We love you back!" she said, laughing.

Frank opened the notebook he had begun carrying and jotted down a few observations. Nouvian winced as though beset by a high-pitched whine.

Jenssen took a seat in the back of the van, looking out the window like a man on a safari. Sparks quickly made her way to his side, Gersten noticed with a smile.

The NYPD escort led them across the city, sirens rising to a scream at every intersection. Gersten thought it fascinating to look out and see pedestrians fighting their way through the July heat to look up at the police escorts and figure out who was in the van and raise their hands in salute. The city was rising up together on a muggy Friday night.

To DeRosier, she said, "I don't think a ticker tape parade is out of the question."

They were sitting together in one of the front seats. He nudged her to look in the back. "You see that?"

He was referring to Sparks and Jenssen. Both clad in fresh threads courtesy of Barneys New York, Ms. Sparks was pointing things out to him as the cross streets went past, giving him a guided tour. Jenssen was not uninterested, in both the city and Ms. Sparks, but she was clearly the more aggressive of the pair.

Gersten said, "Ten bucks it ends ugly."

"It always ends ugly," said DeRosier. "But what does he care? Oh, to be that Swede here in New York. Wonder if he needs a good wingman."

Gersten said, "Think your wife would approve?"

"My wife?" said DeRosier. "She'd be first in line to give this guy tongue. You know what I mean—purely patriotically. In a welcome-home-soldier kind of way. Did you know I used to have blond hair too?"

"And blue eyes?" asked Gersten.

DeRosier frowned. "Goddamn handsome son of a bitch."

Gersten got on her phone, ordering up some more exterior security at the Hyatt. Sawhorses weren't going to cut it. They needed some fencing and mounted officers for crowd control. She requested some more down-market transportation as well. This van was like a tour bus. She called Patton and asked him to secure the hotel's delivery entrance for their return.

Nightline was normally produced at ABC News headquarters in Lincoln Square on the Upper West Side. For this special broadcast, featuring The Six and a New York City–centric story, they returned to the iconography of their Times Square studios.

The producers waiting for them outside the side entrance were overwhelmed by the sudden rush of interest from tourists and savvy New Yorkers. The Six were hustled inside, but not before they got a glance at the big media screens all around the

Crossroads of the World, showing ex-
cerpts from their earlier news conference.

Inside, they were fawned over by the
producers and assorted other people associated with the broadcast. The walls
were lined with people, and it was obvious
to Gersten that not everyone waiting for a
glimpse of The Six was essential personnel. Even normally jaded broadcast employees were swept up by the excitement.

The Six were made up, miked, and led
into the studio overlooking Broadway.
They were introduced to hosts Cynthia
McFadden and Terry Moran, who were
sharing duties for the fifteen-minute segment. Gersten stood back behind the
lights, on the smooth, glossy floor the huge
cameras glided over.

After they were seated, the president of
the network walked in and introduced himself to each of them in turn. After he left,
Cynthia McFadden broke the ice by as-
suring The Six that the network president
didn't drop in to greet just anyone.

The studio was lit, The Six bathed in a
honey glow, seated on high-legged director's chairs in a wide semicircle across from
McFadden and Moran. Moran studied his

notes as the stage manager counted them down, and McFadden launched into the segment. Her introduction cited *Nightline*'s own birth during the Iran hostage crisis, linking that incident of terror to the heroics of SAS Flight 903. She then threw it to a quick package of video of the plane touching down safely in Bangor, with attendant emergency vehicles rushing to meet it. They aired clips from the newly released flight recorder conversations between the captain and air traffic controllers, and then the red lights came back on and the live interview began.

The hosts predictably took The Six through the details of the attack, describing their feelings at the time. Gersten noticed that their answers had become burnished a bit over the past twenty-four hours, as all good stories do. Instead of selfless and self-deprecating claims of unthinking reaction, their heroics were gradually taking on a more deterministic bent. Frank, especially, explained about how he "knew he had to do something," and that if he didn't, "the loss of life would have been tragic."

Gersten got a sour taste in her mouth,

watching a journalist sell his story.

In the interview's most poignant moment, Maggie Sullivan welled up describing her fears as the hijacker overpowered her. Her emotions were true, still so raw, and threatened to overwhelm her. She again spoke glowingly of Jenssen, describing his action as the first man into the vestibule, hurling himself at the Yemeni, wrestling the fake trigger away from him and fracturing his wrist in the process. When the tears flowed and she had nowhere else to go, she turned to Jenssen, seated next to her, and he put his arm around her shoulders, comforting her in silence.

DeRosier, coming up behind Gersten, whispered, "How long until they record their first hit single?"

She smiled, but Maggie's need for consolation touched her—and, she knew, would touch the millions who were watching the program that evening, and the many more millions around the world who would view the clip online throughout the weekend.

Baada Bin-Hezam returned to Penn Station dressed in jeans, black leather dress shoes, a T-shirt, and a casual brown sport coat. He wore a pair of expensive black-rimmed eyeglasses and a trim mustache dyed to perfectly match his hair color. He had trimmed his hair tightly and further distracted from his facial appearance with a fashionable neck scarf. The heat had not diminished as much as he expected, and he was instantly uncomfortable. But to all eyes, he appeared to be a young, upwardly mobile Arab headed out for an evening on the town.

He entered the subway caverns underneath the vast station. The A train, an express, did not stop at 116th Street, his desired destination. The train he wanted was the C, the local. Confusing, but he had rehearsed this day many times in his mind. He had memorized all of his instructions.

He did not know whom he was meeting. He had a cell phone number and a password. *Helilmoya* was the word. It means "Sweeten the water." The countersign was to be *Samak Allah alim*. "Fish God knows best."

The C train came to a stop in front of him. Its doors opened in welcome.

Bin-Hezam looped his arm around the pole in the crowded, lurching subway car as it hurtled north through the tunnel beneath Eighth Avenue. It was rush hour at the end of the week. Each person had a square foot in which to stand or sit, the car packed so tightly that there were no distinct demarcations between one body and another.

Bin-Hezam forced himself to adjust to the sensations of being touched by sweaty strangers, suspending his usual vigilance

about his own flesh, fighting off claustro-
phobia. He closed his eyes and envisioned
a calming night sky beneath a crescent
moon.

He was grateful when the train reached
116th Street and he emerged from below
into the neighborhood, lately known as Le
Petit Senegal. The street, which he had
never before visited, was familiar to him
through his intense study of Google's
amazing Street View feature. He had also
used an Internet site to search for nearby
public telephones, which were a rapidly
vanishing breed.

The first one he encountered was broken, the receiver cracked in half, exposing
wires. He crossed the street to a narrow
market with an interior pay phone installed
above a small ATM machine whose LCD
screen flashed American dollar signs.

He fed the machine quarters and dialed
the number. A man's voice answered
gruffly, "Hello?"

"*Helilmoya,*" Bin-Hezam pronounced
each syllable carefully, thinking it unlikely
that whoever was on the other end of the
call was a native speaker of Arabic.

"*Samak Allah alim.*" He was mistaken. The accent rang true.

Bin-Hezam said, "My instructions, please."

The man responded with another phone number. A local number with the same exchange. Bin-Hezam used his trick of visualizing a number to memorize it, something he had been pridefully good at since childhood.

"Repeat," said the man's voice.

Bin-Hezam recited it back to him. Then the line went dead.

Bin-Hezam had not expected such rudeness, but it did not unnerve him. Perhaps it indicated caution, and caution was good. These were people of a different world, he remembered. Mercenaries at best. If they behaved professionally, he would be pleased.

Bin-Hezam dropped in more quarters and dialed the next number. He gave his code word, and was asked to repeat it before receiving confirmation. This one's accent was much less assured.

"You will walk one block east to Seventh Avenue. You will stand at the curb in front of a barbershop named Meme Amour. You will stand facing away from the shop, toward the street."

Again, a hang-up. Good. Bin-Hezam stepped outside the shop and began walking east right away. He caught sight of himself in a store window and was momentarily shocked at his appearance, forgetting he was wearing a false mustache.

More important, no one moved with him.

The barbershop was small, with photographs of smiling men of varying ethnicities pasted in the window. Bin-Hezam stole a glance inside the shop. No lights. It appeared closed.

He did as he was instructed, standing near the curb, facing the street. He felt visible and vulnerable instantly, and so pulled out his phone and thumbed through different applications, pretending to be engaged.

An oncoming automobile slowed, and in his anxiety Bin-Hezam almost stepped forward to meet it. The vehicle, driven by a woman, sped up again and continued on. It was not his contact. Bin-Hezam felt certain he was being watched by his contact, examined, judged.

Ten minutes passed like thirty. Was this mere caution, or was it some sort of test? If the latter, he was deeply offended. Would his contact stand for a test from him?

Still, he remained. Courtesy was unnecessary in this instance, as was impatience. He realized he had to allow himself to be at another's mercy. He trusted in God.

A man's voice spoke behind him.

"Assalamu alaikum."

Bin-Hezam turned to find a somber-looking black man whose considerable bulk was little obscured inside an all-black nylon Adidas sweat suit.

"Walaikum assalam," Bin-Hezam replied.

The man turned without another word, and Bin-Hezam followed. Instead of entering the barbershop, he led Bin-Hezam into a doorway just to its right.

They entered a narrow, unbroken corridor, like a tunnel into the building, lit only by light from the opaque stained-glass windows in the doors at either end. Bin-Hezam followed the waddling man through darkness, out to a small, fenced yard cluttered with used and discarded appliances. Microwaves, television sets, toaster ovens, bicycle frames, boxy computer monitors. They walked ten yards on a curving path delineated by this junk to the back of a low garage.

The fat man unlocked the dead bolt with a key from his pocket and stood aside, admitting Bin-Hezam.

Inside the garage, the chaos of the junkyard gave way to a meticulously ordered electronics and machinist toolroom. Workbenches were set on opposing sides, running most of the length of the structure. A variety of tools hung from Peg-Boards and from the rafters.

Here were the junk man's works in progress. A small engine in pieces. A television set with a huge screen. Two laptop computers, connected side by side.

Bin-Hezam unwound his thin scarf and tucked it into his jacket pocket, looking around. He feigned curiosity, but in reality was establishing an escape route in case he needed it. The interior smelled of grease and spiced tomato. The garage was windowless and cool.

"A good business," the man finally said, turning to face Bin-Hezam, aware of his scrutiny. "At home, in Dakar, we waste nothing. Here, they waste everything. They leave it out like gifts in the street. A people who do not understand the devices they use do not deserve them." The fat Senegalese crumpled up a food wrapper and dropped it into a pail beneath the counter. "Now, to our business."

He pulled latex gloves from a cardboard tissue-style box. He offered a pair to Bin-Hezam, which he accepted.

The man crossed to the other counter. He moved a pile of gray rags from the shelf beneath it and pulled out a lockbox. He opened it with a key from his ring. He removed a top tray of tools from the inside, withdrawing a cloth bag.

He slid out a nickel-plated pistol with a black rubber grip—holding it openhandedly, offering it to Bin-Hezam for inspection.

"Thirty-eight special. A revolver. It will never jam." The man flicked the release and flopped open the cylinder, showing Bin-Hezam that the weapon was not loaded. "This is what I was told to have ready for you."

Bin-Hezam took the weapon into his hand. A good weight, polished but not brand new.

"Ammunition?" said Bin-Hezam.

The man reached into the toolbox again and pulled out a paper bag containing brass cartridges.

"They told me six," he said. "There are twelve here. I assume you want more, just in case."

Bin-Hezam said, "I will take exactly six."

The man gave him another moment to reconsider, then relented. "Six it is," he said.

The man counted out six bullets with his gloved hands, standing them on the countertop. Bin-Hezam laid the .38 next to them.

"Holster," said the Senegalese. This he pulled down from a shelf, a sling made of Cordura and Velcro. "Fits over your shoulders," he said, miming putting it on—the holster straps were much too small for his bulk. "The butt of the gun is down for clean pull."

Bin-Hezam nodded. He watched the fat man lay the holster down on the counter. He did not need to touch it or try it on.

"Eight thousand," the fat man said.

Bin-Hezam turned his head slightly.

"Eight? I have three. I was told the gun would cost three thousand."

"That was the floor price. The request was for an untraceable late-model thirty-eight caliber with a rubber grip. No serial numbers, not even any which could be raised by chemicals. That meant procuring the weapon directly from the manufacturer. Test-firing it and field-testing it to ensure its accuracy, reliability, and durability. For a tool of such precise specifications, I ask a minimum eight thousand. It is a fair price."

Bin-Hezam neither smiled nor frowned. "You must have known I would not have that much."

"How would I know that, brother?"

Bin-Hezam was not one to show emotion. Part of his preparation for this journey was an exercise in self-control. To do what he was going to do required the highest level of discipline. He was a pillar of restraint.

"I do not have that much money," Bin-Hezam said. "You have wasted my time."

The Senegalese shrugged. "I will remain here all evening. Surely you can get five thousand more."

"I can," said Bin-Hezam. "With five thousand questions and five thousand complaints."

The fat man shrugged again. "I am the best. I will be paid accordingly."

Bin-Hezam pulled off his latex gloves, dropping them into his jacket pocket. He turned back to the door. "Am I to find my own way out?"

The fat man sighed and waddled past him, opening the door to the junkyard. Bin-Hezam passed him and slowed, waiting for the fat man to lock the door with his key. Bin-Hezam then led the way, following the path back to the building. He opened the door himself, entered the hallway, and stopped there, again waiting for the fat man. Bin-Hezam listened for the solid click of the heavy door behind him, sealing them inside the tunnel-like hallway.

"I trust you are not offended—" the fat man began to say.

Bin-Hezam whirled around with his arm bent and crushed the Senegalese's nose and upper mouth with his elbow.

Bin-Hezam followed that with a chop to his throat, the fat man's sweaty skin nearly enveloping his hand. The Senegalese's head struck the side wall, and his great body slid down backward.

He opened his mouth to scream, but the only sound he could get out of his busted palate was "Mmmuuunnhh!"

Bin-Hezam brought the sole of his shoe and the full weight of his body down against the fat man's prodigious neck. Again and again, with little thrusting hops, until he felt the crack of the fat man's neck giving way. Froth bubbled up from his destroyed mouth, a pink mix of saliva and blood. His eyes were open and bulging, becoming fixed.

Bin-Hezam knelt at the dead man's side for a long moment. Uncertain of his surroundings, he listened intently for any sound that might mean discovery.

The building was silent above him. He looked down at the dead man, lit gently through the stained-glass window in the door.

The act of reaching into the fat man's sweaty pants pocket was more unpleasant to Bin-Hezam than the commission of murder. Bin-Hezam discovered and pulled out the ring of keys, warm in his hand. He then pulled hard on the fat man's arm, struggling to roll him over facedown in the hallway. The man's bulk was prohibitive.

Bin-Hezam stood, finding his own shirt drenched in perspiration. He had never killed a man before. He had been well trained in techniques handed down for centuries but had never thought it possible of himself. But he was a new man now. A man on a mission. Giving himself over to a cause, and to God, had freed his soul.

He exited the building, touching the doorknob with his hand inside his jacket sleeve, back in the direction of the shop. He listened outside, then returned swiftly along the path formed by the yard of junk. The key worked in the lock after some wiggling and pulling. Again, he kept his fingerprints from the metal knob.

Inside the garage shop, Bin-Hezam removed his jacket and pulled on the shoulder holster. He inserted the handgun and closed the small retaining Velcro belt. He slipped his jacket back on and felt that the weapon was adequately concealed.

The six cartridges went into his jacket pocket like so many pieces of gold. He checked the fall of his jacket one more time, the handgun tucked securely under his arm. He muttered a prayer of gratitude, then left the garage again, locking the door.

He carried the keys with him, reentering the building, looking once more at the fat man's corpse. Moving it would be difficult and hiding it perhaps impossible. He decided it did not matter, and continued swiftly yet steadily down the hallway to the front door.

He turned the knob with his hand inside his sleeve, then exited onto the sidewalk. He heard a siren and started walking, seeing blue lights approaching along the street.

The siren's wail peaked . . . and then the car was past him, weaving in and out of traffic as it moved uptown.

Bin-Hezam could not take the subway back. Not with an unlicensed firearm in his possession. He dropped the key chain and his used gloves into the first trash receptacle he saw. Bin-Hezam walked two blocks to the nearest hotel, also memorized from Google Maps. There he hired a taxi to return him—though not directly—to the Hotel Indigo.

After returning to the Hyatt through the rear entrance—reserved for deliveries or VIPs, depending on the circumstance—Gersten escorted The Six up to their floor. The exhilaration they had experienced before the interview had bottomed out on the ride back like a sugar crash, and The Six returned the few blocks from Times Square in near silence.

Upstairs, Frank and Sparks lingered in the hospitality suite, unwinding, not talking. The television was tuned to a baseball game, but Patton, the other Intel cop who had remained behind, was the only one really watching it.

Maggie Sullivan returned a minute or two later with two nips of Bacardi from her room's minibar. She mixed them into twin glasses of Diet Coke and offered one to Sparks, who accepted it and drank wordlessly. Maggie took a seat by the window and rested her chin in her hand, looking out at the night.

Jenssen, yawning Aldrich, and Nouvian all mumbled their good-nights and quietly retired to their rooms.

This was Gersten's cue to hand them off to DeRosier and Patton. Gersten's own room was one of the last ones at the far end of the twenty-sixth-floor hallway. She heard cello music from Nouvian's room as she passed, and could easily picture him sitting on the bed, astride his instrument, practicing in his underwear. She imagined the rigors of practice were a balm to him, a man whose life was predicated upon routine. She bet he practiced every night before bed. Gersten had glimpsed his visiting wife earlier, a mouse of a woman who could not have looked any more shaken if her husband had died.

Gersten carded in, unclipped her shield and her weapon, and set everything on the nearest countertop, then went back to double-lock the hotel door.

She kept the lights low, unpacking her toiletries by the bathroom sink, then running water to fill the tub. She checked her phone for messages and then, finding none worth listening or responding to at that moment, shed her clothes. She tossed them onto the made bed, where they lay almost in the form of a fractured person. She pulled a plush white Hyatt robe down from the closet and put it on, and sighed. Nothing like soft, laundered cotton.

She switched on the bathroom fan for white noise, wanting to block out everything for a while. Steam from the hot water drifted up to the dimmed ceiling lights like morning mist. She turned off the faucet when the tub was nearly full, but instead of submersing herself immediately she remained seated on the edge. She ran her hand through the surface, tracing a series of lazy figure eights. The humidity moistened her hands and face. She had been looking forward to this bath for so long, but now . . . now that it was here, it didn't feel right. She made waves in the tub with her hand, hoping this was just a momentary hesitancy, trying to convince herself just to get in . . .

. . . but it was no good. She couldn't do it. Instead, she stood and went back into the hotel room, wandering to the windows. The twenty-sixth floor was not quite high enough for a commanding view of the city, but she could eyeball the building across the street, the people moving in its windows, and all the cars and pedestrians below.

They were the ones keeping her from her relaxing bath, she realized. The people on the street, out and about on a hot Friday night in July. The people Gersten wanted to be.

She went back to her phone, checking again for messages. So difficult to unplug. She hoped for something from Fisk, something to engage her restless mind. She really wanted to call him, but she would only be a bother at this point. She opened her laptop on the workstation desk, but there wasn't anything productive she could do.

Sometimes she hated this job she loved.

She looked at her clothes, the empty

person they described, lying atop her bed. She thought about her future with Intel, her future with Fisk. Where was she going?

She was essentially happy, if not totally fulfilled. Just like all those people out on the streets tonight, she realized with a smile. Things felt right, both personally and professionally. Was that enough?

She realized that these are the thoughts that occur to people stuck alone in hotel rooms on weekend nights.

She found that she was twisting her robe belt into knots, and made herself stop. She returned to the window, like a prisoner hoping for inspiration. After this weekend, she promised herself, she would make some decisions. She would map out a plan. She would define her aspirations and act accordingly.

But right now she was too concerned with the immediate future of those down on the street below to do much of anything.

Out there, somewhere, was the man they were searching for.

PART 6

INTERCEPTS

Saturday, July 3

Bin-Hezam showered, shaved, and was dressed in his dishdasha by 6:00 A.M.

He had consulted the prayer time website for New York City before departing Riyadh. Fajr was at 6:03. He unrolled his rug and reveled in the holy connection of Salah, which he shared at that very moment with a billion and a half of the faithful around the world.

Yet, among those billion and a half, he felt the special light of God shining down upon him alone.

When he was finished, Bin-Hezam rolled up his rug and dressed for the day.

Stonewashed blue jeans, a short-sleeved black cotton pullover, a loose-fitting dark blue nylon Windbreaker, and black Adidas sneakers. He had stowed the pistol, ammunition, and shoulder holster in the closet safe in his hotel room. The combination was set to the month and year of the birthday of Mohammed: 04570.

Bin-Hezam still had plenty of time to fulfill his duties before returning to his room by Dhuhr at 12:35. Too much time, almost. He wanted to act, not to think. Time had slowed down on him. Things would seem different near the end, of this he had been warned. And so he tried to submit to the strange experience, rather than resist it. But it was more important to him than ever that he not miss prayer and the moment of communion that gave him strength.

When he was ready, he left his room, rode the elevator down to the lobby alone, and exited the hotel, turning right on Twenty-eighth Street. The heat was there early, but not the humidity—not yet.

On that early weekend day, the flower shops were just opening, the proprietors carrying buckets of ornamentals to the sidewalk in order to exhibit their wares.

The narrow crosstown street was a canyon of bright colors and fragrant aromas. His senses were wide open, almost as though filters that had been present during daily life were now removed. He was more alive than ever. He moved and the world seemed to move with him.

Bin-Hezam stepped inside a coffee shop. He did not feel a need for food, but he knew he must eat. He pointed out a single pastry in the display under the front counter, and watched to be certain that the clerk grasped it with a wax napkin. He purchased a hot tea as well and paid cash. Bin-Hezam was aware of two surveillance cameras, one aimed at the clerk and the cash register for the purpose of theft reduction, the other on the high wall behind the counter, aimed at the customer.

With practiced self-consciousness, Bin-Hezam was careful not to look straight at the camera. He would let it find him. He was relieved to not be wearing any disguise today.

He found an open table near the stand containing packets of sugar and stirrers, and sat. He pushed the flaky croissant into his mouth, no butter, no jam. He did not look out the window at the passersby, because he did not want to attract the attention of those who might look in. Nor did he make eye contact with those sitting around him. Bin-Hezam imagined himself to be the focal point of the room; the rest were minor figures, like anonymous extras in a film. He was performing, in a way.

Only one thing pierced the haze of his solipsism. It was a television screen mounted at a downward angle from the ceiling. The sound was low, and only occasionally audible.

Following another weather update addressing the weekend heat wave, they showed more footage of the airplane Bin-Hezam had flown aboard. Then video of the five passengers and the flight attendant who stopped the hijacking, standing before cameras like patients undergoing a painless yet intimate radiological medical procedure. They showed the jet again, this time on the ground at Newark. They showed passengers disembarking.

Bin-Hezam watched in apprehension, half expecting to see his own passport photograph on the screen . . . but then the report ended and they did not show him.

He deduced from the graphics that what he was watching was in fact a teaser for a forthcoming in-studio appearance by the group of heroes the media were calling The Six.

Bin-Hezam showed no outward expression. But inwardly he was smiling at the news coverage. He could not understand the entire scenario, but he had intuited enough to know that, as of right now, everything was proceeding exactly as it should.

The tea was oversteeped, foul. He drank only as much as he could tolerate, then rose and disposed of the cup and his wax wrapper. He exited the shop, walking a wide loop of city blocks before cutting back across Eighth Avenue to Ninth, setting his mind to the familiar Street View from Google Maps. This part was like walking through the landscape of a first-person video game in which he was the player.

Bin-Hezam had been taught that each moment was the sum of one's life. That was never more true than each step he took this day.

From viewing its website, Bin-Hezam

knew that the photography and video equipment store was owned and staffed by Jews. Still, upon entering he was shocked by how many there were. Dozens of them, it seemed to him. Patrolling the aisles, backing the glass counters, sitting on high stools at the payment windows. A nest of Hebrews.

Bin-Hezam worked hard to contain his revulsion. A wave of deep tribal mistrust washed over him. These people were The Others. They were less than human. Only by believing that his own God could conquer theirs, and in doing so unite all under Islam, was he able to recover his bearings and continue forth into this foul gauntlet.

He walked carefully around the vast store, locating the photo bags and luggage over to his right. He found just what he wanted, two black messenger bags that were common enough in New York to be invisible.

The desk clerk accepted the bags without a word. The Jew typed the bar code into his register rather than scanning it. The price amount came up on the display and he pointed at it with his finger, too rude to speak.

Bin-Hezam wanted to believe that the

slight was an ethnic one, but he was nearly certain that the clerk had not even raised his eyes. Bin-Hezam pushed the cash to him and the man made change and bagged the items. He slid the bag back across the counter and immediately rose from his stool to attend to some other matter.

Bin-Hezam was heartily disappointed. He wanted to see his own deep hatred reflected back at him. He wanted to find some fault with the man. He wanted to feel the Jew's suspicion. He wanted satisfaction.

He wanted anything other than to be ignored. He wanted the man to look into the eyes of one who was blessed against him.

Back out on the sidewalk, he felt like a spider who had just emerged unrecognized from a nest of flies. He imparted their nonchalance to cultural cowardice and a smug self-satisfaction peculiar to their race. All of which would work to Bin-Hezam's benefit this weekend.

His next stop was around the corner on Thirtieth Street. A hobby shop. No Jews here. A big man wearing a gray work shirt with a railroad engineer's cap atop his unruly white hair sat behind a cash register.

From a raised promontory behind a glass display counter, he presided alone over a roomful of model trains, remote-control airplanes and helicopters, and kits for building aircraft, boats, and cars. A small fan with rippling blue ribbons blew warm air on him from behind.

Suspended from the pipes and ducting under the high ceiling of the narrow store were completed scale models of jets, helicopters, war planes, and a new item, military drones. On the back wall, Bin-Hezam spotted a selection of kits and supplies for model rocketeering. The man at the counter saw Bin-Hezam's eyes fix on this section.

"Rockets?" he said, raising his eyebrows as though he were about to admit Bin-Hezam into a secret club.

"Yes. I want to buy one for my son. He will be nine years old next week. His life revolves around dinosaurs and rocket ships."

"How big?"

"My son?"

"The rocket."

"How big do they make them?"

The man smiled. "They make them pretty big."

Bin-Hezam hid his contempt for this un-washed man and his unclean odor. "How big would you consider a D engine?"

"Big enough. Have a look for yourself," the man said, pleased by Bin-Hezam's interest, yet still reluctant to move from his perch. "We got just about everything. Give me a shout if you need help."

Bin-Hezam made his way past the glues and the rubber cement tubes to the back. The wall rack was immense, and yet he had little trouble finding what he wanted.

An Estes electron beam rocket engine igniter. A launch controller.

On a rack to one side, he found cartons of potassium nitrate fuel pellets. To stay within the legend, he selected an expensive, multipart $350 kit. It included both components, plus a launch stand and the rocket itself, a white cardboard tube a yard long with triangular tail fins and a red plastic nose cone.

The man on the stool brightened when Bin-Hezam returned. A quick sale with almost no effort. "That'll be three hundred and fifty. Plus the government tax."

Bin-Hezam counted out four one-hundred-dollar bills and laid them on the glass countertop. Wind from the fan behind the man on the stool rippled the bills.

"You a Saudi?" asked the proprietor, with an interested smile.

"You can tell this how?" asked Bin-Hezam, assuming that the man was going by his large-denomination bills.

"I worked for Chevron for more than twenty years. Spent a lot of time over there. Took me a while getting used to things, because, man, you all looked the same to me for years. That oil money, it can't be beat. People say they were lucky to be born here in America! I usually just chuckle at that. Luck is one thing. Want to win the lottery? Be born in Saudi Arabia, am I right?"

The man's observation pleased him very much, and he chortled heartily.

"Very nice," Bin-Hezam said, awaiting his change.

The proprietor pulled out a tall bag. "You want to make sure you're the one supervising this thing now. Nine is a little young to be playing with this. Main thing is, you want to come away with all ten fingers. You know how the safety works?"

Bin-Hezam allowed the man in the railroad cap to explain the use of the safety key, a small metal rod inserted into the controller to complete the circuit that provided the current that heated up the igniter and launched the engine. He also showed him the fail-safe, wherein the key had to be inserted and held down.

"Thank you," said Bin-Hezam.

"Anytime, come again," said the man. "And stay cool out there."

He would remember Bin-Hezam, of that there was little doubt.

One final stop that morning. At a medical supply store on West Twenty-fifth Street—not a Duane Reade, but an actual supply store for nurses and home health care workers—he purchased white gauze impregnated with fast-drying calcined gypsum, also known as plaster of paris. He also picked up a box of rolled cotton batting and a sheet of light fiberglass roving rolled into a tube about a foot long. His total purchase came to thirty-eight dollars.

Bin-Hezam returned to his hotel room. It had already been cleaned by the maid; everything appeared to be in order.

He hung the do not disturb sign on the

doorknob and quickly shed his light jacket and sneakers, sitting with the television tuned loudly to some nonsense hotel entertainment channel. His purchases were laid out atop the bed, the loaded pistol removed from the safe and set upon the pillow.

Holy articles. Sacred totems. He had plucked these commonly available items from obscurity, just as God had selected him. Soon he would make them sacred by association.

His greatest duty was yet to come.

He muted the television and performed Dhuhr right on time. Full of gratitude for the flow of this day, he beseeched God's blessing for the rest of it. So far, everything had gone perfectly, as Bin-Hezam traveled in God's own footsteps. With the gift of grace, it would continue, and soon their paths truly would be one.

By midmorning on Saturday, July 3, Fisk was no closer to finding the Saudi from Flight 903 than he had been the day before. Baada Bin-Hezam had vanished into—or from—New York.

At seven o'clock that morning, Fisk scrambled an interdiction team to Flatbush Avenue in Brooklyn. An Arab man matching Bin-Hezam's physical description had been spotted parked in a loading zone and entering a building carrying a satchel. Fisk captained the sweep from Intel headquarters, listening as crash units sealed off the block. The man was taken down without incident upon exiting the building. He claimed to be a jeweler checking on his aging mother before catching an early bus to Atlantic City to play in a five-thousand-dollar minimum buy-in poker tournament.

Verifying his story took nearly two hours. During that time, the man's distraught mother phoned a family friend whose daughter was a lawyer with the Brooklyn office of the ACLU. So piled on top of Fisk's disappointment in the case of mistaken identity, he then had to spend precious minutes on the phone with the ACLU lawyer. He tried sweet talk first, then a straight-up apology, but she would have none of it. An admittedly clumsy appeal to her patriotism was similarly rebuffed. Only dropping the name of her boss, with whom Fisk had dealt some months before in an ongoing surveillance case, prevented her from taking her client's case straight to the media.

At least—he hoped it had. Fisk's only real success so far, in the midst of one of the largest manhunts in the history of the city, was that it was still operating under the media's, and therefore the public's, radar.

He was getting nothing from his people

on the street. Ten o'clock came and went, and the swarm of hourly contact reports from his rakers in the Muslim neighborhoods all turned up negative. Nothing. Not for the first time did Fisk wonder if he had launched a career-killing goose chase.

Maybe the hijacker Abdulraheem really had been just another jihadist looking for a moment of glory in a world that memorialized evil more often than good. Maybe this Saudi Bin-Hezam really was an art dealer.

Of course they had looked into his past. Early hours still, but they found deals he had brokered. Bin-Hezam's name was on a number of transactions, none of them major, none in six or even high five figures. His past travel synced up with the sales and festivals. The few clients he maintained checked out as legitimate sculptors and painters, along with a handful of galleries.

So on paper, he was legit. The question was, was this just a shadow career, meant to pacify exactly such scrutiny into his background? Or was Bin-Hezam simply another of life's minor players, like the vast majority of us, with his own shortcomings, hang-ups, and foibles?

This was a big part of Fisk's job. Being a viewfinder, locating an individual within the vast sea of humanity and bringing him into focus as quickly as possible in an attempt to determine whether he truly was one of the peaceable ones.

On the plus side, he did not believe that, in the real world, the shared kinship between Abdulraheem, Bin-Hezam, and bin Laden could be sheer coincidence. Such a random occurrence was possible but—and here Fisk snapped the ring of circular logic that was squeezing his mind like a tourniquet—realistically improbable.

If thirteen years as a criminal investigator had taught him anything, it was that coincidence was the stuff of Russian novels and television sitcoms. When people converged without any apparent reason, it was only because the objective viewer—Fisk—could not yet determine the reason.

Fisk returned to mouse-clicking the stream of images dispatched to him from the city police cameras. All night, and now into the day, he had been looking at computer-screen pictures of men who looked vaguely like Bin-Hezam. Hell, he's probably in disguise, thought Fisk. That's what I would do.

The cameras could compensate for certain obvious disguises: wigs, mustaches, sunglasses. But he knew that finding the Saudi solely via camera technology was the longest of his long shots.

A few minutes later, Fisk's phone finally rang. One of Fisk's best rakers had information on a taxi driver who claimed to have picked up a man meeting Bin-Hezam's description, but wearing a trim mustache and eyeglasses. It wasn't much, but at this point a tip was a tip.

The raker, a dispatcher for a Brooklyn cab company, said that his driver was a Kuwaiti Sikh. "He picked up a fare uptown. I can get you the name of the hotel. The fare was not a guest, he walked up off the street. How the driver remembers him. He had a mustache and glasses, but he also wore a suit jacket. Something's not right."

"Go ahead," said Fisk.

"Usually he would have refused the man, because you know you want the hotel fares, not the ten-block errand trips. But this was a fellow Arab. He says that he

remembers the man seeming visibly relieved once he closed the door, though he
wasn't out of breath or anything like that.
He gave him an address. The driver doesn't
remember where. They never got there
anyway. Somewhere in the East Sixties at
a red light the fare pushed cash through
the window and got out. Driver doesn't remember the intersection because another
fare got right in."

Most likely the Saudi walked another
block or two and hailed another cab. "I'm
sending over somebody with pictures for
your driver to look at. Meanwhile, get me
the name of that hotel."

Fisk's adrenaline was flowing. This felt
like something. The intercept.

The Capricorn Hotel lobby had Oriental
rugs hanging on the walls. There was no
restaurant adjacent, only a small sports
bar that was, at that hour, still serving a
limited breakfast.

Fisk showed his shield and explained
why they were there. His explanation approached the truth. His people printed out
the register and quickly entered all the
names into the Intel database. Fisk posted

two men in the lobby, just to be careful. None of the registered guests matched Bin-Hezam's description, and none of the staff reacted strongly positively either to Bin-Hezam's passport photograph scan or to another image augmented with a digitally added mustache and eyeglasses.

The cabdriver, on the other hand, made a positive identification. Fisk liked cabbies as witnesses; all cops did. Juries too.

Fisk walked outside to the cabstand, empty at that time of the morning. He watched the cars and people going past, squinting into the rising sun, feeling its heat.

Baada Bin-Hezam had stood there some twelve to fifteen hours before.

The question now was: where had he been coming from?

Gersten was up early Saturday morning, her trusted phone alarm summoning her from sleep. She checked for overnight messages from Fisk but there were none.

He was plenty busy, she told herself. He had real work to do.

Gersten was looking forward to another day as a camp counselor.

She pulled on running pants, New Balance sneakers, and a nylon Windbreaker, and dug her ear buds out of her travel bag. She stowed her sidearm in the hotel room safe, then rode the elevator down to the street. Even that early in the morning, the sticky July heat was oppressive. Any other day she might have reconsidered, or else hopped in a cab to her gym. But she needed the streets, the distance, the workout.

NPR's *Weekend Edition* carried her to Park Avenue and straight up to Sixty-first, where she turned left and then north again on Fifth Avenue, running uptown along the wide sidewalk outside some of the city's best residences, opposite Central Park.

At Seventy-ninth, she turned left into the park itself, cutting back south along East Drive. She ran in the shade when she could. She changed radio stations, riding her presets until she hit disco music. One of her presets was having a Summer of '76 flashback weekend, and it was perfect, just what she needed. The groove carried her south through the park.

A typical Saturday morning: joggers, walkers, nannies, bikers. The sky was clear blue, the rising sun ready to turn brutal in just a few hours. The kind of day air-conditioning was invented for.

She emerged from the park at Fifty-ninth Street, continuing south, stopping for a cold protein shake outside Grand Central before entering the chrome-and-glass lobby of the

Grand Hyatt and riding up to the twenty-sixth floor. Still flushed from her run, yet chilled by the artificially cool air, she nodded to the two new watch cops guarding the hallway and proceeded past the open suite toward her room at the end of the hall.

A door farther down opened as she was passing by, and Gersten saw Maggie Sullivan slipping out into the hallway, still wearing her clothes from the previous night's *Nightline* interview. Her hair was mussed, and her shoes were in her hand.

"Um . . . morning?" said Maggie, giving her a funny look, a cross between embarrassed and giddy.

Gersten realized that the Scandinavian Air flight attendant wasn't leaving her own room. Gersten glanced inside as she passed, and caught just a glimpse of Magnus Jenssen standing near the table at the foot of his bed, shirtless and in boxer shorts, the blue cast on his left wrist. He looked up from checking his wristwatch, his eyes meeting Gersten's in the instant she was passing.

His look was cool and unfazed, showing neither the guilt nor the apparent pleasure Maggie had shown.

Then the door clicked shut.

Gersten stopped and turned back, watching Maggie complete her walk of shame, fumbling her room card into the slot of her door, nudging it open with her hip and slipping inside. Gersten smiled, properly scandalized. What happened to Joanne Sparks? she wondered. The IKEA store manager had been pursuing Jenssen pretty hard last night, but had apparently lost the sweepstakes to the small-town flight attendant.

Gersten continued to her own room, entering, wishing she had someone with whom she could share this fun bit of gossip. She checked her phone first thing, but still had no messages beyond the usual work e-mails she would rather handle on her laptop.

Good for tousle-haired Maggie, thought Gersten, pausing to look at herself as she undressed, the water running for her shower. Not only had she bagged a hot, well-built Swede, but she had also bedded the man who saved her life. Not bad, going from reading romance novels to actually living one.

The shower felt great, and Gersten allowed her mind to wander, as well as her hand, bringing herself to orgasm with a minor fantasy involving shirtless Jenssen and a locked hotel room with a Jacuzzi tub and good champagne. Then out of the shower and into her robe, knocking down overnight Intel reports on her laptop.

Nothing new on the hunt for Bin-Hezam. If not for Fisk, she would be totally out of the loop, marooned here in this midtown hotel.

She dressed and headed down the hall to breakfast, and to relieve Patton. A buffet was set up along one wall of one of the adjoining rooms, and the first person Gersten saw was Maggie. She too had showered and changed, and despite the bags beneath her eyes she looked refreshed, energized. They were alone.

"Good morning," said Gersten, with a smile.

"Oh my god," said Maggie, shaking her head, her smile complicit.

"Sleep well?" asked Gersten.

"Beautifully," said Maggie, dumping eggs and toast onto her plate. "For about two hours."

"What happened?" Gersten wanted to know.

"Too much rum," said Maggie. "Too much excitement, too many emotions."

"Don't take this the wrong way," said Gersten, looking around quickly, "but I thought the IKEA manager . . ."

"So did I," said Maggie. "This . . . this really isn't my style, normally, you know? I think she nodded off maybe. I don't know. He made the first move, and I was like, lead the way." She heard herself say that and laughed. "Oh my god."

"I'm sure you just felt sorry for him. The cast and all."

Maggie smiled. "I was not myself last night," she said. "But the person I was is very, very happy this morning. Should I leave it at that?"

"No," said Gersten. "You should tell me every single detail."

Maggie went away laughing, eating her much-needed breakfast.

Patton came over, anxious to leave. "What was that about?"

"Girl talk, you wouldn't be interested."

"Ask me how I slept," he said.

"Like a baby, I'm sure."

"Exactly. Not at all."

"Things get a little crazy in here last night?"

"A little bit. Lots of giggling in that room. Then snoring. I had the Yankees on, a late West Coast game."

"They win?"

"A-Rod bounced to third with two men on. They lost, four to three."

Gersten looked at Maggie devouring her breakfast. "Well, we can't win 'em all."

"Yes we can," said Patton. "We're the Yankees." He grabbed a muffin off the table. "Hey, one person you need to meet before I get outta here." He led her over to a man wearing a suit jacket that was just slightly too large. He looked like someone who spent a fair amount of each day working out in a gym, yet his chest was bulked out a little more than was natural. Gersten made him as Secret Service before she even shook his hand.

"Tim Harrelson," he said.

Gersten introduced herself. "I take it things are about to get a little more interesting around here," she said.

"It seems so," he said, with a confident smile.

Patton rubbed his hands together and

made for the door. "Have fun, kids. See you later."

Gersten excused herself, leaving Harrelson to return to the head of the buffet table. She smeared cream cheese over half a sesame bagel and carried it into the other room. CNN was running clips from The Six's *Nightline* appearance, but the sound was low. Nouvian stood by the window, his hands in the pockets of his wool pants. Aldrich was working on a clump of bacon, looking grumpy as usual. Frank was rolling through messages on his phone, perhaps already putting out feelers and fielding interest for a book or life-rights deal.

Joanne Sparks, looking sharp in flared pants and a tight blouse, sat on the cushioned arm of Jenssen's chair, nibbling an English muffin. Jenssen looked up as Gersten entered, not smiling or acknowledging her, just looking.

Gersten couldn't look at Sparks. Apparently, she had no knowledge of Jenssen's visitor the previous night. Maggie sat near the window, her legs crossed, sipping orange juice. Things were about to get interesting indeed.

The publicist from Mayor Bloomberg's

office looked like she was in the corner talking to herself, but she was actually finishing up a phone conversation via her Bluetooth ear clip.

"Okay," announced the publicist, stepping forward. "I have your schedule for today, and it's going to be a fun one, something you're all going to remember for the rest of your lives."

Skepticism, rather than enthusiasm, was their reaction. Aldrich and Nouvian eyed Harrelson, who had stepped into the adjoining doorway, warily.

"We are leaving here within the half hour and going a few blocks over to the *Today* show studio for a live interview with Matt Lauer, who is coming in on the weekend especially for you folks, which I'm told he never does. Because you're big stars, right? You deserve the best."

Sparks straightened her back, excited, but most of the rest were waiting to hear what else.

"I want you to know we've turned down scores of offers, some wacky, some interesting. But we don't want to overload or overtax you. So after the *Today* show, you will be heading back here to one of the event rooms, which we will have set up for a pool interview with print journalists. That means the *New York Times,* the *Wall Street Journal,* et cetera, will send one reporter each to interview you all at the same time, rather than parceling out your story over ten, twelve, even twenty little interviews. Those things turn your minds into mush, trust me."

Aldrich said, "I'll talk to the *Wall Street Journal,* but not the *New York Times.*"

The publicist kept smiling while she nodded. "And of course you can answer or not answer whichever questions you like. But your answers will be available to any and all of the participating news outlets."

Aldrich scowled, but seemed satisfied to have had his say.

"And now on to the big event of the day," said the publicist. "No matter where your political sensibilities lie, I think you'll all be both proud and honored to be guests of the president of the United States this afternoon." She kept talking before anyone— Aldrich—could interrupt. "He asks that you join him and Mrs. Obama aboard the aircraft carrier *Intrepid,* which is permanently moored on the Hudson River on the West

Side. President Obama will be delivering remarks honoring the men and women of the armed forces on this July Fourth weekend. You know, of course, he is in town for the One World Trade Center dedication tomorrow morning, July Fourth."

She then introduced Agent Harrelson, who strode to her side with the balance and ease of a man accustomed to handling groups of strangers. "First of all, let me just say that my hat goes off to all of you," he began. "As a man whose profession it is to protect people for a living, I know that what you did on that plane took an immense amount of courage. So first let me add my voice to the rest of the country's in thanking you personally for your bravery, for your selflessness, and for being people of action. You have my respect."

The Six were blown away by the depth of Agent Harrelson's sincerity, the honor his words did them. Gersten thought she detected a tiny bit of flattery in his presentation, which was perhaps advantageous in getting what he needed.

To that end, he held up six sheets of paper. "Each of you must complete a background form, standard procedure for anyone who is going to be in immediate proximity to the president. Yes, I know you have been answering questions and perhaps filling out similar forms since this all went down, and yes, I still have to ask you to do it one more time each. One page only, standard form. All we need to know are your full legal name, date and place of birth, names of your parents and children, occupation, addresses going back twelve years, and the names of three people to whom you are not related and who have known you for at least ten years."

Agent Harrelson distributed the pages as he spoke. Each person took a form without comment. Aldrich, especially, had apparently been sufficiently pacified by Agent Harrelson's praise, and offered no objections to an audience with the Democratic commander in chief.

"Because of the short window of time, I'm going to need you to complete these this moment, so we can clear everybody before the event this afternoon. The speech has a three o'clock start, I believe . . . ?" He looked to the publicist for confirmation.

"We will be leaving here no later than one thirty for the event," she said. "Agent

Harrelson will be part of our team from here on in, until we return from the event late this afternoon."

Agent Harrelson added, "These might help you as well," passing out hotel pens to each of The Six like congratulatory cigars.

Aldrich, his patriotism stirred, went right to work on his form. The others looked it over before starting in. Surprisingly, it was Alain Nouvian, the cellist, who objected, his voice quivering a bit with either emotion or uncertainty.

"What if we—I—no longer want to participate in any of this?"

Harrelson and the publicist looked at each other. The publicist was the first to answer.

"Mr. Nouvian, like it or not, you have become a public figure. I think political differences should be set aside at a time like this—"

"It is not a political issue," he said, rubbing at his forehead with the heel of his hand. "I was very happy to vote for Mr. Obama. I just . . ." He shook the sheet. "Why all this?"

Harrelson showed a little bit of professional suspicion. "Because I require it, sir. This is due diligence."

"And if I would simply like to go home?" This Nouvian directed at Gersten. "I told you . . . I have a performance to prepare for, and I am very tired . . . This is still a free country, isn't it?"

Jenssen looked up from his form, interjecting in his Swedish accent. "Unless you have something it wants, apparently," Jenssen said.

Sparks looked back at Jenssen with surprise and a look of reproach. "I really don't mind doing my part in all this," she said. "But I do agree that this Patriot Act stuff is bullshit. Truly. I mean, look at us."

Nouvian said, "How much of our background do we need to . . . ?" He shook his head. "We are reaching the point where we are being punished for stopping a hijacking."

"Punished?" said Frank, looking up over his eyeglasses.

Nouvian shook his head, appealing directly to Gersten. "I don't like to be on television. I don't need to meet the president. What I need is time to practice my instrument, time to be alone. Is that so difficult to understand?"

Gersten said, "Of course, Mr. Nouvian, you are free to get the advice of a lawyer. Maybe file a writ of habeas corpus. But even that would take time. Until and unless we get a court order, nothing has changed. The ceremony this afternoon aboard the USS *Intrepid* is of course a very big deal. And, as with anything regarding the president, security is paramount. Your choice is to remain with the group and enjoy the afternoon, or I suppose stay here at the hotel. But to be honest with you—*not* going will have the effect of bringing more attention your way, specifically as to why you refused to participate." Gersten checked with Harrelson as she continued. "And regardless, we're still going to need these background checks." Harrelson nodded sternly. "Is that the problem, Mr. Nouvian?"

"No." Nouvian shook his head. "No, it is the general intrusion . . ."

"I'm sorry, but it has to be this way. We have a full morning and afternoon, but as of right now the evening is completely free."

Frank, the journalist, had removed his glasses, addressing Nouvian and Jenssen. "If I can just interject." He stood up to address the group. "It's one weekend. A celebratory occasion, and we find ourselves—rather unbelievably—as the toast of the town. I strongly advocate that we hang tight, play the game, be the people they want us to be, accept what we are offered . . . and at the end of this, all of us, The Six, could very well be set for the rest of our lives. You have children, Nouvian?"

Nouvian nodded.

"You?" Frank asked Jenssen.

Jenssen shook his head and smiled. The smile appeared to be in reaction to Frank's careerism.

"It costs us nothing to participate, but the payoff could be huge." Then Frank turned to Gersten. "But I have a question. About these newspaper interviews, how in-depth will they be?"

Gersten showed him a shrug. "Not my party," she said.

He looked to the publicist.

"As in-depth as each of you chooses to be," she said.

Frank waved it off. "No matter. We can huddle beforehand. I think we should keep our personal narratives to a minimum.

That's what people will want to know about—the 'real' us, the humans behind the heroes. But—never mind that right now. Let's get through this first."

He went back to filling out his form. Nouvian looked out the window and sighed, then picked up his pen and began completing his form too.

A doctor and nurse entered the adjoining room of the suite, and Gersten guessed why they were there. "Mr. Jenssen," she said, "looks like you need to get your arm checked out again. Maybe you can take the form with you?"

Jenssen looked at his blue wrist cast, then pushed himself off the armrest to stand, following her to the doctor.

"Any pain?" asked Gersten.

"Very little," he answered. "It itches, though."

"Going to be tough with this heat today," she said, crossing the hall with him to an adjoining room where the medics had set up a small examining area. Gersten stood aside and invited him through first. That close, she was impressed again by his height and size. He carried himself effortlessly.

"You are a runner?" he said, pausing in the doorway.

"A little bit," she answered, realizing he was referring to their earlier encounter, when she saw Maggie leaving his room.

"Ever marathon?"

"No, never," she said. "Not for me. Tri-athlons are more my cup of tea."

He nodded approvingly. "You are obviously in excellent shape."

Gersten smiled at the compliment and at the obvious flattery behind it.

Jenssen held up his cast. "A triathlon is out, unfortunately. But maybe you will join me for a run before we are through here."

Again she wanted to smile, now at the apparent shamelessness of his flirtation, but could not. She hoped he couldn't see the lightness in her eyes. "I don't think so," she answered, polite but firm.

A crooked smile undercutting his Scandinavian attractiveness. That close, his ice-blue eyes acted like mirrored lenses. Behind them, she realized, was a mischievous little boy. "I'm just looking for a good workout partner," he said.

"I thought you'd already found one," she responded.

"I like to vary my workouts," he said, then continued into the room.

Gersten returned to the hospitality suite, flattered but puzzled by Jenssen's sudden interest. Perhaps it had to do with her seeing him in the aftermath of his night with Maggie. She had caught him at something. He had revealed himself to be a bit of a cad, in contrast to his outward behavior. Maybe that was a turn-on for him.

The others were filling out their forms in silence, the occasional clinking of a coffee cup and silverware the only noise. Gersten stood against the gold brocade wall, shaking off the odd feeling after her exchange with Jenssen. When he had taken his blue eyes off her, she had felt released. His magnetism was unsettling.

Gersten checked her phone again, but still no update from Fisk. She texted him then, one word, "Hello?" realizing only afterward that it made her sound like a neglected girlfriend.

Fisk was back in his car and pulling away from the Capricorn Hotel with the air-conditioning cranking when he got the call. He was at the intersection of 116th and Seventh in minutes.

A resident had called 911 after seeing, from the window of the bathroom in her second-floor apartment, what looked like a child trying to drag a man across a small, fenced yard full of junk below. The boy, she said, was struggling to pull the man's body toward a garage. The man appeared to be dead or unconscious.

A few minutes before police had arrived,

911 received a second call from the cell phone of a man waiting outside the Meme Amour barbershop on 116th Street. The man reported that there was a line of customers waiting to get in for their Saturday morning haircuts, but that the shop was locked. He said that in his sixteen years of coming there for weekly haircuts, the shop had never failed to open, and the customers were concerned.

Arriving officers could do nothing about the closed shop, but quickly gained entry into an adjoining door that led, through a narrow, tunnel-like corridor, to the yard in back. There they met a four-foot-one-inch-tall, thirty-seven-year-old Senegalese dwarf named Leo, who made his living as a barber. He was sweating and red-eyed, and upon seeing the officers raised his stubby arms.

He showed them to the garage, which was locked. Then he showed them to the west corner of the yard, where he had dragged the dead body of the obese Senegalese man who managed the building and rented the garage. Leo had covered him temporarily with cardboard boxes, completely exhausting himself in the process.

Fisk, arriving soon after, learned from Leo that the fat man had last been seen alive late in the previous afternoon, when the barbershop closed for the night. Leo had discovered his body upon his arrival in the morning.

Leo admitted that he believed his friend, who he knew as Malick, was involved in some slightly shady activities, but insisted that he was overall a good, good man.

A homicide detective arrived to catch the murder, and Fisk wasted a few minutes explaining his presence as an Intel officer on the scene, without really explaining anything. He asked Leo what was inside the locked garage. Leo, his short, burly arms barely long enough to cross, said he did not know, but that Malick always carried the key with him.

Fisk was ready to pull on gloves in order to search the dead man's sweat suit pockets when Leo admitted that he had already looked for the key and that it was gone.

The homicide detective agreed with Fisk that they had probable cause to enter the garage. Fisk found a length of discarded rebar in the junkyard and used it to pry off the dead bolt plate, forcing open the door.

The sight of neat workbenches inside surprised him. Machine tools hung on the Peg-Boards over electronics in various stages of repair. Fisk pulled on gloves before entering, ordering everyone else back from the entrance. He was wary of booby traps, though the morning light allowed him a clear view of the interior.

He went in alone. The shop did not appear to have been ransacked, though a lockbox sat open upon the counter, a cloth bag cast to one side of it. Fisk examined the bag, which was empty. He raised it to his nose and smelled polish and solvent. He placed the scent immediately: handgun maintenance.

Fisk went back outside to where Leo was sitting cross-legged on the ground, smoking a cigarillo while he answered the detective's questions.

Fisk crouched down on his haunches. "Here it is, Leo," he said. "I need straight answers, and I need them fast. You tried to cover up a murder and apparently interfered with a crime scene. For all we know you killed this man." Fisk knew this wasn't true—the dwarf's emotions were all too plain—but he needed to cut right to the chase. "Why did you try to hide his body?"

"I . . . I panicked. I don't want any trouble. I didn't know what to do."

"Most people call an ambulance, or 911."

Leo nodded, agreeing with him. "I'm not most people."

"You guys roommates, lovers, what?"

"None! Neither. We worked here."

"His death, his murder—it doesn't surprise you."

Leo took a deep drag on the cigarillo. "He wasn't the sort of man you can warn."

Fisk nodded. "Your late friend Malick—what kind of weapons did he deal in?"

Leo looked surprised but not shocked. "He was a tinkerer. He could take apart anything and fix it up again better than before."

"But I'm not talking about electric razors here," said Fisk. "Malick was killed by someone he met here after-hours. Someone who either didn't want to pay for something or couldn't pay. Malick sold guns. What else?"

Leo shook his head, teary-eyed. "I know nothing about that. Truly. I cut hair."

Fisk believed him, which made him even more frustrated. "What was the last thing he said to you yesterday?"

Leo thought back. "It was 'Au revoir.' He had his mouth full. He always had his mouth full."

Fisk said, "Last question. Answer me directly. Did you ever see any chemicals coming through here? Any strange smells?"

Leo shook his head again. "No. Just food." He stubbed the cigarillo into the ground and began to cry. "Am I going to be taken away?"

Fisk said, "No. Nothing's going to happen to you, you're not going anywhere. So long as you tell us every little thing you know about Malick and his associates."

"I told him he would find trouble."

"It found him," said Fisk, straightening and walking back to the dead man in the black sweat suit. Fisk looked around the junkyard, hands on his hips. A homicide just two blocks from the only confirmed sighting of the disguised Baada Bin-Hezam. This was no coincidence.

But a handgun? It was a dumb weapon, essentially useless for urban terror. There had to be more to it than that.

His phone buzzed on his hip. Intel head-quarters. "Fisk," he answered.

It was someone from the surveillance desk. "We have a street camera image we think might be your target. E-mailed it to you, though you'll want to use your laptop for better resolution."

"Full face? Mustache and eyeglasses?"

"Negative for mustache and glasses."

"Where and when?" asked Fisk.

"Thirtieth and Ninth. Time-coded a little more than an hour ago."

Fisk was already running back toward his car.

The caravan of three black NYPD Chevrolet Suburbans, sandwiched front and back by lit-up NYPD patrol cars, skirted the barricaded streets and descended into a VIP parking area beneath 30 Rockefeller Plaza. There they were met by an assistant producer and her own headset-monitoring assistant, who led them through a warren of corridors festooned with celebrity photos to the makeup salon adjacent to ground-floor studio 1A.

As The Six walked into the long, narrow room of mirrored walls and makeup chairs, the staff lined up along either side applauded. While the group was not exactly used to spontaneous applause, Gersten noted that they were no longer shocked by it and seemed to take the salute in stride.

They had been hastily brushed and powdered in the green room for *Nightline* the previous evening, but here at the *Today* show they sat together three at a time in black leather salon chairs facing a bright mirror thirty feet long for hair spray and primping.

They eyed each other in the mirror, the women smirking as they pretended not to love the attention. Doug Aldrich grumbled when a woman with a diamond nose stud tucked tissue into his collar. "Heavy or light on the rouge?" she asked, and Aldrich gripped the armrests as though he were about to bolt. "I'm kidding!" said the makeup artist, placing a reassuring hand on his arm. "Just giving you some base so you don't look like a ghost in front of ten million people."

"Ten million people?" said Joanne Sparks, eyeing her progress in the mirror.

The makeup artist said, as she brushed at Sparks's cheek, "Probably more, are you kidding? You guys are all anybody wants to hear about! My mom called me today when she heard you were going to be on. My mother *never* calls me."

Sparks said, "I hope a few of my ex-boyfriends are watching."

Colin Frank sat quietly, reading a *New York Times* article about them, his leg crossed at the knee as though getting made up for network television was a routine occurrence in his life. He, more than any of them, was the most interested in the way their story was being framed by the media.

Maggie Sullivan couldn't stop smiling, liking what they were doing to her unruly hair, asking for pro tips. Every once in a while she checked Jenssen in the mirror, probably looking to see if he was looking at her.

When it was Nouvian's turn in the chair, he picked up a sponge and did the area around his eyes himself. The professional stage musician was used to wearing a light coat of makeup.

Jenssen closed his eyes serenely while two of the makeup artists silently fought over who would do his base. Sparks watched from her chair, trapped beneath a black apron, shooting daggers.

The male stylist stepped in, separating the two women with a gentle elbow. He plucked at Jenssen's chopped haircut. "Great TV hair," he said.

Jenssen, his eyes still closed, said, "Must be from watching it all these years."

The stylist and the makeup team laughed like it was the most hilarious thing they had ever heard anyone say in that room. Jenssen opened his eyes and looked around as though he were being put on.

Gersten smiled to herself. For a while at least, everything The Six said and did was going to be amazing or hilarious or deeply wise.

Once they were miked, the group was led outside into the barricaded lane of Rockefeller Center for an outdoor segment. Except for Jenssen, who had never lived in the States, everyone was familiar with the out-of-town tourists waving hello to their friends and relatives back at home. This morning, many of the onlookers had brought handmade signs honoring their arrival, in anticipation of their well-hyped appearance.

GOD BLESS YOU! GOD BLESS AMERICA!
NEVER FORGET!
USA USA USA!
UNITED WE STAND!!

The plaza was shaded by surrounding buildings, but the heat was still an issue. In spite of it, some people had been camped out since before dawn. They went crazy when The Six emerged behind the assistant producer into the heat of the day. Flashbulbs and shouting. For a moment, Gersten expected someone to try to push through the plastic, police-style barricades.

That moment passed, but not the applause. The crowd was still into it even after Matt Lauer emerged and the red camera light went on. Seven director's chairs were set up, though none sat in them. The excitement of the crowd disrupted the flow of the introductions, and the interview started with everyone on their feet. Lauer took them through the aborted hijacking once again, prodding them with questions to keep the narrative flowing, before following up with a softball for each of the heroes.

"Were you afraid?"

"Did you think before you acted?"

"Would you do it again?"

Then, in a surprise reunion brilliantly staged by the show's producers, Scandinavian Air Flight 903's pilot, Captain Elof Granberg, and copilot, Anders Bendiksen, were brought out to Maggie's delighted squeal. They received tearful hugs and firm handshakes from The Six, moving right down the line. The pilots' stories were briefly recounted, augmented with the flight recording of Granberg's distress call. Then they too were prompted to add their own words to the chorus of praise.

The appearance fused the group yet again. Gersten detected a pattern of high and low, and briefly sympathized with the emotional roller coaster they were trapped on. The moments of genuine adulation were transfixing to watch, not only for Gersten but for the entire nation—and Gersten, close as she was to them, could only imagine what it was like to be its focus. In those few moments, the group set aside their individual characters and became the band of everyday citizen-heroes the viewing audience wanted them to be.

The sole note of discord came when

Matt Lauer pointed out the fact that a member of the Secret Service was part of their entourage. "Are you ready to announce your candidacies for the U.S. Senate?" he joked.

Surprisingly, it was Jenssen who answered. "We are meeting President Obama later today," said the Swede.

Matt Lauer said, "Is that the ceremony on the USS *Intrepid*?"

"Exactly."

Gersten saw Harrelson bristle at this public release of information.

Matt Lauer said, "What is that like, to go from private citizens last week to meeting with the president today?"

The others were at a loss for words. Jenssen said, "It is quite an honor, though of course, it would have been nice to have a say in the matter."

Matt Lauer picked up on this immediately. "Are you saying that you would prefer not to meet the president?"

"Not at all, not at all. But some of us relish our private lives and look forward to resuming them as soon as possible. We are being kept under watch at our hotel, believe it or not, except for appearances such as these. I am not an American citizen, but most of us are, and apparently even dutiful citizens—even 'heroes'—are subject to detention."

Matt Lauer crossed his arms, leaning forward for the kill. "You all are being held against your will?"

Colin Frank jumped in as though Jenssen were on fire and Frank held the only bucket of water. "No, no. It's a unique circumstance, Matt. I think what my friend Magnus here is saying is that there are certain compulsory aspects to our current situation, which, I want to stress, we are willing and happy to comply with." He then pulled it back with a smile. "It's all so new to us. It's been a wild ride, Matt."

Gersten watched the mayor's publicist look up at the sky as though praying for lightning—anything to change the topic. The woman reached for her phone before it could ring.

Matt Lauer ended the long segment with thanks to all, linking their brave feat to the anniversary of the country's independence. The audience's applause turned to sustained cheering, and Gersten watched a monitor as the shot was held for a long time. The cameras took in the crowd, finding tears, then came back to the group. Maggie Sullivan spontaneously grabbed Colin Frank's hand, then Doug Aldrich's, raising both in acknowledgment and appreciation. They bowed like members of a Broadway cast, the moment beaming out to a grateful nation.

The others joined the chain, even Magnus Jenssen, who moved around the group so he could lay his good hand on Alain Nouvian's shoulder. The producers held the shot for more than a minute—in television, an eternity—before finally breaking for a commercial.

Some street cameras look like radar guns or radiation detectors. Those stationary cameras are primarily traffic cameras, useful for capturing license plates, car makes, and drivers' faces.

Others are rotational, operated by remote control. Usually these are placed in high pedestrian traffic areas, such as Times Square, around major landmarks, and at Ground Zero.

The third kind of New York Police Department surveillance camera is the globe. These resemble the shoplifting deterrent bubbles descending from store ceilings.

On the streets of New York, they are most often suspended from streetlamp posts like shaded eyeballs.

Fisk stood looking at the one hanging over the intersection of Thirtieth Street and Ninth Avenue, near Penn Station. The globe hung there in plain sight. He glanced down at the color printout in his hand, with the NYPD shield in the lower left-hand corner and a time stamp along the bottom. He looked again at the street around him.

Baada Bin-Hezam had stood in this exact spot less than three hours ago.

No question. Fisk had a zoom-in of his face as well. No disguise. Fisk could just barely make out the dark spot that was the mole on the left edge of his jaw. Bin-Hezam wore a dark blue or black Windbreaker, blue jeans, and black Adidas sneakers. He carried a large plastic generic store bag in his hand, the printed words THANK YOU plainly visible.

Fisk distributed a packet of images, including one of just the bag, and dispatched twelve Intel officers to canvas the immediate neighborhood in an ever-expanding grid. They were to show store workers the image of the bag, and if they got a positive match, then and only then Bin-Hezam's face. He expected to get a lot of bag matches. He hoped to get at least one face match.

But he never expected to be the one to score the positive identification. It did not come from the shop that was the source of the bag, but rather from a store owner who remembered a man matching Bin-Hezam's description carrying such a bag.

It happened at a small hobby shop called To the Moon, sandwiched between an Irish pub and a Thai food takeout restaurant, mere steps from the surveillance camera. The proprietor, a burly man wearing a black-and-white-striped railroad engineer's cap over a bush of white hair, looked up from his steaming bowl of noodles and his open copy of *Model Railroad News* and nearly stabbed at the enlarged image of the THANK YOU bag with his chopsticks.

"The Saudi," he said.

Fisk's eyes widened in surprise. "Come again?"

The man looked at Fisk's shield. "Aw, shit. Tell me he's not a bad guy."

The hobbyist confirmed the full photo of

Bin-Hezam. He even claimed to know what was in the plastic bag: "A satchel or shoulder bag of some sort. I think it was imitation leather, though. I could see right down into it. Please tell me this guy's not a mad bomber or something."

"I don't know what he is, sir," said Fisk, "I'm just trying to identify him." Fisk excused himself for a moment, calling in support, then returned to the man. "When would you say he was in here?"

"Oh, I'd say, about three hours ago? Soon after I opened. That's usually at nine but I got in a little late today—I was up late watching junk."

This guy wasn't a kook. Fisk now had a positive ID on Bin-Hezam.

"Sir, I need to know, to the best of your recollection, everything he said, touched, and bought."

The hobbyist took another mouthful of noodles. "Bought is easy." He came down from behind the high glass counter and walked Fisk to the back wall rack of rocket kits. "He picked up one of these big boys. The full kit. Said it was for his son."

The kit the hobbyist was referring to was

to construct a rocket approximately three feet long by three inches in diameter.

"I went over the safety key for him, on account of his kid. He didn't seem to want to talk much otherwise. Well spoken. Paid cash. Hundreds."

Fisk stood before the display of rockets, running various scenarios through his head. One word kept recurring to him: "fireworks."

The hobbyist said, "This guy didn't have a kid, did he."

In her Bay Ridge, Brooklyn, apartment, Aminah bint Mohammed sat watching her cellular phone vibrate on the kitchen table. She stared at it as though it were a giant mechanized roach, summoned to life.

At first she was paralyzed by a mixture of fear and surprise. Twice before she had been instructed to clear her weekend for an opportunity to be of service. Twice before she had done so, remaining indoors and alone with the phone they had given her, waiting for it to ring.

Twice before, the weekend had passed with no contact whatsoever.

But, far from becoming complacent, in fact she was confident that this third weekend alert would be fulfilled. She had been given explicit instructions earlier in the week. Still, with the phone now lighting up and moving, she fought back panic.

She only hoped she was worthy of the trust they had placed in her.

She was under strict orders not to answer the phone. She was to wait for a voice mail to be recorded, and access that.

The phone stopped moving, but Aminah's hands remained gripping the edge of the table. She watched the device.

A minute or so later a blue light began pulsing, indicating a voice mail.

She stood and wrung her hands, pacing out of the kitchen and then back in. The windows were open, and her fans moved hot air through the apartment. City sounds floated in over the whirring. She had been uncomfortably hot all weekend; now she felt only chills.

She rummaged in a drawer for a pen and paper so as not to make any mistakes, then thought better of it. She closed the drawer, wiping her clammy hands on her long robe.

She went to the telephone, picked it up. She unlocked the screen and dialed voice mail, her fingertip leaving a wet smudge on the touch screen.

It rang, asking for her pass code. She entered the six digits that corresponded to her first name.

It was a male voice. He spoke in English, no words, only a return number. She listened to the message twice, but did not bother to memorize it. The device did that for her.

She redialed the number from her call register. It was the only call she had ever received on this phone.

The call rang once.

The same male voice answered. "You are prepared?" he said. He spoke with a directness of purpose, and the reverence of a prayer.

"I am prepared," she answered. American English was her native tongue.

"The Hotel Indigo, West Twenty-eighth Street. Between Sixth and Seventh Avenues, Manhattan. Top floor, penthouse suite A. Do not come veiled. Not even a hijab. Speak only English. And bring what you have."

She was searching for an appropriate response when he hung up. The line was dead, the call ended.

She pulled the phone away from her ear, amazed. It had started.

Fisk spoke with Intel Division chief Barry Dubin via a secure link from the Midtown South Precinct on West Thirty-fifth Street. He swallowed his food quickly, tucking the rest of his turkey club sandwich out of view of the camera.

His monitor showed a view of the Intel briefing room from one corner of a table. There were others in the room with Dubin, who sat comfortably in his high-backed seat as though conserving energy for the rest of the weekend.

"So what do we know?" asked Dubin,

the former spook. "It's real-world now. We've got a hot situation."

Fisk said, "Bin-Hezam is in Manhattan and on the move. Likely staying here somewhere, since we've turned up nothing off the island. Either a cash customer at a hotel, or else he's being put up by associates."

"I would think he's got to have associates. But so far nothing on that front?"

"Nothing," said Fisk.

They had scrutinized snoop cameras in a three-block radius, searching for more images of Bin-Hezam. They had picked him up on two cameras, but in terms of information, learned nothing more. He was the same Saudi Arabian carrying a plastic bag.

What it did show was that the technology was not infallible: face recognition programs had failed to filter the images and push them to Intel. Nobody wanted to talk about that, though. Sometimes the sentinels wanted to believe in the magic of ultimate security as much as the people they sought to protect.

The other issue was that, despite rumors to the contrary, many of the thousands of

Manhattan's city blocks were not yet wired with surveillance cameras. Camera location maps, drawn and maintained either by hobbyists or First Amendment activists, were available to anyone with an Internet connection—making it easy enough for an undesirable to select a hotel or host apartment on a residential street without electronic eyes.

Dubin said, "We swept up all our questionables in the past week, in advance of the Fourth and the One World Trade Center ceremony. I wonder if maybe we cleared out some of his help? Sure hope so. Maybe this is why he's moving around doing errands on his own? Because otherwise why risk that when he should be laying low? All the effort that went into inserting him here . . . I don't see how he can be a lone wolf."

"Agree in principle," said Fisk.

"So." And here Dubin looked at the others in the room, people Fisk could not see. Fisk assumed there were federal agents among them and was glad he was participating in this meeting via remote. "The big question is, do we take the hunt for Bin-Hezam public? Do we saturate the airwaves this afternoon and evening and put the city to work for us?"

"Or does that start a panic and work against us," said Fisk.

"This is the swaying tightrope we're on now," said Dubin. "Do enough, but don't do too much."

"Not my call," said Fisk, "but I think going to TV does not materially improve our chances."

"What does materially improve our chances, Fisk?"

Fisk shrugged, conceding the point. "Indeed."

"That said," continued Dubin, "I lean your way as well. There's a line of thought that says that if we even introduce this idea into the ether, that compromises the entire fireworks show tonight and becomes the focus. If we scare people away and there's no actual threat or arrest at the end of it, that becomes the story. The fireworks display is a big fucking deal, symbolically."

Fisk nodded. Reading between the lines, he was now certain there was someone from the mayor's office there, perhaps even the governor's. Fisk had spent enough time around Dubin to know that he would pay lip service to his political overseers if need be—but then turn right around and do whatever he needed to do to get the job done right.

"Bottom line," said Dubin, "we put this guy's face on TV, we give him oxygen, we wind up creating a supervillain. We give terror a platform and a voice in tonight's show. We mint an archenemy—and I just don't think we've crossed the fact threshold on that just yet."

Fisk agreed. "We've got nothing from cell phone surveillance?"

As with the camera screening, the NSA cell phone monitoring was being performed by computer. The court order granting permission to digitally monitor cellular towers came with specific conditions, some of which were even honored. But the sheer quantity of Arabs speaking via cell phone at any given minute in the five boroughs was staggering. Each of the five major providers serving those areas had received the judge's surveillance order electronically through a crisis link established after the communications chaos during the World Trade Center attacks.

Dubin told Fisk what he already knew.

"No leads. Lots of garbage. I've asked them to slow it down, go back through records from the morning hours before and after we have him on camera. In case we missed something. Which is entirely possible, even for the best computer systems in the world. I wish we'd gotten a picture of him talking on a phone, so we could zero in on a time. I should tell you, Fisk, there's been some talk about imposing federal priority, but I think you agree, we are best equipped to handle this."

Again, playing to the room. Fisk's role was to be the straight man. And so he nodded yet again.

Dubin was a master at this. When it came to deflecting pressure or criticism, even in the hottest of circumstances, the man was 100 percent Teflon.

Fisk said, "In many ways, this is a statistical exercise. If we keep at it long enough, chances are good we'll get a hit."

"But long enough doesn't get us through tonight, Fisk. Nor through tomorrow morning. Now, what's with this rocket talk?"

"He dropped three hundred fifty cash on a kit. And he was carrying an imitation leather bag or satchel."

"Is this a kid's toy or are we talking air attack?"

Fisk answered, "Yes and I don't know. It can get height. Launch it from the top of a building, you've got true elevation, though not enough power for aim."

Dubin winced. "Air delivery says biowarfare agent to me."

Fisk said, "A small bomb is going to go bang, and that's it. So I agree."

"We're going to have millions of people lined up along a two-mile stretch of the West Side tonight, from nine o'clock until about nine twenty-five. Sitting ducks. It's a massive task just securing the ground on a normal July Fourth, now we have to think air? He launches it from a window or a roof, one of those parachute floaters riding the breeze off the Hudson?"

"It's tough to defend."

"Or is he looking at Sunday morning down at Battery Park? Ground Zero? Dropping a toy rocket full of who-knows-what over the ceremony?" Dubin was getting angry now.

Fisk said, "As an attack tool, it is not precise. It can't travel far, though it doesn't have to. It does seem to indicate some

high-altitude interest. If it indicates anything."

"What does that mean?"

"It means what we know is that we still
don't know much. We don't have any bio-
agent yet."

"Here's what we do know," said Dubin,
sitting forward. "We've got a ceremony this
afternoon on the USS *Intrepid* with the
president. We've got the fireworks tonight,
setting potential victims out along Elev-
enth Avenue like a human buffet. Then
tomorrow morning, the dedication of One
World Trade Center, with not one but two
U.S. presidents in attendance, the sitting
president and his predecessor, also the
vice president, the governor of New York
and *his* predecessor, the mayor and *his*
predecessor, foreign dignitaries, nine-
eleven families, an audience of millions. At
oh-eight-hundred hours tomorrow. That's
about twenty hours from now.

"We've spent the last ninety minutes de-
bating how to call these things off grace-
fully if we don't get this Saudi before then.
That is—how to call it off without appearing
to call it off, because as you know, neither
the president of the United States nor his

staff would ever go for it. It's not his job to make our job easier, it's the other way around. So we're trying to come up with ways to tighten up security today, tonight, and tomorrow, whether we get this guy or not. But guess what? Security is already as tight as can be going in. So we need ideas."

"We need to get this guy," said Fisk. "And you left someone off that list."

"Who's that?" said Dubin.

"You forgot The Six. The ones who foiled the hijacking that was meant to distract us from Bin-Hezam in the first place."

Dubin said, "What about them?"

Fisk saw himself in the smaller monitor window. He checked his logic first, wanting to make sure he didn't come off as crazy. But no—it was just occurring to him now, and it made sense. "What if it's about them?" he said. "What if . . . think about this for a moment. Look at where we are. They are, what—this symbol of hope. Of resilience, of heroism. It's a long shot, but—bin Laden wanted symbolic targets. He was looking to do something big and new. So what if the hijacking was not only a distraction . . . but a ploy?"

Dubin grew impatient. "Not following."

"The hijacker had a weapon, he had wires and a trigger but no bomb. Because he's a nut, right? And he is. But all that gave the passengers time and opportunity to jump the guy. To overpower him. To save the plane."

"You're not casting aspersion on them?"

"No. I'm saying this botched hijacking allowed these heroes to be created. What if that was the plan? Maybe they—I'm talking about Al-Qaeda here—assumed it would be one or two or at most three passengers who acted. Probably not six. But no matter—all they needed was one. One brave citizen to be lauded, celebrated, made famous on this celebratory weekend of fireworks and rebirth. Guaranteed maximum publicity."

Dubin was getting it now. "They wanted to create a situation where a hero would rise . . ."

". . . specifically so they can bring him or her—or them—down. What better way to undermine confidence? By providing a symbol of triumph . . . and then to snatch it away."

Fisk felt like this held water. Dubin was less convinced, but giving it thought.

"We have a lot of odd angles on this," said Dubin. "Rockets and heroes and hijackers. A weekend full of potential targets. What's next for those six?"

Fisk said, "Not sure. I don't have their minute-by-minute schedule. Gersten's on it."

Fisk, after answering, realized that Dubin had actually been speaking to someone else in the room with him. That voice answered, "They're doing the *Intrepid* thing this afternoon."

"Holy shit," said Dubin.

Fisk said, "What's that?"

"They are special guests of POTUS aboard the USS *Intrepid* this afternoon. A military salute."

Dubin said, "If it's military, it's going to be tight already. Gangway metal detectors, canine sweeps, random pat downs."

"We'll have Gersten, Patton, and DeRosier there. We've got to get Bin-Hezam's new photo out to the Secret Service. The pictures from this morning." Fisk checked the clock on the wall. "I can get over to the Hyatt now and brief Gersten's team in person."

"Do that, Fisk. Look, there's no way

around it. We have to get this guy. We need to get very lucky very soon."

Fisk nodded, grabbing his sandwich for the ride. "He's shown himself once. He'll do it again."

Fisk badged his way up to the twenty-sixth floor of the Grand Hyatt only to learn that The Six were down in one of the second-floor function rooms doing a lunchtime presser.

He headed back down, finding Gersten, Patton, and DeRosier drinking coffee inside the high-ceilinged room, the heroes seated along one side of a long table, answering questions from a half dozen reporters scribbling notes and aiming their recording devices back and forth among speakers. The ballroom curtains were drawn and servers stood at either end of the table, attending to the diners' needs.

Fisk said, speaking quietly, "Still complaining about this assignment?"

The Intel detectives turned. Patton and DeRosier smiled and shrugged, Gersten holding her reaction in check.

DeRosier said, "The superheroes are eating Smith and Wollensky. Filet mignon and creamed spinach. And special Scandinavian dishes sent over from Restaurant Aquavit. Jenssen requested lingonberries and meatballs and herring."

Patton said, "And the *New York Times* is eating hotel scampi and pasta."

Gersten held out her cup. "We get coffee."

Fisk shared a quick smile with Gersten before he got serious. "It looks like you guys might actually start earning your paychecks now."

"What's up?" asked Gersten, all three of them ready for action.

Fisk ran down the Bin-Hezam news from that morning. Some of it had come across in action reports, but he wanted them to have the full account. He gave them hard copies of the new photos, and told them to keep them private.

"Twenty dollars says it's anthrax," said DeRosier, in regard to the rocket purchase.

Patton said, "Remember that scenario we drilled on, maybe two years ago? The guy who contracts genetically engineered smallpox and hops over here on an airplane, then just starts walking the streets and eating in restaurants. Not washing his hands. That could be this guy."

Fisk said, "I have a side theory—and it's just a theory now." He talked about the hijacking, and the generally accepted fact that Abdulraheem's chance of success had been practically nonexistent. "Not only was it a distraction, maybe it had a second function."

"What second function?" asked Gersten.

"You don't have to take out the president to shock the country. You don't have to blow up a landmark. You only need to hit people on a gut level. That's what bin Laden was about." Fisk pointed to The Six. "Everyday people. Citizens, like anyone else. These people are the feel-good story of the year. You create heroes? You can wipe them out too. The ultimate sucker punch."

Gersten's mouth hung open. "That's a real high-wire act."

"Here's the thing. They didn't need the hijacking to get this guy in country. Bin-Hezam was not on the no-fly. He was good to go. Now—maybe they didn't know that. Maybe they wanted extra insurance. Or . . . maybe the hijacking was just the magician's puff of smoke, while the real trick was going on in his other hand."

DeRosier was nodding. "I can see that."

Fisk said, "We have zero evidence of this, but I bring it up so you guys will stay on your guard. Don't get comfortable here. This USS *Intrepid* thing, with the president? Play it smart. I know it's only recently scheduled for them. I know it's a highly controlled setting. I'm saying, don't rely on that."

Gersten said, "Obviously, you don't want us to tell them."

"Certainly not. I heard what that guy Jenssen said on the *Today* show."

"About the Patriot Act," she said, nodding. "Yeah. Now there's pressure to let them spread their wings a little. From the mayor's office. He can't be seen as the bad guy. They want to avoid the impression that we're holding them under lock and key."

Fisk said, "Find a way to keep them out of trouble. Come up with some other kind of activity for them."

"Most of them are down with anything," said Patton. "But not all."

Fisk crossed his arms. "Here's the thing. We need to see them through the ceremony tomorrow morning, like six fragile eggs. We get through that, we're good. If this Bin-Hezam starts knocking off the group next Thursday, one at a time like an Agatha Christie villain, it loses impact. He needs to get them this weekend, if ever. Bottom line—we've added them to the target list. The target list of a man we cannot find."

Gersten said to the others, "How about we collapse our shifts. Two of us on at all times. One down in the lobby watching for Bin-Hezam."

Fisk said, "That works."

The reporters had pushed back their chairs, standing, collecting their notebooks and voice recorders, as the presser broke up. They were all shaking hands.

DeRosier and Patton checked their wristwatches. "We leave soon for the aircraft carrier."

"Okay," said Fisk. "Keep them together, keep them moving."

DeRosier and Patton tossed their coffee cups into the trash and went to escort The Six back upstairs. With a quick tip of his head, Fisk stepped out into the hallway, Gersten just two steps behind him. He walked to the far end, turning a corner and ducking in at a little alcove that once held pay phones, near the restrooms.

They hugged there, nothing too physical. It never felt right while they were on the job.

"Honest appraisal," he said.

"Far-fetched," she said, looking at his hand holding hers. "But—so was flying airplanes into buildings ten years ago."

"Exactly," he said.

"Just don't lose sight of the fact that the hijacker got into the galley with a knife. He slashed at the throat of a flight attendant. That was real. He wasn't faking anything. Not so far as *he* was aware. Abdulraheem believed he was taking that plane down. And these people risked their own lives to stop him."

Fisk nodded. "You're right. Good point going forward. I'm not trying to rewrite that. I'm just trying to understand this whole thing. It's something bigger, right? I mean, tell me I'm not just off on a wild-goose chase, overthinking this."

"You're not. What does Dubin say?"

"Hard to tell. He's throwing everything at this. I guess that says it all."

"You okay?"

"I'm better now. This morning, before we'd heard anything and still had no trace of Bin-Hezam, I was not too pleasant to be around."

"Is that why you never got in touch with me overnight?"

He winced. "Yeah. That and . . . you know how it gets."

"I know exactly how it gets," she said quickly, hoping to neutralize the shrill, one-word text she had sent him that morning. "Just feeling stranded here."

"I get it. Wish I had you out there, believe me." He checked his watch. "Speaking of which . . ."

"I know," she said.

"Anything looks hinky here, do not hesitate," said Fisk. "I mean anything. Everything's still up for grabs."

"I'm on it," she told him, as he pulled away from her.

"Sunday night. When all this is behind us, God willing. A bottle of red, right?"

"A big bottle," she said. "But let's get there first."

He blew her a kiss before hurrying out into the main hallway, turning the corner, disappearing. Gersten remained behind a few moments longer, partly so they wouldn't be seen together, partly because she wanted to be alone.

Maybe The Six were the target. Security at the Hyatt was meant to keep away the press and fame seekers, not terrorists. The twenty-sixth floor was basically secure, in that everybody on or off the elevator was eyeballed. The hotel location was an open secret, however. They had been outside at the *Today* show that morning, vulnerable to the enthusiastic crowd surrounding them. The group was easy to spot.

She felt better knowing that she could do something proactive now. She felt like maybe something was finally coming her way.

Gersten rode up to 26 with a bickering family of German tourists staying on one of the higher floors. She walked into hospitality and immediately Patton gave her a strange look, as though surprised she was alone. She assumed he was expecting Fisk.

"Where's Nouvian?" asked Patton.

Gersten said, "How would I know?"

"He didn't get on my elevator. I thought he was with DeRosier, but no."

DeRosier came over. "Nouvian isn't with you?"

"Where'd you go?" asked Patton.

Gersten stepped back toward the door. "You're sure he's not up here?"

Patton gave her a look that showed her his concern was not misplaced.

"Shit," she said, angry with these guys as well as herself. And just after Fisk's warning. "I'll hit the lobby. Try his cell phone."

"Already did," said DeRosier, his voice following her out to the elevator. She pressed the call button and waited an un-usually long period of time. The door opened on the same German family, who had apparently returned to their room for a forgotten item. They rode down in a glum silence, Gersten's foot tapping.

She jumped out on 2, the floor the ball-rooms were on, and strode quickly back and forth along the ornate hallway, just shy of jogging. She returned to the side hall where she and Fisk had spoken, near the restrooms. She knocked on the men's room door and checked inside, then the women's room, leaving nothing to chance. No Alain Nouvian.

She cut back out to the stairs, running down one flight to the lobby. From the top of the escalators, near the construction, she saw down to the street entrance and its revolving doors. No Nouvian there either.

She hustled up into the bar area, which jutted out from the façade, one floor over the sidewalk. The walls, the ceiling, and even the floor were made of glass, affording her a decent view of Forty-second Street, half a block each way. No sign of a fifty-one-year-old cellist with a dyed black comb-over.

Then back down to the reception area, searching the lines of arriving guests waiting to register. The small shop that sold coffee and candy was not busy at that hour, and he was not there. She turned behind the elevator bank, past a few other small hotel retail shops, trying to figure out what her next move was. Call Fisk? Not first. Not if she could help it. But he was her superior, and the point man for this case.

They had talked about things like this, once upon a time. How he might have to ask her to risk her life in the line of duty someday. She told him then and she felt it now: she wouldn't hesitate to make the difficult decision, and neither should he.

And now she supposed that went for fuck-ups too.

Just as she was giving up, and about to head back up to 26 to eat shit, she saw Nouvian walking toward her. He recognized her and there was a moment of surprise in his face—nearly panic—but a split second later it was gone. She wasn't sure what it meant. It could have been pure embarrassment at getting lost.

"What happened?" she said, trying not to sound too angry or relieved.

He was flustered and immediately defensive. "I guess I got on the wrong elevator or pressed the wrong button or something."

"Well . . . you know how hotels work, right? You go back up."

"Of course. I just . . . the door opened on the lobby, and I didn't know where everybody else went . . . and so I thought I'd stretch my legs a bit."

They were directly behind the elevator bank now. A small concourse of shops. "Shopping?"

"No, no. Clearing my head, mostly."

"Stretching your legs, clearing your head." She took his arm and started back around to the elevators. "We tried calling you."

"My phone is still upstairs. Didn't need it for the interview."

Gersten pressed the up button. She quickly called DeRosier's cell, hoping they hadn't called in this mishap. When he answered she said, "Found him, coming back," then hung up. She went quiet then, waiting to see what Nouvian would say next.

"I didn't mean to . . . I hope I didn't alarm anyone."

"Little bit," she said, as an empty car arrived.

They entered and stood on opposite sides as the elevator rose. She glanced at him in the reflective golden doors, sweating him a little. Trying to figure out whether he was just odd or if there was any more to it.

He kept his eyes on the floor as though they were strangers—indeed, they weren't much more than that—and when the doors opened he waited for her to exit the car first, in the most automatically cordial way. She did the same for him at the turn into the corridor, passing the two NYPD cops. She saw him into the suite, watching him enter past Patton and DeRosier, neither of whom addressed him, letting him pass without a word into the adjoining room. Gersten gave them each a tiny shrug that said, "I don't know," then turned and went back to the elevator.

She rode back down to the lobby, turning the corner and returning to the small concourse behind the elevators where she had found him. He had appeared near a small jewelry shop catering to midrange tourists and a souvenir shop with the usual "I ♥ NY" kitsch, tiny Lady Liberties, and New York Yankees gear.

Across from the store was a pair of pay telephones—only, unlike the ones upstairs near the ballroom, these still contained actual phones. A rarity in modern Manhattan—if they still worked.

Gersten picked up each receiver. Both phones gave her a dial tone.

Do not come veiled. Not even a hijab.

Aminah bint Mohammed pulled the twin loaves from the refrigerator. Each was wrapped in wax paper and clinging plastic. She padded the bottom of a large Macy's shopping bag—blue with a big red star—with cotton dishcloths, laying the chilled cakes on top. She covered them with a brown cardigan sweater from the plastic storage bin at the back of her bedroom closet, about five years out of fashion and three months out of season.

Aminah prayed as she packed, giving thanks that the wait was finally over. She continued her prayers while she undressed. She had grown so comfortable with the black burka she had been wearing daily for almost three years that—with the exception of her nursing scrubs—she felt nude in ordinary Western clothes. Especially with her head uncovered—without a hijab, or head scarf.

This was the second time that week she had shed her comfortable current identity for her unfamiliar former one. When she had shopped for the ingredients three days ago, she wore blue jeans, a T-shirt, and a jacket. And it was as though she had disappeared. No suspicious looks on the sidewalks, for a change. No dismissive stares. No tiny pointing fingers from children. Her old style of dress had felt to her exactly like a disguise, symbolizing the completion of her three-year journey from Kathleen Burnett to Aminah bint Mohammed.

Kathleen Burnett had been born to a Methodist minister and his wife in New Bedford, Massachusetts. The youngest of five, she had an undistinguished public school education, trained at a community college, graduated with a nursing degree, and began working at a hospital there.

For twenty-nine years she was Kathleen Burnett. Thirty-two now, she was five feet, three inches tall, with a lifetime of trouble keeping weight off. She had dark curly hair that she believed was her best feature. She had never married. She was not a virgin, but only due to a traumatizing date rape in the summer between her junior and senior year of high school.

Following the death of her mother, less than twelve months after the initial diagnosis of kidney cancer, Kathleen scoured out-of-state employment opportunities and impulsively accepted a job as an emergency room nurse at St. Vincent's Hospital in Greenwich Village. She had relocated to her Bay Ridge apartment five years ago and started her life over with great anticipation, becoming very passionate about saving lives. She was proud that, every time she went to work, someone who otherwise would have died without her did not.

Her first and best friend at the hospital was a physician's assistant named Na'ilah Al-Mehalel, a Westernized Muslim with roots in Jordan. Kathleen experienced a kind of crush on the older, wiser woman. Accepting an invitation to accompany Na'ilah to the Masjid Ar-Rahman mosque on West Twenty-ninth Street had at first seemed more like fellowship than religion. The religious barriers between men and women startled her at first, but she quickly came to honor them as a matter of respect and protection, rather than repression.

What began as her half-earnest pursuit of Na'ilah Al-Mehalel—which was unrequited, and remained Kathleen's secret, more unfocused impulse than reality—led to something much more profound. Two years later, she became a Muslim. The imam asked her three questions:

"Do you believe in one God?"

"Do you believe that Jesus was a prophet but was not the son of God?

"Are you willing to accept Mohammed as a prophet?"

Kathleen Burnett answered yes to all three questions. She had joined the Islamic religion by repeating the imam's next words:

"There is no god but Allah and Mohammed is His prophet."

Like many Western converts to Islam,

she took a Muslim name, Aminah—it meant "Trustworthy"—and bint Moham-med. "Daughter of Mohammed."

For a small filing fee at the Department of Records, Kathleen Burnett's transfor-mation into Aminah bint Mohammed was legalized, and her rebirth complete.

A few months later, Na'ilah's brother, Robeel, was taken from his Queens apart-ment by men claiming to be law enforce-ment, though without a formal arrest. Na'ilah was inconsolable, and Aminah sat with her day after day after day.

Six months later Na'ilah's parents re-ceived a letter from the U.S. government asking them where they would like their son's remains to be shipped. Robeel had committed suicide in the prison at Guanta-namo Bay—or so the letter claimed.

Some months later the father of an-other of Aminah's friends from the mosque disappeared without a trace. Vanished. Na'ilah grew paranoid and embittered, talking ceaselessly about the United States' war against Islam. Aminah was devastated when Na'ilah and her family decamped for Jordan, leaving Aminah an-gry and alone once again.

She came to believe that the accident of her birth had placed her on the wrong side of this conflict. When another American woman from the mosque befriended her and offered her the opportunity to enlist in the army of God, Aminah knew that she could not refuse. She met secretly with this woman, who encouraged her to stay away from Masjid Ar-Rahman due to American law enforcement surveillance. She was told that she would be most valuable to jihad as a deep-cover sleeper agent, though not in so many words. She was to continue to live quietly and pursue nothing out of the ordinary until the moment came when her presence in New York could turn the tide of battle. Asked if she would be willing to give her life for Mohammed, she answered yes, but she was thinking not of Mohammed but of Na'ilah.

In the swirl of this heady cause, Aminah bint Mohammed had found more purpose for her life than ever before. Saving the lives of the victims of street crime at St. Vincent's paled by comparison with helping to bring God's plan into this world. But St. Vincent's Hospital closed in April 2010, and after Aminah's unemployment payments ended, the woman from the mosque offered to offset Aminah's lost salary so that she could keep her Bay Ridge apartment without concern. Most critical, said the woman, was that Aminah remain available and unencumbered for when the call to service arrived.

The first call had come earlier that week. A different man's voice. A different code word.

He had instructions for her. She was to purchase six twelve-ounce bottles of hydrogen peroxide, six one-pint cans of acetone, and a gallon bottle of muriatic acid. Each item had to be purchased separately from different stores in different neighborhoods.

The voice had slowly recited the URL for an Internet site where she would find instructions for blending the ingredients. She wrote it down and read it back to him before ending the conversation and dressing in the strange disguise of her former life.

Chemistry lab had been Aminah's favorite class in nursing school. Following procedures carefully and exactly was second nature to her.

Hydrogen peroxide was a common household antiseptic. The acetone was identical to nail polish remover. When mixed with water, and used carefully with rubber gloves, muriatic acid powder worked miracles on dirty stonework.

Mixing the explosive took her three days. On the counter of her tiny kitchen alcove, she laid out her tools. White, cup-shaped paper coffee filters. A measuring cup. A 60 ml syringe. A pint bottle of household ammonia. Two one-quart glass mason jars that had been in the freezer with her ingredients, as it was necessary to bring their temperature down to thirty-two degrees Fahrenheit.

Using the syringe and measuring cup, she mixed hydrogen peroxide and acetone in a 3:1 ratio in the large glass jar, then put the mixture in the freezer. She mixed the powdered muriatic acid with water in a jar to make 120 ml of a 30 percent solution, and put that in the freezer as well. A half hour later, she mixed the hydrogen peroxide, acetone, and acid in one of the jars, and set it in her refrigerator overnight.

In the morning, she saw exactly what the instructions said she would: fine white crystals in the bottom of the jar. She had derived approximately one-third of the amount required. She strained the liquid through a coffee filter into the empty jar, leaving a residue of white paste. That was the explosive, known chemically as triacetone triperoxide. Finally, she poured the ammonia over the white paste until it stopped bubbling and frothing, further purifying it. She repeated this process until all the liquid was out of the jar, then set aside the coffee filters with the TATP to dry on a newspaper.

The following day, and the next, Aminah repeated this careful process until she had derived exactly one pound. She disposed of the empty bottles and cans nightly in a gas station waste barrel, running fans in her apartment with the windows open to expel the scent. She carefully cleaned the jars, measuring cup, and syringe, but did not dispose of them, just in case she would have to repeat the process of mixing the explosives sometime in the future. She stored the cleaned equipment inside her refrigerator, on the same shelf with the twin loaves of explosive.

The woman Aminah now faced in her bedroom bureau mirror startled her. She wore a long skirt, a blue cotton wraparound that concealed her legs to the ankles, and another of her outdated sweaters, a mock-turtleneck beige pullover. Brown flats completed the disguise.

How odd it was to meet her old self on this fateful day.

She did not feel as brave or as holy as she had hoped. She knew nothing about the larger plan. Indeed, she believed that there were many links in this magnificent chain such as herself, none of whom knew anything other than their own blessed duty. And for some reason this reassured her.

Down on the street, shopping bag in hand, Aminah completed another of her tasks. She returned to the same gas station two blocks away and discreetly ejected the battery from her cell phone and disposed of both in the trash. Jettisoning that device was yet another profound moment for her, a no-turning-back display of conviction.

Two blocks on, she hailed a livery cab. She gave the driver the address of the Hotel Indigo in Manhattan, and as he pulled away from the curb, Aminah sat back against the firm leather upholstery and resumed her prayers. When the driver accelerated onto the Brooklyn Bridge, crossing into lower Manhattan, she closed her eyes, not wanting to view the city of infidels that rose like a fortress against the one true God.

The Six dressed in formal attire for the aircraft carrier event. Four NYPD motorcycle policemen escorted their convoy of Suburbans across Manhattan to Pier 86 on the Hudson River, at the end of West Forty-sixth Street.

Gersten, like DeRosier and Patton, had never before been aboard an aircraft carrier. From the street, USS *Intrepid* looked enormous, rising above them to the height of a twenty-story building. The stern was a quarter mile from its bow. The floating city-weapon inspired pure awe.

Security was reassuringly tight. Unbroken lines of people shuffled up two gangways that led to the middle of the ship in the sweltering midafternoon heat. At the foot of each, zigzagging airport-style queues held more people awaiting metal detector screening.

The Six got to avoid the exterior scrutiny, receiving VIP treatment. Past the gangways, their motorcycle escorts peeled off, forming a perimeter between the three Suburbans and the crowd. They idled for five minutes, cool in their cars, waiting as one of the huge aircraft elevators on the outside of the carrier descended to within twenty feet of the dock. From it, a broad ramp extended to bridge the remaining distance.

The Suburbans drove right into the belly of the ship, unloading inside the cavernous hangar deck, which ran the full length and breadth of the carrier.

Uniformed navy officers saluted as they exited the cars. The group returned the salutes awkwardly, except for old man Aldrich, who snapped off his salute with precision.

They waited in a comfortable officers'

wardroom on the hangar deck for almost an hour. Secret Service agent Harrelson apologized for the delay, yet explained that it was routine. "We have to stabilize the area for at least a half hour before POTUS arrives," Harrelson explained. "You may be the heroes, but he is the commander in chief. Military protocol dictates that the senior officer arrives last."

They sat silently, excitement building, threatening to overwhelm them. Meeting Barack and Michelle Obama had been an abstraction until now. They were actually going to shake the president's hand, look into his eyes, receive his thanks. Gersten saw the realization coming over them.

Aldrich said, "I'll shake his hand, but I'm still glad that I didn't vote for him."

Maggie rubbed his arm, gently teasing him. "Who are you kidding, Doug? You're melting like a polar ice cap. When I come up to visit you in Albany, you're going to have a big old 'Yes We Can' sign on your lawn."

The others laughed—except for Joanne Sparks, who had been noticeably cool to her fellow female hero since the morning. Gersten wondered if Sparks suspected what had happened between Maggie and Jenssen last night, or if she was beginning to. Sparks was not as flirty and attentive with Jenssen either, not at all like she had been yesterday.

Nouvian looked away when he saw Gersten watching her. She noticed that he kept clasping and unclasping his hands.

Two men in suits were escorted into the room, introduced as the Canadian ambassador to the United States, Gary Doer, and the Swedish ambassador to the United States, Jonas Hafström. Ambassador Doer embraced a flattered Maggie Sullivan, a Canadian citizen. Ambassador Hafström shook Jenssen's hand, huddling with him in the corner. Gersten smiled to herself, having the feeling that, following Jenssen's words on the *Today* show that morning, the Swedish ambassador had been dispatched with special instructions to bring him into line. Jenssen was a phenomenal PR opportunity for Sweden as well, as his handsome face could sell quite a few tourist packages to female international travelers.

Jenssen looked wary at first, but after a few exchanges, Gersten watched him activate his native charm. They conversed in Swedish, cordially, mostly question and answer.

When the time came, The Six and Ambassadors Doer and Hafström and their handlers were led from the wardroom, emerging from the towering command island onto the vast flight deck in the baking heat. The broad blue-brown Hudson flowed to their left, the hump of midtown Manhattan buildings rising to their right, windows flashing in the reflected light of the sun. A heat mirage hovered over the city like rising steam.

Once The Six were recognized as they made their way to a riser against the island from which they had just emerged, two thousand people aboard the four-acre flight deck erupted into cheers. Television cameras tracked them as they walked and waved, the ceremony being covered by every cable news network.

The group took its place among the dignitaries, while Gersten, Patton, and DeRosier were relegated to an off-camera area to the side, not twenty feet away.

The whapping approach of a helicopter drew everyone's face skyward. A big green-and-white Sikorsky approached from the north, nose high, its twin turbines loud enough to drown out all other local sound.

The aircraft settled gently into the white circle with the letter *H* at its center, two hundred feet from the crowd, the wash from its rotors bringing a moment of relief to the overheated spectators.

Two marines in dress blues stood at attention at the edges of a red carpet leading precisely to the helicopter's door just behind the cockpit. The crowd cheered, waiting for the president and First Lady to emerge.

But instead, confusingly, the giant chopper's engines howled to takeoff power, as though the pilot had changed his mind. The helicopter lifted off and rose abruptly to an altitude of about one hundred feet, spun sharply on its axis, and flew back the way it had come toward the George Washington Bridge in the far distance.

The fading sound of its engines was replaced with a buzz from the crowd, their puzzled conversations expressing concern, fearing an unfolding emergency. Then fingers pointed into the sky.

A second, identical chopper appeared

over the river from New Jersey, heading toward the carrier. This, everyone realized, was the real Marine One, the helicopter carrying the president.

The first helicopter had been a decoy. With the Saudi still at large in New York, the Secret Service was taking no chances.

The second copter landed, and the crowd erupted with relief and excitement as Barack and Michelle Obama emerged. The reception line included two admirals, a general, Mayor Bloomberg, Ambassadors Hafström and Doer, and The Six—all of whom stood on the raised dais from which Obama would address the audience.

The president and his wife shook hands with each attendee. President Obama stopped and chatted with each of The Six in turn. He had been thoroughly briefed, as he knew each of their names and apparently a little bit of biography as well. Gersten could not hear the conversations from where she stood, but the president seemed intent on making a personal contact with each of them, himself benefiting by association with the heroes of the moment.

Each of the group was perfectly courteous if not gracious. Aldrich, Gersten noted, shook Obama's hand firmly and nodded but said nothing. Still, his chest swelled to the bursting point. Jenssen smiled when it was his turn, answering a question succinctly. Maggie wiped away tears and laughed at herself for doing so, the president smiling and patting her shoulder before pulling her into a hug. Sparks shared a laugh with Michelle Obama. Nouvian exchanged some pleasantries with her, apparently about the cello. And Frank smiled heartily throughout, as though posing for his book jacket photo.

From Gersten's perspective, while Obama appeared trim and fit, just as he did on television, even from twenty feet away she could see the gray in his hair. The job had aged him as it did every other president.

He spent approximately five minutes of his twenty-five-minute speech honoring the heroes.

"We are gathered here today to honor the members of our armed forces who have given their lives in defense of this country in the decade since the attacks of September 11, 2001. It is worth reminding ourselves, however, that in the war against international terrorism, any one of us can become a combatant in an instant. Just forty-eight hours ago, these six men and women, passengers and crew aboard an airliner heading for this great city, banded together to foil a hijacker who intended to seize control of the plane and crash it into midtown Manhattan. Their actions speak of courage, resolve, and a fierce unwillingness to surrender to fear. They acted for all of us. And this is our opportunity to thank them. I want to invite them to join Michelle and me tomorrow morning, as we welcome to this historic skyline a new landmark, a symbol of resilience and regeneration."

The president had just finished his speech when Gersten's phone vibrated. She slipped away to take the call, grateful to get under a sliver of shade, but having trouble hearing Fisk's voice over the whipping river wind.

"How's it looking there?" he asked.

"We're five by five. Did you hear the speech?"

"Nope. Got it on mute."

"I don't know if it's confirmed, but they

just got a personal invitation to the big ceremony tomorrow morning. Not a surprise, really, but there it is. They are the president's plus-six."

"Means you should have a pretty good seat too."

"I'm The Six's plus-one. Anything on the Hyatt pay phones?"

Fisk said, "One call, right around the time you estimated Nouvian was there. He's the musician, right?"

"That's him."

"Local number, just came up. We didn't get it on a subpoena, of course. Came as a favor. It's a New York cell, and we're running it down now. I'm guessing you'd like to see this thing all the way through yourself . . ."

She was nodding excitedly, even though Fisk could not see her. "Absolutely."

"How's Nouvian now?"

"He's like the others," she said. "Could be he's just a flake. I don't know what he was doing. But seemed like he was up to something."

"Who do you think he could be calling?"

"He has his own phone. That's the weirdest part. His own cell. So why sneak away to use a public phone?"

Fisk said, "That's not kosher. Strange enough to follow up on. I'll get you the info once we develop it. And I'll mention to Dubin how you picked up on this. Back at you soon."

Gersten hung up and reemerged into the hot sun, returning to her post just as the dais was being cleared. She paid special attention to Nouvian coming down the stairs, looking flushed and excited like the rest.

It could be that it wasn't even him using the pay phone after all. But no matter: it was enough to get her off this shit assignment for a little while, at least. Even a wild-goose chase was a welcome diversion.

Gersten noticed Ambassador Hafström taking Jenssen aside yet again before the group headed down to the flight deck for the ride back to the Hyatt. They seemed to be having some trouble connecting, but it was in Swedish so she couldn't be certain. They ended in English before the ambassador pumped his hand, sending him on his way.

"It will be a wonderful ceremony, Magnus, and then as soon as you return home we will enjoy many other celebrations."

Hafström held direct eye contact with the schoolteacher, as though compelling him to behave graciously. His wavy blond-silver hair and carefully etched facial lines were patrician, and this was likely a look that had worked for him many times in the past. Jenssen signed off pleasantly, and the ambassador wished everyone well and said he looked forward to seeing them in the morning before stepping away.

"*Politikar,*" said Jenssen, once inside the lift.

"What is that, a curse word?" said Maggie, smiling.

"It is . . ." said Jenssen, with what seemed to be a struggle to remain polite, staring at the closed doors, his eyes low. "It means 'politician.'"

Aminah bint Mohammed did not know what to expect, what to say, what to think. Normally she faced stressful situations by rehearsing her emotions ahead of time, in order to keep them under control, but here she had no idea what she was walking into.

Everything would have been easier for her had she been able to visualize the mid-afternoon cab ride, crawling slowly across the Brooklyn Bridge into Manhattan, the lurching, horn-blaring rush uptown on Sixth Avenue, and finally the loop around the block onto Twenty-eighth Street heading east. As it was, the ride seemed like a haphazard meander, leaving her anxious and confused.

She paid the driver cash. She nodded awkwardly at the bellhop who opened the glass door for her. She hesitated a moment while passing the Hotel Indigo desk clerk, wondering if she needed to say anything or if they would let her walk right onto the elevators. The clerk looked up, smiled, and turned away. Aminah continued through the open elevator doors, turning, avoided the bellhop's gaze as she waited—for what seemed like an eternity—for the doors to close. Once they did, she exhaled and prayed.

She was carrying a pound of high explosives in her Macy's shopping bag.

The hallway on the penthouse floor was surprisingly short. Aminah pressed the buzzer next to the door labeled A—and the door opened immediately.

She was met by a Saudi Arabian with handsome features offset by a nickel-size mole on the left edge of his jaw. His black eyes judged her.

For his part, Baada Bin-Hezam, when he first saw the red-faced, stocky woman, thought for an instant that she was the hotel maid. Then he saw the shopping bag in her hand. She was not what he imagined when he was informed that he would be contacting a sleeper agent in the United States. This American woman held very little intrigue.

There were no passwords for this meeting. Bin-Hezam stepped aside so that she could enter, then closed the door, locking it behind her.

Aminah walked a few paces forward, then stopped. She had not been alone in a room with a man for a long time. She felt even more uncomfortable because of the way she was dressed. Compared to her usual attire, even the most modest of Western clothes drew attention to the feminine figure.

She glanced at his face again and saw that his thick-lidded eyes were downcast, avoiding her face and her body out of respect. This was a source of relief to her.

"*Assalamu alaikum,*" he said.

She did not know whether to continue into the main room or await instructions. "*Walaikum assalam,*" she said.

"Please," Bin-Hezam said, stepping into

the room. He reached out his hand to take the shopping bag from her. Then he introduced himself formally. "I am Baada Bin-Hezam."

"I am Aminah bint Mohammed. Please forgive my presence, and . . ." She did not know how else to say it. She knew he had been expecting a man. She had heard it in his voice on the telephone. She wanted somehow to apologize, not for her gender, but for the awkwardness posed by her presence.

He moved around her into the sitting room. The room assaulted Aminah's eyes with its insistent decor even in the dimness of the light from a single floor lamp and the overhead globe in the entry hall. The drapes were closed, a bright sliver of afternoon sun slashing into the room through the narrow gap where they did not quite meet.

It was indeed a setting for illicit behavior, though not of the kind normally associated with hotel rooms.

On a small, round dining table, she saw two black messenger bags, a large plastic bag of folded white gauze, a small blue box, a curled sheet of plastic, and some things that looked electronic. Through the open door into another room, she saw a bed on which the jacket and trousers of a coffee-brown suit and a folded white shirt were neatly laid out as though in a vestry.

"Sit," said Bin-Hezam, motioning Aminah to one of two purple horseshoe chairs. He removed the sweater from the shopping bag and set it aside, carefully taking out the twin plastic-wrapped loaves of explosives and placing them on the tabletop.

With the tenderness of a man unwrapping a swaddled newborn, he opened one of them. He touched it to test its consistency. It held the impression of his finger when he pushed down. The fresh explosive was as malleable as plumber's putty.

"Yes, you have done well," Bin-Hezam said to Aminah.

Her spirit lifted. "I followed instructions. It is good?"

"Very good."

She wanted only to be useful. God had seen fit that she should be adequate to the challenge today. This feeling would raise her up and carry her through the rest of the day.

He studied the fingerprint impression

he had left in the explosive. Each half-pound loaf was powerful enough to turn a three-bedroom suburban house into a pile of splinters. The blast would kill anyone within a radius of fifty yards and maim out to a hundred yards. Ignited in an open field, it would yield a crater thirty feet in diameter and ten feet deep.

Bin-Hezam gingerly rewrapped the loaf with his fingerprint on it, sliding it into one of the black messenger bags, which he then set apart from the rest of the items on the table.

He put the other slab carefully into the second messenger bag, followed by the gallon-size bag of white gauze, a box of cotton, the plastic sheeting, the model rocket fuel pellets, and the electronic ignition components. Bin-Hezam hefted the bag gently to let everything settle, then checked the interior again to confirm that he had packed it well enough to prevent accidental explosion. Unlikely, but possible. All told, the messenger bag with its contents weighed about five pounds.

"This is for you," he told her.

She was surprised to carry only one. But she did not question his command.

"These things I give you are very important. You have provided the most critical
element of all."

Bin-Hezam took a breath. His most
crucial task was the instructions he was
about to give her. Everything hinged on
this American woman now.

"You will take this bag by taxicab to the
East Eighty-fifth Street entrance of the
Central Park. From there, you will walk into
the park to the south end of the reservoir.
There you will find a granite pump house.
You will wait outside until you are greeted.
Is that clear? Until you are greeted."

"Will it be a man?" she asked.

Bin-Hezam hesitated before answering.
"It is best that you do not know."

"How will I know it is . . . the person?"

"They will find you there and summon
you. You will know them the way you would
know Allah. And then you will follow their
instructions. You may have to wait some
time for the meeting. Maybe hours. You
will be patient?"

Aminah nodded sincerely.

"Perhaps you should bring a book—
a Western book—in order to appear leisurely and occupied. Your contact will

have very little time, so it is critical that you are available."

Aminah felt certain it was to be a man. She believed that Bin-Hezam would have told her if it was a woman, knowing that it would have a calming effect on her.

"First a hotel room, then a rendezvous in the park," she said. "After years of strict observance, I am disobedient at the end."

She was making a joke, but also telling the truth. For the first time since the door opened she looked directly into Bin-Hezam's eyes.

He nodded paternally. He accepted her. That much was enough.

He said, "You have never been more observant than you are today."

"Please forgive me, but . . . can you tell me what it is we will achieve?" she asked.

"This is a perfect plan because none of us except for the last person knows what is to come."

Aminah nodded, then lowered her head. *"Insha'Allah,"* she said.

Bin-Hezam said, "There is no reason for you to delay."

"I have one request," she said, her heart starting to race.

Bin-Hezam looked at her doubtfully. "What is it?"

"May we pray together before I go? Is it allowed in the same room?"

Bin-Hezam appeared warmed by this display of devotion. "It is allowed." He stretched out his arm, pointing to indicate the east. "You must kneel behind me, that is all."

He left the room, returning a moment later with his prayer rug and a bath mat for Aminah. Together, they moved two chairs aside to give them room.

"Do you know the passage?" Aminah said.

"I memorized it as a boy," Bin-Hezam answered. "As a child, when this great day was only a dream."

"I am grateful to you, Baada Bin-Hezam," she said. Aminah closed her eyes and waited for God to flow into her as Bin-Hezam prayed aloud.

"Think not of those who are slain in Allah's way as dead," he intoned in a soft, lilting Arabic that was almost a song, his hands open to heaven, his eyes closed. "Nay, they live, finding their sustenance in the presence of their Lord. They rejoice in the bounty provided by Allah. By Him in whose hands my life is! I would love to be martyred in Allah's cause and then get resurrected and then get martyred, and then get resurrected again and then get martyred and then get resurrected again and then get martyred."

When Bin-Hezam stopped speaking, both of them pressed their heads to the floor. Aminah's cheeks were wet with tears. It was beautiful.

Separately, and yet together, they said their private prayers, pleading for strength and courage.

Bin-Hezam stood for many moments after she left, listening for the elevator ding and the doors to open and close, then sat deeply in one of the purple chairs. He remained still for several minutes, praying silently now. He was grateful for having reached this point in the mission.

The woman Aminah bint Mohammed appeared capable. He reviewed his steps many times, making certain that he had fulfilled each one and in doing so had left nothing lacking, or to chance.

Bin-Hezam stood and walked to the closet. He entered the month and year of the prophet Mohammed's birth into the keypad of the room safe. He removed the nickel-plated pistol and the shoulder holster, and unloaded and reloaded the handgun.

In the bedroom of the suite, Bin-Hezam laid the holster and pistol upon the bed. He stripped to his white briefs and T-shirt, unfolding the freshly laundered white shirt and slipping into it, enjoying the sensation of clean, crisp cotton against his skin.

Next the trousers. He recalled packing them in Stockholm, and the anticipation of boarding the plane three days ago. He clasped the belt at his waist and smiled to himself. Everything becoming totems now.

He began to recite the prayer aloud, his own voice a soothing accompaniment to the *schripp* of Velcro as he arranged the straps of the holster to fit his back and shoulder.

"Think not of those who are slain in Allah's way as dead."

The holster fit perfectly with the butt of the gun on his left flank just below his rib cage. To draw it, he had only to reach across his body, slide his hand under the suit coat, and tug it free.

Free.

"I would love to be martyred in Allah's cause and then get resurrected and then get martyred . . ."

Bin-Hezam lifted the dark brown suit coat from its place on the bedcover, feeling the back straps of the holster tight against him as he slipped it on. He turned to face the mirror over the vanity across from the bed.

Perfect, he thought.

He retrieved his cell phone. He was dismayed at first when he opened the desk drawers and found them all empty—but then discovered the New York phone directories stacked on the top shelf of the closet.

He opened to the middle of the book and flipped pages until he found a listing for Saudi Arabian Airlines. He placed a call to their office on Kew Gardens Road in Kew Gardens, Queens, and inquired about the next available flight departing for Saudi Arabia.

He conversed with them in Arabic. He mentioned that he would be paying cash.

The man on the other end of the line read him the flight number and details, but

Bin-Hezam did not bother to write them down. He hung up once the call was completed, and then set his cell phone down on the ledge by the high window.

Fisk shot back over to Intel, lighting up his grille flashers and siren at red lights to get there faster. At his desk, he was looking over an array of Bin-Hezam photos showing his face from various angles when his computer chimed with a programmed alarm for the Joint Terrorism Task Force e-mail network.

It was an encrypted message, an incident number and instructions to call the JTTF liaison at NSA. Fisk dialed on a secure Intel landline.

The voice on the other end asked for his name, then his incident number.

"We just got a good hit on cell line Arabic per your request, Detective Fisk."

"I'm listening."

"So are we," said the NSA agent. "Call went out of mid-Manhattan to Saudi Arabian Airlines in Queens. We're tracing the originating end now."

"The airline? What flagged it?"

"The voice asked for flight information and wants to pay cash."

Fisk nodded. "A flight tonight?"

"From JFK. In five hours."

"How long ago?"

"About four minutes ago. That's why we haven't traced the source yet."

"Male voice, I'm assuming?"

"That is correct."

"Can I hear it?"

"Not over the phone. I can e-mail you the voice file, but it is in Arabic."

"Yes. Not a problem. Send it immediately, please."

Fisk hung up and waited. An e-mail from an unknown source landed in his spam file. He opened it. The audio file was attached.

Fisk clicked play and the telephone conversation played out of his speakers. He slapped in his headphone jack in order to concentrate.

They had no comparison voice impression from Bin-Hezam. It could have been him. If so, why was he planning to fly out as soon as possible? Because his work here was finished? Or because he had gotten spooked and needed to flee?

Fisk's secure line rang. He pulled down his headphones to answer it.

"Detective Fisk?"

It was the same NSA agent. "How'd you get this numb . . . never mind."

"If you could give me that incident number again."

Fisk found it in his e-mail and repeated it.

"I have a twenty on the other end of that call. The location it was placed from is the middle of the block on the north side of West Twenty-eighth Street between Sixth and Seventh Avenues. GPS zeroes it at the Hotel Indigo."

Fisk did not know the hotel, but he knew the block. Flower shops.

"Don't suppose you have a room number for me?" said Fisk.

"Ha," said the NSA agent. Not a laugh, but the actual word. "Good luck, Detective."

Fisk rushed into Dubin's office to brief him. Dubin scrambled an interdiction team in full extraction armor. There was no discussion about getting a warrant first.

"I'm going with," said Fisk. "That way if something breaks on the photo front, we're already on the island."

The heat wave was doing a real number on Frankie D'Aquila's business. July was usually a slow month—Independence Day was not known as a "flower" holiday—but he had multiple large orders due to be delivered to One World Trade Center that evening, and the heat was just one of many obstacles in his way. They were shutting down the security ring at midnight, but he did not want to risk getting tangled up in fireworks traffic, so he had to find a way to get his blooms down to Battery Park, and another way to keep them from wilting overnight.

He was renting coolers all over town. He even got his hands on two misters like the type they use out in the Midwest. He'd brought on extra staff to help him load and transport.

Frankie had earned his smoke. He stepped out onto the sidewalk and snapped his Zippo, firing up an American Spirit Light. This was only number five of the day—no, he realized, counting the cigarettes left in his pack, six—since he came to work at five thirty that morning. Not bad. His wife would be pleased, if she believed him. Saturday night was normally their date night. Best night of the week. He hoped to be home in time to catch the fireworks show on TV.

Almost quitting time for everyone else on Twenty-eighth. Except the Spanish guys who stayed open until eight. Frankie exhaled the first luscious drag over the sidewalk rows of cat palms and dwarf bamboo partially obscuring his view of the street. He noticed most of the other vendors had been backing away from trees. Too much dead loss, too much work to display. They were using their sidewalk real estate for tourist color, the big bunches of *Alstroemeria* lilies, roses, and mums that gave the district what was left of its visual charm. Frankie was always ahead of the season. A July Fourth heat wave, and he was thinking about fall houseplants and ornamentals.

Frankie reached out and plucked a dry brown frond from one of the palms, tossing it into the gutter. Across the street, the guys at the silk flower shop were already outside furling their awning. Frankie envied them on days like these because they weren't slaves to living plants. And he would never admit it to a customer, but he couldn't believe how beautiful some of the false flowers and fruits were these days. Some even with the fake fragrance. Just like the real thing, until you got close enough to feel them. The human touch always knows a dead thing from a living thing.

Frankie finished his smoke with one last deep drag. He was field stripping the cigarette butt when he saw a blue-and-white squad car pull across the intersection of West Twenty-eighth and Sixth Avenue and stop there, sealing off one end of the block.

Frankie's eyebrows went up. He looked the other way, to Seventh Avenue, just in time to see another NYPD squad car pull across.

No flashing lights. No sirens.

Aw, shit, thought Frankie. There goes date night.

The uniforms were out of their cars in seconds, trunks popping open, cops assembling sawhorse barriers and using them to further block off the street and the sidewalks. A New Yorker's sense of self-preservation prompted Frankie to back into the big, tiled double doorway of International Garden, though he kept watching.

From both ends of the block, men and women in khaki trousers and black Windbreakers fanned out along the sidewalks outside the shops. Definitely cops. And maybe FBI.

Frankie quickly ducked inside his shop. "Pack it up!" he called. "Lock the tills. Some kind of roust going down." He went and used his belt key to lock the cash registers himself, pulling out the big bills first, stuffing them deep into his pockets. "Cops all over the street."

Half the men and women working in the flower district, aside from the owners, were illegals of one sort or another. Clerks, cutters, gofers. Their biggest fear was an ICE raid. Immigration cops.

Ernie went out first, pulling his cap from his back pocket and popping it onto his head, low over his eyes. Then Flacco, Marie and her daughter Jean, then the Asians from the tables in the back where they put together the bouquets and wreaths.

Frankie hustled everybody out, including the store's only customer, then tugged down on the rolling iron gates, snapping the locks into place. He pulled down the rear door of the loading truck, working the lock.

Maybe she'd stay up late for him tonight, Frankie thought. In the meantime, he was worried about the flowers, hoping they stayed cool enough in the truck. This was his livelihood on the line.

Frankie joined the exodus toward Seventh. There, the late afternoon traffic was further tied up by curiosity seekers.

Something big was going on. He rounded the corner by the old fur factory building and spotted a blue-and-white police helicopter hovering high above the intersection. Not good, Frankie thought, weaving between the stuck taxicabs. Not good.

Fisk saw the helicopter he had not requested. He punched in a phone number that patched him into the tactical radio channel. Strict communications discipline was in force. Nobody said anything that wasn't absolutely necessary. He was waiting for a go from the police sniper team trying to get roof-ready across the street from the glass-front Hotel Indigo.

The tactical arrest team consisted of three officers in full armor, armed with M16s and a bullhorn. The uniformed policemen on the bottlenecks listened in but did not speak. Their job was simple: shepherd as many civilians off the street as possible in case this thing went live.

Fisk said, "Sky, this is Detective Jeremy Fisk with Intel. I need you back. Way back." He squinted up at the Bell Jet Ranger helicopter as he spoke.

"Uh, roger that," came back the air cowboy's voice. "Snipe team is installed and prepping."

"All units," said Fisk. "Hold fast. We don't know if we have an official snatch op or not. You are not hot. I repeat," he said, raising his voice for emphasis, "you are not hot. If we are go, we want this guy in a chair, talking to us."

"Roger," said the sniper pair and the arrest team. They repeated their orders. "We are not hot."

Fisk entered the lobby alone through the front glass door. A young hipster in a plaid shirt and Converse sneakers sat on a bench to the right, facing the small reception desk, thumbing the touch screen of his smartphone. There was no bellman. A runway led to a neighboring restaurant, which was empty.

Fisk had not called ahead first to check

on Bin-Hezam's reservation. He could not take a chance at warning anybody at the hotel, on the off chance they might be sympathetic to Bin-Hezam. That was the problem with the helicopter: it ruined any potential element of surprise.

He crossed to the clerk, who was taking a phone reservation. Fisk waved to get his attention. The clerk failed to pick up on Fisk's insistence, showing him one finger before returning to his keyboard.

Fisk pulled out his shield and held it out for the clerk to see. The man looked at the badge with acute interest, not alarm, as though this were the first police badge he had ever seen close up. Only then did he look up at Fisk's face.

He said into the phone, "May I put you on hold for a moment?"

He pressed the hold button on the phone and turned his full attention to Fisk.

Fisk said, "I need to check your reservations."

"Okay. Yes, sir. What is the name?"

Instead of giving him a name, Fisk pulled a scan of Baada Bin-Hezam's passport photograph and ID page from his pocket and unfolded it in front of the clerk. "Recognize this face?" asked Fisk.

"No, sir," said the clerk. "But I came on at two o'clock."

"Okay, check the register for his name. Bin-Hezam could be under *B* or *H*. If the name isn't there, then I want you to check cash customers. And if that doesn't work, we're going to have to close up your hotel and go room by room. There's a chance he could be staying with another guest."

The clerk looked pained, as though he were the one in trouble. "Let me check here."

While he was doing so, his head lowered to within inches of his beneath-the-counter display screen, the lobby elevator *dinged*.

Baada Bin-Hezam watched the numbers descend on the elevator digital display like a countdown while he prayed.

Ten . . . nine . . . eight . . .

". . . and then get resurrected again and then get martyred and then get resurrected again . . ."

Seven . . . six . . . five . . . four . . .

". . . and then get martyred and then get resurrected again . . ."

He prayed to shut out all the other thoughts in his head.

Into the jaws of the lion. Head high.

He adjusted the strap of the messenger

bag across his chest, jostling the butt of the pistol in his holster. This reminded him of the fat man, the Senegalese who tried to cheat him and whom he had had to release into eternity.

Would he meet that man in the afterlife? Bin-Hezam did not think so.

Three . . . two . . .

Upstairs, in his penthouse suite, the helicopter had drawn his attention sooner than he was ready. He had hoped for a little more time to sort his thoughts. To prepare.

But when he looked out and glimpsed men on the roof across the street, one of them carrying a long suitcase, he knew the time had come.

They were there for him. It had all been foretold.

His service was nearly complete. This was the last of his directives. The exit. The way out.

The elevator stopped.

One.

The doors slid open. He immediately saw a young man sitting with a handheld device, scrolling through its contents. This man was no threat.

Then he saw the man at the counter, who turned his head and looked at Bin-Hezam . . . and knew him. He knew him. The man's eyes reacted though his face did not.

This was Bin-Hezam's confirmation that a policeman was already in the lobby.

The policeman turned back to the desk clerk. Bin-Hezam started walking. His legs carried him out of the elevator toward the door, constant prayers running through his head. He passed within ten feet of the policeman, who faced away from him but, Bin-Hezam could tell, was hyperaware of his presence.

The street appeared quiet and peaceful through the glass doors ahead. No traffic. No bellman. No taxis awaiting fares or cars idling at the curb.

An innocent summer afternoon. Bin-Hezam laid his hand upon the cool glass door, pushing it open.

Fisk had made Bin-Hezam instantly. It took everything he had to suppress his astonishment at seeing the Saudi walk directly into his path.

Had he not seen the helicopter? Bin-Hezam did not run. Nor did he hesitate.

Fisk did not like the bag of imitation leather across his back. No disguise, nothing in his hands.

Fisk had made a split-second decision to turn back to the desk. He allowed the Saudi to pass. He wanted him outside the hotel. The arrest team was in position outside, the street was sealed. The desk clerk and the hipster guest behind him were directly in the line of fire if something happened inside the hotel.

Fisk stared at the clerk, fearing he would look up at the exiting guest and point him out to Fisk as the man from the scanned photograph in front of him. The moments moved in slow motion, Fisk listening to the terrorist's footsteps crossing the lobby behind him.

Once the Saudi was past, Fisk glanced over his shoulder. He focused on the bag across the man's back. Could be anything in there, starting with the handgun he had acquired from the murdered Senegalese. Bin-Hezam wore a jacket as well, enough to conceal a weapon.

Fisk slid his phone out of his belt.

The subject pushed open the door to the sidewalk.

The door eased shut behind him, and Bin-Hezam was out on the sidewalk of the oddly quiet street.

"This is him exiting," said Fisk. "I repeat—mark is exiting."

The clerk looked up at him, puzzled. "Excuse me . . . ?"

"Get down on the floor now!" said Fisk.

He turned and grabbed the hipster's shoulder, throwing him down to the floor. "Down!"

The hipster's phone never left his ear as he looked up at Fisk with great offense. Into his phone he said, "Some asshole just shoved me to the floor."

"Stay down!" said Fisk, already rushing to the door.

Baada Bin-Hezam walked out of the Hotel Indigo into late-day heat. He noticed instantly how quiet the canyon of West Twenty-eighth Street was.

Silence in the valley. He savored it.

All for him.

Racked plants and flowers stood along on the sidewalks, but the vendors were all gone. Hose water trickled into the gutter.

Bin-Hezam muttered a prayer of gratitude at that moment, only his lips moving.

Then he sensed another body moving through the glass door behind him.

"Bin-Hezam!"

They knew his name. The voice behind him—surprisingly, given what Bin-Hezam had seen of his face inside the hotel lobby— yelled at him in Arabic, ordering him to lie facedown upon the burning sidewalk.

Joy flowered in Bin-Hezam. He stepped off the curb and stopped.

There, across the street to his left, in an alcove in the front of one of the shops, appeared two men in black jackets and helmets. And from behind a parked car to his right. Rising like spirits, greeting him.

He heard the policeman's voice again behind him, instructing him to lie down before them. Yelling at him now. Commanding him.

Bin-Hezam raised both of his arms in the universal gesture of surrender.

The man behind the car straightened, aiming a large automatic weapon at Bin-Hezam. The two from the alcove slowly advanced.

Bin-Hezam recited his prayer. He knew he would be forgiven for standing.

Fisk saw Bin-Hezam's arms go high, the messenger bag shrugging up his back. He had stopped and surrendered, but he had not begun to lie down.

"There is no god but Allah," said Bin-Hezam. Not a yell, just a statement. An assertion.

Fisk repeated his orders. The crouching black-armored tac team cops moved a few more shuffle steps toward the opposite curb, their footsteps like drumbeats on the pavement.

"Get down!" Fisk yelled, this time in English.

"Mohammed is His prophet!" called Bin-Hezam, now yelling in reply. Fisk didn't like this.

Bin-Hezam was lowering his hands. Fisk instinctively started toward him from behind.

In a single motion, Bin-Hezam lifted the messenger bag off his shoulder and reached across his chest. He drew something from within his jacket under his left arm. Fisk saw it was shiny, nickel-plated.

Fisk yelled, "No!"—both at Bin-Hezam and the tac cops.

Bin-Hezam pointed the weapon first at the cop coming from behind the car. He squeezed the trigger, the handgun leaping in his hand.

He barely got off a second shot before a single 7.62 full-metal-jacket, boat-tail sniper bullet exploded in his brain.

Concurrently, the other tac cop had opened up on the Saudi. The twin impacts drove Bin-Hezam back and down against the sidewalk, collapsing him in a quivering heap. He resembled a pile of rags more than a human being.

What was left of Bin-Hezam's life flowed from the gaping wound in the back of his head, his blood joining the water trickling in the gutter, turning it crimson.

The messenger bag, having jumped from his hand, lay a few feet away.

Fisk stood stunned. Only later did it occur to him that he had unwisely been standing opposite the tac teams' lines of fire. Had they missed Bin-Hezam by just a few inches to the right—unlikely at close range, but possible—Fisk too would have gone down on the pavement in a bloody heap.

As it was, Fisk walked to Bin-Hezam, standing over the dead terrorist. They would get no further information from him. Bin-Hezam had wanted to die. The only consolation was that he never would have consented to be taken alive.

The helicopter reappeared overhead. The tac agents joined Fisk at the curb. They looked down at the Saudi, whose eyes were beyond seeing.

PART 7

DOUBLE-SPEAK

The cab crawled uptown on Sixth Avenue in the thick of early evening traffic.

It hit every light because of the snarl of pedestrians crossing against them on this late Saturday afternoon. The driver had the radio on, 1010 WINS New York. All talk. Traffic on the ones.

The announcer cut in with breaking news. A police barricade in Chelsea had resulted in a shooting. Early reports indicated that it was an antiterrorist operation, but it was unclear at that time whether they were reacting to a confirmed threat or the actions of an unbalanced individual.

The announcer issued a traffic alert for the area around Twenty-eighth Street between Sixth and Seventh Avenues.

"This heat make people crazy," mumbled the driver.

In the backseat, Aminah bint Mohammed felt herself regressing into Kathleen Burnett. As completely as she had pledged her word and life to Allah, her meager training had not prepared her for this.

The man she had met that afternoon had died. He had been martyred on the field of battle—this she knew. Baada Bin-Hezam had known he was walking into death. She realized that now. He went bravely. He went unquestioningly.

As she must now.

This was how she had come to work in the emergency room. Nursing the sick and dying. So much like what she was doing now: saving the world from godlessness and the torture of innocents.

For some time, she had passionately tended her secret life as an Islamic jihadist. That had been enough to soothe her insecurities and fears. But the bottle in which she contained herself cracked now as she understood that she had left a man to walk to his death.

She was his last human contact. She carried the things he provided in the bag he had given her. She was acting for him now.

He had accepted his death. He had passed along his strength to her with the bag and the assignment. She was, as she had never seen herself before, a sacred messenger.

Sacred, yet still scared.

The cab turned right onto one of the larger east-west thoroughfares, then left on Madison Avenue for the run up to the park. She had given the driver the Metropolitan Museum of Art as her destination. The museum was a short walk from the fenced hundred-acre pond officially known as the Jacqueline Kennedy Onassis Reservoir.

Aminah glanced at the red LED digits of the clock on the cab's meter, then her eyes fell to the driver's ID placard below. Aaqib bin Mohammed. "Follower Son of Mohammed."

In the mirror, she saw the eyes of a fifty-ish man whose face had seen sorrow and grief. His eyes flicked up into the mirror and noticed hers staring at him. She wondered what he saw in his passenger. One of those typical New York white women slipping uncomfortably into middle age. Unaware of the simple privileges of birth and geography.

"Can I help you, miss?" he asked. "You are crying?"

Aminah had not been aware of this. She swept away the tears rolling down her cheeks. "No . . . I'm fine. Really." She played at looking out the window. So many people, so many buildings and doors. So much life. "Maybe . . . maybe you can help me. You are a Muslim?"

He glanced at her again, this time with suspicion. "I am, miss. As much as I can be, which is not much these days. It is worse now that everyone mistrusts us. But I . . . I have lost my faith in the heat of its violence."

Aminah felt cold. "The world is violent," Aminah said, reciting one of the most primitive truths. "Is it not?"

"It is. But I remember a time when religion brought us peace without violence. It is so much easier not to believe now. Easier and saner. So I close these windows and I drive." He laughed, a tired smoker's hack all too familiar to Aminah from her nursing days.

"You should have your lungs checked," she told him.

"Yes." He honked twice at a slow passenger vehicle in front of him. "Yes, I know." He glanced back at her again. "You would be surprised how many people cry in taxis. Very surprised. But no one worries about my cough, until you. No one cares."

"Then, may I ask you one more question?" She struggled to get this out. "If you have lost your faith, as you say, then have you also lost God?"

"I have not lost God, miss. What I have lost is the idea that I can ever know what God is. That is why religion has become a curse on the earth. Nobody can know. But everybody presumes. Many are willing to kill without knowing. Without even thinking."

She felt sickened by his blasphemy, because it touched the doubts crowding her mind. She went deeper into herself for strength.

Prayer was like a fence, expanding outward. Protecting her faith.

Obviously, this taxi driver was a test sent by God at her moment of truth. She rejoiced that Allah would strengthen her resolve in this way. So important was her mission.

"The museum," said the driver, crossing both lanes of Fifth Avenue from East Eighty-sixth, pulling up at the curb in front of the massive temple to art.

Aminah reached into her skirt pocket. She carried no identification, only cash, as instructed. She handed a twenty over the seat. The fare was twelve dollars. "Six back," she said to the infidel, a knowing lilt to her voice.

He nodded, perhaps aware of how abruptly she had ended their conversation. He made change, retaining his two-dollar tip. "Thank you, miss."

She looked at him one more time via the rearview mirror, imagining she saw some evidence of the hidden God in his eyes. She nodded to him, charged by the exchange, feeling a surge of gratitude for God's greatness. Aminah slid across the seat to the curb side of the car, the messenger bag still in her lap. She opened the door—but then hesitated, tapping on the

Plexiglas that partially divided the front seat from the back.

In English, she said to the driver, "Peace be upon you."

She exited and watched the yellow vehicle join the others, fading into the flow of traffic. Standing on the sidewalk in front of the museum, she felt her senses reawaken, following their momentary banishment by fear.

It was a beautiful evening, historic, holy. The sidewalk was full of people whose general good cheer was unmistakable. Conversations ricocheted off the stone bluff of the blocklong building as they passed her. The air was scented with the steamy hot dog and pretzel aromas from the vendors' carts on the sidewalk—flavors of her youth. She saw God in the face of every person around her.

Aminah lifted the messenger bag onto her right shoulder like a handbag, turned right up Fifth Avenue, and started toward the entrance to Central Park just a few hundred feet away.

Gersten buzzed the third-floor apartment from the stoop. It was early evening in the city's old Hell's Kitchen neighborhood of Midtown West. She was just around the corner from the firehouse at Forty-eighth and Eighth, which, of all the fire stations in New York City, had lost the most personnel on 9/11.

She had two patrolmen with her. She motioned to them to stay tight against the prewar building, so as not to be viewed from above. There was no camera in the lobby.

"Yes?" came the male voice.

"Mr. Pierrepont?" said Gersten.

"Yes. Are you from Scandinavian Airlines?"

She said, "We spoke a little while ago?"

"Yes. Come on up."

The locked door buzzed and Gersten pulled it open, the cops following her inside. She skipped the elevator—the wait in these old buildings could be an eternity—and instead used the carpeted staircase, climbing to the third floor.

The twentysomething man waiting at the door wore a cardigan sweater over a T-shirt and dress pants, and had a brown mustache. His smile faltered when he saw the uniformed police officers coming up the stairs behind her.

"Is there a problem, miss . . . ?"

"Gersten," she said, showing him her Intel shield. "Krina Gersten. Mr. Pierrepont, the truth is, I'm not with Scandinavian Air, but the New York Police Department." The two cops caught up with her. "Mind if we step inside, out of the hallway?"

After a moment of held breath, he backed inside, allowing them to enter.

The one-bedroom apartment was a little jewel, with built-in bookcases, a rehearsal corner under a skylight with a sheet music holder set upon a small, round Oriental rug, and framed New York Philharmonic posters on the walls.

"I don't understand what this is about," he said, short of breath, pale.

"Are you alone, Mr. Pierrepont?"

"I am, yes."

One of the cops poked his head in the doorway to the bedroom and around the corner into the kitchen, making sure. "You were a passenger on Flight 903, the airliner that was almost hijacked on Thursday?"

"Indeed I was," he said. "You called and said you had a gift for me, for my inconvenience."

"I actually have some questions for you about your seatmate on the flight."

Pierrepont was slow to react, thinking it through. He shook his head, too casually. "I think I've answered every question about the flight already."

"This is about Mr. Alain Nouvian. He was seated to your immediate left. He was one of the five passengers who intervened to stop the hijacker."

Pierrepont swallowed. "Yes?" he said.

Gersten motioned to his rehearsal space. "I see you are a violinist yourself?"

"A violist. I play the viola. Bigger than a violin, smaller than a cello."

"You play professionally?"

"Yes and no. I do, but not full time. I want to play full time."

Gersten nodded. "And is Mr. Nouvian assisting you in that respect?"

Pierrepont began to answer, then stopped himself. "I'm not clear on what rights I have."

"He tried to contact you earlier this afternoon. He left you a message, which you may even still have on your voice mail."

She was wearing him down, but he did not yet give up on playing at incomprehension.

Gersten backed off a bit. "Would you please read Mr. Pierrepont his rights, officer?" she said.

It was painful watching the musician try to maintain his composure while the cop rattled off his Miranda rights.

"Yes," he said, answering the question of whether he understood his rights. He said it in an exasperated why-me? tone.

Gersten said, "Mr. Pierrepont, I don't

want to arrest you." In truth, she had noth-ing to arrest him for, just yet. "I don't want to subject you to any unnecessary public scrutiny. I don't even want to take up too much of your time. But I do want you to answer my questions."

"This is exactly what he said he didn't want," said Pierrepont suddenly. "*Exactly* what he was afraid of."

"Okay," said Gersten. "Maybe you have heard about what happened to another of your fellow passengers? Less than an hour ago, down in the flower district?"

Pierrepont's shocked expression told her that he had. "You mean, that man . . . he was on our flight too?"

"A second terrorist. I need answers, Mr. Pierrepont. I need to know what you two and Mr. Nouvian were talking about."

Dubin had his feet up on his desk, tilted back in his big leather judge's chair. He was the picture of relief. Stopping the Saudi took heat off him from about eight different directions.

"So what do you want, Fisk? A bigger office?"

Fisk smiled, playing along. "This one is nice."

Dubin shook his finger no-no-no. "Maybe if you had caught the bastard alive."

"I know it," Fisk said.

"He fired on officers. This kamikaze shit is the toughest nut of all. Now I've got to put a tac team cop on leave, pending the shooting inquest. No way to keep this quiet, Fisk. This is going out over the news as a big win."

Fisk nodded, though it didn't feel that way to him.

Dubin continued. "Won't know for sure until they test it, but looks like a half pound of TATP in the shoulder bag. The stuff they call 'Mother of Satan.' Remember that Shah attempt in Times Square? Same thing. They love that shit. Mixing it makes them feel like fucking mad scientists."

"But where'd he get it? Traces in his hotel room, but he didn't make it there. Hasn't been in town long enough to mix and cool it."

"The penthouse suite, hmm? Not very Muslim of him." Dubin pulled his feet off his desk, sitting forward. "It was given to him, I'd say."

Fisk said, "A half pound of homemade boom is not much either. Where was he headed with it? And a loaded weapon?"

"All compelling questions."

"And with no detonator."

"Yeah. I don't like that part either. Maybe that was his next stop, where he was headed. Or—you can detonate with a gun, can't you? Even impact. Looked at that way, he did have a detonator tucked inside his shoulder holster. We got the rocket body from beneath his bed. I think he was zeroed in on the fireworks. Forty thousand fireworks for America, one exploding rocket from Al-Qaeda."

"All they need for impact."

"It only takes one. Presumably he was going to do some damage—we don't yet know where—then try to make a late flight back to Saudi Arabia."

"We didn't find the igniter," Fisk reminded him. "For forty-eight hours now we've been straight out, trying to find this guy without any hard evidence he was up to no good. Now we have that evidence—and we still don't really know what's going on."

"The picture will become clearer over the next twenty-four hours, once we unravel this thing. Point is, we got him. We did our job. This is a huge boost to Intel, and ought to silence the naysayers—at least for a couple of news cycles."

Fisk left Dubin with his victory. He flopped into his office chair and awakened his laptop, closing his eyes for a few moments to ruminate on what had happened.

A Yemeni had tried to take over an airliner bound for New York. A flight attendant and some passengers stopped him. Under interrogation, the Yemeni confessed that he intended to crash the plane into midtown Manhattan at rush hour ahead of the July Fourth holiday weekend. Then he clammed up.

Before departure from Stockholm, at least one passenger witnessed the Yemeni talking to a well-dressed Saudi Arabian businessman booked into the business-class cabin. When the Saudi arrived in New York, he avoided the city's Muslim neighborhoods, hiding out instead in Chelsea. He murdered a contact in Harlem on Friday night, shopped for a rocket and a messenger bag on Saturday morning. The rocket body was discovered beneath the hotel bed. The Saudi had explosives on him when he was killed, though not enough for a major attack.

But they still had no idea how or where he procured them. Or where the rocket igniter was.

Fisk opened his eyes and reached for his phone. He needed to update Gersten, but more than that, he needed someone to help him untangle this mess.

Gersten ignored her buzzing phone, standing with The Six watching the news update on the hospitality suite television.

The anchorwoman spoke over footage shot from the corner of Twenty-eighth Street and Seventh Avenue, showing investigators and members of the coroner's office—all in white Tyvek suits—going over the sidewalk in front of the Hotel Indigo. Gersten thought she recognized Fisk to the left, talking with someone from the hotel.

"New York City police commissioner Raymond W. Kelly's office has confirmed that a terrorist plot has been thwarted. A

Saudi Arabian male carrying a loaded handgun and a bag of explosives was shot and killed by police snipers outside a Chelsea hotel a short while ago. Police say the shooting came after an intensive search for the man by New York police. One unconfirmed report states that the dead man was a passenger on Scandinavian Airlines Flight 903, the plane aboard which on Thursday an attempted hijacking was thwarted by hero passengers. We will continue to bring you breaking developments as they come in."

DeRosier muted the television with the remote control.

The group was shocked.

Flight attendant Maggie said, "What the hell does that mean?"

Colin Frank's eyes sparked with excitement. "Means there was an even bigger plot at play here."

Gersten held up a hand to settle them down. "We still don't know for sure, but one theory is that this man was a backup plan in case the hijacking was foiled. I will say that, for a while today, there was some concern that this man's target might be you six."

"Us?" said Maggie, looking at the others.

"Speculation," said Gersten, "but it made sense. Terrorists don't need to demolish office buildings anymore. They want to strike at symbols. This is psychological warfare as much as anything else. And you people are the human equivalents of the tower being dedicated tomorrow. Icons of the new post-nine-eleven America."

Aldrich, the retired auto parts dealer, said, "Jumping Jesus Christ. These animals."

Nouvian also looked shocked. Jenssen, on the other hand, seemed doubtful about the whole thing.

Sparks said, "So what does this mean for us?"

Gersten said, "For you it means very little. Tonight we have the fireworks at nine P.M. Some of you have expressed interest in attending. We have the One World Trade Center building dedication tomorrow morning at eight—but otherwise, and this is direct from the mayor's office, the night is yours. If you want to get a bite to eat, if you want to meet with your family if they are local—great. We request—and by request I mean that we *strongly* urge—that you allow one of us to accompany you if you do decide to head out tonight. Only because it is our job to deliver you to the Ground Zero ceremony safe and sound—and you wouldn't want us to lose our jobs, would you?"

"And then?" asked Jenssen.

"After the ceremony tomorrow morning? Then you're on your own. Cut loose. Released into the wild."

That drew a few smiles.

Frank spoke up. "We definitely need to huddle at some point before we go our separate ways so we have a general game plan. I just want to point out that our bargaining position is much stronger if we stay together, as a team, as opposed to six smaller books on the same topic racing to be the first one out. Some of us have already made plans to get together later for drinks down in the lobby after the fireworks—that seems like a great time to toast the future and get on the same page. If not, then tomorrow morning before the big show."

Gersten nodded. "Those of you who are planning to head over to the West Side to see the fireworks need to be ready to go in a little while. We have a surprise viewing spot we think you'll like."

Gersten stopped outside Nouvian's room in the middle of the twenty-sixth-floor hallway. She was surprised to hear nothing, no cello practicing. She rapped a knuckle against the door.

Nouvian opened. He was wearing a white Hyatt robe, his hair wet.

"No practicing?" she said.

"Soon. I've been asked to perform at the ceremony tomorrow. Maggie's suggestion. On top of everything else. But how could I say no?"

Gersten nodded amiably. "Mind if I come in for just a minute?"

"Certainly," he said, surprised, stepping back. She moved into the room. The sheers were drawn but not the heavier curtains, allowing a gauzy view of the skyline at sundown. The entranceway was humid from Nouvian's recent shower, the bathroom smelling of aftershave. She moved farther inside.

"Go ahead and have a seat," she suggested.

He did, plopping down on the corner of his bed. His cello case stood against the wall near him. He looked a little puzzled.

Gersten said, "Here's the thing. You probably know you've been acting in a suspicious manner."

His interested expression immediately flattened out.

"You went missing earlier today, and when I found you, you didn't seem like yourself," she continued. "This raised red flags, and I checked into what you might have been doing and discovered some pay phones down behind the elevator bank."

He did not know how to react, and so kept quiet.

"I followed up on it, because that is my job. I visited Mr. Pierrepont less than an hour ago at his apartment, and interviewed him."

Nouvian did not know which way to go with this. "I don't know what you're . . ." he started to say, which then gave way to "This is an outrage."

She tipped her head to one side, trying to defuse the situation. "He told me everything."

Nouvian looked down, coming to grips with this. Then he searched her face, perhaps for signs of disapproval, of which there were none. "If he did, then what do you want me to say?"

"You have your own phone." She pointed to it, charging on the nightstand. "Why not call him from here?"

Nouvian shrugged, his eyes misty. "I assumed you had bugged them or tapped them or whatever you do."

Gersten smiled understandingly, shaking her head. "We are truly here to keep an eye on you. But when you start acting—"

"He was panicking that someone would find out."

"He was? Funny. He said you were the one panicking."

Nouvian sighed, looked away. "Well, I am the one with a wife and family. I am the one under a microscope now." He rubbed his hands together. "The Secret Service check. All the questions up in Bangor. I thought, if I can just hang in there . . . if we can just ride this out . . ."

"Those background checks were just looking for red flags. This is a situation where you always want to be scrupulously honest. Trust me. Otherwise—as happened here—the machine turns around on you."

He shook his head. "Easy for you to say."

She moved closer to reassure him. "I don't have any need to go any further with this. I thought you would like to hear this from me. And it is none of anybody's business, about you and Mr. Pierrepont. Except your wife and children."

Nouvian sighed, nodding. "I am at a crossroads, Officer Gersten."

"Detective Gersten," she said. "But you can call me Krina."

"Krina. I know what you are thinking, and believe me, it is what I have been thinking about for . . . it's been almost a year now. I was very unprepared for what happened with . . . him. This affair. That's what it is. I know I don't need to explain anything to you, but I love my children, nothing has changed there. And nothing will ever change."

He looked away, across the room. As difficult as this was for him—and for Gersten—he seemed to want to air it with somebody impartial.

"What has changed . . . is my mind-set. This incident . . . my so-called heroic action . . . in many ways it has decided things for me. I need to act, and I know that now. And now I know that I *can,* you understand? But—in such a way that I can make the best future for my family as possible."

Gersten raised her hands. "Again—your private, personal business. I think you'll do the right thing. But will you do one favor for me? Not a favor—I'm going to insist upon it."

He waited to hear what it was.

"No more scares like that. Okay? Let me and my fellow detectives finish our job here, and then you can go on to face whatever you have to."

Nouvian nodded. "That sounds reasonable."

Gersten smiled. "It does, doesn't it?"

She turned and went to the door. Nouvian did not stand up from the corner of the bed.

"Krina," he said, before she could get the door open.

She turned. "Yes?"

"I don't want to write a book and I don't

want to make any money from this. I just want to play my music and raise my children. And that's about it."

Gersten nodded, feeling for him. "Well then, my advice, if you're asking for it, is to just wait until after tomorrow to tell Colin Frank. Because it's going to break his greedy little heart."

Back inside her own room, Gersten kicked off her shoes, watching NY1 on mute, her phone to her ear.

"Bin-Hezam was just a few blocks from Penn Station, Krina," said Fisk. "He was right here. Can you believe it?"

"You saw his face," she said, envious. "What did it say?"

"Great question." She smiled, waiting while he thought it through. "You know what it said? It said that he knew he was going to die. He knew he was walking to his death. He wasn't just resigned to his fate, he was dictating the terms."

"Wait. After he got outside?"

"No. I never saw his face outside, his back was to me out on the sidewalk. This was in the lobby. The elevator door opened, and I looked at him—and it was like he had arrived at the pearly gates already. He was reporting for death. You just helped me confirm that."

"What does it mean to you?"

"Dubin thinks he was going somewhere on another errand, but I don't. I think he was headed to death. That's the reason he came downstairs."

"With a half pound of homemade acetone peroxide explosives in a bag?"

"Boom in bag, gun in hand. I think he heard that helicopter . . . I don't know, maybe even before that. I mean, he called Saudi Air directly and spoke in Arabic. The first time all weekend he used his native language over the phone. He knew we'd be able to screen for that. He had to."

Gersten chewed on that. "Maybe the helicopter over the hotel told him the game was up. That's what it would tell me. If he knew he wasn't going to get out of that building a free man, then what's left for him? Instead of biting down on a cyanide pill, he went out the hard way."

More silence from Fisk, then, "Another fair point. Maybe I'm overthinking this. Hey, you know what I miss? Cops and robbers. Jesus. Why can't these shitheads just rob a bank?"

"The bad guy is gone. Focus on that. You found him—doesn't matter how now. Bin-Hezam sleeps with the virgins. Call it a win."

"I want to," said Fisk. "But what can I do? I don't feel good about feeling good about this. That's the bottom line. Maybe I need to stop thinking about it for a while. What about you? Catch me up on Nouvian."

She did. Fisk listened.

"I think he's making a big mistake," said Fisk. "Given what you just told me, I bet his book would outsell all the others."

"It was kind of fascinating, though. He sees the foiled hijacking, and his role in it, as giving him permission to change. Like a near-death experience."

"Hmm." Fisk waited for more. "What does that say to you?"

She smiled. She was going to say this. "I'm thinking about maybe transferring out of Intel."

"You . . . what?"

"Like you just said. I miss cops and robbers. Look at me here. I could get shit assignments like this out of a regular precinct. But at least I'd be doing something."

Fisk said, "You're serious."

"I'm getting there," Gersten said. "Maybe it would be better for us."

"For us?" He thought about that. "Maybe it wouldn't, though."

"Not living this twenty-four seven?"

"Look," he said, realizing she wasn't just bitching about this, but that she was serious. "It's been a rough weekend. We need to go somewhere so I can talk you out of this."

"You're welcome to try. Supposedly we're meeting with the group later for a nightcap in the hotel lounge, after the fireworks."

"Sounds totally unprofessional," he said. "I'll be there. Assuming nothing else breaks in the next few hours. Where you headed now?"

"Nowhere. Paperwork is calling to me. I've got to write up everything from the past two days. I'm going to play some music and get into it."

"No fireworks?" he said.

"Depends on you. I've got a nice hotel room all to myself here."

"Ah, you're killing me. I have so much to clean up with this Bin-Hezam thing."

"I know, I know. Try for the drink."

"Sunday night," he said. "That's my goal."

"What are you thinking? Cafe Luxembourg?"

"Like two regular people."

"Sounds marvelous. Only problem is, we'll probably both fall asleep before getting out the door."

He said, "Takeout's okay too."

She smiled. It was good to talk to him. It helped. "Hey—I think maybe his mission was to get blown up and take out a bunch of cops in the process. Including you. So be more careful, all right?"

"Yeah, yeah. I'll see you later."

She hung up, dwelled on the conversation for a few minutes, then set it aside.

Focus on paperwork. Get through this. Table everything else until Sunday.

Back at the Hyatt, Colin Frank sat in the common room, alone with his laptop. He was framing out the story in the form of a book and transmedia proposal. He knew some documentary filmmakers and was considering going that route first, a video document that would coincide with the book's release in six to eight months, each one promoting the other.

He cracked open a second nip of Bacardi and dumped half of it into his Diet Coke, pushing back his ball cap and cycling through e-mails, leisurely reading the ones from prospective literary agents and managers, and a handful of personal introductions from various big-name movie producers.

When it all became too much, Frank at once leaped up out of his chair and gave a Tiger Woods–like fist pump, rejoicing silently in the empty hotel room.

Joanne Sparks put the finishing touches on her face in front of the bright bathroom mirror, smoothing out the cracked lipstick in the corners of her mouth. That bitch Maggie Sullivan was going to the fireworks, and this was Sparks's first—and maybe last— shot at the Swede without the others serving as an audience.

She checked the skirt again—clingy-tight but not desperate-looking—tugging down the fabric at her slender hips and then grabbing her handbag, heading out to Jenssen's room.

She paused halfway out her door, spotting Jenssen in running shorts and a wicking T-shirt down at the far end of the hall, talking to someone. Sparks stared down the hallway, unseen as yet. That far down the hall, she realized, were the cops' rooms.

Detective Gersten.

Sparks watched a few moments longer—long enough—and then stepped back inside her own room, her door closing with a click.

She turned and whipped her handbag at the wall over her bed. It bounced off the headboard and landed on the nightstand, knocking over her alarm clock and television remote.

She returned to the bathroom mirror, face-to-face with her furious self.

"Cocksucker," she said, gripping the counter.

She was done with Jenssen. Or even if not, she sure was going to act that way from now on.

Gersten stood in the doorway to her room, shoeless, feeling short. Jenssen stood almost a head taller than she. One of the sporting goods chains had sent over some swag, and he wore a blue-and-white Adidas shirt and shorts, and New Balance running shoes.

"You're sure," he said, "I can't change your mind?"

Dangerous, dangerous man, thought Gersten. He knew just how to say it, delivering the line with just the right amount of play, in such a way that she felt somehow foolish declining.

At the same time, she didn't appreciate the attempt at manipulation.

"Too much work, unfortunately," she told him. "Appreciate the invitation, though. Nothing like a nighttime run."

"Actually, more satisfying is the cool shower that follows."

Gersten smiled, as much at the sentiment as the cheekiness.

"You're certain I can't change your mind?" he said. "What if I get lost?"

"Tell you what," she said. She had her phone in hand. She quickly dialed De-Rosier. "Detective DeRosier? Mr. Jenssen needs a buddy for a night run."

"Aw, fuck," said DeRosier. "I just ate."

Gersten smiled at Jenssen. "He'd be thrilled to accompany you."

Jenssen smiled wanly. "The feeling is mutual."

Gersten smiled for real. She felt as though she'd gotten the upper hand in this exchange. "Be careful in the dark," she told him, and closed her door.

She felt a little short of breath. She was flattered by Jenssen's attention, and briefly wondered what sort of vibe she was putting out there.

"I hope I brought my sneakers."

The voice surprised her. DeRosier was still on her phone.

"Good luck," she told him, and hung up.

With Nouvian in a self-imposed exile, practicing the cello in his hotel room, flight attendant Maggie Sullivan and retired auto parts dealer Doug Aldrich were the only ones interested in attending the fireworks.

They left the hotel in a lone Suburban, no motorcycle escort, only an off-duty cop driving them and the mayor's office's PR person. The driver used his grille lights only when they hit the barricade on Tenth Avenue.

"Gonna be tough going back to being a regular citizen," said Maggie, looking out at the revelers walking toward the water.

"Wish I was able to bring my grandkids to this," he said.

The Suburban pulled over at a mobile NYPD checkpoint. At the corner was a rectangular box with windows, not much bigger than an SUV. Security cameras and satellite dishes stood on top of it.

"Here we are," said the PR woman.

She opened the door for them and walked them to the enclosure. People looked their way, but nobody was close enough to identify either Maggie or Aldrich.

"In here?" said Maggie.

"You first," said the PR woman.

Maggie entered the hinged door. Aldrich followed, then the PR woman. She had her phone out, but for taking photographs, not calls.

The door closed and the box started to rise. Maggie realized now, she had seen these things before in Times Square. It was like a hydraulic riser, a promontory nest giving a good view of the street below . . . but an even better view of the night sky, from above street level.

"Best seats in the house," said the PR woman.

Maggie laughed hard and hugged Aldrich. "The others are going to absolutely kick themselves!"

Jenssen waited at the twenty-sixth-floor elevators. The police detail on their floor had been reduced from two to just one, he noticed.

It was after 8:00 P.M. now. Jenssen was anxious to get moving.

He heard cello music from Nouvian's room. Jenssen recognized the tune: "America the Beautiful." Interesting, in that it was a patriotic song not about battle or victory or God. It was a song about beauty. Jenssen thought to himself that in today's America, that sentiment could only be taken ironically.

The elevator doors opened, but he was still obliged to wait for the detective. He noticed the camera panel in the interior corner of the car. It was a fact that, while hotel cameras constantly recorded, the images themselves were rarely monitored.

Jenssen was still unsure about the female detective. She watched him at times, but it was difficult to gauge her intent. Had she accepted his invitation, he would have completed an easy two- or three-mile loop and been done with it. Her years as a law officer had given her confidence, but he believed her still insecure about her tomboyish look. She was not a lesbian; of that much he was certain. He clearly recalled how she had interacted with the detective she was paired with in Bangor, Maine. Jenssen remembered thinking at the time that they could be lovers.

So perhaps it was simple desire on her part. Another loose American woman. He needed to know for sure, of course. He had witnessed their alarm at the brief disappearance of the cellist, Nouvian, and noted that Gersten was absent for some time after that, which Jenssen suspected was an assignment resulting from Nouvian's actions.

This was a time to be most careful.

DeRosier, the bald-headed male detective, finally exited his room, walking down the hallway in light nylon pants and an NYPD Softball T-shirt. "You're gonna go easy on me, right?" he said, with a big New York smile.

"I am," said Jenssen. "At first."

They rode together down to the busy lobby of the Hyatt, DeRosier checking his phone, then zipping it into his pants pocket. They exited in the lobby, walking past the reception area and the concierge desk, looking up at the lounge.

"We could just get a drink," said DeRosier, only half kidding.

Jenssen smiled. Just as in Sweden, the slam-and-go drinkers crowded against the long bar, downing cocktails before dinner.

Reflected in the facing windows were the lounge television screens, some showing a baseball game, the others showing helicopter footage from the police investigation of the shooting of the terrorist, Baada Bin-Hezam.

"We nailed that fucker," said DeRosier. "Good weekend for the good guys, huh?"

"Very good," said Jenssen, stepping onto

the short escalator down to the front entrance.

"Oof," said DeRosier, as they exited the revolving doors to the sidewalk and the heat. "This is going to be fun."

"I am fine if you want to stay behind. This city is on a numbered grid, no?"

"No, no." DeRosier was swinging his arms, improving his circulation. "I probably need this."

"Tell you what," said Jenssen. "Let's take the subway part of the way, and just run back. I want to see the park."

"Sounds good to me."

Nighttime Manhattan had its own distinct rhythm. This was Jenssen's first visit to the United States. He followed the detective, moving with the flow of pedestrians heading east on Forty-second Street. Half a block later, they descended into a white-tiled cavern known as the Lexington Avenue subway station. DeRosier sought out a Port Authority officer and badged them through the turnstile.

Jenssen trotted down another flight of stairs to the uptown platform, the smell gagging him, a hideous mélange of piss and dead animals. People crowded near the yellow line, all so nonchalant about the nauseating circumstances in which they found themselves.

Discipline taught Jenssen not to react to every little dissonant note in his surroundings. As always, visualization soothed him. He summoned images of the magnificent Rådhuset subway station on Stockholm's Blue Line, its escalators running from the wide, clean track platforms through dramatically lit solid rock. He imagined himself traveling out of Stockholm on a trip to visit his widowed mother, Hadzeera, in Malmö.

Jenssen had never known his biological father. His mother had met his stepfather, Jonas, when he was a member of a United Nations Peacekeeping Force in Srebrenica. Jonas had discovered Hadzeera hours after she had been raped and left for dead by Serbian soldiers, after instructing her eight-year-old son to bury himself under clothes and blankets in the back of a bedroom closet. Against his own better judgment, as well as the advice of his commanders, Jonas Jenssen fell in love with the brutalized single mother. She and Magnus triggered a caretaking instinct in him that was simply irresistible. His father converted to Islam out of sympathy and love. But the marriage was fated to last less than two years; Jonas was killed in a car accident on his way home from the Malmö mosque after Friday prayers. That was the day Jenssen resolved to be the man in his mother's life.

"First time in New York, right?" said DeRosier. It was an attempt at conversation. Jenssen nodded, but did not take it any further, feigning interest in the arrival of the 5 train, shrieking out of the tunnel beneath Lexington Avenue, stopping at the platform.

Together they boarded the crowded train, standing two seats apart. The riders rocked in silence. DeRosier nodded to him, and the two men exited the subway at East Eighty-sixth Street, reemerging into the heat.

Jenssen checked the street signs in order to orient himself. West was to the left. DeRosier wanted to stretch, so Jenssen went through the motions, keeping an eye out for a tail car. Sure enough, he spotted the other detective, Patton, in an unmarked car double-parked across the street. DeRosier straightened then, announcing that he was ready.

They set off together at a slow lope, like

any of the other weekend evening joggers heading for Central Park. Two minutes in, Jenssen felt his arm beginning to throb against his cast.

When Jenssen tore the bomb trigger from Awaan Abdulraheem's hand in the galley of Flight 903, his forward motion coupled with the impact against the floor caused a fracture of his left distal radius. The minor break had required only immobilization. Jenssen had insisted that the doctor sent by the mayor's office cover only his forearm and the back of his hand, over a soft palm grip stabilizing his palm. He had been taking ibuprofen for the swelling, but disposed of the prescribed pain medication. The pain was bearable.

He picked up his pace, DeRosier breathing heavily behind him. Jenssen reached Fifth Avenue in five minutes. He jogged in place waiting for the light to change and the detective to catch up. He noticed the unmarked car waiting a few vehicles back at the light. DeRosier came up panting.

"Good?" said Jenssen.

DeRosier waved at him to continue on as though it was no problem.

They jogged up Fifth Avenue to Ninetieth

Street and crossed the four-lane boule-
vard with the light, between stone pillars
flanking the park entrance. Inside, sloping
paths led up to the reservoir two ways—
left and right. Jenssen picked up his speed,
consulting the map he had committed to
memory. He needed to veer to the left. He
turned back twice and saw DeRosier fading into the dimness of the evening.

"Wait up!" said DeRosier, waving to him.

"All right, then!" Jenssen yelled back to
him, pretending to misunderstand.

He continued to cut left along the path.
After the first turn he went into a sprint, the
motion and the breeze feeling excellent
after the past few days of stasis.

He left the path when it was safe to do
so, racing between trees until he rejoined
another path at the top of a rise. Confident
he had left both DeRosier and Patton well
behind, he downshifted so as not to attract
attention, jogging steadily past dozens of
New Yorkers and energetic tourists out
walking.

The loop around the reservoir provided
not only exercise but some of the most
magnificent views in the city, especially at
night. The bursts of colored light above

the trees to the southwest told him the fireworks display had begun. Pedestrians stopped to watch, lovers holding hands.

Jenssen kept on. Ahead of him, the lawns of the park gave way to the skyscrapers of midtown Manhattan. The illuminated monolith of the Empire State Building rose from their midst. Since the fall of the Twin Towers, it had resumed the role of the tallest building in New York City. Come tomorrow morning, when One World Trade Center was officially opened for business, the Empire State Building would slip back to second place.

For Jenssen, these spectacular views served only as geographic landmarks as he circled the body of water. This reservoir no longer fed drinking water to the inhabitants of Manhattan Island. It had been decommissioned in 1997 because of its vulnerability to terrorist attack. Now its one billion gallons fed other ponds in the park through a glittering schist and granite pump house located at its south end.

He ran for another quarter mile before again veering off the gravel path, this time onto an unlit trail to his left. The trail took him down a grassy slope to a bridle path covered with pine needles under overhanging trees. Jenssen followed it for two hundred yards, turning right at the southern end of the reservoir, near the rear loading docks of the Metropolitan Museum of Art.

To his left were the former stables now used as sheds for gardeners' equipment. Jenssen tucked himself into the shadows between two adjoining sheds. His vantage point gave him a full view of the front of the pump house, topped by a large clock face.

Jenssen saw her right away, in silhouette. He made out the messenger bag on her shoulder, tucked close to her body beneath her elbow. He saw the outline of her skirt. Even from that distance, he could see that she was anxious. As she should have been—she had waited for some time. She looked from the clock to the bright explosions in the western sky.

Jenssen walked to the bottom of the broad cement stairs leading up from the bridle path. She was overweight, but otherwise extraordinarily plain. He waited until her scanning eyes passed over him.

Her head panned right, past him, then back again. She had seen him. Jenssen nodded. She looked around, for the moment a caricature of furtiveness. Jenssen winced and motioned to her with his hand.

She made her way down the stairs self-consciously, like a woman gripping her handbag in a bad neighborhood. He waited until he was certain she was coming his way, and then drifted back toward the gardeners' sheds, waiting for her to follow.

He was waiting for her when she rounded the corner into the dim light behind the shed. Here, they were completely hidden from the reservoir path and the bridle trail.

She came to him like a sinner, hesitant, seeking release.

"*Assalamu alaikum,*" she said, in a meek voice.

"*Walaikum assalam,*" he said in reply.

"I am sorry," she said. "I was so nervous, waiting this long. And the fireworks . . ."

"You are indeed blessed," Jenssen said, then quickly spun her around and clamped his wrist cast against her throat.

Jenssen was a big man, his grip seeming to envelop her completely. Her body shook, her hands coming to his cast. She pulled at his fractured wrist, his pain hot, severe. When he did not relent, her grip came away from his arm, her hands reaching out in front of her. In that way, she gave herself to him. He imagined she was looking to the colored bursts in the otherwise dark night sky.

She understood what had to happen, and released herself to God.

Gurgling sounds came involuntarily. Her hands fell to her sides. Her legs sagged, her body listing beneath his grip.

He held on until he was sure of her death, then set her down on the ground. He pulled the bag from her shoulder and dragged her into the shadowed recess between the two sheds, all the way to the rear.

He gripped his cast, having rotated his wrist in the strangling. With great effort and pain, he twisted it back into place. The pain flared and then—slowly—passed. He felt a bit of the woman's saliva on his cast, but nothing more.

He picked up her bag by its handle and started away into the trees.

Jenssen pulled a plastic Duane Reade bag from a trash can before hailing a cab on Fifth Avenue. He wanted to run the full forty blocks back, but he needed to preserve his energy. He dismissed the cab before Rockefeller Center, jogging the last ten blocks back to the Hyatt.

He went around to the service entrance, the one The Six's motorcade had been using. A pair of young garage workers looked up casually, one of them recognizing Jenssen as one of the group of heroes, admitting him with a wave. Jenssen shook their hands, apologizing for the sweat. His entry was not questioned. He went up the stairs they had taken before, stepping into a service elevator that rode up the same shaft as the guest cars but opened on the side of the elevator bank.

Jenssen strode out onto the twenty-sixth floor, drugstore bag in hand, and nodded to the officer sitting on a chair before the hallway.

The corridor was empty. He had succeeded in beating the two detectives back to the hotel. Jenssen moved swiftly past the hospitality suite so he would not be drawn inside. Only the journalist, Frank, was inside, clicking away at his laptop.

The hallway was empty. Jenssen plucked the room key from his sweaty sock and fed it into his door. He was waiting for the green light and the click.

A door at the far end of the hall opened. Jenssen froze a moment, then had to turn.

It was Detective Gersten, rolling out a room service tray.

She was three pairs of doors away. Jenssen had no alternative but to acknowledge her. He waved his key card.

"How was your run?" she asked.

"Good, good."

"How did DeRosier do?"

"I will ask him when he comes back."

She laughed, and Jenssen pushed inside on the joking remark—but not before the female detective's eyes fell upon the white plastic bag hanging from his wrist cast.

Jenssen pushed inside his room, closing the door behind him. His face showed fury, but he allowed no further demonstration of that emotion. He quickly stowed the bag in his hotel safe, then eased back out into the hallway—quiet, empty again— eager to resume his cooperative presence.

He was drinking his second bottle of water and stretching a bit at the waist when Detectives DeRosier and Patton entered the hospitality suite. DeRosier was still sweating, and Patton looked angry. Jenssen wondered if Gersten had phoned them after her exchange with Jenssen in the hallway.

"What happened?" asked DeRosier.

"Nothing," said Jenssen, feigning confusion.

"Why didn't you wait?"

"I was supposed to wait? Why didn't you keep up?"

DeRosier reached for a bottle of water. "Because I couldn't."

"Beautiful night, no?" said Jenssen.

"No," said DeRosier, between gulps.

Perhaps Gersten had not called them after all. Perhaps she had thought nothing of the bag, or its contents. Jenssen would remain attentive to her in order to make sure.

Fisk awoke suddenly, hearing his alarm clock.

Only, he wasn't in bed. He had drifted off at his desk.

Shit.

And—this wasn't his alarm clock ringing. It was his phone.

He stood and shook out of his befuddlement. Felt like he had been asleep for hours, but without the refreshment benefit.

He checked the time. Maybe twenty minutes had passed since he'd put his head down.

He answered his phone just before it went to voice mail.

"Hey, it's Reg. Great get today."

Reg was an NYPD detective assigned to the Joint Terrorist Task Force.

Fisk said, "We got lucky. Thanks to the NSA."

"Nah, I heard you were on this guy from the jump. Which is why I'm calling. We got a look at this bomber's phone. It's a domestic carrier, which is weird for a Saudi art dealer. No international plan."

Fisk said, "He had a cell phone and plan under his name. But the GPS didn't ping. Must have had the phone powered down. In any event, it wasn't the one he brought to the U.S."

Reg said, "He placed a call earlier today, before the inquiry to Saudi Air. Cell to cell. The number is registered to a Kathleen Burnett. We have a Bay Ridge billing address. Giving you a heads-up in case you wanted to hitch a ride over there."

Fisk absorbed this. "Bay Ridge? Who is she?"

"Don't know yet. Common name, but nobody under it is listed in Bay Ridge. But we just got this read, it's that fresh. Had to scan the phone for booby traps first. All developing."

Fisk said, "E-mail me the address. I'll meet you there."

Back behind the double-locked door of his hotel room, Jenssen drew the heavy shades. He made yet another full sweep of his room, examining lamps, the telephone, the ceiling smoke detectors—anything and anywhere a camera or other recording device might have been installed while he was away. Nothing appeared to have been tampered with.

He opened the room safe and pulled out the bag. They would come for him in less than two hours. Skipping the get-together at the hotel lounge would raise suspicion, inadvisable at this late stage.

He could stall them awhile, and he would need to. Time was of the essence.

After months of planning and training, and secrecy that had cost lives and won glory, the hour of action was upon him. Jenssen was the apex of a holy pyramid that had begun when Osama bin Laden initiated a call for victory in the name of Islam and the Wahhabi caliphate. His sacrifice only furthered the mission and the dedication of those called to fulfill it.

Jenssen's primary concern was to protect the explosives. He first removed the small loaf-shaped parcel, unwrapping the foil and wax. Inside, the TATP explosive was pliable and appeared to be well-prepared. He had trained with the substance and felt familiar with it. With care, it could be molded into any desired shape.

He quickly inventoried the rest of the contents of the Duane Reade shopping bag delivered to him by the woman. He examined a Ziploc bag of gauze impregnated with plaster of paris. When wet, it would be formed into a new replacement cast for his arm.

Next, a box of rolled cotton batting.

Then a sheet of fine plastic a foot square.

It could be cut and shaped, forming a partition between the explosive and the gauze. The new cast would be damp for a few hours before drying. But if the TATP became wet, the explosive would have only half its potential force as when dry.

Then the pellets wrapped in tissue paper, from which protruded the vinyl-covered antenna wires. The twin igniters.

And a wireless trigger the size of a can of sardines.

Everything he needed.

He stood and disrobed, throwing the exercise clothes into the corner of the room. He went into the bathroom and turned on the ceiling fan and the shower. He then pulled the sharp steak knife he had purloined from their lunchtime interview from its hiding place beneath the bathroom sink, and went to work cutting his cast. He worked from his arm out. The hardened batting sliced cleanly, but the blue exterior proved a much more difficult task. His wrist ached as he went at it savagely.

One thing they had not accounted for was the color of the cast. Jenssen had requested plain white, but the orthopedist only brought blue. It was an anomaly that would have to be accounted for.

The hard blue casing flaked shavings onto the vanity as Jenssen sawed away, nicking his forearm six or seven times but drawing little blood. When he got half of it cut, he placed the cracked cast against the edge of the vanity and pushed down on it.

The only result was pain.

Jenssen felt the husk give a little, and so grabbed a fresh cotton hand towel and stuffed it into his mouth. He positioned the open seam of the cast against the counter's sharp edge, and on the count of three thrust down against it with all his weight.

The cast cracked open with a shocking crunch. Jenssen's scream vanished into the baffling of the towel, which, after a few moments of lingering agony, he then spit onto the floor.

His wrist throbbed. He thought he might have refractured the bone and feared it would swell anew. He held still, holding it, hoping the noise of the cast breaking did not raise any alarms.

Jenssen remembered meeting the doctor in the hours before the departure of

Flight 903. A tourniquet was applied to his arm just below his shoulder, rendering it numb in minutes. He remembered the doctor—assuming he was in fact a licensed physician—lifting his dead arm and laying it atop the heavy workbench with his hand dangling over the edge. "Avert your eyes," said the doctor, with more than a hint of a smile in his bespectacled eyes. Perhaps the man was in fact an experienced torturer. Jenssen had turned away and closed his eyes. He heard the crunch and felt the workbench shudder, but he felt nothing. A local anesthetic was applied by syringe. Again, he felt nothing, and in a few more minutes, with his fingers swollen and red, the tourniquet was released. The dark anticipation of the pain had left him drenched in sweat, but once the pins and needles faded the anesthetic worked effectively. He was given anti-inflammatory medication for the swelling, and had his sleeve rolled back down and buttoned for him. Then he walked out to the car that would transport him to the airport.

When the renewed pain receded, Jenssen grabbed the trash can and dumped the broken cast inside, sweeping the blue shavings off the counter. He stepped into the shower and washed himself gingerly but quickly, the jets painful against his swelling left wrist.

He focused his mind away from the pain by mentally rehearsing the next few hours. He ticked off various potential disasters that might bring down the plan, anticipating them and preparing himself to avoid them.

I am safely concealed, he reminded himself. I will not fail.

Insha'Alla.

Fisk had spent a fair amount of time as an Intel cop in Bay Ridge. The streets there were as bucolic as any in the five boroughs. A light night breeze off the Verrazano Narrows was the only relief from the lingering heat of the day. This corner of Brooklyn had absorbed waves of Irish, Italians, and Norwegians—and, more recently, Arabs.

The address was only fifteen minutes away with lights and sirens, in a neighborhood that had recently been christened "Little Palestine." The JTTF called ahead to the Sixty-eighth Precinct station house, which had two units idling at Seventy-ninth and Shore Road, just a block away. No lights, no show. Not sealing off the area, but present and available if needed. Reg arrived with an interdiction team of his own, four SWAT-trained tactical officers in full extraction armor, two FBI agents, and a linguist.

The location was a converted brownstone, lights in the windows on the first and second floors. The front door was unlocked. The listing on the lobby plate for the third-floor apartment in question read "bint Mohammed," not Burnett.

Fisk waited while Reg and the FBI agents went around with the linguist, rapping on the doors of the three ground-floor apartments, then the two on the second floor. The only person who gave them trouble was an elderly woman who refused to be forced outside unveiled. She took her place sullenly on the sidewalk in front of the stoop with the other families, pointedly turning her back on the FBI agents and police detectives.

Reg said to Fisk, "What do you think? Pick it or kick it?"

Fisk said, "If she's home, there's a good

chance she knows we're here already. Bin-Hezam wanted suicide-by-cop and got his wish. So kick it. Hard."

Reg gave the signal, and the four-man interdiction team then went up the stairs in close-quarters combat formation, advancing and covering two-by-two. Boots soft on the wooden floor, commands mimed in silence. Fisk and Reg and one of the FBI agents went up one floor behind them, the linguist remaining on the stoop with the other FBI agent.

At the third-floor apartment door, one of the tactical officers unslung the heavy-weighted steel tube from his back, gripping its handles. Another man aimed a 12-gauge shotgun at the door hinges as backup, counting him down in silence.

The officer swung the breach tube hard, striking the dead bolt above the door handle. The lock plate and the door frame splintered and the door whipped open.

The other three men flooded inside. In a matter of seconds, they cleared the tiny apartment. The fourth officer signaled Reg. There was no one home.

The team flipped on light switches. The main concern now was booby traps. They cleared the place for trip wires, and only then were Fisk and Reg allowed inside.

Reg went immediately to a stack of mail upon a small corner desk. Fisk went straight to the bedroom.

There, draped over a straight-backed chair next to a single bed covered with a paisley spread, he found a deep blue burka. The room was monastically tidy. At the foot of the bed, a worn red prayer rug was neatly folded.

Fisk brought out his phone, dialing Intel. He realized he needed the spelling of her name, and walked out to join Reg.

"I need you to access the city records database," he told the agent who answered. He spelled the names "Kathleen Burnett," confirming it from her cell phone bill, and, reading from a catalog label, "Aminah bint Mohammed." "Assuming it's a name change, but need to confirm they are the same person. I need a photograph ASAP."

He hung up and went looking for photographs. The single bed and Spartan appearance said single occupant, and those people rarely put out pictures of themselves.

In the front room, between a pair of overstuffed chairs facing a small flat-screen television on a rolling table, he scanned a single bookshelf. Korans in English and Arabic, and a single photograph of a man and woman dressed for something formal standing next to a 1980s Buick sedan. Parents. Probably deceased.

Two windows, one left open approximately eight inches. A stack of newsletters in Arabic, and some newspapers. Reg booted up a small netbook plugged into the wall.

Reg said, "What do you think? Girlfriend? Handler?"

Fisk turned in a slow circle, taking it all in. He moved to the kitchen. No dishwasher, a drying rack in the sink. A short refrigerator.

The interdiction team rigged up a bungee cord, opening the fridge from around the wall. No bang. Fisk went in, wishing he had gloves on. He tugged his sleeve down over his fist and moved containers of low-fat yogurt and a deli tub of dates.

Two empty glass mason jars. He got down low, trying to see up through the wire shelf rack. He saw what looked like white crust residue in the lid threads.

He moved everybody back. To Reg he said, "Get a dog over here stat."

Applying a cast to the arm of another person was a relatively straightforward procedure. Applying a cast to one's own arm was as difficult as one-handed surgery. But Jenssen had trained for this repeatedly. Though only once with real explosive. And never with a broken wrist.

He sat near the table. His swollen arm looked pinkish gray, like dead skin abraded with a square of fine sandpaper. He rubbed it gently, indulging himself in a moment of itch relief, tempered by the tenderness of his wrist and the clotting cuts where he had punctured his skin with the tip of the steak knife.

The new cast would take three hours to fully harden. The first time he attempted this, he had applied the plaster gauze too snugly and could not tolerate the pain for even one hour before ripping it off. Now with his wrist and forearm swollen and already tender, he knew he had to be careful.

On the other hand, he would only have to stand the throbbing ache for a few short hours.

Jenssen addressed the moment of greatest peril first. He unwrapped the roll of TATP and held it in his good hand. In practice, he had used ordinary putty of a similar consistency, and once a professionally firm slab of the real thing. This substance was gummier and stickier. It clung to his fingers.

He cleared his mind and went to work. A mistake could ruin months of preparation and devotion by many people in a fiery instant.

Using both hands, though generously favoring his left, he began to work the half-pound roll of whitish-gray explosive. He stretched the substance to roughly the distance from his thumb joint halfway to his elbow. Too much squeezing with his left hand produced a stabbing pain, and he stopped, calmed himself, focused, and continued.

With the heel of his good hand, Jenssen gently and patiently flattened the explosive to a thickness of about a quarter inch. He had seen what the TATP could do, detonated by a gunshot in an abandoned barn in a field in Sweden. The image of the structure splintering in a dynamic blast of flame still made him flinch, his body remembering the shock wave from 250 meters away.

Halfway done.

The explosive clay sweated moisture as Jenssen manipulated it. He had not anticipated this. The mixture was damper than expected, weeping a substance that smelled like chemical sweat.

Did this mean that the mixture was no good? More unstable? Less effective? He wondered: Was the woman in Central Park the chemist? Had she prepared this like shortbread in her kitchen, and mismeasured an ingredient?

He couldn't concern himself with that. He continued to mold the TATP, using bathroom tissues to soak away the moisture. What had been a loaf no larger than the cardboard tube of a roll of toilet paper was now a trim sheet that would cover the heel of his hand, his wrist, and his lower forearm.

Jenssen took a break to clean up the tabletop. In the bathroom he splashed cold water on his face.

Next, he removed the cotton batting and wound a thin layer over his tingling arm, securing it with a small steel clip at the end. He had almost forgotten the fabric softener sheets, and rose to remove them from his luggage. They were to aid in masking the scent of the explosive, in case of dogs. He then laid his cotton-clad arm on the table, palm down, and with his good hand slowly peeled the sheet of explosive dough from the tabletop. It did not come off as smoothly as expected. He molded the TATP onto his left forearm, feeling it compress the cotton. Then he patched and repaired with bits left on the table.

He was sweating but had nothing handy to wipe his brow. At one point he shook his head violently, spraying sweat around him.

Jenssen took the two igniter pellets from the messenger bag. He made sure that their antenna wires were laid cleanly on the edge of the explosive, then embedded one near the heel of his hand, the other at the opposite edge. He pressed them gently but firmly, ensuring they wouldn't chafe, but also flattening them against his arm as much as possible.

It looked good. Now the plastic. The sheet of thin acetate fit his forearm well. It had to, in order to insulate the explosive from the wet gauze impregnated with plaster of paris. He pulled it from the ice bucket, shaking off excess water.

This part was most essential if his work was to stand up to scrutiny. He began at his hand, following the same pattern of winding as he had with the cotton batting. He formed a grip across his palm like the old cast, and as he wound, he transferred the layers of remaining gauze from one side of his arm to the other, passing it underneath and above.

He was most careful not to be too fastidious, and in doing so wind the gauze too tightly. The process took him a half hour.

His initial disappointment—the white cast appeared bumpy—gave way to encouragement once he regarded his work in the mirror. The makeshift cast was evenly layered around his arm. It would further set over the next few hours. Right now, it felt neither too tight nor too loose.

Then he heard a knock at his door. He swallowed to make certain his voice was clear of any audible distress. "Yes?"

"We're heading down to the lounge." It was the journalist's voice, already wobbly with drink. "Party time! Let's go, Magnus!"

The usual overfamiliarity of the liquor-addled personality. "Getting dressed. I will be along in a bit."

"If you don't, we're gonna have to bring the party to you!"

Exactly what Jenssen did not want. He listened to Frank thumping away down the hall. The original plan had anticipated and accounted for one or two fellow heroes to join him, most likely after the fact. No one expected that four other passengers would leap into the fight. Jenssen had told himself that there was increased safety in numbers, and he had faded into the group well enough, but the price paid was having to put up with their self-inflated egos.

The truth was, it was difficult to converse with pawns and treat them as equals.

In the silence that ensued, Jenssen heard the street noise rising to his window. Car horns and bus hydraulics and a faraway siren. The hotel ventilation system clicked on automatically, sending a rush of cool air at him from a vent over the door. The sounds of life.

He fingered the wireless trigger. The bomb he had just built into his cast would explode a microsecond after ignition, vaporizing every shred of his body and destroying every living thing within fifty yards of detonation. He would feel and hear nothing other than God's grace. There were many worse deaths than that.

At 11:00 P.M., the Lounge at New York Central—the Hyatt's second-floor bar, extending from the hotel façade over Forty-second Street, adjacent to the entrance to Grand Central Terminal—was full of post-theater nightcappers.

The hotel had cleared the far right corner for the heroes, and the mayor's office was picking up the tab. Antipasti, shrimp, and plates of french fries sat on the corner table. The mayor's PR person lingered just long enough for one glass of Chablis. She and Maggie and Aldrich crowed about the fireworks, then she received a text and abruptly said her good-byes.

Gersten arrived, feeling fried from a few hours of recapping the past forty-eight in cop language. DeRosier was drinking Diet Coke, still sore from his run. Patton chose to live dangerously with an on-duty O'Doul's.

Gersten's attention first went to Colin Frank, the journalist sipping a vodka-and-something while engrossed in knee-to-knee discussion with a very attentive—and aggressively attired—Joanne Sparks. Gersten wondered how that had happened, then decided it was probably Sparks's way of showing up Jenssen.

If so, the effect was not as intended. Jenssen sat at the far corner of the bar, nursing a club soda and lime. Maggie Sullivan, his other entanglement, was laughing with a male stranger while alternately watching the Yankees game on the overhead televisions.

Aldrich sipped bourbon on the rocks, chatting with Gersten and Patton. He was an amiable enough guy, more so after two drinks, and he loved to talk about auto parts. Nouvian sat next to Jenssen, drinking one of the lounge's cocktail creations, though it seemed like neither had much to say to the other.

Maggie politely excused herself from the stranger and came over to Gersten. "I'm finally one of the popular girls at the school dance!" she whispered, laughing.

"Slow down, girl!" said Gersten.

Maggie fanned herself with her hand. "It's a roller coaster, I'll tell you. I don't know what to make of myself." She sipped her Seven and Seven. "I met the president today!" she exulted. "This hand." She looked at her hand. "Who am I again?"

She was the one Gersten would miss most of all. Maybe the only one. She was the most real, somehow, and the most joyful. Gersten thought to tell her that, but now wasn't the time, and here wasn't the place.

Maggie picked up on Gersten's appreciation somehow, throwing her arm around her. "Nice to see you detectives as people, for a change."

Patton killed his nonalcoholic beer. "We got peace in the valley tonight."

Gersten smiled and nodded, because it

was expected of her. But Fisk's suspicions weighed on her mind. She sipped her water, desperate for a real drink, hoping Fisk would arrive soon.

"Everybody!" Maggie called people to attention with the ease of a woman who, as a flight attendant, had been politely but firmly instructing strangers for her entire adult life. "A toast to the nice people who have been putting up with our shit over these insane last two days. To your health."

"Here, here!" said Frank from the corner, his free hand rubbing Sparks's bare knee.

"And," said Aldrich, standing unsteadily, "to their comrades-in-arms for blasting the sand out of that terrorist today."

"To heroes everywhere!" exulted Maggie.

"Heroes," intoned all, glasses raised.

Jenssen caught Gersten's eye as the others' glasses came back down. He tipped his drink to her individually.

Gersten nodded back, then turned toward the lobby, making another quick scan for Fisk.

Aminah bint Mohammed's neighbors described her in glowing terms. Conscientious and quiet. She told people she was a nurse, and indeed had been called upon to stanch a neighbor's kitchen knife cut a few months ago, yet hadn't seemed to work or at least keep regular hours for perhaps a year or more.

No, they had never seen suspicious-looking men visiting her. They had never seen any men, or women, as guests.

Fisk took the inconvenienced neighbors' negative views of law enforcement into consideration, yet he still believed they were telling him the truth. None of them had ever heard of a woman named Kathleen Burnett.

The photograph on her expired Massachusetts-issued driver's license showed an unveiled American woman with brown, maybe reddish-brown, hair and a smiling, plain face. Her New York license under her Muslim name showed a flatly smiling, somewhat heavier woman with shorter hair. For obvious reasons, New York driver's licenses forbade veils in photographs.

He had the more recent photo sent back electronically to Intel, and was preparing an alert. He wavered on whether to call Dubin directly, and decided he probably would.

Forensic chemists were taking the mason jars to be tested. Fisk was back inside her apartment, exhaustion and bewilderment setting in, combining to make him feel as though he were in a dream. Part of him believed she might show up at any moment and walk in the door. Another part of him wondered if there was an unassuming-appearing Caucasian woman out there acting on behalf of Al-Qaeda.

Aldrich wisely made his way out of the lounge a little while later, smiling, patting shoulders, shaking hands, and making very little sense. DeRosier walked with him down the stairs, holding him by the arm, ready to catch the unstable senior citizen as he wove his way toward the elevators.

Gersten noticed Jenssen stealing looks at her, using the bar mirror. She suspected he was lingering at the bar because of her. Flattering, but also a little weird. She still hadn't heard from Fisk. When Nouvian got up to answer a phone call—"Hello, honey," he said, passing Gersten on his way out of the lounge—Gersten made her way down toward Jenssen's end of the bar.

She cruised the food table, picking through the crispy french fry butts remaining on the crumb-strewn platter like cigarettes in a dirty ashtray.

She felt Jenssen's eyes on her. So why not play the game.

She eased in next to him. The seat afforded her a better view of the street below, a good vantage point from which to watch for Fisk's approach.

"No drink?" she asked, holding up her water for the bartender to refill.

Jenssen smiled, tinkling the ice in his glass. "Pure poison. What's your excuse?"

"Still technically on duty."

"Oh? Still keeping an eye on us?"

"Still your camp counselor. Do they have camps in Sweden? Summer camps?"

"Oh, yes."

Her fresh water arrived. "So you never drink? All organic?"

"Never say never." He smiled. "But in general, I find alcohol to be a useless complication."

Gersten glanced over at the corner where Frank and Sparks were now openly making out.

"Exactly," she said, with a smile. "The world is complicated enough."

She shifted in her seat, bumping his knee accidentally. "Sorry, sorry," she said. She moved her chair back a few inches in order to ensure that it wouldn't happen again. In doing so, she felt a spot of wetness on her thigh, and at first thought she had spilled some of her water. But no— her leg had been beneath the bar ledge.

"Do you feel something under there?" she asked, bending back to see beneath the bar. She saw Jenssen's arm resting on top of his leg, the sleeve of his shirt buttoned over his fractured wrist. "Something leaking?"

"I think it's my cast," he said, pulling it halfway out for a look. "They told me to shower with it wrapped in plastic so it doesn't get wet. I had a drugstore shopping bag I thought would do the trick, but apparently I wound up soaking it."

"Oh," she said. "That doesn't sound good." She tried to get a better look, but he returned his arm beneath the table, rather protectively. "Do you want me to call around, see if we can get someone here tonight, or tomorrow morning most likely, to look at it?"

"No, it's fine. It will hold until after the ceremony."

Gersten's phone vibrated on her hip. "You're sure?" she said. "It looks sore." He was holding it oddly, almost hiding it beneath the bar, perhaps out of embarrassment.

"It is tender, but once the cast dries again it will be fine. I am certain."

Gersten checked her display. Fisk, finally. "Excuse me," she said, standing quickly. "I have to take this."

She made her way down the short flight of steps, turning left into a short corridor leading to the restrooms, seeking a quiet spot.

"Hey," she answered. "Where in tarnation are you?"

"Are you sitting down?" he said.

"No. What is it?"

She listened while he told her about the Bay Ridge apartment raid.

"She mixed the Bin-Hezam boom?" said Gersten.

"Looks that way. So where is she now? And how much more does she have?"

Gersten's head was spinning. "Maybe his call to Saudi Air . . . was for her?"

Fisk said, "If so, nobody came in late and paid cash for a ticket. Already checked. That flight's already departed. She wasn't on it."

Gersten blocked her open ear with her free hand in order to hear better. "You have her picture, though. We have a face."

"We have a face, we have two names, we have a Social Security number, an apartment full of fingerprints . . . but we don't have a location."

Gersten shook her head. She turned to scan the lobby. "So now I have to watch for a Caucasian woman . . ." She thought about the exposure of the lounge, with its glass walls and floor hanging over Forty-second Street. And a woman with a backpack full of TATP standing on the sidewalk below . . .

"I'll try to wind up The Six, or those who are left."

"You're still at the lounge?" said Fisk.

"Yeah," she said. "Waiting for you."

"Ah," he said. "No chance now."

"It's cool. You've got a job to do." As she was looking back toward the lounge, Frank and Sparks walked down the short stairway together on their way to the elevators. Sparks glimpsed Gersten on the phone and shot her what could only be termed a nasty look, leaving Gersten wondering, What the hell was that all about? "I need her photograph."

"Alert sheet should be in your inbox now."

"So she's a fundamentalist convert. Maybe a radicalized sleeper agent? An assassin?"

"If so, then her cover here is airtight. I mean, she looks for all the world like a cat lady, only substitute jihad for cats. She's involved, that's all we can know for sure. How involved? That information died with Bin-Hezam."

"So what if . . ." She let her thoughts trail away for a moment. "What if Bin-Hezam, not the hijacker, was the real distraction? What if . . . this whole weekend . . . when we thought we were tracking the real bad guy, we were chasing his decoy?"

"A double deception? It's . . . possible, I guess. At this point, anything's possible."

"You took it to Dubin?" asked Gersten.

"Had to. Waiting to hear back now."

"He's going to go public with this one. No more secret hunt."

Fisk said, "He should. This has gone too far. It's gotten out of hand. We need to find this woman."

She lost part of the word "woman" because he was getting another call.

"That's Dubin," said Fisk. "Gotta go."

"Good luck. Talk tomorrow morning if you can."

"If I can."

And he was gone.

Jenssen sat rigidly at the end of the lounge. He could no longer see Detective Gersten, who had disappeared around the back of the bar and down some stairs. He had to fight the urge to stand and observe her.

He was certain she was talking to Fisk, the other one she arrived with in Maine. The detective with dark hair and eyes, whom she seemed closer to than the others. Whom Jenssen had misled by linking Abdulraheem to Bin-Hezam in the airport lounge in Sweden.

He was the lead investigator. What was she telling him?

The Swede has changed his cast?

She had played it cool, but Jenssen could not be too careful now. His background was impeccably respectable—but if they harbored too many suspicions, they would exclude him from tomorrow's ceremony simply as a matter of precaution.

His arm ached, as with every throb against the hardening cast, the pain increased. The only reason for coming down to this gathering was to avoid suspicion caused by his absence. Now he was certain he had drawn suspicion and imperiled his mission by attending.

The shirtsleeve over his cast felt damp now. Given the pain, he imagined it was bright red with his blood, but a peek beneath the bar showed him it was clear. A combination of moisture from the setting gauze and perspiration. The faint chemical smell was masked by the musk and social desire of the lounge setting.

The flight attendant, Maggie, was the last of the group to leave, avoiding Jenssen either out of embarrassment or shame. She left with Detective Patton, chatting as casual companions. The IKEA manager,

Sparks, was the more dangerous woman of the two. Clingy, prying, predatory. Taking the flight attendant back to his room had been a most effective way to neutralize the manager's smothering desire.

And it had worked. God would forgive Jenssen for taking the flight attendant. Jenssen had been forgiven many times in the past.

So the rest of them had retired to their dreams of great fortune and fame—all to be dashed tomorrow morning. They had wasted their last night on Earth with drink and self-congratulation.

Jenssen scowled again at the old man's toast to Bin-Hezam's murder.

A few moments later Detective Gersten returned, walking the length of the bar—slowing a bit when she saw they were the last ones there. It looked like she was still distracted by her phone call.

"Late, huh?" she said.

"You look troubled."

"Do I?" She was disappointed that her expression had given her away. "Just tired. Got to get up early. So do you."

"Indeed," he said, putting forth his best

smile. "Still, I hate to see a Saturday night in the city come to an end. I am thinking I will make an exception on this fine night."

Her eyebrows rose over a grin. "An exception to what?"

"I think I might order a nightcap after all. If you will join me."

Her grin spread into a smile. She looked away, only inches, out the window behind him. Then back to him. "Magnus?" she said.

"Yes, Detective?"

"I'd like to. I really would. I'm flattered. But—I just can't."

"Can't we both make an exception to-night?" he said, smiling, pushing. He laid his good hand gently on top of hers.

She smiled at the gesture, and he saw that she was teetering on the edge of yes. But just at that moment, the clocks over the entrance to Grand Central began to chime. The twelve notes of midnight. These tones decided the matter for her, and she slid her hand out from underneath his.

"Good night, Magnus," she said.

She turned to go away, but Jenssen could not read her thoughts. What had her look said to him? That she knew? Was she toying with him? Keeping him close to her—and yet at arm's length?

He decided he could not let her go without knowing.

When he offered himself for recruitment in Malmö, they had promised him that the honor of martyrdom would be his. Jenssen, having had time to think deeply about the afterworld, wasn't convinced about the details. But dying in an act of vengeance against the Western powers that had corrupted and destroyed the lives of his family was the best way to end his own life. A desire for blood revenge ran deep in Jenssen. He embraced the dawning of the day of his own death, as he believed he'd soon be reunited with his mother and father.

When he accepted the mission, they made him memorize the martyr's prayer, which he repeated in his head as he rose from his bar chair.

Think not of those who are slain in Allah's way as dead . . . I would love to be martyred in Allah's cause and then get resurrected and then get martyred, and then get resurrected again and then get martyred and then get resurrected again and then get martyred . . .

Upstairs Gersten laid her Beretta 84FS Cheetah on her bedside table. She slipped her cell phone from its pouch inside her suit jacket and checked it for messages. Nothing more from Fisk.

She opened the scramble alert for the woman known as Aminah bint Mohammed, just to look at the convert's face. Not the face of evil. The woman's eyes said nothing. That was the scary thing, the thing that kept people like her up at night: the limitations of profiling. Not every terrorist fit the bill.

She darkened the screen to show just the clock and the date. Just a few minutes into Sunday, July 4. After Christmas, this was probably her favorite holiday. Cookouts and parades and Popsicles. It took her right back to childhood. She had a sudden craving for orange soda.

Later that day, there would be a ceremony marking the opening of One World Trade Center, the new tallest landmark in New York City. Taking the place of the ones that fell on that day that changed everything. That gave her the job she had now.

She turned and caught a look in the mirror. She pushed away a rogue strand of hair and wondered what exactly had so entranced the tall, blond, and blue-eyed schoolteacher from Sweden. Tempting, that one. Something about his face and the inflection of his translation of his own words from Swedish to English, giving them a formal politeness that contrasted with the diffidence of his personality. Perhaps, she realized, she ought to play hard to get more often.

Then she heard a knock at her door. She frowned, assuming it was either DeRosier or Patton—and if so, it meant something else was up, and bedtime was that much further away.

Or was it Fisk? A long shot, but . . .

She looked through the eyehole. None of the above.

It was Jenssen. So tall, the top of his head was not quite visible.

Christ. Apparently she hadn't been firm enough downstairs. He had crossed the line from flattery to boorishness. Time to drop the hammer on this frisky pup, and send him back to his room.

The bolt was thrown, and the door opened. Jenssen saw her stern expression and, below it, her uncovered neck.

He was on her immediately, before she had a chance to speak or cry out. He used the element of surprise to take her down fast. Even one-handed, his six-foot-four-inch, 210-pound frame was too much for her. He threw all his weight on her as the door closed behind him.

The momentary shock passed and Detective Gersten realized what was happening. She fought him, though Jenssen already had the advantage. He had her on the floor and forced his good forearm against her windpipe, up hard into her jaw. She gripped his arm with one hand, but was not strong enough to pull it away.

With her other, she balled her fist and aimed for his groin first. Then his throat.

Jenssen pushed back mightily against the top of her throat, feeling her thrashing beneath him. She kicked his legs but not with much force. He only worried about an impact to his cast, which could ignite the explosive prematurely.

She tried to call out, but her voice was caught beneath his forearm. Her eyes bulged, moving within her incapacitated head as she searched for a weapon, any-thing.

Jenssen put all his weight into her throat, grinding the top of her skull into the car-pet.

She struck him against his ear. The pain was sharp, and knocked him off balance. She squirmed out from beneath him, one hand to her throat. She was trying to scream, but only a whisper came out.

He reached for her neck again. She kicked him in the side, and he struck her temple, knocking her head into a low cabinet.

She was crawling, dragging herself around her bed toward her nightstand. And her handgun.

Jenssen gripped her leg and yanked hard, pulling her away. He climbed up her back, forcing her against the carpet. She kicked at the floor—eager to make any noise, raise any alarm. With his explosive cast held out at his side, he jammed his good arm beneath her neck, feeling the architecture of her throat as he squeezed, whispering the martyr's prayer into her ear.

PART 8

MOMENT OF SILENCE

Sunday, July 4

Fisk received a call around 6:00 A.M. from an overnight captain who had a call from one of his detectives. He had just come off a homicide in the park, near the Met. "He came in and got a look at your alert. The decedent resembles this bint Mohammed lady. Said the resemblance was strong enough that I should call."

"Dead in the park?" said Fisk, jotting it down. "Who found the body?"

"Didn't get that part. That time of night in Central Park, you probably don't wanna know."

Fisk hung up. Before he could call the Office of Chief Medical Examiner, the overnight coroner rang through to him.

"I just heard," said Fisk. "You have pictures?"

"Not for a while now. Backed up. Three suicides, a motorcycle accident, and an overdose."

Fisk knew he'd have to appear in person to make the positive ID anyway. "On my way right now," he said.

Fisk called Dubin from the cold basement on First Avenue near Thirty-second Street, beneath the pavement of the East Side.

"It's her," he said.

Dubin said, "You're sure?"

"DNA will confirm, but"—Fisk again looked at the dead eyes staring out of the head protruding from unzipped plastic—"it's her. Strangled in Central Park. Time of death, approximately twelve hours ago."

"Murdered? Christ."

"Nothing found at the scene."

"Christ," said Dubin again, with more emphasis this time. "Where does it end?"

"With whoever killed her, maybe."

Dubin said, "Cameras in the park? I'm assuming there's zero witnesses."

"Cameras take time. The One World Trade Center dedication starts in two hours."

"You still think it's that?"

"I can't imagine what else it could be."

Dubin said, "Am I missing something? About how all this makes sense?"

"Same thing we're all missing. There's a piece we haven't seen yet."

"Goddamn it. Next step?"

Fisk shook his head, at that moment the only living person in an overlit room of seven corpses lying on seven stainless steel tables. "Call off the bint Mohammed alert. Raise the threat level."

Dubin said, "Raise it to where? We're already doing traffic checkpoints looking for car bombs. We've got men with automatic weapons stationed all over lower Manhattan. We towed away parked cars all day yesterday. Rounded up undesirables midweek. We're running random bag searches, radiation detectors. And a cell phone blackout starting at eight A.M. down around Ground Zero."

Fisk waited patiently for him to finish the

list. "If this is about the boom, one pound or thirty isn't going to matter to that building. The target isn't the structure itself."

"It's something to do with the ceremony," said Dubin. "Terrorism is theater. And the curtain rises in two hours."

At 6:30 A.M., the heroes were loaded into the Suburbans in the VIP parking garage beneath the Hyatt, their motorcycle escorts' engines burbling outside the already-raised chain-link gate.

Secret Service agent Harrelson was back with them today. He came up to DeRosier and Patton after spending some time with his finger pressed against the radio in his ear. "We gotta get moving," he said.

Patton hung up his phone. "Still nothing."

"Her cell?" said DeRosier.

"What?" said Harrelson.

Patton said, "Gersten, the other detective. Can't raise her." To DeRosier, he said, "I tried the room phone a couple of minutes ago."

DeRosier needlessly checked his watch. If The Six didn't get down to Ground Zero in time, it was their jobs. "Maybe she got hung up in the lobby, getting coffee?"

Harrelson shook his head. "We've got a specific window for penetrating the security bubble downtown. We miss it, we're fucked. All of us. So we're not gonna miss it."

DeRosier said to Patton, "I'm not getting written up because she decided to sleep in. When did she leave the bar last night?"

Patton shook his head. "She wasn't there when I left. But I don't remember her saying good night either."

"Ask Jenssen," said a voice from the lead Suburban.

The Intel detectives turned. The rear window was halfway down, and DeRosier looked inside and saw Joanne Sparks sitting forward in her seat, her head in her hands. Hungover.

"What's that?" asked DeRosier.

"Ask Mr. Sweden where Gersten is."

DeRosier and Patton exchanged looks,

then went and did just that. Patton tapped on the closed window of the second Suburban, and it was lowered. Journalist Frank sat with his head tipped back, sunglasses on. Maggie Sullivan sat on one side of him, Magnus Jenssen on the other.

"Mr. Jenssen?" said Patton.

"Yes?" answered the Swede, looking apprehensive.

"We're wondering, do you know what time Detective Gersten left the lounge last night?"

He thought about it, then slowly shook his head. "She left to take a call on her telephone at one point. I never saw her come back. I left a short time later."

Patton and DeRosier nodded, backing off. "Okay. Just wondering. Not a problem. Thanks."

They stepped away, not wanting to get the group riled up over nothing. Harrelson looked over at them from the first vehicle. They nodded to him.

DeRosier said, "I'll call Fisk en route, let him know."

Patton climbed into the front passenger seat of the second Suburban. From the back, Maggie asked him what was wrong.

"Nothing," he answered. "Just looking for Detective Gersten. Could be she went in ahead of us," he lied.

Agent Harrelson climbed into the middle row, sitting in front of Jenssen. As they pulled out of the garage, Jenssen eavesdropped on Harrelson's coded exchanges with the Secret Service detail at the first checkpoint.

Except for the missing Gersten, everything was going according to plan.

Fisk zoomed up FDR Drive and was on the Queensboro Bridge on his way to Queens when DeRosier finally reached him. "Gersten didn't make the trip."

Fisk said, "What? Why not, what's wrong?"

"Don't know. What's wrong is she was a no-show. We couldn't wait. Not answering her phone."

Fisk was not expecting this. He tried to think of the last time he spoke with her. "Nothing happened overnight?"

"No. Nothing to speak of."

Fisk knew she wasn't one to oversleep. "No word at all?"

"Nada."

"You knock on her door?"

"Couldn't. No time. Didn't realize she wasn't coming down until too late. And this leg of the journey is the Secret Service's show."

"Okay. So you guys are gone."

"We are in the chute."

"No worries. I'll follow through. You guys got the update on bint Mohammed?"

"Another dead Muslim," said DeRosier. "Not the kind of pattern you want to see on a day like this."

"Listen, stay alert, okay? Look sharp."

"You think The Six are at risk?"

"Somebody on that dais is. You and Patton have a privileged vantage at this thing. I don't know what we're looking for, but chances are you'll be in the best position to see it."

"Shit. All right. You got it."

Fisk rang off. Trying her cell was the most obvious first thing to do. His call went right to voice mail.

"It's me," he said. "Where are you? Call."

He hung up and checked his call register, remembering trying her once late last night, getting her voice mail. That was at 12:13 A.M.

No call back from her. No text. No nothing.

Not that unusual, the gap in communication. But now it formed an inconvenient hole in time.

He tried his own apartment landline. Covering every base.

After four rings, voice mail.

"Hey. It's me. Trying you here. Give me a call."

He was off the bridge, and now faced with a decision. Either go back to Intel, make one last run at his rakers for street information, and keep waiting for Gersten to announce herself. Or check on her back at the hotel.

It went without saying that he truly had no time for this errand. But in the end, the two choices melded. There was that little voice inside of him saying that the two were related.

Fuck it, he thought, hating to give in to the paranoia. He switched on his grille flashers and banged a U-turn.

* * *

Fisk dodged a few early Sunday travelers towing suitcases to the reception desk, making his way to the row of a dozen golden elevator doors. One opened to his right and he pushed inside, half expecting to find Gersten exiting, instead making way for an attractive woman with a Prada shoulder bag who glared at him with the hard-edged confidence of a hooker on her home turf.

The doors opened on the twenty-sixth floor. Fisk turned left into the hallway, and realized that he did not know Gersten's room number. He ducked into the hospitality suite and found a woman clearing away food-stained dishes. He asked her if she knew anything about the room arrangements on that floor, and she answered him in a dialect of Spanish that Fisk did not understand.

He quickly went back down to the front desk. A young female clerk examined his shield and summoned security. A thin, almost frail-looking man who looked about twenty-five emerged from a door behind registration, wearing gray slacks, a blue blazer, and regimental striped tie. Fisk guessed that Sunday mornings were the training shifts for new hires.

This guy had a clip-on ball microphone on his lapel, the black wire running from the back of his neck to an ear bud. He took a look at Fisk's credentials a beat longer than he needed to, and pretended not to be intimidated.

"What can I do for you, Detective Fisk?"

"You have a master key, right?"

"Of course."

"Gersten, Krina. Twenty-sixth floor. Under her name, or maybe registered to NYPD or the mayor's office."

The clerk found it and looked up. "Twenty-six forty-two."

"She didn't check out, anything like that?"

"No, sir. And the room hasn't been cleaned yet."

"Last accessed?"

"Last room card read was . . . twelve-oh-seven A.M., this morning."

"Let's go," said Fisk, starting back to the elevators at a brisk pace.

The young security guard followed close behind. "Can I ask what this is about?"

Fisk ignored the question until they were alone aboard an up elevator with the doors closed.

"You know who is registered on twenty-six?"

"Yes. The airline heroes. The Six."

"A detective assigned to their security detail is . . . is missing." The word bumped Fisk. It was difficult for him to say. Was she missing? If Fisk walked into her room and she was sacked out in bed—who would be more embarrassed, Gersten or him?

"When you say missing . . ."

"I don't know if she's missing. She missed her ride this morning, I know that much. And I have very little time. So let's go see, okay?"

The guard picked up on Fisk's anxiety and just nodded. As they watched the numbers rise, something occurred to him. "I have to let somebody know what I'm doing," said the guard suddenly. "That okay?"

Fisk nodded. "Sure."

The guard tilted his head toward his lapel mic. "This is Bascomb. I am keying into room . . ."

"Twenty-six forty-two."

"Twenty-six forty-two. I am with an NYPD officer—I mean, detective—at his request." Bascomb turned toward the corner camera. "Yes, George. I saw the man's badge. Fisk. Intelligence Division. I'm not sure." The doors opened, Bascomb following Fisk down the hallway. "I'll let you know. Not at this time. I will advise."

At the door, Bascomb pulled out the master key card attached to his belt by a lanyard. He slid it through the slot, and the interior lock whirred, the light turning green. Fisk opened the door, Bascomb stepping back to allow him to enter first.

Fisk stopped a few steps inside. He did a preliminary scan of the room, then realized he was looking at this as a crime scene.

The bed had been roughed up, the pillows dented. It looked slept in. No lights on, windows closed, television off. No sign of a struggle or anything amiss. Just an empty hotel room.

Still, Fisk had a tight feeling in his gut. A psychic scent. The feeling that something bad had happened here.

Fisk took a few more steps inside. Bascomb appropriately hung back. On the dresser to Fisk's left was a handful of change next to a half-empty bottle of designer water from the minibar. A metal corkscrew sat on the desk blotter.

"You don't have any gloves, do you?"

Fisk asked, hating these words as they left his mouth. But he was a cop, and any enclosed space had the potential to become a crime scene. And too many cases were lost forever due to the arriving officer's clumsy first steps.

"No," said Bascomb, a note of worry in his voice.

"Fuck," said Fisk, more about the general situation than the lack of gloves. "Do me a favor, Bascomb, and stay right where you are, okay?"

"Yes, sir."

"Thank you."

Gloves or no gloves, Fisk went to the dresser. He opened the six drawers one at a time. Gersten's underwear and two unopened packages of panty hose lay in the first one. A sweater, a folded white blouse, and a pair of blue jeans lay in the second. The rest were empty.

Fisk found her carry-on suitcase in the closet, closed but unzipped. He pawed through it quickly, finding nothing of note.

He walked to the side of the bed, studying the carpet for signs of disturbance or staining. Nothing.

On the nightstand was the usual iPod

dock and digital radio combination alarm clock. He opened the drawer in the night-stand, finding a Bible and various table tents advertising hotel services. He had seen Gersten do that before, gathering up the triangle brochures upon check-in and stuffing them into a drawer, out of sight. Seeing this familiarity gave Fisk a burst of optimism.

Inside the bathroom, he found a stack of fresh towels on the rack. No used ones on the floor. Clean water in the bowl. He recognized the flowered pouch Gersten used for her cosmetics and toiletries.

No puddles of water on the counter, the sink, the shower floor. Everything was dry. The bathroom showed no sign of having been used that morning.

That was troubling. Where would she go without washing her face or her hands first?

Fisk came back into the main room, avoiding Bascomb's curious gaze. Fisk decided to change it up for a moment, fo-cusing on what he had not yet found.

Her shield. Her weapon. Her phone.

He pulled his cell and checked for mes-sages from her. He dialed her again, hoping he would hear a ring if her device was somewhere in the room.

No ring. And the call went right to voice mail.

He put away his phone. His hand was shaking a little. He stood still in the center of the room. He didn't want to give in to panic, but this wasn't right. He had no evidence of foul play—none whatsoever—but Gersten was no flake.

He had always considered the fact that, in their line of business, he might have to face something like this someday, a professional incident that would cross into personal territory.

Don't get ahead of yourself. He forced himself to think like a cop.

Was this connected to everything else that had gone on that weekend? It had to be. This was too large of a coincidence.

But—as with everything else—how? What was the link? Was there something about this antiterror case that could have blown back on Gersten? Was it indeed a threat to The Six? Had she discovered something last night?

No—she would have followed up on it. She would have taken it to him, to Intel.

She would not have gone off half-cocked. Unless . . .

Unless she had stumbled upon it unknowingly.

Fisk turned to the security guard standing just inside the closed door. "Bascomb. Here's what's going to happen. I need you to alert your security group to initiate a search of the entire hotel. Start with the construction areas and any closed floors. This is going to mean inconveniencing people. This is a New York Police Department detective you're looking for. Have your group dial 911 as well so we can get some uniforms in here."

Bascomb nodded and turned to his microphone. Fisk gave him a brief description of Gersten to repeat.

When he finished, Fisk said, "Now you and I are going to open every door on this floor and check every room."

Traffic heading south through Manhattan was horrible, even with NYPD motorcycle escorts. The gridlock was such that there was nowhere for them to go. Nothing to do but wait for the clots to work themselves through.

They crawled down Seventh Avenue past Penn Station, affording everyone a look at the still-closed block on West Twenty-eighth where the terrorist Baada Bin-Hezam had been gunned down.

Then past the Fashion Institute, across Twenty-third, across Fourteenth, into Greenwich Village where Manhattan Island narrowed into the thumb of the old town. As they left behind the cool shadows of the midtown skyscrapers, the heroes became aware of the magnificence of the morning. The sky was Magritte blue, almost fairytale perfect. Sidewalk pedestrians wore sun hats, ball caps, and shorts, watching the Suburbans roll by with cups of iced coffee in their hands.

They crossed Houston Street, moving toward Canal. They rolled past a massive electronic checkpoint, demarcated by tactical operations vans, a generator truck, and rows of screening stations. People waited calmly in line, as though having taken a special vow of cooperation that morning. Despite the heat and the long wait time, no one appeared to be complaining.

Once gates were moved and the Suburbans were inside the security perimeter, movement was easier. They rolled along an open lane toward the staging area for the ceremony near Trinity Church at the intersection of Broadway and Wall Street.

Frank had the Sunday *New York Times* with him, and was reading the front section concerning the building dedication. "There's Trinity," he said, looking up at the brownstone neo-Gothic cathedral. "See the steeple? Says here it rises two hundred eighty feet. Until the end of the nineteenth century, it was the highest point in Manhattan. Now—it's this."

They looked the other way, high up toward the top of the soaring One World Trade Center. Not only New York's tallest building—including its spire, rising 1,776 feet tall in honor of the year of American Independence, it was the tallest building in the Western Hemisphere, and the third tallest in the entire world. Its sheer glass façade shimmered in the hot July sun.

"The first twenty floors above the public lobby are all base," Frank said, scanning the article. "Then sixty-nine office floors, including two television broadcast floors and two restaurants. There's an observation deck opening soon. And it's a 'green' building with renewable energy, reuse of rainwater, all that."

Maggie looked out with her hand covering her throat. "What about safety?"

"Yup. Structural redundancy, dense fireproofing, biochemical filters. Extra-wide stairs, and all the safety systems encased in the core wall. Probably the safest building in the world, I would imagine."

"Would you go up it? All the way to the top?"

"Absolutely," said Frank. "You?"

Maggie shook her head. "I think I would wait a few years. What about you, Magnus?"

Jenssen glanced at the building. "Why not?" he said.

"Ha," said Frank, still reading. "Says here there's a waiting list to become a window washer."

"*Never,*" said Maggie.

Frank folded his newspaper and said, "I'm with you on that one."

They had parked, but were kept waiting in their vehicles for a few minutes by agents in sunglasses talking into the cuffs of their suit jacket sleeves. Maggie Sullivan was wearing her flight uniform, and Magnus Jenssen took note of two pins on her lapel, one of an airliner set against the Canadian flag, one of an airliner against the American flag. He noticed the detectives wearing flag pins also.

When they were allowed out of the vehicles and assembled before the security checkpoint, Jenssen stood in line behind Maggie Sullivan.

He watched the agent run his wand over and around her legs and outstretched arms. He paid special attention when the wand passed near the twin metal pins clipped to the breast of her uniform. No beep.

He stood next, holding the same pose. The wand traced the outline of his body, over and around his left wrist, inside of which were the two short wire antennae. No reaction. Over his breast the wand *blipped* ever so softly as it crossed a pin he had put on one-handedly while dressing that morning. It depicted the flag of Sweden, given to him by the clueless ambassador aboard the aircraft carrier the day before. The screener wanded it again, just to be thorough. Another gentle *blip*.

He moved on, unaware that the device was actually registering the small trigger device inside his breast pocket, with a tiny pebble-size battery.

Jenssen stepped through. Before he could relax, however, another security agent wearing blue gloves waved him over.

"Hold out your arm for me, sir."

Jenssen extended his wounded left arm,

presenting his cast for inspection. The agent touched it very lightly, then asked him to rotate his arm at the elbow. His wrist and forearm were quite sore, but Jenssen complied, masking the pain.

"Bend it back for me, please." Jenssen bent his elbow as though about to drive it into the face of the screening agent.

The man visually examined the arm edge of the cast, then nodded.

"Thank you, sir."

When the rest were cleared, Harrelson, who had also been wanded—and who, along with the detectives, had to unload and present his sidearm for inspection—stepped to the fore.

"Hard part's over," he said. "Now everybody follow me."

Fisk went into every room on the western half of the floor, finding no one and nothing having to do with the disappearance of Krina Gersten. He then moved on to the other half of the hallway, which was closed for renovations, inspecting each room and each half-finished bathroom with the same results.

No sign of Gersten, no sign of anything amiss.

Another, more senior security guard was in the hallway now, as was a uniformed cop. Fisk returned to one of The Six's rooms, the one with the cello inside, belonging to

THE INTERCEPT   557

the musician. Nouvian had left his television on with the sound muted, and Fisk
stared absently at CNN's coverage of the
hour leading up to the memorial ceremony
at Ground Zero.

He checked his phone again, wishing
she would just call and end this thing—
thought he couldn't for the life of him imagine where she could be. He backed up his
thought process again. What did it mean
that she was gone?

If the threat involved The Six, nothing
had been accomplished here at the hotel.
They had all gotten into the cars and were
en route to the ceremony, no problem. So—
why would someone, anyone, need to put
Gersten out of the way somehow? As the
group's shepherd, she posed no direct
threat to anyone trying to harm them . . .

Unless the threat was from within.

But that defied logic. What would be the
point? One of The Six? Or—even Patton
or DeRosier?

Never mind the fact that they had their
chance to do great damage yesterday,
when they shook Obama's hand. No Al-
Qaeda agent would have passed up an
opportunity like that . . .

Unless the sitting president wasn't his or her target.

On the television screen before Fisk, former President George W. Bush and his wife, Laura, descended from a private jet at LaGuardia Airport. They shook hands with greeters at the bottom of the stairs, waved at the cameras, then disappeared into a waiting limousine with U.S. flags fluttering on the rear bumper.

Fisk stared. He thought way back to Ramstein, to the discovery of Osama bin Laden's directive, discussed in the months before his assassination. Bin Laden of course did not know he was going to die as a result of a special military operation initiated by President Barack Obama. His prime antagonist at that time was perhaps the sitting U.S. president. But his sworn enemy was the man who, in his eyes, had conducted a crusade of brutality on the Islamic world for the previous ten years.

Bin Laden's number one target was George W. Bush.

Fisk's mind reeled. The Yemeni hijacker, the elusive Saudi art dealer, and the fundamentalist convert sleeper agent in Bay

Ridge, Brooklyn. All participants—and all
decoys.

Maybe the hijacking had been ordered
to insert, not Baada Bin-Hezam into the
United States, but one or more of The Six.
The weakness they had chosen to exploit
was the American celebrity machine, and
its love for ceremony.

Fisk looked around the cellist's room.
He had gone through each of the heroes'
rooms, but quickly, searching just for clues
to Gersten's disappearance—not for indications of the presence of a terrorist.

He went back through them now, tearing
through each room, looking for something—
anything—that could support if not confirm
his theory.

Security guard Bascomb followed at a
distance, as Fisk went rifling through rooms
without explanation. Overturning mat-
tresses, emptying out luggage. Ordering
that each room safe be opened.

Bascomb said, "We're not allowed to do
that without a specific search warrant."

One hard look from Fisk persuaded him
otherwise.

Only a few were locked. Fisk was standing next to Bascomb in one of The Six's rooms, watching him key in a master code on yet another empty safe, when Fisk noticed a stain on the top of the table he was leaning against.

Closer inspection revealed that it was more like a burn in the veneer. He ran his fingers over it, feeling the roughness. He bent down and sniffed the oblong mark.

It smelled vaguely chemical.

"Whose room is this?" Fisk asked.

Bascomb did not know. While he called into his shoulder microphone to find out, Fisk went into the bathroom, checking it again, but more closely this time.

In the corner of the floor underneath the ledge of the vanity, he found a dusting of blue-colored flecks, accumulated there as though brushed away by hand.

He touched them with his fingertip. They felt hard, almost plastic.

He knew whose room it was even before Bascomb reported the answer. Fisk remembered the Swede's blue wrist cast.

"Magnus Jenssen," said Bascomb.

Blond, blue-eyed Scandinavian. Schoolteacher, was it? Fisk couldn't remember anything more specifically about Jenssen.

He knew that none of the passengers had self-declared themselves as Muslim. He also knew that the Islamic population of Sweden stood at a little more than half a million, approximately 7 percent of the population—up from nearly zero just thirty years ago. The trend was similar throughout Scandinavia and Europe.

Still, religion was only an indicator. Rarely was it the sole factor in profiles of terrorists.

His mind raced. Had the Swede truly fractured his wrist during the attempted hijacking? Or earlier, before he even boarded the aircraft?

With care, he could have hidden such an injury. The backscatter scanner at airport security would not have revealed it. The terahertz photons used in those machines were just below infrared on the frequency spectrum, and well below true X-rays.

There was no time to pursue this theory now. Fisk had to work with what he had in front of him.

A chemical in Jenssen's hotel room, staining the furniture. What could it be? Had he hidden it inside his cast?

TATP. More boom.

He wondered what sort of scrutiny the heroes would face inside the Ground Zero security bubble. The answer was: once they were inside, very little, if at all.

And, by his clock, they were already inside.

Fisk had to get down there. He had to leave this place, even with Gersten still missing.

He went to Bascomb. "Give me your phone."

The guard started to ask why, then instead simply pulled it from his belt. He turned it on and thumbed in his pass code, then handed it to Fisk.

Fisk quickly went to his contacts and punched in his own cell phone number, and his last name in all caps. So that there would be no mistakes. He thrust the phone back at Bascomb.

"I could give this to the cop, but I'm giving it to you. If they find anything about the missing detective, you call me right away. It's critical, understand?"

Bascomb responded with a trembling nod.

Fisk ran to the elevator.

* * *

Fisk had left his car at the cabstand with his grille lights flashing. He realized he didn't have DeRosier's number, so he first tried Dubin.

Immediate voice mail. Fisk dialed Intel directly.

They told him that Dubin was down at Ground Zero. Cell phone service within the bubble had been jammed in order to prevent any remote control bombs being detonated using cellular technology, a favorite tactic of terrorists and insurgents.

Fisk informed them about Gersten's apparent disappearance. He said that The Six had to be sequestered for their own safety—phrasing it that way because, without Fisk there personally, if they tried to collapse on the heroes with force, Jenssen could detonate immediately, killing everybody within range.

If, like Bin-Hezam, he had a half pound of TATP on him, the death toll would be incredible.

He told them to do everything they could to get the message out, then asked to be patched through to DeRosier's cell phone. That call also went immediately to voice mail—confirming that The Six were already inside the security bubble, and Jenssen with them.

Fisk leaned on his horn, grille lights flashing, willing the traffic to move. He was now in a race against time and gridlock to get from midtown down as close to Ground Zero as he could.

"Holy shit!"

Flight attendant Maggie Sullivan came bursting into the hospitality trailer where the rest of the group, as well as their minders, Detectives DeRosier and Patton and Secret Service agent Harrelson, were waiting with some other VIPs.

Maggie held up her hands as though about to burst into song. "Paul Simon just shook my hand on my way back from the Porta-Potty."

A woman from the mayor's office said, "He's here to sing 'The Sound of Silence' at Mayor Bloomberg's request."

"He recognized me," said Maggie, amazed. "Me! He said, 'Great job.' *Great job!* I was tongue-tied."

Sparks said, "I hope he washed his hands."

Jenssen sat deeply at the end of a suede-covered couch. A flat-screen television played on the opposite wall, above a small buffet with chafing dishes of Vermont maple bacon, a strata with sausage and egg-soaked bread, hash brown potatoes, and French toast. Carafes of coffee and orange juice were set before trays of cardboard cups.

The pain in his arm was intense. He had neglected to take any ibuprofen, and now the swelling beneath his bomb-laden cast was radiating pain into his fingertips. Droplets of blood appeared from the seam of his palm, which he was discreetly swiping onto the suede fabric beneath the sofa.

The pain was a significant distraction, forcing him to retreat into prayer. It was his sole consolation, yet it isolated him from the rest. He felt their scrutiny and wondered how much of it was mere paranoia on his part.

He focused also on the television images. The Americans had memorialized their own defeat with two giant holes in the ground at the foundations of the destroyed Twin Towers. The inside of each was sheathed in black stone, the names of the dead etched into panels at waist level along their perimeters. Water ran down all four sides of each hole, emptying into reflecting pools at their bottoms.

The view shifted to show the new tower, rising into the sky. Jenssen, for his part, saw it as a headstone.

The camera panned a surrounding garden of oak trees and pathways to the ceremony dais. Tiers of platforms were flanked by a pair of giant broadcast screens like those seen in sporting arenas. Panels of bulletproof glass walled the speaker's podium at the center. A choir of singers attired in long blue robes stood in ranks to the left and right of the podium.

Jenssen shivered once, due to both the pain and the profundity of the moment. The spirit of hundreds of millions of American viewers would be shattered forever after the live television assassination of their former leader. Obama and the rest were in play as collateral damage, but not necessary. Jenssen had shaken the man's hand yesterday. He had looked into his eyes and smiled. He had done all this with murder in his heart.

He did not have to assassinate Obama. In the days and weeks and months to come, the photograph of the sitting U.S. president shaking the hand of an Al-Qaeda terrorist would be his undoing.

All he cared about was the infidel Bush. He was somewhere near Jenssen right now—perhaps already within blast range.

A new streak of pain up to his shoulder shook him, Jenssen going rigid and briefly leaning forward in compensation. He wished to leave the cramped trailer for fresh air, but he remained inside the trailer where it was safe.

Explosive-sniffing dogs concerned him. He needed to remain sheltered until the last possible minute.

There had been contingency plans. If Jenssen and other passengers on the plane had for some reason not achieved the celebrity status anticipated to get him onto this stage, then Jenssen's orders were to get as close to the ceremony as he could and detonate. If, today, he had attracted too much scrutiny at the security checkpoint, he would have detonated immediately. Even if he had failed to get Bush, the explosion would have led to many casualties and reminded the United States that it was not invulnerable.

But everything had gone close enough to plan. All he had to do now was remain alert and focused in the face of increasing agony from his improperly cast arm—and he would succeed with glory.

"Magnus?" Maggie Sullivan sat next to him, on the edge of the couch in her uniform and blue cap and flag wings. "Are you all right?"

"Fine," he said, a terribly incompetent response. "Overwhelmed."

"Sure," she said, understandingly. "You look ill, though."

"Tired." Go away, you heathen bitch.

She touched his knee gently. "Before things get too crazy and we go our separate ways, I just wanted to take the opportunity again to thank you for saving my life—for being the first to act. I really . . . I think you are an amazing person. Your courage, I'm in awe of it. And . . . as to what happened between us, two nights ago . . . I don't regret it, I just . . . I don't know if it's complicated things, or what. But I want you to know that it hasn't changed my opinion of what you did. I was feeling . . . well, I don't know what I was feeling. It's a little embarrassing, but I'm okay with it—I just hope you are too."

He swallowed with difficulty, the throbbing of his arm accompanied by a kind of screaming in his head. "Yes, yes," he said abruptly.

She nodded, waiting for more. "Are you sure you're . . . ?"

He nodded quickly.

"Okay," she said, offended—but done. "I'll leave you alone then," she said, and stood, stepping away from the sofa.

He resisted an urge to howl. He checked his left palm, and smeared a bit more blood on the underside of the sofa.

On television they were showing a child pointing up at the new monument of America. Jenssen had been the child of a pariah, a refugee woman who never ascended from the trappings of poverty, despised in a country where poverty was nothing less than a sin. Magnus grew up in the brick hives of immigrant ghettos, where every race hated every other race. His growth spurt came late, after years of childhood bullying. He knew what it was to live in constant fear. To escape further bias and beatings, he and his mother worshipped as Muslims in secret, alone in a largely Christian ghetto. After two years in a manual trade school, studying highway surveying and engineering, he instead pursued school-teaching as his profession. It was a way to live quietly and at the same time pursue his own self-education—his true avocation—in solitude.

Removing this evil from the earth—Bush, the radical Christian leader of the American crusade against Islam, the unprincipled thug—was the greatest victory a martyr could claim. Taking Obama at the same time—were it to be God's plan—was an added glory. The sitting president was a man who had heard Islam's voice and turned from it. Curse both of them to hell.

Jenssen again trembled in pain. He had reviewed their approach on the way in. They would follow a pathway through the tree garden, over which a pipe scaffolding covered with blue tarpaulin had been constructed. This was so that during their walk to the stage, the president, former president, and fellow dignitaries would be shielded from potential snipers in any of the thousands of windows overlooking the Ground Zero construction site.

Jenssen reached into his jacket pocket, having transferred the trigger mechanism there. He fondled the small plastic rectangle, running his thumb over its simple switch.

The components were virtually foolproof. The trigger was a simple inertial generator, sending a single pulse of electricity to the wire antennae of the twin igniters. Only one of the igniters had to work. There would be a gap of about a half second between the trigger and the flash: a blue blast from his arm, then a rush of flame consuming all oxygen in the air.

In that split second, all would die.

His thumb pressed against the trigger, toying with it. The fire in his arm was such that he could not wait to detonate and be free of pain. His vision of becoming the most glorious religious martyr in the history of the world was the only thing that allowed him to rise above the weakness of his flesh.

The mayor's office's liaison entered. She was going over arrangements after the building dedication. Jenssen smiled grimly before tuning her out. There was nothing to arrange after the ceremony. Jenssen would take care of all that.

THE INTERCEPT   579

Fisk was still in the car four blocks from Chambers Street when his phone rang.

"Uh, hi. Detective Fisk?"

Fisk's heart sunk. "Bascomb. What do you got?"

"We, uh . . . somebody, a guest, reported seeing a woman's shoe out on the lower-level roof in back of the hotel."

A chill ran up Fisk's spine. "You found a shoe?"

"We went out and got the shoe . . . and we found a woman's body."

Fisk blanked out. He was still driving but he wasn't seeing anything and he could not speak. He had to remind himself to breathe.

"I said . . . we found a woman's body. On the roof. It looked like a suicide, until we saw her throat. Really badly bruised."

"Are you sure it's . . . ?"

"We found an empty gun nearby. A Beretta. Somebody said a service piece. I . . . I took a picture and just sent it to this number as a text. I hope that was okay. If you want to . . ."

"Hold on," said Fisk, nearly a whisper.

He worked his phone to his messaging queue. He opened the one from Bascomb.

It showed Krina Gersten lying against a bed of roof gravel. Her eyes were open, her upper neck purpled with deep contusions.

Fisk stared at the image for a long time. Somehow when he looked up, he was still driving, and hadn't crashed.

He brought the phone back to his ear. "What are they doing for her?" he asked.

"They're . . . it's a crime scene. I'm sorry to be—"

Fisk waited. Someone or something had cut him off. Fisk was in shock. When Bascomb didn't continue, Fisk looked at his phone display.

Dropped the call. No bars. No reception.

Because he was now inside the security cell blackout.

The traffic came to a dead stop ahead. It was a virtual parking lot in the street. With nobody honking, it only added to the unreality of the situation as Fisk sat there staring straight ahead—stricken by heartbreak.

Fisk put the car in park. He got out with his phone and walked on, abandoning the car where it was.

Despair gave way to rage, and soon he was running. She was dead. Krina was dead. She had found out something. Her murder was connected to the fucking Islamic terrorist decoy asshole motherfuckers he had been chasing all weekend.

That trail ended with The Six. Magnus Jenssen. A human bomb who was ready to detonate himself outside One World Trade Center.

Fisk reached the lines of people waiting to be screened for entry. So many people wanted to be near the new building, despite the heat. They wanted to be a part of the healing.

He had to find a way to the front. He started pushing his way through.

"Sorry, sorry." He said it in that New York way, where he didn't really mean it, but was just letting others know that he had a good reason for being rude.

He reached the front. A few grumbles but no real complaints yet. He faced dozens of police cadets wanding for weapons. Fisk picked out the youngest and approached him with his badge wallet held at shoulder level, right in the cadet's eyes.

"I'm sorry, Detective," said the kid. "Nobody armed gets inside this morning. That's right down from the commissioner. Even your shield won't get you in with a piece."

"Your lieutenant. I need him. Now." Fisk was breathing heavily, not from the exertion of running but from hyperventilating with emotion.

Now people started to get on Fisk for holding up the line. "Hey, what is this?" "Who the hell is this guy?" "Commmmoonnnnnnnnnn."

A patrol lieutenant in dress blues walked up, expecting trouble. Fisk read him in a glance. Old school, not terribly bright, honest. A cop's cop. Showed up every day, made no waves, took all the tests and made lieutenant. The guy looked at Fisk's credentials and repeated what the cadet said.

"Not getting in with a piece," he said. "Nobody enters with a weapon after seven A.M. No exceptions."

Fisk felt himself getting shrill, and pulled back, keeping in control. Asking these guys to let him pass with his firearm was asking them to put their careers in his hands, something that wasn't going to happen.

"I gotta get in there," said Fisk. He showed the lieutenant his open hand. "Lou. Look at me. I'm reaching."

The lieutenant looked suspicious. "Okay. Slow."

Fisk went into his jacket and pulled out his Glock 19. He turned it butt-first, slid out the magazine, kicked out the round in the chamber. He handed it all to the lieutenant.

"Good?" said Fisk.

The lieutenant still wasn't sure. "St. Clair," he said. "Wand him."

St. Clair did. Fisk was clean for metal.

"Okay?" said Fisk.

The lieutenant took the wand from St.

Clair. "You accompany Detective Fisk wherever he is going. When you get him there, you report back to me on the double. Clear?"

"Yes, sir," said young St. Clair.

"He is to remain in your line of sight at all times. Clear?"

"Yes, sir," St. Clair said again.

"Good?" the lieutenant said to Fisk.

"Good," said Fisk.

Before the lieutenant had even finished nodding, Fisk was through the checkpoint and running at a loping trot down Greenwich Street, trying to figure out which way to go.

St. Clair sprinted after him, catching up with him before Vesey Street at the very perimeter of Ground Zero.

Fisk heard the strains of the NYPD Pipe and Drum Band running scales, warming up. They were to play a medley of patriotic tunes during the live broadcast.

Hearing them meant that he was close. And that the ceremony hadn't started yet.

Even the upbeat song sounded like a dirge. Fisk had always hated bagpipes. Bagpipes meant cop funerals to him.

Gersten loved bagpipes. This memory struck him with the force of a cramp. She always teared up. Must have been that cop gene of hers.

Across Vesey, the crowd thickened into a shoulder-to-shoulder mass that was difficult to see over. The entrance on the north side of the Ground Zero memorial was a hundred yards ahead. Fisk knew he had to stop The Six from going into the ceremony proper, because once the players were in place, then the central podium area would go into full lockdown—with Jenssen sealed in place, ready to blow them all to kingdom come.

More than a hundred plainclothes NYPD officers, FBI men, and Secret Service agents meandered among the throng. Fisk darted into the crowd, quickly outpacing St. Clair, who yelled behind him, "Wait, wait!"

Fisk ran toward the sound of the bagpipes. Tears burned his eyes. To his distant left, he saw a blue tunnel leading from a small staging area full of trailers.

He heard yelling and noticed a few of the lawmen pointing him out. Others began running in his direction. He hoisted his shield high as he went so as not to be shot down.

His anxiety was electric, apparently; it

drew people his way. He was yelling, "Fisk! Intelligence Division!" because no one there knew him, and even if they did, they could barely see his face as he darted around strangers in his path.

As he got closer, he saw that the tunnel was merely a series of tarps knit together, lashed to arched pipe scaffolding, the fabric rippling in the Hudson River breeze. Fisk looked left and made for the staging area.

"Hey, hey, hey!" said a cop as Fisk blew another security barricade without stopping. He gave up showing his shield. Imitation tin was just a couple of dollars online.

What Fisk had going for him was his years on the job: he looked "cop." That, more than his shield, was what kept fellow officers from shooting at him on sight. He ran past a quartet of Porta-Potties and a hospitality tent manned by support staff. He darted around civilians wearing access passes on neck lanyards, searching wildly, then he saw a trailer with an open door.

In the window of the trailer, propped up against the drawn shade, was a printed sign reading, THE SIX. Fisk raced to the door and burst inside.

Food table, empty couches, a television.

Empty.

A person ran to the trailer door behind him. Fisk whirled around.

It was a cop with his sidearm drawn. Patton.

"Fisk?" he said.

"Where are they?" said Fisk.

"They're . . . on their way in," said Patton, pointing. "Where's Gersten?"

"Obama? Bush?"

"Outside the core. They go in last."

Fisk grabbed Patton and spun him around, pushing him out of the trailer door. "Keep them out of here!" he said. "However you can. We have a man with a bomb!"

In any other setting, such a claim would require further evaluation. But in this tinderbox of antiterror paranoia, such a warning was treated as verified until proven inaccurate.

Fisk leaped off the top step of the trailer, waving gathering cops out of his way. The pipes and drums had started their medley, being carried throughout the staging area via speakers.

He looked to the blue tarpaulin archway tunnel ahead. The crowd parted a bit, just enough for him to see and recognize the older man starting inside. Aldrich, the auto parts dealer, was entering the ten-foot-wide tunnel. Behind him went the journalist, Frank. Walking one at a time, like entrants at a wedding. Alphabetically. Which meant that . . .

Fisk saw the next entrant, tall and blond, wearing a light blue suit. A coordinator wearing a headset nodded to Magnus Jenssen.

With a long, determined stride, the Swedish terrorist started into the tunnel.

Fisk glimpsed Jenssen's left hand. The part of his cast visible beneath the sleeve of his suit—it was white. It was not blue.

Fisk yelled, but his voice was drowned out by the music of the pipes. Jenssen was on his way to the stage.

To Jenssen's ears, the bagpipers' bleating was like the furious drone of an overturned beehive. It sawed into his head. His left arm was little more than a weapon grafted onto his torso now—and one his body was rejecting.

He was in the blue tunnel. Fabric rippled as each plodding step brought him closer to glory. Ten paces ahead, the journalist Frank swept his hand through his hair, grooming himself as he made his way toward the stage.

Jenssen stumbled once from the dizzying pain. He was carried along by the will of God and the generous spirit of Osama, who through Jenssen was returning to the altar of victory as a marauding soldier of Allah, at the site of his greatest victory.

. . . and then get resurrected and then get martyred . . .

Ahead of him: daylight.

Ahead of him: glory.

The vague sounds of a commotion behind him barely breached the great commotion ongoing inside his own head. Was it about him? If so, they were too late.

He was inside the heart of the beast. He had reached its soft, sentimental core.

He pulled the trigger from his pocket with his good hand and rubbed it with his thumb like an amulet, a holy object.

Fisk was yelling Jenssen's name when law enforcement converged on him, stopping him before the entrance to the tunnel.

That was as far as he could go. No one entered the chute who wasn't cleared to be on the stage. He could have persuaded them eventually, but there wasn't enough time. Fisk backed away from the hands that wanted to restrain him. "He's in there!" yelled Fisk, past all sense now.

Alain Nouvian, the cellist, was next to go in. He turned in alarm at what was happening, recognizing Fisk. He said to the nearest official, "That's one of our police detectives."

The coordinator was lost in her headphones, the ceremony's choreography the defining principle of her life at that moment. "Go," she told him. "Now!"

Nouvian, unsure, did as he was instructed, starting slowly into the tent, checking back over his shoulder.

Joanne Sparks and Maggie Sullivan joined the fray near Fisk, echoing Nouvian's words. "What's happening?" said Maggie. "Where's Detective Gersten?"

The mention of her name gave Fisk a sudden burst of strength. He pulled away from the cops and raced around the two female heroes, in essence using them to set a pick, allowing Fisk to get free and go around the entrance to the side of the tunnel.

He ran along it, trying to guess Jenssen's position inside. He shielded his head with his arm and cut sideways into the tunnel, bracing for impact against the unseen metal rib cage.

He struck a cross-pipe just a few inches away from a conjoined vertical post. The force of his impact ripped the blue tarp from the side bar, setting the entire tunnel wriggling like a giant blue worm.

The pipe held firm, but exposed a weakness at a connecting joint above, dislodging the frame.

Fisk fell sprawling into the tunnel, landing hard on the gravel path. He looked up fast and saw a body stumbling to the side. The dislodged pipe had struck Jenssen on the right side, nearly throwing him to the ground.

Fisk righted himself. Jenssen did not. He looked up, wild-eyed, his cast hand held out from his side, his right hand open and empty.

He was searching the gravel path around him frantically.

Fisk slipped on the gravel with his first step toward the larger man.

Five paces behind Jenssen, Nouvian stood in shock. He was looking down at something at his feet.

A small white device lay in the gravel. He started to reach for it.

It was the trigger.

Fisk yelled at him, "Don't touch it!"

But Nouvian already had it in his hand. He straightened, examining the strange device—then saw Jenssen running at him.

The Swede let out a howl, charging the cellist like a bull.

Nouvian's eyes saw Fisk beyond Jenssen, pointing, yelling, "No!" Then back to Jenssen coming at him.

The cellist's eyes cleared of all confusion. As Jenssen reached him, Nouvian tossed the trigger device away, toward Fisk.

Jenssen crushed into Nouvian, driving him to the ground in an open-field tackle.

Fisk caught the trigger with both hands, receiving it as gingerly as a newly laid egg. Jenssen turned from where he was crouching on top of Nouvian, seeing that the device was in Fisk's hands now.

He got up, then pitched hard to one side, holding his cast arm as he staggered.

Fisk saw that the Swede was near delirious with pain and panic.

Jenssen pitched himself toward Fisk, attempting another mad dash. But after a few uncertain, unbalanced steps, Jenssen stopped.

Voices echoed in the rippling tunnel now. Police were rushing toward them from the staging area. People were massing outside the tarpaulin, pressing against the fabric walls.

They were closing in. Failure was collapsing on Jenssen.

He held out his broken wrist, looking at the explosive cast. Fisk saw blood dripping off the man's fingertips to the ground.

Gunfire now. Two rounds thumped the ground near them, tearing through the tarp.

Somebody had given the sharpshooters orders to fire blindly into the tunnel in an attempt to stop the threat.

Fisk remembered that TATP could be ignited three ways: electronic pulse, fuse, or impact.

Jenssen knew that he could not reach the trigger in Fisk's hand in time. Now he turned, looked for the source of the gunfire. He wanted suicide-by-cop like his comrade Bin-Hezam.

Only—Jenssen wanted impact on his arm. He wanted detonation.

Fisk saw a wild thought come into the terrorist's blue eyes. The Swede, who had killed Gersten, stepped to the side of the tunnel. There, he reared his forearm over his head.

Fisk started toward him but could not close the gap in time.

Jenssen brought his cast down full-strength against one of the metal support bars.

A massive *crack* . . . but no flash. No explosion.

The pain from this desperate act crippled Jenssen. He fell to his knees as though struck, holding his cast out in front of him as though it were consuming his arm.

For the moment he had lost all awareness of Fisk.

Fisk lowered his shoulder, hurling himself at Jenssen. He struck him low against his ribs, laying him out. The terrorist stared up at the wind-rippled ceiling of the tunnel. He was trying to get his cast arm up. He was still trying to detonate.

Fisk gripped Jenssen's elbow, forcing the cast back into the terrorist's throat. He had seen the bruises on Gersten's neck. Fisk was choking him with his own weapon of mass destruction.

The terrorist's eyes bulged and his lips turned blue, his mouth open, breathless.

Fisk used his free hand to reach into his

pocket. Not for the trigger. He found his phone and held it before the terrorist's dying eyes.

He wanted him to see. Gersten's picture. Krina's dead body.

Fisk wanted this to be the last thing Jenssen would ever see.

Krina Gersten was posthumously promoted to Detective First Grade. She was buried six days later on a knoll overlooking the Verrazano Narrows at St. Peter's Cemetery on Staten Island. Police officers from all across the city and the country attended the Saturday morning service, more than a thousand men and women in full-dress uniform.

The NYPD Pipe and Drum Band played "Amazing Grace." Fisk didn't hate the bagpipes. Their song was beautiful. Their plaintive cry was his cry.

The long blue line of mourners filed

past the open grave and Gersten's griev-
ing mother. The Six—now five—attended,
though Fisk tried to avoid any contact with
them.

They were obviously devastated, both
by the death of a person they had come to
know and by the duplicity of a person they
had believed to be one of them.

The flight attendant, Maggie Sullivan,
was especially shaken. As was the cellist,
Alain Nouvian. He was the only one who
made a point of seeking out Fisk, perhaps
guessing at his relationship with Gersten.
Nouvian's arm hung in a muslin sling,
thanks to his scuffle with Jenssen. He had
broken his hand, and his future with the
New York Philharmonic was in doubt.

His status as an American hero twice
over was not.

Later, Fisk shared a private moment
with Gersten's mother, following the long
and emotionally exhausting tribute. Afterward he honestly could not recall a word
either of them had said. The way Jenssen
had felt when the pain in his improperly
set arm overloaded the nerves throughout
his entire body—that was how Fisk felt
now. He too wished he could self-detonate.

Fisk found Dubin standing with the commissioner after the service. Fisk had been out that entire week.

"I don't know if I can come back," he told his boss.

Dubin laid his white-gloved hand on Fisk's uniform shoulder. "Take some more time. You'll come back. We need you."

Fisk did not respond. He had stared into the icy blue eyes of a fanatic. He had crushed his windpipe. But nothing had ended, he knew that. Like a virus, the killing desire had merely jumped into a new host. The defeat of one soldier of jihad gave rise to ten more.

Fisk's biggest regret was not having killed Jenssen. He almost did. He would have, if not for the cops who converged on them, dragging Fisk away from Jenssen's unconscious form. They had saved his life, but not his arm. Jenssen was in a military cell now. His arm had been amputated. Supposedly he had already given his interrogators information on the terror cell in Scandinavia, Nordic-looking jihadists existing beyond the limits of crude profiling techniques. The future of antiterrorism had begun its segue from ethnic and religious power struggles toward conflicts of pure ideology.

Fisk didn't care. The big picture didn't interest him anymore. This was a war waged by damaged individuals, making victims of the innocent. Trying to be the catcher in the rye, as Fisk had, was insanity.

Then again, despite the Sisyphean aspect of the job, somebody had to do it. Or at least try.

A few days later, Fisk found himself inside the Metropolitan Museum of Art, staring at Monet's sunflowers. He remembered how it all started, back in that hangar on the airfield at Ramstein Air Base: the digital images that hid the messages to and from bin Laden.

Fisk wasn't what you would call a museum-going person, but this was as good a place as any to try to figure out his life. Gersten's life had ended forever, and it wouldn't seem right to him if his didn't veer off in some unknown direction now. That is what occurred to him as he thought about the digital rendering of this artist's vision of an object in nature.

No one knew about him and Gersten.

That was a good thing. It allowed him to mourn her alone, and at his own pace. But that was also a bad thing. Everyone understood that he was distraught over the loss of a fellow cop. No one understood that he was also distraught over the loss of a love.

When he stopped hearing the bagpipe music in his head, then he would know it was time to move on. Then he would know the next step.